ALSO BY BARBARA WRIGHT

Easy Money

Plain Language

A NOVEL

BARBARA WRIGHT

A TOUCHSTONE BOOK
Published by Simon & Schuster
NEW YORK LONDON TORONTO SYDNEY SINGAPORE

TOUCHSTONE
Simon & Schuster, Inc.
Rockefeller Center
1230 Avenue of the Americas
New York, NY 10020

Designed by Colin Joh
Text set in New Caledonia

Manufactured in the United States of America

ISBN 0-7394-2908-6

For Frank

ONE

The buckskin gelding pawed the ground and tossed his head back. Alfred urged him on, but the horse moved in quick side steps without going forward. The horse had an Indian background and a stolid temperament. It was not his nature to be nervous. But something was upsetting him.

Alfred looked out over the windy plains of eastern Colorado. Broad hillsides sloped into grassy bottoms dotted with spiny yucca, prickly cactus, and thistle. The land was barren of trees, except for the occasional gnarled scrub cedar clinging to a rocky bluff, or the scraggly cottonwoods that congregated near the creek beds. He saw nothing amiss. Closer in, Alfred checked the ground. No rattlers, gopher holes, or other dangers a sharp horse like Sage might detect.

Alfred clenched his jaw and heard a familiar crunch. Grit. What he didn't breathe in through his nose, he took in through his mouth. Grains of sand lodged in the crevices of his teeth. It was a condition of working on the dry, brittle land.

Six months earlier, when Alfred had bought the ranch, no one had put a name to the long dry spell. He had been living in Mexico for eight years and had read about Roosevelt and the hard times across the country. People had put a name to that: the Depression. What were the odds that, hard on the heels of massive unemployment, would come the misery of drought—for that was the word everyone now used: drought.

The wind picked up, and the air took on a bilious yellow cast. Alfred had grown up on a ranch in the Rocky Mountains and was not yet familiar with weather patterns on this terrain. He had not yet learned to read the currents and eddies of dust, the way an experienced canoeist could read a river, could tell by the roar of the water, the height of the spume, and the churn of the foam, the exact degree of danger the rapids held.

Overhead, ducks dragged their purple shadows along the backs of the grasses. Sage whinnied and shied back.

"Come on, pal. Help me out here."

Alfred was not in the habit of talking to his horses. Sure, a word or two—"Good boy," "Giddy-up," that kind of thing. Yet here he was, speaking in full sentences.

He didn't have time for a balky mount. He was losing patience. He thrust his heels into the horse's side, and Sage moved reluctantly forward.

Alfred needed to get home and clean house to prepare for the arrival of his bride. At that very moment, Virginia Mendenhall was on the train from Mexico. She would arrive in Denver the next day and they would get married at the Quaker meetinghouse. It was impulsive to bring Virginia to this desolate land. They were both older and had worked at other jobs—he as an organizer for the YMCA in Mexico, she for the American Friends Service Committee, a Quaker organization based in Philadelphia. She knew nothing about ranching but was game to try. Her enthusiasm reassured him, though he knew, deep down, that she had no idea what she was getting into. If he had been more prudent, he would have waited to see if he could make a success of ranching before bringing her out. But he was not prudent. He was in love, and love and prudence were not compatible. So he abandoned the sense of responsibility that throughout life had been both his curse and his blessing, and asked her to marry him.

Alfred heard a sound like a freight train and looked behind him. A massive cloud rolled toward him, muddy tan at the top, black at the base. Before he knew it, the cloud caught up with him. The wind hit like a tornado, blowing dirt so violently he could not see beyond the brim of his hat.

A dust storm. Sage had known, had tried to warn him. Perhaps it was the static in the air, or some high-pitched signal, some disturbance in the natural order of things that his horse could pick up, while Alfred, with all his reasoning and intelligence, could not.

The cloud guzzled up the light. He could not see beyond the back of Sage's head. All he knew was that home was east, directly into the wind, and miles away. He pulled his bandanna over his nose and turned the horse in that direction.

The wind came at them with unrelenting fury. It stirred up particles and hurled them through the air with such force that they scoured his face. Dirt crept down his pants, like insects. Tumbleweed spinning crown to head flew at him from out of the darkness, grazed his face, then moved on. Sticks, gravel, and flying debris pelted him full force. The wind pushed his hat further onto his head, as if a giant hand were pressing against it. His thoughts were not for himself but for Sage. It was cruel to have an animal out in this.

His best bet would be to go to the old sod house. It had been left there by the original settler who had proved up the claim. The roof was caved in and the windows gone, but it huddled against a rise and would offer some protection from the storm.

He turned Sage around. Now the wind flogged their backs as they made their way toward shelter.

Suddenly something spooked Sage—a darting animal or

some wind-borne debris. The horse reared up and pranced backward. Alfred heard a crackling sound, like a rifle shot. The weight of the horse fell from beneath him. He jumped clear as the horse crashed to the ground. Alfred got up, but Sage didn't. Sides heaving, the horse kicked his feet and strained his head upward, to no avail. Alfred knew from the terrible sounds of pain that the animal was in trouble. He circled Sage and approached from the back so he could check for damage without getting kicked. Blinded by the dust, he felt the animal's lower pastern for the bone between the hoof and the fetlock. All he could feel was gelatin.

He had to act quickly, before he lost courage. The saddle pitched and yawed as the horse flailed about. Alfred had trouble unstrapping the rifle. When he finally had it in his hand, he came around in front of the horse and aimed between the eyes, getting up close so that he would not miss. Sage tossed his head, caught the barrel of the rifle, and sent it flying. Alfred groped in the dust until he felt cold metal. The better target was behind the ear, he decided. He changed position. The horse's anguished neighs lacerated Alfred's insides. His hand shook. He concentrated on steadying his hand. He cocked the rifle. It didn't catch. He tried again. No use. The thing was jammed. The dust had clogged the mechanism.

Alfred's stomach turned nut hard. The wind cuffed his ears and numbed his face, but not his heart. Working the ranch alone, Alfred had done about everything a man could do. But this was one chore he had not counted on. He thought of every way to get out of doing it. Perhaps he could go get help. Perhaps the horse could be saved. But as the wind screamed and the dust built up, he knew what he had known in his gut from the beginning. He had no choice. He was wasting time, trying to save himself from the unpleasant chore, thinking about himself and not Sage.

He pointed the rifle into the air and tried again, just to make sure. Nothing happened. He took off his bandanna. Should he tie it over Sage's nose or eyes? Nose, he decided, so that for the last few moments, the horse could breathe dust-free. Even this close, Alfred could not see Sage's eyes. For that he was grateful. It was because of his liquid, intelligent eyes that Alfred had selected Sage from the many wild horses that the trader Caruthers had for sale. He felt the plush warmth of Sage's nose against his palm.

He got out his knife and crouched behind the horse's head. His lips burned, and his skin felt cracked and abraded, like old shoe leather. For his own safety he could delay no longer. Before putting on his gloves, he gave Sage one last pat. Each moment was another moment the horse was in pain. He held his breath, closed his eyes, and pulled the blade across the horse's throat. The knife caught at first—why hadn't he sharpened it more recently? He changed his grip and pulled harder. He felt the blade slide across. The neighing stopped. The legs went still. Sage's head flopped to the ground. Alone with the wind, Alfred backed away in horror and held up his palms to his face. This close, he could smell his gloves, which were darkened with blood. The wet fingers were a magnet for the dust. In disgust, he threw the gloves into the whirling dust. Then he flung the knife after them.

He turned into the wind and he headed toward home. His chaps scraped against the low-growing cactus and sagebrush. Without his bandanna, he had nothing to keep the dirt out of his face. Sludge coated his tongue. He spit out a wad of mud. Flying grit scratched his eyes. He lowered his face into the crook of his elbow to protect his eyes. Suddenly he thought: *His eyes. I should have covered Sage's eyes.*

As doubt set in, he began to lose his sense of direction. To get his bearings on the ranch, he depended on visual relationships, how one thing lined up with another—that butte across from that gate, this hillock in relationship to that gully. But he could not see an arm's length in front of him. He was walking east, directly into the wind and in the direction of home. But suppose the wind had shifted, even slightly, so that he was actually walking southeast, into the vast open range? If a ship veered off course even a few degrees, it would miss an island.

Too much thinking interfered with his homing instincts—whatever it was in man that told him where on the earth he was, which direction to go, and how to get home. Everything around him was the same. He could be walking in circles, for all he knew.

If something happened to Alfred, no one would miss him for days—weeks, even—except Virginia. And what would she think when he wasn't there to meet her at the train station? She knew no one in Colorado. She didn't even know where the ranch was. All she had was a rural-route address. The only other person who might miss him was the postman, who would notice the mail collecting in the box—any letters Virginia had mailed from Mexico that would arrive after she did.

Up ahead he saw sparks traveling waist high, in succession, cutting their way horizontally through the dust. A trail of stars, each one fading before the next lit up. Was his mind turning feeble? As he got closer, he realized that he had reached a barbed-wire fence. The wind was so strong it generated electricity that jumped from one barb to another along the length of the wire.

A fence spitting stars. Its strange beauty calmed him. Cutting a wide berth, he followed the fence until he came to a gate. He climbed over the weathered plank boards to the road. He chose a direction—left—knowing he had a fifty-fifty chance of being right. Now he traveled by the feel of the ground beneath his feet, sensitive to any change in elevation. When he felt himself going down into the bar ditches, he regained the high ground. When he came upon the curved metal mailbox, he was home free. From here he knew the way by heart.

Without eating supper or taking a bath, he fell into bed. Tomorrow he would take care of everything. Tomorrow he would get married. Now, the only thing he sought was sleep.

❀   ❀   ❀

Sleep did not come to Virginia until deep in the night, after the border crossing. She had passed most of the time in the tiny curtained sleeping compartment, listening to the rotation of the train's wheels, fast for long stretches, then slow, pulling her toward her new life. The future hung shining before her, without a hint that anything could tarnish it.

After a few short hours of rest, she freshened up as best she could in a bathroom that wasn't much bigger than a telephone booth. She wore her long blond hair the same way she had for the past ten years, up in a bun, which made her look a bit too severe, but it had the virtue of being a quick hairstyle. She had never been one to waste time in beauty parlors. As she wound the thin ponytail at the nape of her neck, the train lurched around a corner and she was thrown against the side of the lavatory. The hairpins in her mouth fell to the floor and scattered. She washed them off and started over, then pinched her cheeks and looked at herself in the saucer-sized mirror.

She was not a beauty—her forehead was too high, her nose too big, her cheeks not defined. But she had a pleasant face. With a touch of mascara, a bit of red at the lips and some powder on her nose, it would even be a handsome face, but she had never gotten in the habit of putting on makeup, and when she did, she felt like a stranger to herself. So even today, on her wedding day, she wore none. But she felt beautiful and knew instinctively that her face had a special glow. Not even lack of sleep could keep loveliness from her face. Not today.

She found a seat on the train and gazed out over the flat New Mexican desert. Low scraggly bushes gave the terrain a nubby appearance. Adobe houses the same color as the earth fit against the hillside. Near the front of the car, several men read newspapers, and a mother tried to quiet her two small children. Cigar smoke wafted through the window from another car.

Virginia unfolded a handkerchief on her lap and got out a roll she had saved for breakfast. After she finished eating it, she carefully brushed the crumbs from the pleats of her purple crepe dress—her best dress. Not new, but of solid quality. She could not afford a new dress for her wedding.

She thought of Alfred, dear, sweet Alfred, waiting for her at the station. Would she even recognize him? She pictured his strong jaw, his square chin, and his eyes, which were . . . which were . . . What color were they? She couldn't remember. This flustered her. She had only seen him twice in her life—once eight years ago, in the Washington, D.C., train station, and once six months ago, in Mexico. After that, they had gotten to know each other through the mail. Over the months, the details of his face had blurred, and the only thing that stood out was the lightning-shaped scar that divided his forehead. Taut and shiny, the scar did not tan the color of the rest of his skin, and made his face look lopsided. But his eyes. She closed her own—would he be able to say what color they were?—and tried to picture his face.

She felt a stab of apprehension as it occurred to her that she did not know him at all. She had no idea what it would be like on the ranch, far from her family, who gave her strength; from Quaker meeting, which grounded her; and from the Quaker work that gave her life meaning. She was giving up everything she knew in order to go to a place she had never seen, to marry a man she had known for less than two days. The folly of it hit her with full force.

The apricot-colored desert jerked by the window in flits and flashes. The rocking of the train made her queasy. She began to question her judgment. A rancher's wife? She was afraid of horses and didn't know a thing about cattle. She was a complete greenhorn. And the thought kept returning to her: she did not know the color of his eyes. She was marrying a man and she didn't even know the color of his eyes.

She had first met Alfred in 1925. She was on her way to graduate school at Haverford, a Quaker college near Philadelphia. She had never traveled outside of North Carolina. Her father was worried about her long train ride alone, and he had come up with the idea that she should travel as a pregnant woman. No man, no matter how unsavory, would bother a pregnant woman, he had reasoned. Her mother had made a special pillow that Virginia fastened beneath her slip. The strings hung down against her bare skin and tickled her back.

During the intervening eight years, she had traveled frequently and had come to love train stations, those cavernous spaces that are made intimate by all of the human drama of partings and arrivals. But the trip to Philadelphia was her first, and she was terrified by the world, so unimaginably large and different from Whittier, North Carolina.

She had to change trains in Washington. Unaccustomed to her new body shape, she kept bumping her elbows into her padding as she dragged one suitcase a few yards, then went back to get the other. As she advanced slowly down the platform, a tall, attractive man in cowboy boots approached her.

"Please, ma'am, let me help you with those," he said.

Remembering her father's stern warning, she pulled the suitcases to her. "No—no, thanks. I'm fine." He was handsome, and therefore dangerous.

"You shouldn't be lifting heavy things in your condition."

"Oh—right." She had forgotten she was supposed to be pregnant.

The authority and command of his physical presence made an impression on her. She was tall for a woman, and measured five feet nine in her stocking feet. This placed her eye-to-eye with most men she knew, and she gazed over the heads of most women. With Alfred, she looked directly into his neck, where the top pearl-snap button of his Western shirt opened to accommodate his tanned, hairless neck.

"I'm sorry. I haven't introduced myself. Alfred Bowen." He shook her hand. "Where are you headed?"

"Philadelphia." She looked around her and realized, with growing panic, how confusing the station was. "I don't know where the train leaves from. All these different tracks. I had no idea."

"No need to worry. I've got a long layover. I'll make sure you get on the right train." He tucked his worn cardboard suitcase under one arm and picked up her two bags. He had muscular forearms and thick wrists, and he moved with an easy athletic grace.

She took off her glasses so Alfred could see her eyes—her best feature, with long lashes and slate-colored irises so large there was little white visible. As she walked beside him, she hunched her shoulders forward, but no contortions could hide the large bulge at her midsection.

They walked to the main terminal. Light streamed through the large glass windows and scattered onto the floor among the bustling crowds. She and Alfred stopped for a moment at the big board. She squinted but could not read the timetable.

"Your train leaves in two hours. Is your husband going to meet you at the station?"

She looked at him in confusion. People swarmed around them.

"The baby's father," he said.

"Oh, yes. Well—" She blushed and clutched the handle of her purse. Her fingernails dug half-moons into her palms.

She did not want to lie, but then her whole masquerade was a lie. Surely her father, a devout Quaker, had not foreseen this predicament when he came up with this ridiculous scheme. "I'd rather not go into it, if you don't mind," she said.

"You should be careful traveling alone," he said. "You never know who you might meet."

Here was a man who would get along with her father, she noted.

He invited her to eat with him in the dining room. They sat at a corner table overlooking the street. She felt comfortable around him. He had a gentleness and a sense of confidence that reminded her of her older brother Jonathan, before his head injury.

"Where are you going now?" she asked, after deflecting several questions about herself. An inexperienced liar, she had no idea how to assemble the structure of falsehoods in order to make the lie of her pregnancy blend in with the rest of her life.

"Mexico."

It seemed unspeakably adventurous and exotic. She was nervous about going to Philadelphia, and here he was off to another country where they spoke a different language. "Why Mexico?" she said.

"I love children. Especially adolescents. I worked at the YMCA in Chicago for years, and when they asked me to open a branch in Mexico, I jumped at the chance."

"You worked in Chicago? Do you know Jane Addams?"

"Not personally. But I've been to Hull House. I was looking into doing some joint programs with the Y."

Her eyes widened. She knew all about Jane Addams's settlement house for immigrants. She wanted to model herself on this pragmatic woman and her brand of democratic social ethics, which had less to do with handouts and more to do with helping immigrants help themselves.

"I can't believe it. Jane Addams is my hero. She's the reason I'm going to graduate school in social work."

"Graduate school?" he said. Two creases formed at the bridge of his nose, like a chute his lightning-shaped scar might slip through.

"Yes. I mean, eventually. When the time is right." She felt herself floundering. Pregnant women did not go to graduate school. Period.

When the time came for her train to depart, he paid for her meal, accompanied her to the train, and made sure she was settled.

"You take good care of that baby," he said, like an affectionate uncle.

She watched him through the window as the train pulled out. He did not turn around, did not wave, did not see the tears of disappointment that dropped from her cheeks and onto her collarbone.

She had felt such a connection to him. He was idealistic and adventurous. He had been to Hull House. There were so many things she wanted to find out about him. He was ten years older than she, and so much more advanced in his knowledge of the world. But every avenue of conversation led to a potential trap that would unmask her ridiculous disguise. What a stupid idea. A fraud. She should never have consented to it.

When the train was outside the city, she went to the lavatory. It was stifling inside the tiny cubicle, and the smell made her nauseated. The window was tilted open, leaving a small space at the top. She lifted her dress, untied the pillow, and stuffed it through the window. Standing on her tiptoes, she watched it tumble down the steep embankment like a giant marshmallow and land in the reeds.

Years passed, and she thought of him often. She finished her degree and worked for five years as youth coordinator for the American Friends Service Committee in Philadelphia. Her job involved seeking placements for Quaker youth in settlement houses, Indian reservations, prisons, and reform schools across the county. She eventually visited Hull House. In 1933, she went to an Appalachian mining town to organize a Quaker-sponsored child-feeding project. After an incident she couldn't bear to let herself think about, she suffered from nervous exhaustion, and went to Mexico City. A friend's aunt, an English Quaker who had married a Mexican anthropologist, graciously provided a place for her to recuperate.

A few months into her stay, Virginia was walking on a

crowded commercial street with the maid's eight-year-old daughter, Claudia. Among the jumble of signs in Spanish, she saw the familiar letters YMCA and thought of Alfred. On a whim, she went inside. A Mexican youth behind the desk was moving his lips silently as he read a book called *Speak English Today.*

"Do you know an Alfred Bowen?" she asked.

The boy marked his place in the book with his finger and looked up at her. "El Señor Elfego Bowen? He is very very big man? Giant size?" He raised his hand over his head to show the height.

"Yes, that's the one. Is he here? In this office?" Virginia said.

"He is to go in America," the boy said. Apparently he had not reached the chapter on verb tenses.

"He's gone?" Virginia said.

Virginia turned to Claudia, who knew more English than the boy behind the desk. After several exchanges, Virginia was able to determine that Alfred was leaving for Colorado the next day. The boy went and found an American, who gave them instructions to Alfred's house.

She and Claudia took the tram across town. They found Alfred's house and Virginia knocked on the door. A tall man answered. When she saw the lightning-shaped scar on his forehead, she knew it was Alfred.

"May I help you, ma'am?"

She remembered how odd she felt when he had called her ma'am in Washington.

"Hello. I'm—I know this will seem very peculiar, but I met you many years ago. My name is Virginia Mendenhall."

He looked at her without recognition. She blushed furiously but continued on. "In Washington, D.C. You were on your way here. Oh dear, it was too many years ago."

"I'm sorry. I can't say that I remember." Suddenly it became clear to her. In the intervening years, she had been preoccupied with him and he had not given her another thought. There was no reason for him to remember every single person he had helped in his life, particularly not a pregnant woman traveling alone.

"On the train . . . I was . . ." She held her hands out in front of her stomach.

His face brightened. "Oh yes, of course." He glanced at the dark child beside her. "And this is your daughter."

"Oh, no. This is the maid's daughter. Actually, I don't have a child."

"I'm so sorry," he said and looked down.

"No, I mean, I wasn't—it was all a ruse. My father's idea. It was . . . a put-on. He was afraid that, well, you know, that a strange man might talk to me." She smiled at the irony.

He led Virginia and Claudia across a courtyard to a small room that was empty but for an open trunk and some odds and ends scattered on the floor.

Alfred pulled a doll from the trunk and gave it to Claudia to play with. "It's for a friend's child," Alfred explained. Claudia beamed with pleasure and ran off to the courtyard to play.

"I'm sorry I can't offer you a place to sit," he said to Virginia. He closed the trunk, and she leaned against it. He sat on the floor.

"Where are you headed?" she asked, and remembered that she used those very words, or ones similar, when she had met him in the train station.

"Colorado, where I'm from. I'm going to start a ranch."

He told her, with great enthusiasm, about his plans, and the time passed quickly. Before she knew it, the light began to fade. Outside, the pepper tree in the courtyard shimmered with movement from hundreds of wild parrots, tiny drab birds unlike their colorful relatives that Americans kept as pets. As if on signal, the birds flew away all at once, rising in a magnificent racket and joining swarms of other parrots until the pink sky became stippled and dark like a day-old beard over sunburn. Virginia was filled with happiness, until they exchanged addresses and said good-bye, when she realized that for the second time in as many meetings, their crisscrossing paths would lead them to different countries.

His first letter arrived the day after he left. He had mailed it before boarding the train. She sat down immediately to respond. They began corresponding every day. Because the mail was picked up three times a week on the ranch, some days she would get several letters and some days none. She lived for the post. She cherished his letters, which arrived with a thin line of grit in the bottom of the envelope.

Each afternoon when she sat down in front of the tissue-thin stationery, she found herself loosening up. The blank page drew words out of her that she had never said to anyone, certainly not a man. In her squat, manly handwriting, she confided in Alfred, the way strangers on buses and trains had opened up to her. Convinced she would never see him again, she felt free, unbound, as if the laces of a corset had been snipped. Gone was the self-consciousness, the shyness she felt around other men. Her letters were filled with her thoughts of the past, the future, what she saw around her in Mexico. She fell in love with the person she was on paper, and the way she felt when she wrote to him.

His letters were practical, plainspoken, filled with details of ranch life. He exuded decency and integrity, and this commanded her respect. But she longed for a bit of poetry, a romantic, heartfelt confession or some raw unguarded revelation.

When he proposed, he wrote, "I would be honored if you would be my wife. Together we could make this ranch prosper. I can do it on my own, but I'd prefer to do it with you, if you can stand it."

He had actually said that. Not "I love you," but: "If you can stand it." So much for poetry.

But she could not accept his offer, for there was one thing she had failed to tell him during their courtship (she was not even sure while it was going on that courtship was what it was, since he had never offered any clue to his heart's feeling). The thing she had not told him was this: she could not have children. That was what the doctor in Philadelphia had told her after the women's problem she had experienced in graduate school. She had to let Alfred know. If she had been forced to tell him face to face, she was not certain she could have done it. A letter was hard enough. She crumpled up page after page, dissatisfied with each version. She did not know which affected her more, telling him in the first place, or knowing that doing so would cause him to reject her.

His response came quickly: "Dear Virginia, I read your letter with great sadness . . ." She could read no further. Tears dropped onto the page, dissolving words into pools of blue, dissolving pools of blue into each other.

She did not have the courage to finish reading the letter until the following week, and then she had to decipher the words through the smudges: "Dear Virginia, I read your letter with great sadness, knowing what you have had to suffer. But I love you, and want *you*, not a progeny. So if you are still willing to have me, this poor old heart will not have to break."

She realized that what moved her was not flowery language or romantic flourishes, but a heart's honesty.

Remembering this, her fears fell away and her thoughts turned giddy and girlish. Today was her wedding day. She was ready to meet the future, whatever it held for her.

By the time the sun cast its first light over the plains, Alfred was out with the two drays and a wagon, searching for Sage. The virgin dust created a strange but beautiful sheen in the early morning sun. Dunes had appeared overnight, rippled on the surface like the rib cages of starving cattle. Smaller drifts had formed around tumbleweed, cactus, driftwood, and bushes—anything that trapped the traveling earth. Somewhere, in the vast sweep of prairie totally reordered by the storm, Sage was buried aboveground.

Alfred surveyed each drift, looking for the one that had, at its heart, the remains of his horse. When he saw a hoof protruding, he stopped the team. In a strange reverse of the burial process, he dug around the horse until the weight of the dirt was reduced enough for the drays to pull Sage out. Covered in dust, Sage had a petrified look, as if he had been there since prehistoric times. If an archaeologist uncovered this horse and found the animal's throat slit, what assumptions would he make about the behavior of man and animals, Alfred wondered.

He had no great affection for horses. He had been bitten, stepped on, and splashed with urine. Horses had rubbed him against trees and blown out their stomachs to keep him from properly tightening the cinch. But Sage was an exception. He was a first-rate cutting horse, range-smart, with cattle sense bred into him. He could hear or scent cattle before Alfred could. He knew how to keep order without stirring up the herd. He could outrun a cow and turn it back in a quick, smooth motion.

Alfred had admired Sage's athletic prowess. More importantly, the horse was attuned to Alfred's moods and compensated for his deficiencies so that together they operated far more efficiently than either could with another partner. In Alfred's experience, this true understanding with an animal came rarely. He felt a deep sorrow at his loss. Hat in front of his heart, he stood by the newly formed dune and paid silent tribute to his beloved horse.

He had not felt this way since he lost his first horse. Streaker was a black gelding with a splotch of white on his forehead, as if someone had hit him between the eyes with a snowball. Alfred's father had given him the horse on his twelfth birthday—a rite of passage. He adored Streaker. Like all first loves, this one was passionate and unguarded, his heart still unscarred by loss. His father mocked him for pampering the animal. In his father's view, a horse was utilitarian, period. One day, when Alfred was helping his father repair fences, Streaker got tangled in a bale of barbed wire. The more he thrashed about, the more the barbs ripped his flesh. Alfred watched in horror. He was paralyzed. He turned to his father, who knew what to do. Always.

"Shoot him," his father said and handed him the rifle.

Alfred had been brought up with guns, had been hunting since he was a young boy, but he could not bring himself to shoot Streaker. "I can't," he said.

"It's your responsibility, son," his father said.

The wire thorns sliced through the horse's black coat and into the glossy red muscle beneath. Alfred screwed up his face and closed his eyes tight, as if to keep out the tears. Images reeled before him: Streaker carrying him bareback across the meadow; Streaker's tongue sweeping his palm for sugar; Streaker coming when he was called, like a dog.

Alfred opened his eyes. "Please help me," he pleaded. For his father, shooting Streaker would have been no more difficult than killing a rattlesnake or a coyote.

"He's your horse. Man up to it."

No, no, no, no. Alfred repeated silently to himself, hoping his voiceless screams would drown out the horse's cries.

"You'll thank me later," his father said.

He didn't want to cry in front of his father, but he couldn't stop himself. He wiped his nose on his sleeve. The horse was screaming. The boy cursed his own weakness. His older brother, Shrine, could have shot the horse, no problem. But Alfred couldn't do it.

Losing patience, his father said gruffly, "You can shoot him or stand here and watch. Your choice." He walked away.

Silently cursing his father, young Alfred raised the rifle. His hand quivered against his cheek. The lick of white between the horse's eyes marked the target. He fired. The screams stopped.

He turned for his father's approval, but all he saw was his father's back. His father did not turn around. He did not come back. He just kept walking.

Alfred hated him.

He curled up on the ground, making himself small beneath the immense blue sky.

Nothing else would ever approximate the grief he felt at the loss of his horse. But the tears stayed inside him, safe from ridicule. He would not show weakness again, at least not in front of his father. From then on, whenever he felt any emotion surface, he would swallow it, as if he were swallowing his own vomit, and the taste was just as acrid.

He never felt that way about a horse again. Better not to risk the pain of loss. Of course, nothing bad ever happened to any of the horses he didn't care a whit about. Then came Sage. He forgot himself, became attached again. And now it was as if the mere act of loving that horse had marked it for loss.

Alfred dragged Sage to the bone yard, then headed home. The grit under his clothes scratched his skin. On the front porch, he took off his clothes and shook them out. Buck naked, he hauled the tin tub to the kitchen and took a bath, cleaning places he usually didn't bother cleaning. The channels of his ears had collected sand, like the chambers of a conch. He gently lifted his private parts and washed. Grit had collected in the folds. It would not do to bring sand to the wedding bed.

He thought of Virginia's body. Tonight he would see it for the first time. They would be husband and wife, and it would no longer be unseemly to think of her in such a way.

As he lay folded in the tub, he looked at his own body and wondered how it would appear to her. He was forty-three, no longer a young man. Though his muscles were taut from physical labor, he had more soft spots than he would like to admit.

After his bath, he prepared the house for Virginia's arrival. Alone, he had not paid much attention to housecleaning. He had bought the ranch from the bank. The previous owners were bachelor brothers who had leveraged the property in the late twenties and invested the money in stocks. When the market crashed, they lost it all. The two-room house stood abandoned for several years, and the prairie winds pushed the dust through the cracks and crevices of the house. When Alfred moved in, he shoveled the accumulated dust out of the rooms, but he did little in the way of improvements or serious cleaning. There was a bed on which to bunk down, and a stove to keep the place warm. The only thing of value to him was a grand piano that his grandmother had brought across the country in a covered wagon. His mother had taught him to play on its stiff keys. The hard action had forced him to develop great strength in his fingers.

Alfred wanted everything to be pristine for Virginia. First impressions were important. Every woman he had ever known was particular about cleanliness, and he didn't want to start off on the wrong foot. He dusted the piano and the other furniture and carefully swept the rooms. Yet he knew that during the two days he would be gone on his honeymoon, a layer of dirt would collect on the furniture and floors.

Suddenly he had an idea. Virginia's mother and sisters had sent out a trunk packed with tablecloths and sheets. He would simply cover the two small rooms from wall to wall with the linens, and when he and Virginia returned from Denver, he would leave her in the truck while he rushed inside and removed the sheets. Then he would carry his bride over the threshold—if, in fact, that's what she wanted. He didn't know much about these Quakers. His general impression was that they were a little odd. Maybe being carried over the threshold wasn't a Quaker thing.

After he packed and dressed, he opened Virginia's trousseau and covered the rooms with cloth.

The train slowed down as it approached Denver. Virginia looked out the window and saw some dilapidated brick buildings and the backs of a few wooden houses that overlooked the railroad and had been left unpainted. One neatly kept backyard had crisp white sheets bleaching in the sun. Virginia smiled as she thought of the trunk of linens her mother had shipped to Colorado. Virginia could picture her mother the way she had seen her so often in childhood, with a wooden embroidery hoop in her lap, picking at the taut fabric with a needle, in and out, in quick movements.

A ninth-generation Quaker, her mother believed in plainness, and spurned worldly goods. The Quaker concept of plainness had nothing to do with homeliness or ugliness. It was a form of genuineness. Her mother did not spurn beauty, only frivolity—anything that was not necessary. Their house was spare, with a few well-made pieces of furniture. There were no knickknacks or porcelain figurines to clutter the room. No wallpaper covered the walls. Books added the only hint of color.

Virginia's mother believed that anything useful should also be beautiful. This included embroidered pillowcases, pitchers, and furniture. Honesty was a quality she expected of objects as well as of people. She had lovingly prepared a trousseau of embroidered sheets, a damask tablecloth, crocheted runners, and pillowcases edged in tatting. Virginia had never had patience with a needle, and the thought of starting out her married household with her mother's exquisite handwork filled her with delight.

The train pulled into the station and hissed to a stop. Virginia took her bags from the overhead rack and carried them to the platform. People milled about, and the crowd parted to make room for a porter's cart. She heard a man shout, "Vivian," and her heart leaped. She looked in the direction of the man's voice, thinking that perhaps it was her name that had been called. Then she was bumped aside by a young woman in a red suit and hat who was striking enough to be a movie star. The woman zigzagged her way through the crowd and rushed into the open arms of her lover. They kissed fervently, oblivious to the surrounding observers. Virginia blushed and turned away.

The crowd thinned out, and still she did not see Alfred. Suddenly she was seized by a nameless panic. What if he had changed his mind? What if she had gotten the day wrong? But she thought better of it. Alfred was not a man who made careless mistakes. There was a reasonable explanation, she was sure.

She made her way to the main terminal, a cavernous room with high-backed oak pews set in rows facing each other. She spotted him across the room. He was wearing a cowboy hat and a suit with a string tie. His hat turned this way and that as he searched for her. She waved to get his attention.

Beneath her breastbone, her heart felt stiff and twiggy, as if a bird's nest had lodged there. The intimacy of their correspondence had created an illusion of closeness, but now, confronted with his physical presence, she felt awkward.

When she reached him, he tipped his hat and quickly took her suitcases, tying up his hands and erasing the need for physical contact.

She felt a touch of disappointment, thinking of the wild abandon of the lovers she had witnessed earlier on the train platform.

"Your eyes are brown," she observed.

He cocked his head slightly. "Yep," he said and waited for her to explain herself. When she didn't, he said, "Sorry to be late. I had to take care of some unexpected chores. Did you have a good trip?"

"Yes, lovely," she said. There was an edgy politeness between them.

In the parking lot, they found his navy-blue truck, which was sandblasted into the mottled color of sun-bleached asphalt. He put her luggage in the bed of the truck alongside some rusted machine parts and several burlap feed bags.

She opened the door, and dust dribbled down the window. She brushed off the seat with her hand. Seeing this, Alfred quickly pulled out a red bandanna and dusted off her seat, with apologies.

"I'm fine," she said, sensing his embarrassment. She hiked up the skirt of her best crepe dress and climbed into the dusty truck. She didn't want him to think she lacked the mettle to be a rancher's wife.

They drove to the Friends' meetinghouse near the university and met briefly with the Quaker elders who had agreed to oversee the wedding.

At the appointed time, Virginia and Alfred went into the meetinghouse and took their places near the front on one of the plain wooden benches arranged in a square.

Virginia sat in the stillness of the meeting and let the dappled sun warm her skin. Unadorned windows looked out over a yard shaded by enormous oak trees. Squares of sunlight fell across the unoccupied benches. A vase of purple phlox on the center table sweetened the room with its scent. Around her, people sat with heads bowed, hands clasped, faces quiet and composed. These Friends had come for an opportunity to worship and to extend the fellowship of celebration to another Quaker.

In her travels, she had worshipped in silent meetings all over the country, and she felt comfortable amidst people of like mind, united by the conviction that the inner light, or "that of God in every man," revealed itself directly to each individual. The people who were gathered in the room believed, as she did, that religion was a personal experience and that no intermediary, such as a minister, was necessary to communicate with God. She waited in the silence, warmed by the fellowship she had come to expect of Quakers, though today, on her wedding day, her excitement made it impossible to ease into prayerful meditation.

After people had settled down and several minutes had passed, she nudged Alfred to get up. They stood by the table in the center of the square, faced each other, and said their vows.

They returned to their seats, and the ceremony continued in steady silence. Birds chirped outside, and the smell of smoke drifted through the open windows. A cat meowed and scampered under the benches. It approached Alfred and rubbed against his leg. Several of the members smiled.

Alfred reached over and felt the edge of his hat, a familiar object. He lifted his head and glanced around him, careful not to be too conspicuous. He saw bowed heads and expressions of calmness and serenity. Virginia had explained to him that a Quaker wedding was a silent meeting for worship in which a marriage took place. This struck him as an odd way to conduct business, but he was indifferent to religion and didn't want to deny her.

As the minutes ticked by, Alfred fidgeted. He felt like an alien presence in the room. Sitting still was unnatural for him. He was a man of action. The only time he was still was when he slept. He tried in vain to keep from jiggling his leg. He thought what a curious act it was to sit in silence. At one's own wedding, no less. He thought of all the things he could be accomplishing. On the ranch, there was more work than one man could possibly do. He was always pushing forward, never relaxed. No matter how much he did, it was never enough.

As the silence progressed, the muscles in his neck lengthened out, his breathing became steady and regular, and his shoulders dropped. At some point, without realizing it, he let the outside world loose and went inside himself to a place where he existed in a timeless state of grace. He had experienced similar moments at the piano as he marshalled all his faculties to interpret the music. When he funneled his thoughts and feelings into an intense concentration, the exterior world fell away and he reached a realm of pure communion where he and the music became one. It seemed to him that creativity, like worship, was a form of concentrated focus.

When an academic-looking snowy-haired man in wire-rim glasses stood up and started to speak, Alfred was startled out of the deep place where he had come to rest, and was surprised to find himself at his own wedding.

The man spoke of the patience to endure the weaknesses and human failings of the other person. Alfred thought this a dispiriting thought to introduce at a wedding. Once again he was reminded what a foreign setting this was. Sitting by his new wife, surrounded by this queer fellowship, he felt embraced but out of place. His life had taken an inconvertible turn, and wherever it would lead, it would lead them together.

TWO

Alfred looked out the truck window at the bleak landscape that unrolled in drab shades of brown: brown grass, brown brush, brown dust. The land was fissured with dry creek beds that had open lesions and curled leathery pieces of dried mud where water had once been. Stony outcrops and ragged buttes interrupted the monotony. At certain points, you could look for miles with nothing to interrupt the sightline. In other places, a rise by the road put the horizon an arm's length away.

He was driving Virginia to the ranch for the first time, after two wonderful honeymoon days in Denver. Virginia had loved City Park, with its swan-filled lake and a dramatic backdrop of mountains that kept their snow crowns even in the heat of August. They had attended a summer stock production of *Cyrano de Bergerac* at Elitch's Gardens. During the quiet moments on stage, they could hear the tinny tunes of the merry-go-round through the theater walls. Everything about Denver had delighted her. But now city life was far behind them. They had been driving over dirt roads for an hour, and Virginia had been conspicuously silent. The truck was stifling inside, but Alfred dared not open the window. Enough dust seeped in through the air vents to make his skin itch and his throat feel chalky.

He had hoped for clear skies today. He wanted the land to put on its best face for Virginia, so her first impression would be favorable. Instead, everything had a jaundiced cast, made worse by the wind, which stirred up the topsoil and dirtied the air, the way a clear pond becomes muddy when the bottom is disturbed. Wind roamed over the land and, at certain spots, turned on itself to form a dust devil. Its rattlerlike tail whipped this way and that, scooped up tumbleweed, sticks, small pebbles, and loose soil and carried them aloft until it ran out of fuel and deposited its contents randomly on the plains, far from where it originated.

It was people's misuse of the land that had caused this dust-choked mess. The prairie was a delicate system, not to be tampered with. The roots of the grasses ran horizontally under the surface, where they were protected from drying, grazing, trampling, fire, and frost. The fibrous roots descended eight inches and were so thickly matted that the settlers had carved out bricks and built houses with them.

Underneath the sod layer, the soil was rich enough to grow crops. In this part of the state, farmers had peeled back the protective covering of the prairie and had planted wheat and corn. When the Great War increased the demand for grain, more and more people converted the grasslands to fields. But with the sod layer gone, there was nothing to hold the soil in place, and when the wind skimmed the fields, it sheared off a layer of dirt and sent it traveling for miles.

In Alfred's letters to Virginia, he had described in the bleakest terms the dust, the drought, the difficulties of daily life. But he also mused, on paper, how they would work together to transform this dry corner of Colorado into something they could be proud of. He was only faintly aware that he was doing a salesmanship job.

In his youth, he had followed his fortunes haphazardly, just to see what would turn up. When he left the ranch to go to college against his father's will, he sought out courses in literature, history, and the arts—all subjects his father had no use for. He majored in music, driven in equal measure by his mother's love of the piano and his father's scorn. He discovered, upon graduating, that the only jobs available to him were church choir director or private music teacher, and neither of these appealed to him. He tried for several years to give private piano lessons, but only succeeded in forever ruining his enjoyment of "Für Elise" and the *Moonlight Sonata,* two perfectly fine pieces of music when played by skilled hands. He worked for many years with the YMCA youth program before he was asked to open up a branch in Mexico. He jumped at the chance to learn a new language and experience a different culture, without a thought of the future. And he did not regret it. But now that he was older, his life was more directed. When he wanted something, he went after it. And he wanted Virginia.

He glanced nervously at his new bride. Her blond hair was pulled up in a twist and secured by combs. He loved her graceful neck, with its swells and indentations at the nape. It pained him to see the red lines where she had scratched herself. The way the air dried out the skin took getting used to, he knew, as did the tickle of dust that felt like the brush of gnats against the skin.

She fanned a handkerchief against her neck. "Is it always this dusty?" she asked.

"Can be," he said. "Today's a bit worse than normal."

They pulled within view of a two-room house and a windmill on a hill, with not a stick of greenery in sight. The white sun was a metallic smear in the sky and made everything look ashen. The dirt yard was packed as hard as cement. The outbuildings were made of scrap wood the color of driftwood. At one time, the house must have been painted white, but the grit had sandblasted much of the paint away. Squares of plywood, hinged at the top and held at a tilt by sticks, shaded the windows. Alfred had never paid much mind to the house. It was a place to bunk for the night, nothing more. But looking at it now, alone on a barren hill, he wondered what Virginia must think.

She looked around, alert and bright-eyed. It was this gleam of curiosity that had so touched him in Mexico. Things made an impression on her. She was willing to embrace new things. But this was a lot to adjust to.

He parked the truck by the house. "Stay here. I need to check on something," he said.

As he walked to the porch, the wind worked its way through the grass, and all of the land seemed to be moving, a phenomenon that had created in some pioneers a queasy condition very much like seasickness. He felt that way now. What was he thinking, bringing this cultured, educated woman to an isolated two-room house that lacked running water or electricity?

Inside, with the furniture draped in white linen, the rooms had a ghostlike quality. He quickly pulled off the sheets and tablecloths, balled them up, and kicked the pile under the bed. The place looked spotless, just as he had planned.

He returned to the truck. Suddenly he was overcome with shyness. It seemed silly to carry her over the threshold. Instead he said, "Would you like to see the house?" and led her through the door by the hand like a burro.

Virginia looked around the two rooms with the cold eye of one evaluating a rental property. When she saw a trunk at the foot of the bed, her face softened and she rushed over to it.

"Oh, this is the trousseau Mama wrote me about," she said with more animation than she had displayed since they left Denver. She opened the trunk. It was empty.

"What happened to the linens?" she said.

A bad feeling that had been building in Alfred now reached its full proportion. He considered lying. But that was no way to start off their new life together. Sadly he lifted the edge of the bedspread and with his boot swept the pile of dirty linens from underneath. They both stared at the dingy mound.

"I covered the furniture to protect it from the dust. I wanted you to walk into a clean house," he said despondently.

She collapsed on top of the pile and pulled a tablecloth up around her face. Her shoulders shook, her chest moved in small convulsions, and he heard strange sounds coming from her. His mind sped into the future, and frames of a disastrous marriage flipped past. It wasn't until moments later that he realized that what he was hearing was laughter.

He looked at her curiously.

She was laughing so hard she was crying. She wiped her eye with a corner of the tablecloth. It left a muddy smudge.

"Silly me," she said as she looked into Alfred's stricken face. "Attached to some old pieces of cloth."

"You mean you don't care?"

"The dirt will come out, I'm sure," she said.

He joined her on the pile, and they tumbled about in the dirty laundry, exuberant with the promise of a fresh start.

Virginia was ill equipped to define, or even conceive of, romance. Long ago she had declared herself beyond it, above it, or at any rate far from it, and she doubted that she could even cobble together a rough picture of what romance might include. What she now had with Alfred was not romance but something more exquisite: a joy in everyday things, shared with someone else. She loved the way Alfred's face lit up when he returned home after a day on the ranch; the way he observed her like a strange but cherished curiosity; the way he was always humming without being aware of it, and when she asked, "What's that tune?" he'd act startled, as if caught in an illicit act.

She was thirty-four, far past marrying age. "Spinster" was not a word she had ever used to describe herself, but others no doubt had. Even the open-minded Quakers. After she finished graduate school at Haverford—one of only three women in the department of social work—she was offered a position with the American Friends Service Committee in Philadelphia. When she accepted the job, Mr. Darby, a distinguished gray-haired Quaker with an aquiline nose and dark bushy eyebrows, looked at her and said, "We're so glad you're joining us. We've had problems with young women who take the job and then get married within a year."

Alone, she had lived a full life. She traveled frequently for her job, had a lot of friends and more dinner invitations than she could accept, was active in Quaker meeting, and sat on too many committees. She was an avid reader of newspapers, Quaker journals, and novels. At night she liked nothing better than to slip into different fictional worlds, live inside characters' heads and get to know them in a more intimate way than was possible in real life. But she had never become inured to that moment when she closed the book, turned out the light, and settled back into her pillow—that moment before sleep when the chilly fingers of loneliness touched her in an unwanted caress.

At different stages of her life, Virginia had come in and out of being herself. As a child, she had been spirited and adventurous. Then life intervened, and she turned serious-minded, a little dour. On the ranch, she felt her true self emerging—an aspect that had remained concealed for most of her adult life, until she met Alfred. She was still the same person she had been when she was alone, but a part of her that had frozen was now melting—water instead of ice—the same substance, but a different form.

One thing she hadn't done when she was alone was laugh. With Alfred, she laughed all the time. When he came in from work and found her in the kitchen, he would lift her from behind and say, "How's my *bonita Cuaquerita*?"—his pretty Quaker. Sometimes he called her Shoo-fly. She laughed with delight when she felt her feet leave the ground. With the air under her soles, she took in the salt, hay, and leather smell of him. When he set her down, she would put her hands on his shoulders and stand on her tiptoes to taste his lips, which were briny from the day's work.

She had never developed the gift of being merry. Optimistic, yes, but not merry. With Alfred, she was merry. They teased each other, nuzzled, and frolicked. It was ironic that despite the deep vein of seriousness that ran through both of them, what love brought out was a playful, childlike quality. Each allowed the other to be silly. And that was another thing Virginia had had very little of in her life: silliness.

One evening shortly after her arrival, she and Alfred had come upon a prairie-dog town. From afar they watched the rodents gambol in the dust like young pups. Alfred put his finger to his lips and they stood stock still, watching as two prairie dogs stood face-to-face on their hind legs and clicked their teeth together in a tender, affectionate moment. When the wind changed direction, one of the animals let out a warning cry— half whistle, half shriek. The others dropped to the ground, chased their black-tipped tails, and dove into their holes.

As she and Alfred got to know each other she often thought of those prairie dogs. Like the animals, they, too, kissed, prodded, and poked, establishing ties through a kind of playful dance.

Every evening after supper, Alfred took her to a different part of the ranch. He wanted her to discover the land with him. Being from the East, she yearned for tall trees, overhang, cover. Here everything was exposed; there was no place to hide. The flat expanse of patchy brown grass, yucca, and low-growing shrubs reminded her of some mangy animal pelt. The land did not stir her soul. What stirred her was Alfred's love of the land, the fact that it was not a separate thing from her, but included her.

She could not believe her good fortune—for there was no other explanation. What would have happened if she had found herself isolated in this barren corner of Colorado with a difficult man? When Alfred asked her to marry him, all she had to go on was several months of daily letters and a deep connection that she trusted but could not explain. Now they were two strangers joined by—by what? A mysterious bond that had nothing—or everything—to do with marriage.

The two-room house she now called home had once been a bunkhouse. When the main house burned down, the bachelor brothers had converted the bunkhouse's rickety side porch into a tiny kitchen and moved in. Leaky windows surrounded the kitchen on three sides. A hand pump drew water from a cistern in the basement. An air-ventilated cupboard with screen shelves served as the only refrigeration. The cast-iron stove was in the main room, where it doubled as a heater in winter. To cook, Virginia had to shuttle back and forth from the kitchen. There was so little space that sometimes when she backed up from the stove, she would bump into the grand piano. She could not move the piano back. The two reading chairs and the desk were already crowded against the wall, giving the room the feel of a storage closet. When she and Alfred read at night—by the same lantern, so as to conserve fuel—the flame's lurching reflection against the piano's curved sides created a cozy feeling. But by day, the strange-looking piano dominated the room. Horseshoe-shaped gashes scarred its ebony lid. Shaggy logs held up the piano, like the massive legs of dray horses. Alfred was very attached to that piano and coddled it as if it were a priceless Steinway. He kept a pail of water underneath it to protect it from the dry air. Periodically he rubbed it with the same linseed-oil-and-root mixture that gunsmiths used on guns. Often he would open the lid and flick his fingers lightly over the surface to remove dust. Then he would close the lid carefully as if the piano were a rare treasure box. But he never played it.

The only possessions Virginia had deemed worthy of shipping to Colorado were her books. She could not live without them. In addition to her beloved novels, she also had Quaker diaries, journals, and essays. Reading was one of her main sources of spiritual strength. She was a firm believer in the "inner light" and knew *Faith and Practice* by heart. The cover of her leather Bible was worn through to the suede on the spine, and the gilded edges of its tissue-thin pages were now as dull as unpolished brass. The Quakers, so well known for their silence, were a verbose lot when it came to writing. Virginia drew strength from the lives of Quaker women, who were strong and had been treated as equals since the seventeenth century, when George Fox trembled before the Lord and gave the Quakers their name. She admired the seventeenth-century Quaker Margaret Fell, a mother of eight, who served time in English prison for her beliefs. The book she wrote there, *Women's Speaking Justified,* was never far from Virginia's bedside. Her main role model, the reformer and social worker Jane Addams, was born to Quaker parents and maintained close ties to the Society of Friends. Another role model, Elizabeth Fry, opened a school for women prisoners in London before coming to America in the 1820s. Virginia also admired women like Susan B. Anthony and Lucretia Mott who exemplified the Quakers' belief in action rather than thoughts.

She unpacked her books and set them in columns around her. The bookshelves were already filled with Alfred's books. She read the spines: Tolstoy, Shakespeare, Henry James, Thucydides, Herodotus. All books of substance, but they were not hers. They did not warm her soul like the quiet parlor observations of Jane Austen or the passionate intensity of Emily Brontë and other books that had taken her in as a guest between their covers. Setting out her books gave her dominion over the room in a way nothing else could. She stuffed as many books as she could fit in the glass-fronted bookcase, then put the rest on the high shelf that ran along two walls.

Virginia never thought she would find housekeeping fulfilling. As a working woman she had viewed any time spent cleaning as time wasted. But now she had more than a place to live; she had a home, and the urge to clean blossomed inside her.

As she organized the house, she felt her mother's influence looming in her. Her mother was a fervent housekeeper. While she was growing up, their house had always been messy, but immaculately clean. Her mother encouraged artistic and imaginative clutter and left any ongoing projects undisturbed, whether paints and brushes scattered over a table, or an ever-expanding fort of sheets, chairs, scarves, and shawls, or the many volumes and papers of her father's historical research projects. But underneath the clutter reigned a sense of order that contributed to the warmth, familiarity, and affection that made home home.

On the ranch, the water that the windmill pumped for the cattle was too "hard" to use in the house, Alfred had told her. She had never heard water referred to as hard, though she had noticed a white crusty ring around the pail under the piano. For use in the house, Alfred drew water from a distant watering hole and hauled it to the cistern in a special tank that fit in the back of the truck. He searched for holes that had frogs—the water from these tended to be the safest. But cistern water was too precious to use for cleaning, so they took the laundry to town, an hour's drive away.

Virginia felt sure Alfred was being overly cautious. How would he know whether the livestock water could be used for mopping? The dear man had worked so hard to make the place clean for her, but he clearly had never taken a pail of water to the floor. She fetched a bucket of salty windmill water and sloshed it along the pine planks. The water beaded up in clear bubbles. When she submerged the mop in the pail, the mop's floppy tendrils wouldn't even absorb the water. She ended up spreading the water around on the floor and leaving it to evaporate.

So she couldn't mop the floor. Surely she could take a bath. Again, she trudged back and forth from the cattle tank to the main room and poured the water into large pots on the stove. She moved the kitchen table aside to make room for the large tin tub. With clothespins, she attached sheets to the clothesline

35

above the windows in the unlikely event that a visitor should choose this moment to be neighborly. After filling the tub, she lowered herself into the water. To her disgust, she found herself coated with a translucent film that made her skin as slippery as if she were bathed in mucus. She lathered up to rid her skin of the creepy feeling, but the water would not rinse off the soap. Finally, she rose from the tub and rubbed the minerals and soap off her skin with a towel.

Scarcity she understood—of food, clothing, shelter, money, jobs. The country was in the middle of a depression, and people lacked many of life's necessities. But water was one thing she had always taken for granted. No longer.

Once, and only once, did she use cistern water for laundry, and she hoped she would never have to again. On that morning, she had been collecting eggs in the broken-down henhouse by the windmill. Across the rafters, the bachelor brothers had tacked up old burlap feed bags as insulation. The burlap sagged with something heavy and lumpy. Curious, she stood on an empty crate and pulled the frayed edges of burlap away from the nails that held them. Suddenly she was pelted with dozens of rotten eggs. They broke against her head, splattering on her shoulders and slithering to the ground. The fetid smell penetrated into her pores the way bad kitchen odors seep into a cutting board. Horrified, she ran toward the house, dripping with greenish slime. As she reached the door, she thought better of entering: she could not introduce that sulfurous smell into the house. So she dragged the washtub to the cattle trough, filled it with water, got in, clothes and all, and dunked her head under. The slippery water did not get rid of the horrible smell. With no thought to modesty, she removed her wet clothes and walked, stark naked and dripping, before God and all the livestock, to the house. She washed again in the kitchen, this time with precious cistern water, and used the same water to launder her clothes.

She usually loved to tell Alfred the details of her day. He was amused by her improvisations but never made her feel diminished, and he listened with a respect for her attempts to overcome things with pluck and good humor. But this incident she preferred to keep to herself.

That evening, Alfred came home late. Before he had even shed his boots and hat, he wrinkled his nose and said, "Do you smell something funny?"

"That's an odd thing to say, for someone who comes in reeking of manure every day," she teased.

"No, I could swear . . . I can't identify it. It's familiar." He left his boots by the door and walked around in his stocking feet.

"It's strange. It smells like the refineries in Denver." He pulled his denim jacket over his hand and, using it as a potholder, took the lid off the iron kettle on the stove and moved his nose toward the steam. "That's not it," he said and replaced the lid. "It almost smells like rotten eggs."

She could keep her secret no longer. She told him.

He laughed. "Chickens like to hide their eggs where they won't be found." He looked at her with admiration. "I'm just lucky you're good-natured."

"Stinky, but good-natured."

"That's a combination I can live with."

Three times a week, the mail arrived. Virginia loved walking the half mile to the mailbox, anticipating what it might hold for her. She received letters from her family and Quaker friends. The American Friends Service Committee sent her journals, minutes, and papers. Magazines served as her link to the outside world. She pored over the Sears catalog for ideas she could adapt for her house before the book found its way to the outhouse, where its pages made a more suitable toilet paper than newsprint, which left gray smudges. One catalog that was spared that fate was Barnston & Sons, which featured pure copper branding irons, capsules for eliminating bots, docking pincers, teat oil, louse killer, ear-notching punches, bull rings, and a frightening gadget called an emasculator.

The *Denver Post* arrived several days late. She always read the newspapers thoroughly to keep informed of the country's economic situation and the Roosevelt administration's programs. She had been hooked on the news since her student days at State Normal College in North Carolina, when she joined the Suffrage League, which was dominated by Quakers. She and her mother had traveled to Raleigh and stood in front of the legislature, in a group several thousand women strong, holding up brooms and a banner that said A CLEAN SWEEP. The women hoped to persuade the General Assembly to cast the deciding vote to ratify the Nineteenth Amendment. North Carolina declined, but Tennessee voted in favor, and the amendment passed. She was not accustomed to being allied with the winners. Quakers, with their pacifist stand and their championing of the underprivileged, rarely found themselves on the winning side.

Admittedly, her part in the victory was small, but her sense of power was large. Along with thousands of women, she had won the right to vote. Being informed was part of being a good voting citizen, and she took her new responsibility seriously.

During autumn, dust was less of a problem on the ranch. Every so often there would come a rare day of perfect clarity, when the wind was still, the earth stayed in place, and the plains were bathed in the kind of light that only falls in autumn, when the air catches and distributes light with perfect equanimity. What a thrill, what a privilege it was to be alive on days such as this, she thought one morning on the way to the mailbox. She had been married a month. Alfred already teased her about her sentimentality. But surely the world was no worse off for her happiness, and if that was sentimentality, so be it. On this perfect day, with the sky so blue, the air so clear, this private, secret moment was hers and hers alone.

How different the land seemed to her when she was in this

kind of mood. She took in the broad sweep of the plains and loved it all, without reason or distinction: the birds she could hear and see but could not name, the grasses that bent over and allowed the silver to shimmer along their backs, the scruffy cottonwoods with bark like the thick tread of tractors, and the leaves that turned brown and fell off early, without a nod to the beauty of autumn.

As the days advanced, she encountered more and more things she had to master. She decided that the household needed milk. Alfred hated milk cows. In his estimation, they ranked only slightly above sheep. But Virginia convinced him that they could sell the cream in town and earn a few extra pennies.

"If you're willing to milk the cow, I'll get one for you," Alfred said.

"Sure. I'll do it," she said confidently.

"You don't know anything about cows."

"I know more than you think," she said. She hated to be told she couldn't do something. Sure, she had grown up in a town. When she needed milk, she went to her father's grocery store or waited for Mr. Ellerby to deliver it in the wagon. But she was a quick study. She would learn.

"How many upper teeth does a cow have?" Alfred asked.

"I don't know—about sixteen," she guessed.

He laughed. "Go count them."

"Not on your life." She was afraid of animals, if the truth be known. But she did want milk. That did not necessarily mean she was willing to stick her hand in a cow's mouth on some ill-advised research project.

Alfred laughed. "A cow doesn't have any upper teeth. Only jaw teeth way in the back."

"Just because I'm not a dental expert doesn't mean I can't learn to milk," she said. "What side do you milk from?"

"The left," he said.

"Okay, I'll figure it out," she said, with a confidence she did not feel.

The following day, Alfred came home with a Holstein cow and her calf and put them in the shed. There was no barn on the ranch. The shed contained a few stalls for sick animals. All the other livestock lived outside.

She felt nervous about milking. Alfred would be gone in the morning, and she would be alone with the cow. But she was not one to shirk from a challenge. The year before, when she was in Appalachia, she had learned to drive a car in a single morning. She and Alice Cadbury, a Quaker in her forties, had moved to the mining town of Swan Hill to organize an American Friends Service Committee project to feed the children. They had inherited an ancient Ford that stood idle in front of the house. The right front fender hung loose on the frame, and the ripped canvas top had been hastily patched in several places. The car belonged in a junk heap, and, in fact, that's where it had come from. A Quaker from New York had combed the junkyards along the East Coast to find reasonably priced, if not reasonable, transportation for the Quakers to haul food to the isolated towns.

It wasn't until they dressed to go to town for bulk supplies—Virginia in a dress, Alice in her good gray twill suit and white gloves—that they discovered that neither knew how to drive. Each assumed the other could. They stood by the front bumper and stared at each other, both aware of the gravity of their plight. If they didn't get to town, the children would have nothing to eat.

Virginia volunteered to try. Many years earlier, she had convinced her brother to let her drive their father's new car on the back roads. She vaguely remembered two pedals, a clutch, and a brake. But which was which? The gears posed another problem.

The town was built on a mountainside, and the road in front of the house was steep. The Ford was pulled so close to the house that if Virginia made a mistake and put the car in forward instead of reverse, she would crash into the porch. The only thing to do was to roll the car back and then try to get it in gear.

Alice took off her hat and gloves and set them on the passenger seat and joined Virginia at the nose of the car. They leaned their palms against the radiator grill and pushed. The car stayed in place. "Harder," Virginia said. The pearls she wore drooped down from her neck and rested under her nose. They pushed harder. The car did not budge, even though it was on an incline. Finally, Virginia got behind the wheel and examined the various sticks and levers. Something she did in the next few moments of frantic pulling and poking released the car, and it started rolling backward. "I don't know what to do next," she cried in a panic.

A crowd of young boys in tattered clothes walked by, carrying their books in straps. Alice ran at them, waving her arms and crying, "Shoo, shoo." The boys scattered as the car rolled back.

Virginia slammed her foot on a pedal, but it went straight to the floor and the car kept rolling. She jerked the steering wheel to the right and, by luck, maneuvered the car onto the road, but it was still rolling backward. The boys flung their books onto the side of the road and ran squealing after the car. Finally Virginia tried the other pedal, and the tires locked, sending the car skidding in a cloud of dust.

Now she was stopped on another steep incline, pointing in the wrong direction. Her dress was soaked with perspiration, and she was exhausted, and she hadn't even started the motor. This was ridiculous. She had no intention of rolling backward all the way to Stoutville.

She turned the key. It produced a terrible grinding sound. What had her brother told her to do?

She looked ahead and saw Alice walking briskly down the hill, surrounded by a band of boys. Virginia looked behind her. A row of outhouses was built by the creek. A few on the end had collapsed, spilling their weathered boards down the steep banks. A narrow bridge crossed the creek, then the road dropped again until it evened out in front of the company store.

How could she possibly put together all the steps on such a steep grade? At least she now knew where the brakes were. She didn't need the motor. She simply rolled a few yards, then pressed the brake, working the pedals like the mangle she had once used to iron sheets. In this way, she rolled down the mountain backward in a jerk-and-stop motion until she reached the flat ground by the company store.

She sat in the driver's seat, trembling. The unemployed miners on the store's porch glared at her with hostile faces. None of them offered to help. They still harbored suspicions that she worked for a union.

Virginia took a deep breath. She would have to figure this thing out on her own. And somehow she did. She never knew how, but eventually she put the steps together that were needed to get the motor running. After practicing on the flat ground by the company store, she and Alice followed the narrow mountain road, with its hairpin turns and steep drop-offs, and made it to town and back with the bulk supplies.

Surely milking a cow could not be as hard as driving a car. However, a car could not kick or bite her. The following morning Virginia went to the shed. The black and white cow stood placidly in the stall, and the calf sucked at her teats. It was still dark, and Virginia hung the lantern on a nail. She got a tin pail and a wooden stool and stared at the animal. "I'm not afraid of you," she said, drawing a deep breath. "You're just a big, dumb old cow."

Alfred had said you milked from the left, but was that the left as you faced the cow, or the cow's left? She picked the side nearest the light, planted the stool in the hay, and put the pail under the cow's bulging bag. She yanked on a pink teat. Nothing came out. She tried again. Eventually, after a lot of exertion, she was able to get half a cup of milk, barely enough to make the bottom of the pail white. From the other side, the calf was noisily sucking and swallowing. She watched the calf. Obviously, there was more milk on his side. Virginia swatted the calf away and reached for the teat on the far side. No milk came out. The cow munched hay, unconcerned. Finally, the calf trotted around to her side, butted her off the stool, and grabbed the last of the milk.

That evening she and Alfred sat down to a supper of corn bread, beans, and rice.

"I'm surprised we're not having milk tonight," Alfred said and took a sip of water.

"Well, I went head to head with the calf this morning, and I lost."

"And what happened this evening?"

"This evening?" she said, the sauciness gone from her voice.

"You've got to milk a cow twice a day."

"You didn't tell me that," she said, with a sinking feeling. If she had known that, she would not have been so enthusiastic. "What am I going to do?"

"You'll figure it out," he said with confidence.

"You're not going to help me out?" she said with dismay.

"I don't want to venture where I'm not welcome," he said with the hint of a smile.

"Alfred Bowen! You're going to make me beg, aren't you?"

"A simple request would do the trick. I don't know why you're so stubborn. Milking's not something people are born knowing how to do."

"Okay. I give in. Will you teach me?"

"With pleasure."

After several lessons from Alfred, she got the hang of milking. Each day she got slightly more milk. She loved to go to the shed on cold mornings and rest her forehead against the cow's warm side. The first jets of milk broke against the pail with a startling sound. Then, as she settled into a rhythm, two noisy lines of milk flowed steadily into the pail, one high pitched, the other lower. The milk gave off a grassy smell, and steam rose from the foaming white liquid. She strained it into the separator, a large tin can on legs, which they kept in the root cellar. Each evening, she turned the crank for about twenty minutes. Cream rose during the night. Through a faucet, she drained off the milk, which was so thin it was blue. With the cream, she made butter. The extra cream she canned and sealed in pint jars to sell in town.

The days slipped by quickly, and though she was often frustrated, she was also exhilarated by hard work. She had been brought up to value economy and thrift, which put her in good stead on the ranch. But the core value of Quaker simplicity did not have to do with hardship, it had to do with a state of mind: putting first things first and focusing on what was important. It involved a quality of the soul that her teacher at Haverford called "unclouded honesty at the heart and center of the man." On that point, her personal searching came up short, for she kept a secret close to her heart. She felt deceitful not telling Alfred. Then again, why should she? She did not want to burden him with her every shortcoming. But her reticence was tinged, she well knew, with a strong measure of self-interest. If she told him, then what she cherished most—the tenderness, the closeness—might disappear.

On their honeymoon, she had remained wooden, frozen, afraid of being found out. On the ranch, she dreaded the nights. While she waited for him to come to bed, she remained rigid, expectant, alert under the covers—the same feelings she remembered from playing hide-and-seek as a child, when she held her body in total stillness, her heart pumping rapidly as someone approached, wanting to remain hidden, but wanting, at the same time, to be discovered.

She was afraid—not of him, but of the passionate side of herself, which she had been unable to control once before. To give herself up, to completely let loose, would be a reward too rich, and she was not worthy.

Sometimes, caught unawares, she found herself slipping into pleasure. She would feel his calloused hands, shyly at first, almost apologetically, and then with more confidence, follow the curves of her body to her secret places. Then she would move toward him, involuntarily, surprised by his ardor, confused by her own. Afterward, as she fell asleep beside him, his warmth radiating toward her, she experienced a feeling of deep, deep peace, such as she had never felt before.

On nights when Alfred was too tired, or not interested, she felt let down. Dismayed by her longing, she did not allow herself to approach him. That would be too forward, too unladylike. On these nights, she went to sleep with a faint feeling of regret.

Once, in the brief moment before sleep, when her mind loosened itself from her control, an unwelcome sound unmoored itself from her memory and threaded through her thoughts: multiple voices chanting in unison, *Siam the mayan Thomas, siam the mayan.* She struggled to keep from losing herself, like a drowning person batting the water and fighting for air, but she was too tired to raise herself into consciousness, and the primitive chant surrounded her: *Siam the mayan Thomas, siam the mayan*—until she finally slipped through the dense thicket of words into sleep.

THREE

Fence mending was Alfred's least favorite part of ranching—but it was a substantial part. He had miles and miles of fences to keep up. The ones he shared with the sheep rancher Gerald Dalton caused him the most trouble. Dalton was lazy about rotating his herd and left his sheep in the pasture so long that they stripped the land of grass. The hungry sheep lined up along the fences and tried to reach the grass on Alfred's side. More and more sheep leaned on the fence until eventually the staples popped out, or the posts sagged over, and the sheep filed into his pasture. They chomped the grass off close to the roots, making it harder to regenerate. The only thing worse, Alfred thought, would be for a neighbor's bull to get loose in his herd.

He took his responsibility to his cattle seriously. They depended on him. Dalton tended to cut corners. Alfred looked down on people like that.

One day in November, Alfred parked the truck by a sagging section of fence. The back of the truck was filled with wooden posts and big spiny hoops of barbed wire. He got out a shovel and started digging. The ground was devoid of moisture and was compressed into a substance that resembled soft rock. He didn't dig so much as chip away at the earth. He pitied the grave diggers. Everyone's life had been touched by the drought. Even the dowsers. They planed their forked sticks over the sun-baked earth while anxious landowners waited for the rod to start twitching. The twitching never came. The long dry spell had lowered the water tables.

Alfred shaded his eyes and looked up. The cloud's gray underside was shadow, nothing more. Light and dark played tricks on his eyes, putting him in mind of rain. But it was all a cruel mirage. Today's clouds were decorative puffs.

Sometimes Alfred dreamed of water—never rain, only water: lakes, streams, waterfalls, ponds. In the dream, he was always in the water. What stayed with him when he woke was not the imagery but the clean, pure feeling of water against skin.

As he was ruminating, Dalton rode up on horseback.

"I could use a hand here," Alfred said. The work would go twice as fast with two people working.

"Can't now. Coyotes took down a couple of my sheep along here," he said.

Coyotes survived mostly on mice and insects, but a hungry pack could do a lot of damage to a herd, picking off the weak calves or sheep. Alfred went home to get his gun.

Virginia was sitting on the bed, brushing her hair, when he arrived unexpectedly in the middle of the afternoon. Her long blond hair was filled with static electricity and crackled with each long, steady stroke. She bent at the waist and brushed away from the nape of her neck, careful that her hair not touch the floor, for no matter how hard she worked, she could not get rid of the dust. Every day in the middle of the afternoon, she took out ten or fifteen minutes to brush her hair. The rhythmic strokes of the brush lulled her into a dreamy state, and she let her thoughts wander. By nature, she was a doer. She approached things full bore and was not satisfied until a job was done, and done well. But she regularly carved out a few minutes of private time to indulge her dreamy side. Now she was embarrassed to be caught in such an idle pastime. But Alfred didn't seem to notice. He headed straight to the basement and returned a few minutes later with a rifle. Virginia looked alarmed.

"I didn't know you kept a gun in the house."

"Yep." He cocked the rifle, and an empty shell popped out.

"What are you going to do?"

"I saw Dalton in the north pasture. The coyotes got a couple of his sheep."

"You're going to shoot the coyotes?" She used three syllables to pronounce coyotes, betraying her Eastern roots.

"Aim to." He reloaded and picked the empty shell off the floor. Coyotes were a rancher's scourge. The Navajos called them God's dogs, though to his mind there was nothing godlike about them. Alfred had no patience with people who romanticized them. His father was the only other person he knew who actually liked coyotes—or, rather, admired them. They were tough and independent, like him.

"Why don't you just trap them?" she said. Her hair, full of body, hung loosely about her head.

"They're too smart for that. The rare one that's dumb enough to get trapped will gnaw off his own leg to escape." Just the other day, he had watched a mousy-colored three-legged coyote hobbling along the perimeter of the ranch.

"Alfred, I won't have guns in my house."

"*Your* house?"

"Our house. It's against Quakerism. We believe in nonviolence."

"Well, we believe in survival." He did not have time for ridiculous arguments. He started out the door.

"Alfred, hear me out. Please." She didn't even know what she had to say, but it infuriated her that he was ignoring her.

He stopped and rested the butt of the gun on the floor. "Okay, tell me."

In the three months she had been at the ranch, everything was new to her, and she had tried her best to learn quickly. But by reinventing herself into this new person—the rancher's wife—she had left the old person behind. And she missed the old person. The Quaker beliefs she held so dear were an important part of who she was, and she was not willing to give them up. But she abandoned all attempts to explain this to him. It all seemed so complicated. Instead she said, "I'm not exactly sure."

"Something along the lines of, you'd rather let the coyotes pick off the stock. Because that's what'll happen if I don't kill them first."

"You're not respecting my beliefs." She whipped her hair over her shoulder.

"And you're trying to remake me in your image." They stood glaring at each other. He was the first to break the glare.

"This is ridiculous. I have to protect the herd. What do you expect me to do? Wait for a coyote to rip out the cow's insides? What does Quakerism say about that kind of violence?"

She had never seen this side of her husband. But then again, they had never had a fight. He was too proud, or too stubborn, to concede any points.

"Guns are a necessity on a ranch," he said and looked out the window to the west. He thought of the dust storm, when Sage went down, his rifle jammed, and he was forced to slit the horse's throat. He had needed a rifle then.

"If you cared about my beliefs, you wouldn't use guns and you wouldn't have them in the house," she said and yanked the hairbrush through her hair.

Alfred suppressed a sigh of frustration. The argument was going nowhere.

"I'll be home by dark," he said and started out the door.

She stopped brushing her hair and looked at him incredulously. "Did you listen to what I just said?" She hated to be dismissed.

"You don't want the gun in the house, so I'm taking it outside."

That did it. She lost control and threw the hairbrush at him. It whizzed by his shoulder and ricocheted off the wall. Her mouth dropped, and they looked at each other in shock.

"Not a bad aim, for a Quaker," he said and slipped out.

Alfred fumed as he rode his horse to the area where the coyotes had last been seen. His jaw set, he tried to calm down. Her sanctimonious nature was insufferable. It was insulting how little Virginia understood him. She was acting as if she were the only one in this marriage. She didn't even make an attempt to see things from his point of view. Treating him as if he were some kind of murderer, just because he wanted to go after a critter that was a threat to his livelihood—and hers. Each pregnant cow represented the future of the herd. He had to protect them.

The day passed slowly for Virginia. Little noises sent her to the window to check for Alfred. She could not do any work. She was ashamed of the way she had acted. In defending one Quaker belief, she had ignored another that was just as deeply held: the ability to stand in someone else's shoes and see things from his or her point of view. She knew she had a harsh, moralizing streak in her. In his better moods, Alfred made fun of it. As well he should. She tried to keep it in check, but she was not always successful. She wondered if he regretted marrying her. Their first months together had been such bliss that she assumed that the whole of their marriage would be all light and no shadow.

It was past dark when Alfred returned. He had not found any coyotes. The entire afternoon had been wasted. And there were still fences left to mend. His first argument with Virginia had upset him. What if their good times together turned out to be an aberration—simply the honeymoon period?

He didn't understand marriage. The most unlikely combinations worked. His parents, for example. His mother loved music and literature, yet she married an uncultured man whose only interest was livestock. When his parents were together, they filled a room to the point that it had made him feel left out as a child. His father loved to hug his mother and playfully pinch her on the behind when he thought no one was looking.

In winter, when there was less to do on the ranch, his father banned the children from the house for hours at a time. When they came back, his parents would be fixing dinner, laughing together, joking. What happened in those large blocks of time he did not understand until he was older. But he understood, even as a child, how it buoyed them up and sustained them.

Growing up, he had lived in fear of his father's temper, but he had never seen his father get angry at his mother. He wondered if they ever fought, and if so, how they resolved an argument. Alfred still seethed with anger at Virginia.

When he returned home, the dim lantern light pulsed from the bedroom window. He was in no hurry to see Virginia. He took his time rubbing down the horse. In the saddle room, he aired out the horse blanket, then put the saddle on the ground. He would sleep here tonight and show her. He made a pallet on the floor. Propping his head on the saddle, he tried to get comfortable in the straw. He felt a pain in his stomach, but he would rather go hungry than go inside. Exhausted, he fell hard asleep. Some time later, he woke up. The wind seeped through the cracks in the shed. Outside, he heard a strange clanking noise coming from the direction of the windmill.

Virginia had gone to bed early. She knew he was back. She had heard him ride up. She waited and waited for him to come inside. When he didn't, she went to bed. She had been ready to forgive him, but if he was going to act like that, she had no use for him. Let him suffer out in that leaky shed. She lay on the bed, arms crossed over her chest, limbs stiffened. She remembered her mother's advice: Never go to bed angry. Well, Virginia did not have her mother's magnanimous spirit. She was not about to apologize. He was the one who should apologize. Treating her as if her beliefs meant nothing.

But alone in the bed, she felt an aching emptiness. She was used to going to sleep beside him, her legs fit against his, feeling his warmth radiate to her. Without him, the bed was cold and lonely.

She got up and pulled on her bathrobe. He had not eaten dinner. He must be hungry. She would set a plate of food for him by the saddle room. She didn't have to talk to him, but she couldn't bear the thought of his spending the night hungry.

Without lighting a lantern, she slipped out in the moonlight and looked across the prairie. In the distance, a few lights winked, like boats at sea. Somewhere a coyote wailed, its wild voice filling the night with regret.

She found the pallet he had made in the saddle room. It was empty.

He had left to check on the windmill but found nothing amiss. The sky was dull—another night without stars. He missed the sense of pattern and order the stars lent to the night sky. If only it were rain clouds and not dust that erased the stars. He looked at the dark house, the windows blacker than the walls. He found himself thinking about the hairbrush and smiled. He was surprised, and secretly pleased, if the truth be known, that she had it in her to throw the brush. Even in his anger, he had noticed how beautiful she looked that afternoon, the light making spun gold of her hair. He decided to swallow his pride and go to their bed. He would ask her forgiveness. He had been unreasonable.

He slipped inside the front door and went to their room. The bed was empty.

He lit a lantern and could see in an instant that she was not in the two small rooms. He called her name, checked the basement. What could have possibly happened to her? Had she left him? Where would she go? Surely she would not start out on foot across the prairie. On the other hand, she was just independent and ornery enough to try something like that.

He would go after her. But what direction would she go in? He tried to think like Virginia and realized he had no idea what went on inside her head.

When he went to get a saddle and a bridle, he found Virginia on the pallet, asleep. The cold plate of food sat beside her. A piece of straw was stuck to her cheek, and she looked so beautiful that he stood and stared for a few moments. Then he picked her up like a small child and carried her back to the house and across the threshold. He would always remember this as the true beginning of their marriage.

Rattlesnakes were more plentiful with the drought, and Alfred had warned Virginia to be alert on her walks. It was a myth, he said, that the snakes rattled before striking. In fact, this happened only half of the time.

When she went outside, she carried a knife in case she needed to slice into her skin and muscle to release the poisonous venom a snake releases through its hollow fangs. At first she was vigilant, looking at the base of gateposts, behind every bush, in the bar ditches, knowing that it took only a split second for the snake to strike. But she never came across a rattler, and soon she let down her guard.

Then one late November day, Virginia went to the cellar to get some Mason jars. The ceiling was too low for her to stand upright. As she moved in a stooped position toward the shelves, she saw an enormous snake coiled in front of her. She screamed and jumped back. Her head knocked against the ceiling studs. The snake was the same color as the dirt floor and barely visible in the dim light, but she knew it was big. One end—was it the head or the tail?—curved underneath a table. Her heart was pushing against her rib cage as she reached for a shovel. Using all her strength, she brought the sharp edge down hard. It bounced off the thick skin, and the snake jerked into another position. She repeated the action over and over. She was bent at the waist, and her head was perilously close to the snake's twitching and writhing. Finally it went still. In horror, she dropped the shovel and fled up the steep stairs.

When Alfred returned that evening, she told him about the snake.

"A rattler?" Alfred said.

"I don't know. It's downstairs. I left it for you to clean up."

She hoped he would be proud of her. She had encountered a problem and taken care of it herself, though she had been shaky for the rest of the afternoon.

He came upstairs with the snake in a burlap bag. Holding it up, he said, "This here was Miss Nellie."

"Miss Nellie?" she said.

"Yes, a bull snake. A good snake. Kept the mice away."

"I didn't—I had no idea . . ."

"I thought Quakers were against violence," he teased her, but she did not hear the lightness in his voice.

"I'm so sorry," she said, ashamed to look at him.

"You've got pluck. I don't know many women who would have taken on a snake like that, thinking it was a rattler."

"Did you mean what you said about violence?"

"Here's the bait." He held out his left hand with the tips of his index finger and thumb pressed together. "And here's Virginia." He moved his right hand toward his left and snapped. "You know I can't resist teasing you. It's too much fun."

He picked her up by the waist. "*Bonita Cuaquerita*," he said, and by the time he set her down, she was laughing.

Virginia had fears, like everyone else, but she did not think of herself as someone whose life was defined by them. Some fears were healthy, necessary for survival. Rattlesnakes fell into this category. Some stemmed from previous experiences—bee stings and poison oak, for example—while others were of unknown origin. But overall, her life was not ruled by fear. Most times she could conquer fear by action, like milking the cow. But one thing she had not overcome was her fear of horses.

She knew her phobia was silly, but she had felt that way ever since an accident in the autumn of 1917, when she was seventeen. The United States had recently entered the war on the side of the Allies. Quakers had a long history of pacifism. Many had refused to fight in the Revolutionary War and the War between the States. With the prevailing war fervor, Virginia's mother worked on the peace and social concerns committee to secure conscientious-objector status for young men in the meeting.

In the Mendenhall family, Jonathan was viewed as the smart, responsible child who never got into trouble. As a senior in high school, he was a member of the Forensic Society and won prizes in Latin and math. He also excelled at sports. The competitive spirit was not part of the Quaker tradition of consensus and cooperation, but sports, though not endorsed in their household, were not forbidden, except for football. Her parents drew the line at football. Jonathan lettered in track and tennis.

Virginia, on the other hand, was always getting into trouble. When she got two C's on her report card, she came to Jonathan for advice. She had experimented with various ways to make a C look like a B, but all looked doctored.

"You're too smart to get C's," Jonathan said. "If you want to act up, do it in some way that doesn't hurt you." His reproof stung, and she vowed to work harder. In her family, women were expected to achieve—one of the positive legacies of Quakerism.

"Mama's going to kill me."

"Time for the warm vinegar cure," he said.

It was a private joke between them. Their mother thought vinegar was a solution to everything. Dirty stove? Warm vinegar. Sore throat? Gargle with warm vinegar. Aching bones? A warm vinegar bath. Bad grades? Warm vinegar.

"I think I'll just soak my whole personality in warm vinegar," she said.

"That's not going to get you into college," Jonathan said.

He worried about her. She liked that about him. It made her feel protected. If she had not had Jonathan as a brother, she would not have felt secure enough to be mischievous.

When Tommy Turnbull, the handsome redheaded son of the local doctor, invited Virginia to come see his father's new horse on Saturday afternoon, Virginia asked Jonathan to help her sneak away.

"That Tommy's a mean son of a gun," Jonathan said. "Why do you want to go out with him?"

"You sound more like Mama than Mama," she said.

On Saturday morning, Virginia surveyed the dresses in her closet. Drab. Drab. Drab. She wished she owned something stylish, like the dresses she saw in *Vogue* or *Ladies' Home Journal,* which were brightly colored and a scandalous six inches above the floor.

When Virginia and Jonathan left together to go downtown to meet Tommy, their mother didn't ask any questions.

"Can you keep a secret, Ginny?" Jonathan said as they passed the courthouse. He had pale skin and dark wavy hair that fell into his eyes—"a poet's eyes," her classmate Mary Ebbits had called them. Mary had befriended Virginia as a way to get close to Jonathan.

"My lips are sealed," Virginia said. It was a warm autumn day, and dried leaves crunched underfoot.

"I'm applying to Harvard."

She had never met anyone who went to Harvard. She wasn't even entirely sure where it was, only that it was far away. She couldn't imagine losing Jonathan. He was her closest friend.

"Have you told Mama?"

"If I'd have told her, it wouldn't be a secret."

She felt special, being his confidante.

There was a festive air downtown. Red, white, and blue bunting wrapped a platform that had been set up on the square. People on blankets watched a boxer sparring with a straw-stuffed effigy of the Kaiser. A few children had climbed the bronze statue of Nathanael Greene for a better view. Some of the horses nearby had tiny American flags stuck in their harnesses.

Everybody was going to war, it seemed: the Albertson kid from across the street and Virginia's friend Jennifer's older brother Jack, who was a freshman at State. The boys did look handsome in their uniforms, Virginia had to admit. Take an ordinary boy like Jimmy Straits, who, though not downright homely, had not been given the gift of looks. He was transformed by a uniform.

Virginia and Jonathan stopped in front of the five-and-dime, where Tommy had arranged to meet Virginia. Jonathan stared at a poster of a young man in a bow tie looking wistfully out a window at the passing soldiers. Large red letters at the bottom said: ENLIST.

"Sometimes I wonder which side of that window I'm on," he said to no one in particular.

"What did you say?" she asked, fussing with her hair.

"Never mind. I'll meet you back here at five."

"You're not staying with me?" Virginia said, alarmed.

"No way. This is your show." He left.

Before long, Tommy arrived. He wore a belted coat and a houndstooth cap. His pale freckles gave his face the mottled look of wind on water. She had never seen anyone so handsome. He looked at the poster in the window. "Has Jonathan signed up yet?"

"Oh, hi—hi," she said shyly. "We're Quakers. We don't believe in war."

"You're kidding? Not even when the Kaiser's kicking our butt—I mean, uh—"

"It's okay." The dirty language made her feel naughty, and she liked it.

They walked to his house. He did not introduce her to his parents, as she expected, but took her directly to the barn behind the house. Inside, it was dark and smelled of manure. She made her way carefully, mindful not to soil her newly polished high-top shoes.

In the middle stall stood an enormous horse the color of cement. The tall beast flared his nostrils, and his ears twitched back. When Tommy slipped the bridle in place, the horse reared up and the leather reins whipped out of his hands. The horse's front hooves clattered against the wall of the stall.

"Stupid animal," Tommy said and kicked the horse in the stomach. "That'll show him who's boss."

He hoisted Virginia onto the horse's bare back, then got on behind her. They followed a road leading out of town. Now the houses stood farther apart, separated by fields. Tommy and Virginia did not encounter another soul until they turned onto the old Jamestown Road and saw her neighbor Mr. Elliot in his straw hat and bow tie, out for a drive in his open model T. He honked and waved. Startled by the horn, the horse whinnied and reared back, then pounded down the road.

Terrified, Virginia leaned down low and clutched the horse's mane. Trees passed by in a blur of orange and red, and tiny rocks pelted her ankles. She pressed her cheek against the horse's neck.

Behind her, Tommy let out a whoop. "We're in the cavalry," he said and spurred the horse on.

She did not see the fence, but the horse did, and stopped short. Virginia went over the horse's neck and landed in a patch of poison oak on the far side of the fence.

Shaking, she got up on one elbow and tried to move her arms and legs. Nothing was broken. Her cheek was wet with the horse's sweat. Burrs clung to her dress, and her red hair ribbon hung on some waist-high weeds, like a surveyor's marker.

The horse stood on the other side of the fence, his sides heaving. The broken head stall dangled at his side.

Tommy was sprawled on the ground several feet away from

Virginia. He rolled over on top of her and planted a big wet kiss on her lips.

She had never been kissed before, and even in her day-dreams she had never imagined it would feel like a piece of raw liver smashed against her lips.

She pushed him off with what little strength she had left.

"Nobody's watching," he said.

She sat up abruptly. He yanked her toward him. She lost her balance and fell back, catching herself on her elbow. She righted herself and locked her arms around her knees. She had made a terrible mistake by coming here.

"Is kissing against your religion or something? You don't go to war, you don't kiss. What kind of people are you?"

"Not the kind you'd understand," she said and started the long walk back.

After school the next Monday, Virginia passed by a circle of boys near the gym. She stood on her tiptoes and saw Jonathan and Tommy at the center, crouched low and circling each other. She caught the words, "Your sister."

"Take it back," Jonathan said.

"Whatcha gonna do about it?" Tommy said. "Come on. Let's see what you got." He punched his fists in the air.

"I don't have to fight to prove I'm a man," Jonathan said.

"Is that why you ain't enlisting?" he said. Virginia cringed at his grammar, though she had not noticed it before.

From the crowd came shouts of "Chicken!" "Yellow-bellied coward!" "Traitor!"

Tommy shoved Jonathan hard on the shoulder and Jonathan fell on his rear. Tommy turned to the crowd and said, "See, he's a Quaker. He can't fight." She looked at her brother. His face was purple with shame. She had never loved him so much.

Jonathan got up, dusted himself off, and then, without warn-ing, lunged at Tommy. They fell to the ground, a windmill of legs and arms. Jonathan did not know how to fight, but athletic prowess was in his favor. He did not stop until several boys separated them. Tommy held the back of his hand against his nose as blood ran over his wrist. Jonathan picked up his jacket and pushed his way through the crowd.

At dinner, the family gathered around the table, but Jonathan's place was empty. Virginia had come down with a terrible case of poison oak, but could not ask her mother how to treat it. She made fists under the table to keep from scratching herself. Perhaps warm vinegar would stop the itching.

As they waited for Jonathan, her father said, "Doctor Turnbull's new stallion died this weekend."

"Of old age?" her mother asked.

"No, abuse. His son gave him some violent exercise and then allowed him to drink all the water he wanted when they got back to the barn. The horse got colic and was found dead in the stall."

Virginia stared at her lap and tried to control the wave of nausea that came over her. Much as she despised Tommy, she knew it was not fair to allow him to take the blame, when she had had a hand in killing the horse, as surely as if she had pulled the trigger. She had to own up to her part in the caper. The sneaking out, the deceit—those had been momentary lapses of youthful enthusiasm, but not to take the blame would be a much more serious failure of character. She hesitated. The itching beneath her dress distracted her. She would wait. No, that would not do. Anything short of complete disclosure would be dishonest.

She cleared her throat and, focusing on the place mat, said, "I have something I need to tell you."

She looked up, expecting all eyes to be on her. Instead, her mother and father had turned toward Jonathan, who was standing in the doorway. His left eye was hidden in the center of a puffy donut the color of a thundercloud.

"What happened to you?" her father said.

"After dinner, we'll put a warm vinegar compress on that," her mother said.

The vinegar cure. Virginia met her brother's eyes, but he was not smiling.

"I got in a fight with Tommy Turnbull," he said and took his place at the table.

"Did you win?" their father asked. Their mother glowered at him.

Jonathan smiled proudly. "He thought since I had never fought before that I'd be a sissy."

"Jonathan, there are peaceful ways to solve a dispute," his mother said.

"What was I supposed to do? Stand by and let him insult my sister?"

So she was right. The fight had been about her.

"Amanda, if that's the worst thing—" their father said, trying to smooth things over. He hated conflict.

"Actually, it's not," Jonathan interrupted.

Virginia prepared herself to act surprised when he told them about Harvard.

He kept his face down and said quietly, "I've decided to enlist in the army."

Outside, the deep, round sound of the whippoorwills could be heard above the ruffle of crickets. The wind carried the cries of neighborhood children who were in the midst of an after-dinner game of hide-and-seek. But around the table, no one said a word.

Finally his mother spoke. "Jonathan, thee knows war is wrong." She never used Quaker plain language except in moments of extreme emotion, and it had a powerful effect.

"Is it right for the strongest country to trample weaker ones? Somebody's got to stop the Kaiser, Mama."

Her mother did not answer immediately. Her jaw twitched.

Virginia felt a tightness in her chest and realized that she was holding her breath. The itching tortured her.

"If thee feels thee must serve thy country, then work in an ambulance unit, help feed the refugees. The Philadelphia

Friends are negotiating with the government to allow Quakers to perform alternative service." Now she was almost pleading.

"If I were inventing a world, I wouldn't come up with the idea of war. But it's here. We have to face it. It's cowardly to turn our backs." He sounded exasperated but looked scared.

"Please keep an open mind," she said.

"You don't have an open mind. You've already decided that I shouldn't go."

His mother bowed her head and shut her eyes.

Jonathan left the table. Virginia excused herself and fled outdoors. In the arbor, concord grapes fell onto the cement in purple star bursts. On the trellis by the kitchen window, the blue trumpets of morning glories bloomed from the tangled, dried-up vines. It was her fault. If he hadn't gotten in the fight to save her honor, he never would have been shamed into enlisting. Remorse for her recent prank was replaced by a deeper, stronger guilt, one that could not be so easily alleviated: Jonathan was going to war because of her.

If her mother knew it was Virginia's fault, she would . . . she would . . . what?

She found her mother in the living room, sitting in the teal rocker, with her hands resting on the pages of the open Bible in her lap.

Virginia had always felt a deep connection to her mother through silence. She knew the different kinds, from the deep worshipful silence of prayer, the tumescent silence before her mother was ready to speak in Quaker meeting. And now this misshapen silence as her mother tried to create a space inside herself that was large enough to contain her grief.

Virginia approached her. "Mama . . ."

Before she got more than a few words out, she fell at her mother's feet and buried her sobs in her mother's skirt.

Her mother smoothed Virginia's hair. "I know, sweetheart. I know. We'll all miss him."

The next week, the family gathered in the front hall to tell

Jonathan good-bye. Virginia had prepared herself for this moment so that by now she was all steel. Nothing would affect her. She did not hug him or even shake his hand. If she allowed the least bit of emotion to leak out, she would unravel. But she could not avoid his face. He looked proud, confused, and most of all old beyond his years. It would be a full year before she understood the true gravity of that look, but even though she could not put words to it, she felt, in that moment, the end of her childhood.

FOUR

Alfred rode west to the windmill pasture. Frost sparkled on the tumbleweed trapped against the fence, and the early morning light caught the tiny specks of sand embedded in the earth. His horse, a sorrel mare he bought to replace Sage, had acquired a shaggy winter coat. Though not athletically gifted, the horse was even-tempered and sure-footed. Alfred had not yet named her, and had no inclination to do so. He called her the Sorrel, and for now that was enough.

The sun created a halo through the whirling windmill blades. Overnight, ice had formed in the tank. Alfred unstrapped his ax and took it out of its leather sheath. The wind picked up out of the east. He pulled down the fleece flaps on his cap and raised his collar. The cattle munched on saltbush along the far fence.

He scattered ash on the skirt of ice at the base of the tank where water had overflowed. He hated to see water wasted like that, but he couldn't disconnect the windmill or the pipes and hoses might freeze. When he found a spot where he could stand without slipping, he brought the ax head down hard on the ice in the tank. Glittering chips flew from beneath the blade like sparks. Several cows drifted over and eyed him with interest, their heads tilted and alert.

Before long, sweat was rolling down his back, and he took off his jacket and cap. When he broke through the ice, water splashed on his leather gloves and soaked his jeans. He lifted out the large ice chunks he had loosened and heaved them away from the tank.

As soon as he finished, a few aggressive cows moved in, plunged their noses into the icy water, and drank until their sides bulged. The more timid cows waited their turn and then shyly approached, skimming their noses along the surface and flicking the water into their mouths with their tongues.

The wind was too high for him to work on the windmill blades, so he rode over to the section of the ranch that he had leased from the school. By the time he got there, his jeans had frozen stiff. When he dismounted, his jeans cracked like boards at the knees. The fingers of his leather work gloves were stiff and woody, like an old gnarled root. His woollen underwear hung damp about his legs and chest and gave him a deep chill. Before he started his work, he gathered some driftwood and brush and started a fire. He held his hands close to the flames, palms up first, then down, waiting for the sensation to return. When he was able to move his fingers again, he warmed his lunch of leftovers on the flames.

Lunch was not something he looked forward to. One thing about Virginia—she could not cook. Not that he was complaining. At least, not to her. Lord knows, she tried. That was one thing he admired about her—how much effort she put into things. But she did not take naturally to the kitchen the way his mother did, or, for that matter, the way he did. He had cooked for himself for years, before Virginia arrived, and he was not a bad cook, if he did say so himself. Most of his bachelor friends never fixed a dish with more than one ingredient: hot dogs, rice, potatoes. Virginia wasn't that bad, but how anyone could ruin nature's humblest and most delicious offering, the potato, was beyond him. Her boiled potatoes were soggy, her mashed potatoes had the texture of Cream of Wheat, and her baked potatoes shriveled up and pulled away from the skin. Her cornbread tasted like sawdust, and the meat she fixed, regardless of the cut, reminded him of the long brown slabs of chewing tobacco in Dave's General Store—no matter how much you chewed, it never dissolved.

In his years of cooking for himself, he had picked up a few pointers. An onion could improve anything. Salt pork added flavor to vegetables and meats. Friends in Mexico had taught him how to spice up dishes with garlic and red pepper. But Alfred didn't pass these suggestions on to Virginia, for fear of insulting her. She was insecure about her cooking. Instead he tried to encourage her with enthusiastic comments that were misleading without being downright dishonest, such as, "This really hits the spot," or, "Mashed potatoes—my favorite!"

But he didn't dwell on her cooking. After all, she had improved his life in so many ways. Nothing had prepared him for the pleasures of marriage. The great physical discomfort and isolation of ranch work became so much more bearable, knowing that she was at the house waiting for him. At the end of the day, he ached—bone, muscles, joints—yet still he felt energized as he headed home. It surprised him how longing could regenerate a body that had been pushed beyond its endurance. Emotions embarrassed him. Physical pleasure did not. It was so pure, so uncomplicated.

After four months of marriage, the newness had not worn off, and he delighted in discovering things about her. He admired her willingness to tackle new projects, her ability to laugh at herself, to make him take himself less seriously. There was something very masculine about the way she went about her business—purposeful, set on getting the job done so she could get on to something else—an approach that worked well for housework and chores, if not for cooking.

She was opinionated without being pushy. When choosing a book to read aloud, she would try to interest him in those spunky English heroines she liked so much. He proposed Thucydides, but he understood how she, being a Quaker, did not want to read about the Peloponnesian War. They came together on Henry James.

She was mildly eccentric without crossing the line into down-right peculiarity. He found it endearing how, over a game of Lexikon, she would stick out her tongue—just the tip—when concentrating on the letter tiles on the board. And the way she got her back up over a small transgression of the rules.

He suspected that, having lived alone for so many years, he had developed his own share of odd ticks and traits. When he was growing up, he had known a fair number of crotchety codgers who lived in remote mountain cabins, cut off by snow for months at a time. Not one would pass for what you might call normal. Hard life and isolation had honed their eccentricities to a fine point. He thought of Juke, who had more toes than teeth, or one-eyed Joe, who braided his beard in a pigtail. Old man Bollinger grew out the fingernail on his little finger until it curved over his wrist like a scythe. Men without women were a strange lot. It was hard to say whether they had turned strange being alone, or whether they were strange to begin with and therefore unable to attract a woman.

Alfred suspected that he, too, might have been susceptible to profound weirdness, had he remained alone for many more years. Perhaps all men who lived alone had that potential. His father certainly did, having quit school in the seventh grade to help his crippled father on the ranch; but he benefited from the softening influence of his wife, a cultured woman who traded a job as a piano teacher for the hard life on a ranch. He had encouraged her interest in music. He wanted her to have a semblance of the intellectual and artistic life he could not provide. But when she taught young Alfred to play the piano, Alfred's father became enraged. Music was not a manly pursuit. It was not a worthy way to spend one's time when there was so much work to be done on the ranch.

Alfred resorted to deception, and his mother was a willing collaborator. She gave his father the impression that school let out an hour later than it did, and Alfred would sneak home and practice the piano before going to help his father and brother on the ranch.

One afternoon, his father returned unexpectedly to the house. Alfred was practicing a Chopin nocturne, a slow, lyrical melody of the kind that is challenging because there are no technically demanding passages to cover up any other failings. He looked up and saw his father standing in the doorway. Alfred's fingers went limp, as if his tendons had been severed.

"I do believe you have your mother's gift," his father said. "Pity you weren't born a woman."

Alfred wanted to continue practicing, just to show his father. But he could play no more. He simply could not move his fingers.

His father was wrong. He lacked his mother's gift. He was moderately talented, nothing more. He did not pursue a career in music, but he never thought he'd want to go into ranching. And then in Mexico he began to yearn for the cool, high meadows, the ice-tipped peaks, the trout stream, the aspen groves, and the pine forests of his father's mountain ranch.

So he returned from Mexico after a long absence, hoping his father would take him in. But time and distance had done nothing to improve their relationship. While his mother fluttered and fussed over him, his father remained distant. At the dinner table on the night of his return, Alfred's mother asked him about his future plans. Alfred said, "I've been thinking about going into ranching."

His father pushed his chair back and crossed his arms. He was a not a large man, but he had a large effect. "How are you going to do that?" he said. He did not countenance fools, sissies, intellectuals, or sheep, and his son was suspect on three of the four counts.

"I've got money saved up," Alfred said. "Land is cheap, especially in the eastern part of the state."

His father laughed. "Sure it's cheap—dirt cheap. And there's a reason."

Alfred had forgotten how effectively his father could cut him down to size with a few well-chosen words. He would have thought, after so many years, that he'd be out of practice, the way Alfred's fingers had lost their dexterity after being away from the piano.

His mother rushed in to smooth things over, as was her habit. "You've been out of the country and haven't read the papers. Every week it seems there's another article about ranchers on the plains selling out and moving on."

"We're lucky we've got water from the mountains," his father said. "But out east, the land's just drying up and blowing away."

"I can't afford mountain land," Alfred said.

It was the perfect opportunity for his father to say, "Why don't you come work with me on the ranch?" That's what Alfred had hoped for. He hadn't counted on it, for damn sure he'd never ask, but he had hoped. After all, Alfred's father had worked on the mountain ranch with his own father until he died, when Alfred was ten.

But clearly Alfred's father had no intention of carrying on that family tradition. He cleared his throat, mumbled something under his breath, and excused himself from the table.

Alfred's mother patted his hand and said, "We have complete confidence in you, whatever you decide to do." It was an old trick of hers, to include his father in her "we"—"We love you. . . . We're fascinated by your letters about Mexican culture. . . . We can't wait for you to return to Colorado." Surely she knew that his father did not fit comfortably under the umbrella of her "we."

"He doesn't think I can do it," Alfred said.

"Of course he does. You're his son. Being a cattleman is in your blood."

He did not contradict her, but got up and left. He would show the old man. He'd make a go of it on his own, even if it killed him.

If his brother, Shrine, were alive, he'd be working at his father's side. No one had mentioned him since Alfred had returned from Mexico, but Alfred felt Shrine's presence in the house.

Shrine's real name was Samuel, after his father, but everybody called him Shrine. He was two years older than Alfred and was adored by his father. Shrine was quick and athletic. He was mutton-busting by the age of five—a pint-sized fellow riding a sheep like a bucking bronco. As a child, Shrine carried a rope looped over his shoulder and lassoed everything in sight—fence posts, yucca bushes, bales of hay fitted with a stuffed-fabric cow's head. He soon moved on to calves. His coordination and sense of timing were exceptional, and as he grew up, he excelled at roping calves, breaking horses, and cutting cattle.

As a child, Alfred had been dreamy and shy. Because he had inherited his mother's love of reading and music, he had been tagged a sissy. Both Shrine and his father belittled him. If Alfred made a mistake, it was proof of his incompetence. If Shrine made the same mistake, he was just having a bad day.

Alfred shrank from competition: Shrine thrived on it. Shrine had a fierce need to win even the stupidest game—many of which he invented—as long as it was something he wanted to be best at. Whenever Alfred won an award at school for the best speech, the best essay, or the best soloist in the chorus, it did not bother Shrine, since these were not things he respected.

One Sunday morning in spring when Shrine was sixteen, the brothers went trout fishing on Wolf Creek. The water ran fast and glassy over rocks several feet beneath the surface before it dropped off into a spectacle of sound and spray, rapids and falls.

Alfred was at an awkward stage of adolescence. Though he would soon surpass Shrine in height, his torso at that point had not kept pace with his gangly arms and legs, and he felt ashamed of this jumble of body parts. He was in awe of his brother, who was in magnificent shape. When Shrine's shirt was wet, it outlined the contours of his muscles. No doubt about it—Shrine was a man.

That day, Shrine staked out a place on the bank. Alfred took up a spot on the humpbacked rocks that jutted near the center of the fast-moving water.

Shrine called out, "The fish are here. You'll have better luck on the bank." He always offered tips that Alfred ignored, even though he usually proved to be right.

"I'm fine here," Alfred said, shouting to be heard over the water.

"Your loss, not mine," Shrine said.

They fished most of the morning. Shrine's basket overflowed. Alfred's was empty. Just as they were getting ready to leave, Alfred looked down and, from behind a ledge of the rock, saw a large moving shadow. He selected a fly and, with several whips of the wand, cast it onto the water. The leader and fly landed first, barely breaking the surface. Before long, the rod jumped in his hand, and the supple tip bowed over into a goose neck. Every nerve in Alfred's body was alert as he let the fish make a run for deeper waters, then coaxed it in, repeating the process several times. The spray grazed his face, the sun warmed his skin, and the shadows of the lodgepole pines darkened the water in spires, but he was oblivious to everything except the intense tease between man and fish. Eventually Alfred brought the fish in.

"Shrine, look," he said and held the catch up with two hands. It was a trophy fish, fit to be hung above a mantle. He carefully carried the fish to the bank.

"So you think you're a big shot." Shrine looked at him through narrowed eyes.

"No, just lucky." Alfred unhooked the fish, already imagining what his father would say. The fish was too big to put in the basket, so he cradled it in his arms like a newborn. The trout's skin was soft and smooth. Reflecting the blue of the sky, it gave off hints of iridescent color. Alfred had never seen anything so beautiful.

"Let's see how much that weighs," Shrine said and took the fish from Alfred.

"What are you doing?" Alfred said in disbelief.

The fish slipped out of Shrine's hands and plopped into the backwater, where a brownish froth had gathered on the surface, speckled with pollen and insects. Alfred watched in horror as the fish disappeared beneath.

"You did that on purpose," he said.

"You can't prove it."

Alfred lunged at him. Caught by surprise, Shrine slid on his back across the sand. In a surge of pure energy, Alfred pummeled him. Shrine soon got out from under Alfred's smaller body and, without much trouble, threw Alfred on his back. He slipped free from his brother's hold. This angered Shrine, and he pinned him down again. Reaching beside him, he grabbed a jagged rock and brought it down hard on Alfred's forehead. A red stream dripped into his eyes and down his face, as if he were weeping blood. Shrine cocked the rock above his head again, ready for another blow, but this time he hesitated. Alfred stared into his brother's eyes and, in a moment of terrible clarity, knew that Shrine would die before he would.

Having second thoughts, Shrine threw the rock into the river, picked up his basket, and left.

That evening, their mother fried up Shrine's trout and served it for dinner.

His father took a bite and said, "Mmm, delicious. Did you boys catch these?"

"Shrine did," Alfred said. His father turned his way and noticed, for the first time, the big white gauze patch in the middle of Alfred's forehead, like a miner's light.

"What the hell happened to you?" his father said.

"I hit my head on a rock." Alfred did not look across the table at Shrine.

His father raised his brows. "I didn't know fishing was a contact sport. Better leave it to your brother," he said, smiling proudly at his eldest son. "He's the real fisherman in this family."

Alfred made his stomach hard to keep back the rage.

Later that evening, Alfred's mother came to his room and sat beside him on the bed. "Let me take a peek at that dressing," she said in a soothing voice. He groaned slightly, too tired to talk.

With an iodine-soaked cotton ball, she dabbed at what oozed from the edges of the jagged scab. "Ever since you were a little boy, you've been able to understand how other people feel. That's a real gift." She sponged a cool cloth on his face. "Not many people have that. Shrine doesn't."

He closed his eyes and felt the coolness against his cheek and neck. Why was she saying this? She couldn't possibly know what had happened. Shrine would never tell her.

"You can forgive him, because you understand him. I wouldn't ask that of Shrine, but I can ask it of you."

"I'll forgive him when he admits he's wrong."

"That's not forgiveness. That's pride—disguised, but pride nonetheless." She wrung out the cloth in the bowl.

He turned his head away. He could always depend on her to understand him. Yet here she was, taking Shrine's side.

"Well, I'm not the one at fault," he said defiantly and turned back to her.

"No, but by holding on, you'll do yourself more harm," she said and put a fresh piece of gauze on his forehead.

That night, he promised himself he would never again have anything to do with his brother. But when the scab healed, it left a jagged scar, a white lightning bolt in the middle of his forehead, that served to remind him of his brother's hold over him, in the same way a brand seared into a cow's hide leaves a clear mark of ownership.

By senior year, Alfred was one of only two boys in his class. The others had dropped out to work. Alfred was painfully shy around girls, even Shrine's girlfriend Rosie. She was a spirited girl with black hair and flashing eyes who excelled in all subjects, especially math. Her father owned a neighboring ranch, and there were no sons in the family. If Rosie married Shrine, they would one day run an enormous operation. Alfred was furious at Rosie for wasting her intelligence on Shrine. She should go to college—be a teacher, or even an accountant.

Alfred was determined to go to college. The Sunday before graduation, he went to his father's office, a small room with a desk where his mother did the bookkeeping for the ranch. She also kept the birth weights and calving histories of all the cows so they would know which to sell and which to keep. In the family, however, the room was known as his father's office.

His father sat at the desk, going over his mother's figures.

Alfred leaned against a bookshelf. His father pushed his chair back and swiveled toward him.

"I've been offered a scholarship to the University of Colorado," Alfred said.

His father crossed his arms and leaned back in the chair. His face was deeply tanned up to his eyebrows, but his forehead was milky white where his hat protected it from the sun. "You don't see Shrine running off to college."

Alfred was tired of being compared to Shrine. "He's never been interested in school."

"No, he's a rancher, and he's learning it the only way you can—by doing it. Every day I go out on that ranch, I figure out what I've got to give. Then I give a little more. I see that kind of drive in Shrine. I don't see it in you."

"I'm no good at ranching. That's what you're always telling me."

"You're a fine rancher."

"What do you mean? You're always saying, 'It's like teaching a chicken to fly.'"

"Son, I'm trying to get you to push yourself, excel at something. But you accept defeat. Look at you and Shrine. You never even try to beat him. You don't test yourself. How are you going to wake up in the morning and live with yourself for the rest of the day if you don't know what you're capable of?"

For once, Alfred saw what his mother found so attractive about his father. He was a man to be admired. Feared, but also admired. But Alfred had made up his mind about college.

"I can excel at music. It's not something you understand, but it's something I'm good at."

"Leave that to the womenfolk. Your mother—she enjoys that kind of thing. I like to see her happy. But you—you're a man."

"But it's what I want to study."

"You won't be able to ranch someday if you've got any quit in you."

"I'm not quitting. I'm just getting an education," he said, and left.

Every summer, the Bowens rounded up the steers and herded them to Bear Park, where they grazed, by government permit, on Forest Service mountain land. From the time he was sixteen, it had been Alfred's responsibility to look after the herd. Shrine always accompanied him on the two-day cattle drive, helped him set up camp, then returned home for the summer to help their father look after the breeder cows and calves, which flourished better at lower than nine thousand feet.

A high plateau between Flora Peak and the Jefferson Range, Bear Park was paradise to a dreamy young man like Alfred. While the herd fattened itself on the knee-high bunch grass, Alfred stretched out by the glistening trout stream and read. The rolling meadows were glutted with purple spikes of penstemon, brilliant-red Indian paintbrush, and blue lupines in season. Groves of aspen grew at the border, their heart-shaped leaves so delicate that the slightest breeze flipped their silvery underside to the sun. Beyond, the darker juniper, spruce, and pine rose at steep angles. The snow-tipped mountains of the Jefferson Range nudged their noses into the clouds.

On the annual drive over the mountain paths, Alfred and Shrine rounded up the cattle and herded them in tandem. As always, Shrine rode point and Alfred brought up the rear, where the sick, weak, or lazy steers collected. The tumbled rocks and boulders that filled the gashes in the mountainside revealed where avalanches had occurred the winter before.

They arrived on the mountain by evening of the second day. Shrine helped Alfred unload the supplies and set up the canvas tent. Before starting back, Shrine insisted on going deer hunting. He was an excellent hunter and knew that deer would be plentiful in the uninhabited section of Bear Park that the Forest Service restricted for grazing until midsummer. The brothers rose before dawn and set out on foot into the unfamiliar territory. At first light, they came upon three deer grazing on the edge of a high meadow. Two of the bucks raised their heads, alerted to danger, and darted into a dense stand of pine. Shrine took down the third in a single shot. It was an older buck, judging from the points on its antlers, which had not yet reached their full year's growth. They tied its legs over a pole and carried it back, each brother supporting one end of the pole on his shoulder. Alfred would smoke the meat at the campsite, and that, along with the fish he caught, would hold him for a good part of the summer.

Shrine led the way—it was one of the unspoken rules between the brothers. Rather than follow the path, Shrine took a shortcut, forging his own path down the steep mountain. Alfred kept slipping on pine needles and had trouble matching his gait to Shrine's.

"Don't be a sissy," Shrine said. "Pick it up."

They continued on for a while, until suddenly the ground gave way beneath Shrine's feet. There was a terrible clatter, as if someone had pulled over a shelving unit, and he disappeared into an opening in the earth. Alfred felt the weight of the deer shift from his shoulder as it slipped into the hole after Shrine.

Alfred stared in front of him. Dust rose from the opening like smoke. He cautiously peered over the edge. Shrine had fallen into an old mining shaft. Along its length, old boards and beams stuck out like broken bones. The gauzy light reached down thirty feet or so, and as the dust settled, Alfred was able to make out the deer underneath the debris. Its legs were still bound together, and its head was wrenched so that it faced its tail. But Alfred could not see his brother.

"Shrine. Shrine. Can you hear me?"

"Yep." Shrine was a man of few words, but it only took one to give Alfred a sense of relief.

"Are you hurt?"

"Can't tell if this damned blood's from me or the deer." His voice, through the darkness, was barely audible.

"Don't move. I'll go get help." Alfred would always remember that phrase—*don't move*. How stupid.

"It don't look too good," Shrine said. Alfred knew from his slack voice that his brother was in serious pain.

"I'll lower my canteen down."

"Don't bother. My arm's pinned in here."

As Alfred moved closer to the edge, he loosened some dirt. There were a few seconds of silence before the dirt pattered on top of the debris.

"Get back or you'll fall in, too." Shrine was still ordering Alfred around—a good sign.

Alfred had no horse or rope—only his rifle, which was completely useless. He fired it several times in the air, out of frustration, though he knew it was unlikely anyone would hear.

"I'm going for help," Alfred shouted, standing back from the edge but canting his body forward so his voice would carry into the hole. "You find any gold down there, I don't want you cashing out on me, you hear?"

There was no reply.

Alfred tied his bandanna on a branch to mark his place, then scrambled down the mountain so fast that pebbles and dirt clods tumbled in front of him. He picked up the trail and slowed down, aware that he would have to pace himself if he were to last. He was out of breath when he reached the tent, partly because he was not used to the air at this altitude. Quickly he saddled his horse and followed the trail down the mountain. It was excruciating to go so slowly. As he nudged the horse forward, he couldn't shake the feeling that there was some way he could have prevented the accident. If he had been the one at the bottom of the hole, Shrine would have devised a way to get him out—he was sure of it. Shrine was better at everything.

Once he reached the road to Rock Haven, Alfred pushed his horse hard and arrived in town in a swirl of dust. The horse was foaming and panting. The down-in-the-mouth settlement consisted of a few flimsy pine-fronted stores, an unpainted post office, a saloon, and, off the main street, a scattering of houses. But the town did have a doctor. For that, Alfred was grateful, though less so when he was told he would find him in the saloon.

The doctor was an overweight man with a white beard and a red pitted nose. Purple veins branching across his cheeks gave his face a purple glow. He did not seem drunk, but his wheezing cough made Alfred wonder if he could make it up the mountain.

The doctor, more willing than able, found another volunteer, a man named Deke. After gathering supplies and a fresh horse for Alfred, they returned to the base camp. From there, Alfred led the group up the mountain. On the way down, Alfred had kept himself alert, knowing he would have to retrace his steps. But now he was exhausted, and from horseback, everything looked different. Finally, by luck, he caught a glimpse of his red bandanna through the trees.

They tethered their horses below and scrambled up the mountain. Shrine was still conscious, but weak.

"A good sign," the doctor said. "He hasn't gone into shock."

They still had a few hours of light left. With the rope, Alfred made a lariat and dangled it down the hole. From so far up, the rope was impossible to control. When he tried to lower it over the deer, it dangled out of position. Finally, after many frustrating tries, he worked the rope over the deer's neck and pulled it taut.

"Hang in there, Samuel. We've almost got it," Alfred shouted down into the darkness. He never used his brother's real name, but now it slipped easily out of his mouth.

He tugged the rope hard, but the deer didn't move. It, too, was pinned under beams and wood.

They wrapped the rope around a tree to get more leverage. Even the doctor, who had avoided any physical exertion up until this point, now helped pull the rope. With all three straining together, there was a sudden give in the rope and they staggered backward. The rubble shifted.

"You okay?" Alfred shouted down the hole.

"Good enough."

They slowly raised the deer. Its antlers scraped against the sides of the shaft and loosened the dirt, which rained down into the hole.

"These damned feds," Deke said, grunting as he pulled the rope. "Gave a mining claim to any fool that could put an X on the dotted line."

Finally they got the animal out. Its forelegs had snapped off and its antlers were tipped in blood.

Now Alfred could actually see his brother.

"Can you move?" Alfred called down.

"Got a chest of broken ribs, and one arm ain't good for nothing, but I'm breathing," Shrine said.

"That's one brave fellow down there," the doctor said. Alfred felt proud of his brother.

They lowered the lariat down again, and using his good arm, Shrine fit it as best he could around his waist. When they had pulled him halfway up, Shrine passed out, and Alfred went white.

"Don't worry, son. It's the pain. He'll be all right," the doctor said, and they continued to hoist him up. They pulled Shrine over the edge, and the doctor felt for his pulse. The indentations from the deer's antlers were stamped into the side of his face.

The doctor cut through the bloody right sleeve. Alfred took one look and turned away. The open gash in Shrine's arm was surrounded by mush, like meat that had been chewed and spit out.

"Is he going to be all right?" Alfred asked, breathing through his mouth. The smell was overpowering.

"He ain't going to be any better with you nattering at me," the doctor said. "Now get a fire started."

His authoritative tone gave Alfred a brief moment of confidence, but it disappeared when he said, "This arm's going to have to come off."

At that moment, Shrine stirred awake. "Who are you?" he said groggily.

"The doctor."

"You cut that arm off and I'll, I'll—" He passed out before he could finish.

The doctor turned to Alfred. "I'm going to need your permission, son."

"Do you have any anesthesia?"

"No."

Alfred winced. "What are the options?"

"Way I see it, he can live with one arm or die with two. Your call."

"Are you sure?"

"I can't write you out a guarantee, but that's my professional opinion."

"Give me a minute."

"Not much more," the doctor said.

Alfred went over to the ridge and looked over the edge of the mountain, into the open space that was now filled with grainy light. The evening was quiet. A hawk soared above an outcropping of rock. If only he could reason with Shrine, make him see there was no other way. But when he returned, Shrine was still unconscious.

"Do it," Alfred said.

That was all. He couldn't bear to watch and went back to his place on the ridge. The hawk was gone. He sat for a long time and watched the cliffs on the other ridge turn molten. When he was certain enough time had passed, he got up to leave. It was then that a scream carried over the mountain, a sound that would haunt Alfred for many nights when he most needed sleep. He closed his eyes, and when he opened them, his face was turned upward, and he was praying. He looked at the swollen clouds, hoping to find some answer to his plea. But all he saw was a sky so red that it seemed to have absorbed Shrine's blood.

Alfred stayed on the mountain that summer, though he made several trips back to visit his brother. Shrine had fully recovered, but was slow at learning to use his left hand. Pain he could take, but not incompetence. There were so many things he could not do. He could not rope, brand, or dehorn a calf. He could not calm a nervous stallion or pull a backward calf from the cow, at least not without patience, which he did not have.

On the other hand, there were many things he could do if he tried. But he was used to being the best at everything. He could not stand the humiliation. So he did as little as possible. Sometimes Alfred would see Shrine riding across the meadows, his right sleeve flapping like a windsock. Mostly Shrine spent his days on the porch staring toward the mountains.

That fall, Alfred put off going to college in order to help on the ranch. His father's grief was a palpable if insubstantial being that kept company with the other ghost that was always with them: the ghost of Shrine before the accident. Every time Alfred did a task, his father compared him to the old Shrine, and found him to come up short.

Alfred had no idea what his brother had told his father about the accident, but he was sure that his father blamed him.

One weekend Alfred stayed on the ranch to repair a harness while the rest of the family went to town to do errands. He heard a horse outside and came to the door of the shed, thinking that someone had forgotten something.

He saw Shrine's girlfriend Rosie coming up the road. She rode like a man, but she certainly didn't look like one in her split skirt and white blouse that showed off her thin waist and generously curved body. Her thick hair flowed luxuriously behind her. She rode up to Alfred and asked where she could find Shrine.

"You just missed him. He's gone to town."

"I'll wait," she said, dismounting.

"It might be a while. They said something about eating lunch at the café."

She tied up the horse and came over to him. "You can keep me company," she said, smiling coyly. "That is, if you don't mind."

He felt self-conscious. At the monthly dances in Roaring Creek, she never looked his way. From the sidelines, Alfred had watched her with envy as she danced, so completely in tune with Shrine that they seemed to move as one being. Shrine had not been back to the dance hall since the accident.

To pass the time, Alfred suggested to Rosie that they ride to Wolf Creek, the prettiest part of the ranch. She agreed. He left a note at the house, saddled up a horse, and took her across the meadows, around the base of a mesa, and to the part of the creek where the waters ran too fast to fish. They found a dry patch of ground set back from the edge of a deep pool in front of the falls.

"I thought you'd be in college by now," Rosie said, stretching out on the rock. "I always admired how smart you were."

He didn't think she had ever noticed him in class.

"I'm putting it off for a while. Dad needs me around here now that—well, you know."

"It's hot out," she said, twisting her long hair around her hand. She produced some hairpins from her pocket, lowered her head, and pinned her hair up. Alfred stared at her lovely long neck.

"Do you ever go swimming here?" she asked.

"Shrine and I used to come here as kids. We'd race to the other side. He always won."

"Sounds like Shrine." She stood up. "Want to go swimming?" Splatters of light quivered on the rocks.

"We don't have swimming suits."

"Who needs them? Here, turn your back."

He faced away from the water. He heard the rustle of her blouse, the whoosh of her skirt as it dropped at her ankles, and the gentle shush of water as she waded in.

"You can turn now," she said.

She was treading water in the middle of the pool. Her pale head and shoulders gleamed above the smooth water like a marble bust. He stared at the tantalizing whiteness that fell below her shoulders, refracted by the water. He had never seen a woman without clothes.

"What are you waiting for? It feels great."

He stripped down to his underwear, got in the water, and swam upstream to where the chute of water hit the pool in a revelry of bubbles and spray. He stood underneath and let the force hit his chest, hoping to get rid of the stirrings he could not control.

Then he returned to the deeper part of the pool, stopping

before he got too close to Rosie. The water swirled in eddies from her shoulder as she paddled to stay afloat.

"Did you ever wonder what it would be like to kiss me?" she said.

"I think we better be getting back. Shrine will be home any minute."

"You said he'd be gone for hours."

"With him, you never can tell."

"No one will know," she said, smiling as she glided slowly toward him. The water rippled away from her cupped hands.

"It doesn't seem right," he said, but felt the thrill of the forbidden.

She playfully pecked him on the cheek, then backed up.

He ducked underwater and emerged, farther away from her.

"You look like a snake just bit you," she said. "Was it that bad?"

He shook his head. She moved toward him and kissed him again, this time on the mouth. He reached for her skin, but found himself flapping to stay afloat. Water splashed around them. He pulled her closer to the edge, where the water was waist-high and his hands were free to run across her slippery skin. Her breasts slid against his chest, and he sought out her mouth.

Just then, he heard trampling through the underbrush. As they pulled apart, he saw Shrine towering above them on horseback.

Alfred and Rosie scrambled out of the water. Rosie crossed her arms in front of her breasts and ran to the pile of clothes. Alfred's wet underwear bore the outline of a swelling at his groin.

Shrine got off his horse and approached Alfred, who was struggling into his pants.

"I can explain," Alfred said, glancing over at Rosie. Her blouse had turned flesh-colored where it stuck to her wet skin.

"It's an arm I'm missing, not an eye," Shrine said.

By now, Rosie had struggled into her skirt. She went over to Shrine and laid a hand on his shoulder. "Shrine, please."

He shrugged her away and turned to his brother. "You thought you'd even things up, taking my arm."

"I didn't have a choice. You know that."

"Like you didn't have a choice to take my girl."

Shrine folded his one hand into a fist and walked toward his brother.

Alfred backed away.

"You think I can't fight because I'm half a man. I'll take you with one arm."

"Forget it, Shrine."

"Everyone pretends they don't notice."

He fumbled with the snaps of his shirt. When he finally got them undone, he shrugged his shoulders to get the shirt off, and threw it on the rocks.

His chest and arm were pasty white, never exposed to the sun, but his hand was tanned a deep mahogany, so it looked as if he were wearing an old work glove. His right arm was gone below the shoulder. On the end of the stump, the skin was drawn together into a little flap like the tied end of a balloon. Alfred's heart broke at the sight of it.

"Come on, Shrine. We both need to cool off. Let's go back to the house."

Alfred put his arm on his brother's shoulder. The bottom edge of his hand slipped under the stump, and Alfred felt the wrinkles of the bunched-up skin. He drew his hand back as if he had been stung.

"You son of a bitch." Shrine started pounding on him with one fist. Alfred did not fight back, but tried to stop his brother's moving arm. When that didn't work, he walked away.

"I'll kill you with one arm," Shrine said and took Alfred from behind, his good arm around his neck. Kicking ferociously, Shrine was like a wild animal. In his pure rage, he was a force to contend with. When Alfred finally got Shrine's arm off his neck, he ran away from him.

"Don't you dare pity me," Shrine called after him. His chest heaved.

Alfred returned and punched him in the nose. "There, does that make you feel better?"

"I just don't want pity," Shrine said, wiping the blood from his nose with his stump.

"Nobody pities you as much as you pity yourself," Alfred said and walked downriver toward the horses.

Several weeks later, the postman was riding on the old toll road through Greystone Gulch and came upon a horse tethered to a tree. He stopped and found Shrine underneath. Shrine had finally found something he could do with his left hand, and as was typical of everything Shrine set his mind to, he had done it well. He had shot himself through the heart.

Rosie did not attend the funeral, but the rest of her family went, along with friends from neighboring ranches. Shrine lay in the coffin, his arm over his chest, as if reciting the Pledge of Allegiance. The other sleeve lay at his side, as flat as a paper doll. Alfred had never seen his father cry—not when he separated his shoulder in a riding accident, nor when he was hooked by a bull's horn and fashioned a girdle out of his shirt to soak up the blood. But standing beside the casket, he wept without shame. Alfred did not. He stared into the casket, wooden and unfeeling.

That Christmas, he announced to his father that he was going to the university.

"I could use you around here," his father said.

"You can hire someone to help. I need to get away for a while."

"You didn't even like him," his father said, speaking of Shrine for the first time since the funeral.

"No, but I loved him," Alfred said.

Alfred turned to go, but his father stopped him. "If you walk out of here, don't bother coming back."

Alfred walked out.

FIVE

Spikes of light angled out from the low-slung clouds as Alfred rode to the west pasture to check on the bulls. These days, rain, when it existed at all, evaporated before it reached the ground, creating a spectacular pattern in the sky that teased.

He always watched for rain, hoped for it, prayed for it, knowing full well it never came at the right time or in the right amount. It came down too hard, in the form of hail, or in vertical spears that washed out roads and ran off the pastures without soaking in. It came too early or too late. More recently, it didn't come at all.

There was a saying among the ranchers who gathered at Dave's General Store in town to grouse about the weather:

> Out in the West, where men are men
> And it hasn't rained since God knows when.

He was starting a ranch in the driest year on record—barely nine inches of rain instead of the eighteen needed to grow wheat. A blistering August had seared the hay crop. The static electricity in a midsummer dust storm had charred his neighbor Ebberson's wheat fields like some science experiment gone awry. That fall, some ranchers had liquidated their herds because they couldn't afford to buy feed to carry the cattle over the winter. As a result, the market was glutted with livestock, and prices were down. Since this was Alfred's first year, his cows would not calve until the following March and April. He had to see his cows through the winter and portion out the hay he had, hoping he could make it last until spring.

He was playing with close margins. He had to have a good calving season in the spring. He just had to. Otherwise . . . he couldn't even think about the alternative. Drought or no drought, he could not allow himself to fail. All he needed was a little rain. Just a little. Not snow, for then he would have to start feeding the cattle—but rain. Even though it was too late in the season to help this year's hay crop, the rain would replenish the water supply. Now as he looked west, where the rain remained trapped between the earth and the clouds, he was once again reminded of how powerless he was.

Growing up on the mountain ranch, he had never worried about rain. His family had senior water rights to Wolf Creek. Fed by snowmelt, the creek ran from headwaters on the Continental Divide and crossed the ranch in the northwest corner on its descent to the valley. Through a series of head gates and ditches, the water irrigated the hay fields. His father conserved water, as he conserved everything else, but he had never suffered from a drought. On the plains, Alfred had no choice but to depend on rain to fill the dry creek beds and wash through the wide draws that drained the land when the flash floods came.

Astride the Sorrel, Alfred popped a couple of rocks in his mouth. He kept them in his pocket, like candy, and sucked on them to reduce his thirst. He thought of Virginia at home. He did not tell her about his preoccupations. He didn't want to worry her. The less she knew, the better. But he could feel himself pulling back, ever so slightly.

His body could withstand physical fatigue, but this mental weariness was new to him. At night, he felt so drained he barely had enough energy to read aloud. But he forced himself to, because Virginia seemed to enjoy it so. The evening before, he had worked on his accounts, which always put him in a foul mood. The figures added up—or didn't, in this case—to a bleak picture. The big question mark was how much hay he would need, and that depended on the snow. In bed that night, he felt too exhausted to make love. When Virginia curled her foot over his and rolled to him expectantly—the first time she had initiated lovemaking—a panic seized him. The possibility that his body might fail him was as horrifying as financial ruin. But this time, his fear was unfounded. Once in motion, his body became invigorated through ardor. Afterward, he lay beside her, grateful and replenished, his body the full length of hers and tracing it curve for curve, so familiar, yet still unfamiliar in its softness and warmth, and he thought: *I will never forgive myself if I disappoint her.*

The wind blew every day on the prairie, and Virginia soon became accustomed to its background noise, which sometimes resembled a hum, or sometimes a moan or a howl, and other times the gunning of a motor. The ill-fitting windows rattled like dancing bones and admitted enough dust into the house to form ripples in the floor if left unattended. This was not the light fluff that formed dust kittens under furniture and that, at the slightest gust, floated across the room on a cushion of air. No, this dust was more like pulverized glass, and it blasted the paint off buildings, scoured the color from license plates, and drew blood when it collided with bare skin. It was impossible to sweep up. Some women used red cedar sawdust treated with oil, but Virginia couldn't justify the expense.

So much of her time was spent cleaning. Every morning she had to wash the separator, fill the kerosene lamps, trim the wicks, and clean the blackened chimneys. But most of her work was created by the dust. She was determined to make her job easier. Once hungry for news headlines, she now turned first to the *Post*'s women's page for a column called "Henrietta's Helpful Hints." Dust became her preoccupation, and consumed her time. She solicited advice from neighbors and from store clerks in town. One woman swore by the use of rags stuffed into cracks. Rags could be washed and reused. Another woman advocated the use of oilcloth on the window sills. One article recommended covering window cracks with the gummed-paper strips used to wrap packages. Henrietta suggested hanging wet sheets over the windows and doors. Every person had their remedy, and each remedy had its drawback. Virginia decided to cover the windows in muslin, a more permanent solution.

On Tuesday, her errand day, she made the hour-long drive to town. On the way, she passed a cemetery surrounded by a low wrought-iron fence. Workmen were clearing the dirt that had accumulated between the gravestones. Even the dead could not escape the dust.

In town she delivered the cream, which she sold for nine cents a pound, and eggs at ten cents a dozen. Then she parked the truck in front of the bank on Main Street and went next door to get stamps. People had lined up in front of the post office to get the flour, sugar, corn, and peanut butter the county gave out once a week. Most wore clean, freshly ironed clothes. They had dressed up to stand in line. These were hard-working people for whom self-reliance was everything, but hard times had forced them to accept handouts. She was aware of how thin a line separated her from them. A few setbacks and she, too, would have to wait in line—on Main Street, no less—in full view of neighbors and strangers. Her heart went out to them. She wanted to relay to them that there was no shame in their situation. But who was she kidding? Of course there was shame. It was stamped on their faces, reflected in their eyes, which they averted as she walked past. When she finished her errand and emerged from the post office, she crossed the street to avoid walking by the line again. From now on, she would come to town on Wednesdays, not Tuesdays.

Dave's General Store was across the street from the bank. Inside, it smelled of kerosene, salt cod, spices, and apples—an odd mixture that brought back pleasant memories of her father's grocery store in North Carolina, though Dave's had a dustier, more haphazard look. Hundred-pound burlap bags of coffee, sugar, beans, and cornmeal sat along the wall. Loose tobacco and brown slabs of chaw were kept under glass. From the ceiling hung bibless overalls, galvanized tin buckets, leather work gloves, and yellow rope. Bolts of calico and oilcloth angled in any free space.

Virginia got out her list, which she made not to avoid forgetting an item, but to keep her from buying anything extra. She eyed the soft sticks of red licorice that Dave kept in big glass jars by the cash register, just like her father had in his grocery store. When she was a child, her father always let her take a stick when she stopped by after school. The candy stained her mouth, like carelessly applied lipstick.

She coveted the red glossy ropes of candy but resisted buying any. Candy was not on the list. Muslin was. As Dave measured out the number of yards she requested, she tried to get her mind off the licorice. The more she thought about the candy, the more she craved it.

At the cash register, Dave totaled the items. "Will that be all?" he asked.

She stared again at the big glass jars of candy. She had a few extra coins from the eggs and cream she had sold. What was wrong with treating herself to a few pieces of candy?

"And four sticks of red licorice," she said quickly.

Dave smiled—had her voice sounded as guilty as she felt?—and opened the glass jar to let her reach in.

She went outside and sat on a bench across from the bank and took out a licorice stick. She felt ashamed that she had given in to her sweet tooth.

She sucked on the end of the licorice, letting it soften before she took a bite. Suddenly she found herself surrounded by four small children ranging in ages from four to eight. Their faces were clean, but they wore patched sweaters and were without coats. It was a cold December day, and the little girl's lower jaw quivered from it. Her towheaded brother put his arm around her to warm her. The children stared at Virginia with large eyes.

She put the bag of candy under her arm. "Are your parents around here?" she asked.

The children did not respond. Their eyes did not leave her.

"Why don't you run over and find them?"

The children did not move. They did not smile. They only stared.

"Would you like some candy?"

She gave the two oldest boys a stick apiece and then divided the third piece and gave the halves to the towhead and his sister. They scampered off to rejoin the line in front of the post office.

Virginia sat on the bench and finished her piece of candy, but it did not taste as good as she remembered. Before long, a woman in a thin sweater pulled two reluctant children by the elbow up to the bench.

"Go on. What do you say?" the woman said, pushing the little towhead forward. His face bore the smeared lipstick look familiar to her from childhood.

He lowered his head and held out a sticky palm, returning what was left of the candy. His sister did the same.

"That's okay. You can keep it," Virginia said and tried to return the candy.

"We don't need no handouts, thank you," the mother said stiffly.

"You'd be doing me a favor. I'm just going to throw it away. I hate to see it go to waste," she said.

"What you do with it is your business," she said, grabbing the children, and returned to the post office line. Virginia put the candy inside the brown bag and left it on the bench.

As she was pulling out of her parking place, she glanced back. The bag was still there.

After completing her other errands, she took the laundry to Ida Pinska, who lived alone in a ramshackle house at the edge of town. Ida was a simple soul who looked older than her nineteen years but acted younger. She had an ample bosom and plump arms. At quick glance, one might be forgiven for finding her fat. In fact, she was as solid as a plum, her muscles toned by the demanding physical labor of laundry. Every day she lifted heavy clothes out of boiling vats of water with a pole and scrubbed them on a corrugated metal board. She ferried flatirons back and forth from the fire for reheating, hauled water from the pump, and carried wood to the fire. Her clothes reeked of meat grease and lye, which she used to make soap. She had the wizened hands of a sixty-year-old, from working with the corrosive lye.

Ida's parents had immigrated from Bohemia and home-steaded nearby. They had eleven children. Ida was the middle child and only girl. Her mother died in childbirth when Ida was twelve, leaving Ida to care for her father and ten brothers, including a newborn. Ida was not blessed with intelligence and had not gone to school beyond elementary school. Though she could do simple, repetitive tasks, she was not capable of caring for such a large family. Her father quickly remarried. As soon as Ida turned fourteen, her stepmother insisted Ida be sent to town to work. The Lutheran Church, knowing what happened to single girls alone in town, took Ida on as a project. They found her a house, set her up in business, and made sure she was provided with a food basket at Thanksgiving and Christmas.

When Virginia drove up, she found Ida sitting on the front steps surrounded by cats. One was draped around her neck like a boa and another was luxuriously stretched out in her lap. A black cat with white paws that looked like spats lengthened himself along the top step. On another step, a gray cat exposed its stomach to the sun.

Ida was known about town as the Cat Lady. She took in the sick, wild, discarded, and unmanageable cats. Everyone in town brought their animals to her. Some cats would appear on their own, as if they had been given Ida's address. She fed and cared for them all.

When Ida saw Virginia, she scooped up the tabby kitten and bounded to the truck. Everything she did, she did with the uninhibited enthusiasm of someone much younger.

"Mrs. Bowen, come meet my newest beauty." (She called the cats her beauties.) She held the tabby kitten up for Virginia to pet. Tufts of fur grew from the kitten's oversized ears.

"Let me put this down first," Virginia said, her arms occupied with dirty clothes.

She set down the laundry in the kitchen, then petted the kitten. Ida brought her the Bowens' freshly washed clothes, folded and tied in a neat bundle.

Virginia gave her a dollar. Ida held the bill in her hand and looked at it.

"Do you have change?" Virginia said.

"Change? Oh, yes. Of course."

She went to the bedroom and returned with a blue willowware chamber pot. She put it on the table and opened the lid. It was filled with money—smaller coins, but quite a few fifty-cent pieces, silver dollars, and wadded-up bills. It was an astonishing amount of money for such a young woman to have.

"Take the change," Ida said and pushed the chamber pot toward Virginia. The coins clinked against each other like castanets.

Suddenly it occurred to Virginia that Ida might not know how to count. She tested her theory: "Why don't you give me the change, Ida."

"I was never a bit good with figures," she said.

"How do you keep track of the cats?"

"Oh, no problem at all. I know the gray one's gone, the black one's missing, the tabby hasn't eaten."

"Ida, it's not a good idea to show this money to people," Virginia said as she fished out the change. Hard times sometimes brought out the worst in people. Ida was especially vulnerable because she was not that bright and was totally trusting.

"Why not?" Ida said.

Virginia didn't try to explain. Ida's simple mind could not grasp human failings—which was one of the endearing things about her. Instead, Virginia made Ida promise to hide the chamber pot in her bedroom and put a handful of coins in a smaller bowl for customers to make change.

Virginia strived for simplicity in her life. A core concept of Quakerism, this simplicity involved paring away what was unimportant and focusing only on things that mattered. Simplicity was not to be confused with shallowness. Some of the simplest of Christ's sayings had a bottomless depth to them. Simplicity meant not artlessness but its opposite: elegance. Only what was needed. Nothing more. All one needed to know about simplicity could be learned from a rose. There is nothing extraneous about a rose. Everything that should be there, is. Everything unnecessary is gone. Man muddles things by adding extras.

On the ranch, all of Virginia's time was spent cleaning house, doing chores and putting meals on the table. These things were necessary but left her unfulfilled. She longed to do something that mattered. But she had no extra time.

At her job with the American Friends Service Committee, she had managed twelve projects and forty young Friends and their families, and juggled complicated logistics. She made everything run smoothly yet still had time for an occasional museum during lunch hour, and dinner and the theater with friends. On the ranch, she could barely manage to clean house, do the chores, and put meals on the table.

She had high hopes for the day's project: covering the windows with the muslin she had bought at Dave's General Store. By keeping out the dust, it would reduce the time she spent cleaning. She cut the material into large squares to fit the windows. She dipped the fabric into a heavy solution of laundry starch and fitted the wet cloth to the wooden frame. The starch served as a glue. As the fabric dried, it shrank and created a drum-tight covering.

She waited for a sunny, still December morning, then repeated the process on the outside. She shuddered to contemplate the muddy mess of dust blowing against the wet paste.

In the week after she had finished the job, she did notice a slight reduction in her workload. But she also felt the walls closing in on her. She had not realized how much she depended on the view out the window. The feeling of boundless space made her life in the tiny house tolerable. She needed a connection to the outside, like sailors who live in cramped quarters but retain a feeling of immensity, surrounded as they are by ocean and sky.

She ripped the muslin off of one window. Stiff from the starch, the fabric cracked like a sheet of ice when it fell to the floor. Instead of saving work for herself, she had created more of it, for she now had to take down the muslin from the other windows, then soak and scrape off the frayed threads that clung to the window frames.

Her closest neighbors were Gerald and Eugenia Dalton, who lived on the sheep ranch to the north. Eugenia tested Virginia's Quaker tolerance. A wide sturdy woman with flushed cheeks and a shiny nose, Eugenia looked as if she was descended from pioneer stock, but surely the pioneers never rattled on like Eugenia. The woman was born without the ability to get to the point. If Virginia were to speak her own thoughts as they occurred to her, with no selection whatsoever, she would be as boring as Eugenia, no doubt.

When Virginia saw Eugenia ride up and hitch her horse out front, she began to look around for an excuse to cut the visit short. Eugenia came inside and set a jar of canned tomatoes on the kitchen counter. "These might come in handy," she said.

Eugenia knew that Alfred had not put up any fruit or vegetables for the winter. The woman did have a good heart. Virginia felt small and petty for not liking her more.

In the living room, Eugenia ran a finger across the piano lid, leaving a visible trail in the dust. "It's so difficult keeping things clean around here."

"I haven't started cleaning today," Virginia said, hating herself for feeling inadequate. Why hadn't she left up the muslin window coverings? Perhaps Eugenia would have found her clever and industrious.

"My goodness, what else do you have to do? Without children, I mean."

This hit on a sore point. Virginia did not respond immediately. "I manage to keep myself busy," she said, though she could not think of a single worthwhile thing she had done.

"You poor thing," Eugenia said. "Here all day without a living soul to talk to. You must get so lonely."

Any truth, coming from Eugenia, cut extra deep. Alfred left before daybreak and did not return until dark.

"Are you and Alfred planning a family?" Eugenia said.

"I have a family."

"I mean—you know, children."

"I know what you meant." She resented Eugenia for bringing up what she had tried so hard to forget.

"Silly me. Rattling on. I didn't mean to pry. It's just that I can't imagine life without my little ones. They're the joy of my life."

"I'm sure they are." Virginia stood up abruptly and headed for the door. "I need to get the mail."

"Oh, we can ride there together," Eugenia said.

"I'd prefer to walk, thank you."

"It'll take a good half hour, just to get there and back." She looked around the room as if to imply that perhaps there were more productive ways Virginia could use her time.

"Actually, I don't know how to ride." She immediately regretted this admission, but could not retract it now.

"Now, I don't make it a habit to meddle in other people's business, dear, but you really must learn to ride if you're going to live on a ranch."

"I intend to."

"But when? You've already been here close to five months."

"When I'm ready." They walked outside, and Eugenia unhitched her horse.

"I'll tell you what. We have a sweet old mare we call Lady. The children all learned to ride on her, but they're accomplished horsemen now, and she's really a beginner's horse. Since you're a neighbor, I'm sure Gerald would be willing to give you a good price."

"Thanks. I'll mention it to Alfred."

Virginia returned to the house and wiped the lid of the piano, erasing the trail Eugenia had left with her finger. So what if Eugenia thought she was a bad housekeeper. She was sick of dusting. It was a thankless task. She whacked the cloth against the piano. The air filled with swimming particles that darted through the air like minnows. They fishtailed downward and settled on the shiny black surface, forming a thin layer between her and her reflection.

How could one person touch on all her fears and inadequacies in such a short time? She knew she should learn to ride, but had not yet worked up the courage. But Eugenia had lanced a deeper wound. Virginia could not have children. She poorly understood her own need to replicate herself, to form an indissoluble link to the future. It was an abstract want, an ache that filled her with a sense of loss. Alfred had told her that having children was not important to him. She had taken him at his word, because she never knew him not to speak his mind. But in the throes of love, it had been easy for him to overlook her problem, she suspected. Alfred loved children. He had spent fifteen years working with them in the YMCA. Now that she and Alfred were so happy together, would the yearning for a child visit him as strongly as she was coming to realize it had visited her? And yet she had married him anyway, knowing that at some point he would regret it.

She looked out over the flat, unforgiving land that stretched to the east with nothing to break the monotony. This was run-on land. Human presence was not meant for this kind of brutal landscape. Suddenly she was overcome by a feeling of menace.

She needed someone to talk to, but Eugenia was the only neighbor for miles around. How she missed her female friends. She thought of Alice Cadbury, dear Alice. She would understand what Virginia was going through.

Alice was a legendary figure among the Quakers at the American Friends Service Committee. She helped organize the Quaker *Speisungen*—Quaker feedings—in Germany after the war, when the Allies kept the blockade on Germany and starvation was rampant. At its height, Quakers were feeding more than a million children a day. Afterward, Alice worked in Russia. The government allowed the Society of Friends to do relief work there after the Revolution, long after other groups had been asked to leave.

Alice was in her mid-forties and had never married. She was a tall, big-boned woman with broad shoulders and mannish hands, but she had a soft feminine face framed by gray-streaked brown hair. Though not classically beautiful, she projected an unforgettable presence with her regal bearing, upper-class British accent, and impeccable manners.

She was from the Cadbury chocolate family of Birmingham. The early English Quakers, like other nonconformists, were barred from universities and could not enter the professions of law or medicine. Their pacifist beliefs kept them from joining the military, so they directed their talents toward banking and commerce. The banking families of Lloyd and Barclay were Quakers.

Part of the Quaker charge of social responsibility was to help those less fortunate. Alice's uncles had built the town of Bournville for Cadbury employees, an early experiment in subsidized housing. Each house had a large garden where fruits and vegetables could be grown to supplement wages. Growing up, Alice had spent many hours teaching adults to read in the Birmingham slums—another cause her uncles bankrolled.

When Virginia applied to work for the American Friends Service Committee's project to feed children in Appalachia, she was thrilled, though a bit intimidated, to find she would be paired with Alice. Alice epitomized everything that Virginia had worked toward and believed in. She wondered if Alice could ever be her friend. But then Quakers were known for treating everyone as equals. Early Friends rebelled against the inequality inherent in the language of seventeenth-century England, where commoners were required to address royalty and social superiors with the formal "you" but use plain language—"thee" and "thou"—with members of their own class. Quakers insisted on addressing everyone in plain language, including the aristocracy, in keeping with the Quaker belief that each person was equal in the eyes of the Lord. Nowadays, Friends reserved plain language for rare moments of deep emotion, but the idea of equality remained.

Alice treated Virginia as an equal, and that was even more evidence of her superiority. Virginia felt diminished in the presence of such competence and goodness. As a result, Virginia was not herself around Alice. She was too anxious to please, and as a result lacked her usual spontaneity and sparkle.

Virginia moved with Alice to Swan Hill, Kentucky, in 1932—a mere year and a half ago, though so much had happened in the interim it seemed like the distant past. The effects of the Depression were particularly brutal in the Appalachian mining towns, which were torn by labor strife and mine closings.

Swan Hill was a dreary place with a boarded-up movie theater and an empty community hall. The mine's tipple angled up the steep mountain to a small hole that led to the coal deposits. Squalid, unpainted houses were braced against the denuded mountain by wooden stilts. Many stood empty, and tin cans collected in the packed-dirt yards.

Shortly after they arrived, Virginia and Alice visited the schoolhouse, a natural place for the feedings, since it was where the children could be found. The drab board structure stood beside a spur track that was filled with rusting freight cars.

The schoolroom was thick with the smell of unwashed bodies. Very little light came in through the window, and the children squinted over their schoolbooks. The children in the back row could not see the blackboard at all. Some of them were barefoot, their feet red and raw from walking over the cold ground. Others wore shoes without socks. Many shivered in the unheated room.

At recess, they talked to the teacher, May Swinton, who had a beautiful head of flaming-red hair. She agreed to let Virginia and Alice use the schoolhouse for the feedings. She also recommended they visit Rema, who lived at the end of a row of two-room shacks on the other side of the tipple.

Virginia and Alice found Rema at home. She invited them inside. The house was filled with the sour smell of tallow, but it was spotless. The unpainted plank walls were insulated with old newspapers, cereal cartons, and cardboard advertisements for products she couldn't afford: insurance, aspirin, Jell-O, cigarettes. A collage of happy housewives, well-dressed models, smiling babies, and a Santa Claus beamed at them from the walls.

Alice looked around the room and picked out the one beautiful thing—a baby's quilt, hanging at the foot of the iron bed. "Did you make this?" she said. "The stitches are so small." Alice found something to admire in everyone.

Rema lovingly fingered the quilt. "I made it in better times. When my Harley was still alive." Her husband had died in a mining accident two years ago, she told them, crushed by a slab of rock that sloughed off the ceiling of the mine. "Now hit's just me and the young'uns," she said and looked fondly out at the boys playing in the packed-dirt yard.

"Those are two fine-looking boys. How old are they?" Alice said.

Virginia watched with admiration as this English woman with refined manners and an upper-class accent connected to this backwoods country woman. Virtue rested as gracefully on Alice as a bridal veil, which adds mystery but does not disguise a bride's inner glow. Virginia wanted to learn from Alice. Be like Alice.

After Rema told them about the boys, Alice explained about the Quaker feeding project. "Several people mentioned that you'd be a good person to coordinate the cooking. I understand you organized the wives during the strike."

For the first time, Rema smiled. A cavity had eaten a brown-edged hole in her front tooth. It looked like a fresh pine board with a knot that had fallen out.

Her smile left as quickly as it had come. "Look at me. I ain't even got nothing decent to wear." She smoothed the skirt of her dress, which was made out of old flour sacks.

"I've got an idea," Alice said, her cheeks flushed. "We have a shipment of clothes from the Service Committee. We need someone in charge of redoing the clothes to fit. If you take care of the project, you could have first choice for you and your boys."

"I can't—"

"Don't try to convince me you can't sew. Look at that quilt. I've never seen such beautiful handwork."

She looked proud. "Alrighty, I reckon I could try."

She insisted on serving them tea, and by the end of the visit, she had agreed to organize both the cooking and the sewing projects.

After dinner that night, Alice spread out her accounts on the kitchen table while Virginia did the dishes. "I've got some book-keeping to do here. Would you mind going to see Joseph McCulvey, the owner of the mine? He might be willing to let us use one of the empty houses for cooking."

"Alone?" Virginia was flabbergasted that Alice would trust her with such an important job. She wanted Alice to think of her as competent and brave, but the prospect of approaching Mr. McCulvey left her cold with terror.

Alice laughed. "You act like he's a monster."

"Well, look at this town."

"He's struggling, too. With the price of coal down, he hasn't got an easy job."

"Surely he could do better than this," Virginia said, drying the last plate.

"If the light shines in every man, that includes the coal oper-ators as well as the workers," Alice said and reminded Virginia that the Quakers had been asked to do the project because they had a reputation for not taking sides.

Virginia pleaded with Alice to go along with her, and after the dishes were done, together they climbed the hill to a one-story Victorian house with a wraparound front porch. The mine owner answered the door. He was a small man of Alice's age with a heavy stubble beard that gave his cheeks the look of smudged coal. Everything else about him—his starched white shirt, his vest, his creased trousers—was impeccable.

"You'll have to excuse this mess." He kicked aside a toy truck and showed them into the living room, with its dark velvet drapes and ornate Victorian furniture.

A little girl dashed through the room, pigtails flying. Her brother ran after her. "Betcha can't get me," she taunted.

"Enough, children. Time for bed," Mr. McCulvey said.

"Not 'til you read me a story," the boy said and tugged at his father's hand. He was three, maybe four.

Mr. McCulvey looked apologetically at the two women. "Their mother died last year, the governess quit, and our housekeeper is away. I'm afraid I haven't learned to manage alone."

He started to leave the room, but Virginia sprang to her feet. "I'll read to them, if they'll allow me."

She went upstairs and read the children a story, and soon they were asleep. When she returned downstairs, she found Alice and Mr. McCulvey deep in conversation. They sat on the Victorian sofa with a photo album open between them. The tilt of Alice's head and the attentive way she gazed at Mr. McCulvey made Virginia understand for the first time that she had idealized Alice as an accomplished woman who did not seem to need a man. Given the choice—and a possible choice was seated beside her—it was clear that Alice would prefer to spend her life with someone. Standing in the doorway, Virginia suddenly felt the hollowness of her own future, with no husband and no children. Helping other people, commitment to purpose and truth—all were worthy goals, and she had convinced herself that these alone would be enough. But in this one moment, she grasped the true durability of loneliness.

"Here's a picture of Mr. McCulvey's wife, Helen," Alice said when she looked up and saw Virginia standing there.

Virginia looked at the sepia photograph of a woman with fat cheeks and a heart-shaped mouth. "She's beautiful."

Mr. McCulvey closed the tooled-leather cover and placed the album on the coffee table. "I worry about the children growing up without a mother. They were so young when she died. Do you think they'll remember her?"

He talked about the troubles of raising children alone, and for an hour Virginia and Alice offered womanly advice, completely forgetting the purpose of their visit. When Virginia glanced at the clock on the mantle and noticed it was getting late, she said, "We got sidetracked about why we're here. I'm sure you've heard—we're setting up a program to feed the children." She looked at Alice, signalling for her to jump in, but

Alice seemed reluctant to break the warmth that had developed between herself and Mr. McCulvey.

"Yes, I look at the little ones and think: Where are they going to work when they grow up? There won't be any jobs here in the mines," said Mr. McCulvey.

"The future is a worry, I'll admit, but we're more concerned about the present. They don't have enough to eat."

This was a statement of fact. She didn't mean to offend him. She wouldn't have spoken at all, except Alice seemed incapacitated.

"You can blame me all you want, but the fault's in price slashing." He got up and started pacing in front of the fireplace. "Purchasing agents for big industrial plants play one operator against the other until the price is down so low no one can dig coal for profit." The empty copper scuttle on the hearth rang out when he accidentally kicked it. "I can't ask the power company to cut its rate. I can't ask for a reduction on spikes or copper wire. I have two choices: I can shut down the mine or ask the workers to take a cut."

Virginia wanted desperately for Alice to smooth things over, but Alice sat silently with her hands folded in her lap, and Virginia had no choice but to continue. "We're not pointing fingers. We only want to feed the children, and we need your cooperation to do it."

"What do you need from me?" he said hostilely. She should have been intimidated, but a sudden rush of anger prevented it. He should know, as a parent, what it meant not to be able to give one's child something as basic as food.

"A place to cook and prepare the meals. There's no shortage of abandoned buildings." She didn't recognize this forceful person she had suddenly become.

"No one is dying."

"Not from starvation, no," Virginia said evenly.

He drew his shoulders back and came toward her angrily. "My Helen died of tuberculosis, and she never set foot in a mine. Death happens. It's horrible when it does, but it's natural."

"Is it natural for slate to slough off the roof of a mine and crush a man?" She couldn't believe she was saying this. Her job was to stay neutral, but there were some things she just couldn't let pass. Not after seeing Rema struggle to raise two boys without a husband, in a drafty unpainted shack.

"You sound like one of those union fellows." He looked at her suspiciously. "I wouldn't put it past them to send in the ladies."

The sound of hymns drifted up the hill from the church. Finally Alice spoke up. "We're not here to take sides."

"It sounds like you're taking sides to me," he said.

"I don't know who's to blame, but I know one thing for sure—it's not the children," Virginia said fervently. Power, she realized, came from conviction and passion. In the heat of the moment, she had shed her fears and self-consciousness and said exactly what she wanted to say, with utter sincerity, without showing off, without worrying about what Mr. McCulvey thought or what Alice thought. And she was convincing. She could tell by the way Mr. McCulvey reacted.

"Well, I'll check my inventory of buildings," he said stiffly and stood up.

Virginia did not want to leave without a commitment. "That's kind of you. There seem to be so many unused buildings around. Why, near the school there's that long narrow structure with boarded-up windows."

"That's the old bunkhouse," he said, tilting his head as if suddenly remembering. "The kitchen hasn't been used for years, but the pots and pans are still there. I suppose there wouldn't be any harm if you wanted to use that."

"Oh, Mr. McCulvey, you're too generous!" She forgot her decorum and gave his arm a squeeze before she and Alice took their leave.

During the next few days, she and Alice cleaned the bunkhouse kitchen from top to bottom. They swept up the mouse droppings, scraped the amber grease splatters from the wall, and scoured the chipped linoleum floor. They set traps under the sink. "I won't have the mice gorging themselves on the children's food," Alice said.

The teacher had been right—Rema was a born leader. She went door to door recruiting volunteers and scavenged the town for planks and sawhorses to make tables. By the time they were ready to turn out daily meals, there were more volunteers than equipment to accommodate them. The women stood at the makeshift tables, chopping onions and potatoes. Bacon grease, hog jowls, and, on the rare occasion, a chicken were used to flavor up the soups. The kitchen was fragrant with the smell of sage and thyme.

The feeding project was a wild success. Every day at noon Virginia rang the iron bell by the schoolhouse and children appeared from all parts of town—the young in their mother's arms, the older children spilling out from the schoolhouse. Word spread quickly through the hollows, and mothers arrived with their children strapped on their backs or in wheelbarrows.

The exhausted volunteers stood with soiled aprons, blistered feet, and gnawing stomachs and smiled at the bright eyes of the children lined up with their dented tin cups, waiting for bread and soup.

With each passing week, the number of children grew. Virginia and Alice had underestimated the number of families willing to walk miles for a free meal. No matter how much food they made, it never seemed to be enough. Virginia started making regular trips to Stoutville, and Alice wheedled the milkman into traveling many miles out of his way to make daily deliveries.

Looking back on the Kentucky project, she realized how much she had missed the heady satisfaction that comes from a sense of purpose. She could see the fruits of her labor in the eyes of the unemployed miners who no longer stared at her with vacant looks, but smiled and tipped their hats. She could see it in the children's shining faces. But she also remembered the Kentucky nights. After the children were fed, the kitchen cleaned, the next meal organized, and the bookkeeping done, she was totally, completely alone. She compared that to the jump she felt in her heart when she saw Alfred returning from work. And she knew she had made the right choice, coming to live on the ranch with Alfred.

SIX

Alfred separated the pregnant cows from the heifers and moved them along the fence and across a grass field to a pasture closer to the corral. To keep the herd moving, he crisscrossed behind the line. The wind deadened his hearing, and he could barely make out the bawling and complaining of the cows as they moved forward into the wind. In the middle of the herd, several cows bunched together and tried to double back, but Alfred moved his horse quickly and got them turned around and headed into the wind again. The sun appeared as a gaseous orb through the cold dust. He dropped back to the end of the line but kept his eye on the cow with an ear chewed off. She was a leader and a troublemaker. If she got spooked and turned back, the others would follow, and he'd have a situation on his hands. He pulled his hat low and raised the bandanna over his nose. The inside of his mouth felt like burlap. He pitied the cattle. He didn't like the wind any more than they did. It was the wind that drove homesteaders off the land. It made some of them crazy, though if he had to choose which was worse, wind or dust, he'd pick dust.

Every evening, Virginia read the Bible and recorded her spiritual thoughts in a journal whose brittle spine had broken off to reveal the string binding, crusty with glue. She held the covers in place with a grosgrain ribbon wrapped around the journal and tied in a bow. When she was ready to write, she would untie the bow as if opening a birthday present. Alfred never asked what she was writing, nor was he curious. It was important to her—that was all he needed to know.

"I've been thinking," she said one evening after she finished her journal entry. "Maybe I'll start a Quaker meeting." She held the ribbon in place with her thumb and looped the ends to make a bow.

"I didn't know there were any Quakers around here," he said, unhooking his glasses and setting them atop his book.

"You don't have to be a Quaker to attend a silent meeting. I could invite Eugenia, for instance."

"And have her spend an hour in silence? That would be the Lord's miracle itself."

"I could write the neighbors and post a notice at Dave's." She jotted down a few ideas on the back of an envelope. "I'll fix a simple meal for afterward."

"You're going to serve food?"

"I can't very well expect people to travel forty miles and not give them a bite to eat."

"Land alive! You're going to attract all the tramps, riffraff, lunatics, and reprobates in Trinity county. In these times, people will do anything for a free meal."

"Why so negative? Don't worry, I don't expect you to come."

"I just think it's a crazy idea. Besides, how are you going to round these folks up?"

"It's not a cattle drive, Alfred. I'm not going to round them up." She smiled. "But I may need to water them when they get here."

He looked sheepishly down at the book in his lap.

"Seriously," she continued, "how many people do you think are going to show up? No more than three or four is my guess. We can move the piano into the corner."

"That piano won't budge. It takes three grown men to move it." The tree trunks that held up the piano looked as if they had grown up through the plank floor.

"Maybe we should get rid of it. You never play it."

Alfred drew his shoulders back. He was hurt that she did not understand how much the piano meant to him. Granted, it was ugly, several keys stuck, the action was hard, and the pedals had never worked properly. But he loved that piano. There had been a time when he played it every night after work. His callused fingers and chapped hands could still coax a heartbreaking sound out of the rough keyboard when he was in the right mood. It was not the quality of the instrument, but the heart, through the hands, that could be so devastating.

"This belonged to my grandmother," he said, running his hand along the lid of the piano as if smoothing out wrinkles. "Faith was her name. Beautiful name. I always wanted to name a daughter Faith." He caught a glimpse at Virginia's sad face and realized what a blunder he had made. He quickly launched into the story, anxious to distance himself from his thoughtless remark.

Faith was from an upper middle class Boston family, he told Virginia. She dropped out of conservatory to marry a crippled Welsh immigrant with no family or prospects. Her father warned her against marrying him, but she did it anyway.

"See, I come from a line of headstrong women," he said. "I have some background in dealing with the likes of you." He playfully squeezed her knee, then continued the story.

When Henry's leg injury kept him from fighting in the War

between the States, he decided to go west, where courage, inge-
nuity, and hard work counted for more than family ties. Faith
agreed, on one condition: that she be allowed to take her piano.
They took off the legs and hoisted the piano into the covered
wagon, wrapping it in flannel to protect it from dust. The curved
edge reached the top of the canvas, which was pulled taut over
semicircular hoops.

The wagon train gathered at the Missouri River, the ancient
boundary between East and West. Here, the lush grass to the
east that grew to up to eight feet gave way to the shorter, stur-
dier grass that topped out at four. The prairie gradually climbed
to the foothills of the Rocky Mountains. It had once been a prehistoric sea. When the sea receded, it left a less-fertile soil of
shale and limestone good for grazing cattle and sheep, but not
much else.

The wagon train followed the Platte River across Nebraska.
One morning outside of Ogallala, the group was preparing to
leave. The wagons at the front of the line had pulled out, while
at the back, people were still breaking camp. Someone kicked a
buffalo skull, and it rolled across the prairie, resounding like a
drum. Spooked, the oxen at the river started running. The
movement set off a stampede. Mules and cows scattered. The
hitched-up oxen took off without drivers. Some wagons overturned, and the panicked oxen dragged them on their sides.
Women and children screamed as they zigzagged across the
prairie, dodging one wagon, then another. Faith was closest to
their wagon. She kept her wits about her and threw a blanket
over the oxen's heads and thrust a pole between the wheel
spokes. The animals snorted and jerked under the blanket but
remained stationary. The wagon overturned. The piano spilled
out onto the prairie, and the lid clacked open. The legs slid
across the grass and into the path of an oncoming wagon.

The mayhem was over in minutes, but, like a tornado, it left a
wide swath of destruction. Ruptured barrels, dented milk cans,
guns, bonnets, dolls, tools, lanterns, and pans were strewn

across the prairie for hundreds of yards. The grass was flattened like thrashed wheat.

Women and children spread out over the prairie, combing the ground for any belongings they could salvage. Faith and Henry were lucky. Most of their belongings had stayed in the wagon. Miraculously, the sounding board of the piano remained intact. The detached piano legs were ruined, so Faith and Henry used them as firewood.

The wagons limped to Denver to restock. Henry and Faith decided to continue on by themselves. A week later, the wagon got stuck on a steep incline. They pushed from behind while the oxen strained in front, but it was no use. The wagon was too heavy. Henry told Faith they would have to leave the piano behind. By this time, Faith was demoralized and tired of traveling, and said, "Henry, I will not go a step farther. This is where we will stay."

Henry negotiated to buy ten miles of a creek bed in Greystone Gulch and opened a toll road. He attached crude log legs to the piano. His pregnant wife could not very well lie on her stomach to play a Chopin polonaise.

Alfred's father was born in the small house they built by the tollgate, and they lived there until he was in the seventh grade. That year, the Colorado Central Railroad opened up, and business on the toll road fell off. With the money he had saved, Alfred's grandfather bought a ranch in the nearby mountains. Alfred's father quit school to help his crippled father raise cattle.

When it came time to get married, Alfred's father chose someone very much like Faith—an educated woman who loved music and books. They met one fall when he was in Denver delivering cattle. She visited the ranch and was fascinated by the unusual piano. "I fell in love with the piano before I fell in love with your father," she was fond of telling her boys.

Alfred's mother had taught him to play on that piano, and when he finally settled down after years of living in Mexico, she surprised him with it. The piano arrived in a flatbed truck, a rope pulled taut from each of its legs, holding it like an immobilized animal. It took three men to get the piano inside the tiny house, and now it was there to stay.

"What a wonderful story," Virginia said. "Do you realize I've never heard you play?" The reflection of the lamp's flame bounced against the dark sides of the piano like a buoy in water. "Will you play something for me?"

"Some time. But not now," he said, and stood up abruptly. "I need to check on that carbureter I patched back together." He took the lantern and headed for the shed, leaving her with a vague disappointment that the moment could not last longer.

Alfred rode over the hillocks and watched the light play across the plains in ever-changing patterns. He had learned to appreciate the land's subtlety. Anyone could be taken in by the insistent beauty of the snow-capped mountains that surrounded his father's ranch. But he had come to prefer the stark beauty of this isolated land. Green was a color in short supply. The land was a mixture of brown, tan, gray, sorrel, palomino—the rich colors of horses' coats.

Alfred was not pleased about the prospect of having a Quaker meeting at his house on Sunday, his one day of rest. But faith was important to Virginia, so he would learn to live with it.

Religion was not something he gave much thought to. Growing up, he lived far from town and had not attended church. But he had a deep reverence for nature and had no doubt that some larger power was behind something as complex and elegant as the prairie. As for issues of good and evil, justice and mercy, and some of the more traditional religious quandaries, he had not wasted much time pondering them.

If he had a religion, it was grass. When he rode across it, walked through it, or looked over it, he was held in wonder at its complexity, its subtle and mutable beauty. He loved the grass for being indestructible, for having an insistent will to survive.

Everything on the prairie had that toughness: the jackrabbits and prairie dogs that could survive without water, the scraggly spruce, the twisted junipers, and the cottonwoods, which lacked grace but struggled to go on living, no matter what.

On the ranch, animals were born, lived out their lives, and died, only to be absorbed back into the earth, where they decomposed and enriched the soil to produce the grass that nourished the animals, continuing the cycle. And if the cycle was disturbed by drought, fire, or flood, that was not evil but part of nature's plan. Man was the interloper, with mere squatter's rights.

Early Christmas morning, after doing their chores, Alfred and Virginia traveled to the mountains and spent the day with Alfred's parents. The weather was clear, and the predawn sky was perforated with stars. By first light, they had started to climb. It was Virginia's first trip to the Rocky Mountains, and she looked out the window in awe. Her eye, drawn horizontally on the plains, was now swept vertically, following the deep-green spires of spruce and pine, and the rock cliffs, which were a beautiful shade of red—like her North Carolina dirt, only peachier, with a dusting of sparkles when the sun glanced off the rock face. The snow-capped mountaintops, like all the other features in the landscape, pointed heavenward, leaving less room for the sky.

They traveled along Alfred's grandfather's old toll road. Virginia was nervous about meeting Alfred's parents—mainly Mr. Bowen. Whenever she cared what kind of impression she made on others, she became self-conscious and usually ended up making a fool of herself, and she well knew there was no place for fools in this family.

The ranch buildings were nestled in the valley. The main house was built of logs. Inside, smells of turkey and cinnamon filled the air. Elk antlers on the wall held an assortment of cowboy hats and hunting hats. Alfred's mother came out from the kitchen, wiping her hands on her apron, and warmly greeted them.

Soon the hall was crowded with children and adults, all being introduced to Virginia at once: Mr. Bowen, a couple of ranch hands, Joe and Sue Williams and their two small children from the neighboring ranch. Mr. Bowen was a small balding man who seemed an unlikely candidate for the irritable, mean-spirited codger at the center of Alfred's stories. His body was a catalog of ranching accidents—a finger cut off at the second joint, a crooked nose, a slash at the neck. He welcomed her, took her coat, then led her to the dining room.

The table was covered with a white cloth and set with good china. Alfred's father held Virginia's chair for her to sit down. His courtly manners did not fit the picture Virginia had formed of him.

The women brought out pheasants that the men had hunted on the ranch.

"Who's going to say grace?" Alfred's mother said and looked at the Williams' eight-year-old daughter. "Tully, would you like to?"

"No—ask her," the little girl said and looked at Virginia.

"She's a Quaker, and they don't say grace," Alfred said. "They have a silent blessing."

"I want to join that church," Tully said.

"Then you'd have to sit in silence. I'd like to see *that*," her little brother Robbie said.

"How do you know about Quakers?" his sister said crossly.

"Paw-paw told me the story about the Quaker rancher," he said, turning to the end of the table.

Alfred leaned over to Sue Williams and whispered, "Paw-paw?"

"The children don't have any grandparents and so they have sort of adopted your father," she said.

"Tell it, Paw-paw," the boy said. The light-brown curls around his temples gave him an angelic look, but he had mischievous eyes.

There was throat clearing and nervous looks around the table.

"Not right now," Alfred's father said and set the carving tools alongside the platter.

"Please, Paw-paw. Please," the boy said.

"First we have to have the blessing," his mother said. People bowed their heads while she said grace. Afterward Robbie said, "Now, Paw-paw. Tell the story—you know, the one about that Quaker."

"Father, aren't you going to carve the birds?" Alfred said, moving the pheasants in front of him.

"Please. Go ahead and tell the story. I'm curious now," Virginia said.

Mr. Bowen looked at Alfred, then at the little boy, and leaned back. "Well, there was this Quaker rancher who comes home to find that the notorious gunslinger Black Bart has slaughtered his cows, burned down his barn, and murdered his family. The Quaker goes back to town and finds Black Bart at the bar. He goes up to the outlaw and says, 'Were you the one who killed my family, slaughtered my cows, and burned my barn?' 'Yep, that'd be me,' says Black Bart, belting back a whiskey. The Quaker looks at him and says, 'Well, I wish you'd cut it out.' "

Virginia laughed, and everyone at the table seemed relieved.

Robbie crossed his arms over his chest and frowned. "Now I forget why that's so funny."

Another round of laughter broke out, this one more heartfelt. From then on, the atmosphere relaxed, and they all talked boisterously. Everyone at the table was opinionated and insisted on being heard on the subject of county politics, the local cattleman's association, or problems on the ranch.

At the end of the meal, Alfred said, "Mother, do you ever get the chance to play the piano anymore?"

Robbie looked at Alfred and said, "She's your mommy?"

Alfred nodded. Robbie turned to Virginia and said, "Whose mommy are you?"

"I'm Alfred's wife," she said.

"But whose mommy?" He had a pouty look on his face as he tried to figure it out. "She's my mommy," he said, pointing to Sue Williams. "And she's Alfred's mommy." He pointed to Mrs. Bowen. "But whose mommy are you?"

"I don't have children. I'm not anybody's mommy."

As soon as the words were out, she felt a wave of emotion cross over her. The table chatter sounded far away, as if underwater. Her breaths came fast, one after the other. *Hold it together,* she told herself. *You can't have a come-apart at the holiday table.* She stood up abruptly and started clearing the dishes.

"Oh, leave those. You're a guest—the first time," Alfred's mother said.

Virginia felt an upward tug on her lip, twitches in her cheeks. She looked around, desperate for a diversion. Robbie's words had struck a nerve. She was nobody's mommy. She would not have a son or a daughter, a little baby to hold, its damp curls to kiss, its buttery rolls of fat to poke. She felt dangerously close to breaking down. And right beside Alfred's father, whom she had so wanted to impress. The table fell quiet, and she felt as if all eyes were on her. In desperation, she turned to Alfred's father and made a stab at conversation. "I didn't expect the ranch to be so big," she said. Her voice was shaky, and she wore a false smile. "How many head of cattle do you have?"

He coughed and looked down. "Well, depends on what time of year you're counting," he said. His tone was measured, but the effect was sharp. Somehow she had made a terrible misstep.

"Winter, for example," she forged on.

Alfred stood up. "Virginia, help me get some wood."

She leapt up, grateful for an excuse to leave the room. Outside, Alfred walked briskly, his jaw set. She quickened her step to keep up with his long legs. He did not speak. He, too, was put out with her, and she had no idea why.

They followed the winding road that led out of the valley where the ranch and outbuildings were nestled. The air was damp and smelled like snow. The bare orange willow branches stood out against the dark evergreens. Virginia and Alfred climbed in silence. She stumbled on a rock. Alfred stalked ahead.

"Are you going to wait for me?" She felt a shortness of breath from the altitude.

He turned, crossed his arms, and waited for her to catch up to him. "Do you want to tell me what's wrong with you?" she asked.

He let his long arms drop to his side. "I know you didn't mean to, but you insulted my father."

"I couldn't have said more than two sentences the entire dinner." She had been careful when she spoke to his father, acutely aware of how language could betray her. She might call a pasture a meadow or she might say heifer when she meant cow.

"You don't ask someone how many head of cattle he has," Alfred said, exasperated. "You might as well ask him to open up his bank book."

"I can't translate head of cattle into dollars." Her ears stung, and white smoke followed her words out of her mouth.

"It doesn't matter. It's rude."

"But I didn't mean to be." She was surprised that Alfred was so upset. His father had not seemed all that offended by her remark, but then again, she didn't know him well.

"Did you see him with Robbie?" Alfred said.

"I thought he was very sweet with him," Virginia said.

"He was never like that with me," Alfred said bitterly.

"He's probably mellowed with age."

"Paw-paw. Really! He's not the child's grandfather."

"But he'll never have his own grandchildren," she reminded him. Again she found herself awash in sadness. She could no longer keep her composure. She turned abruptly and went back the way they had come.

"Where are you going?" he called after her.

"Back to apologize to your father," she shouted without turning around, afraid he would see her tears. "If I made a fool of myself, it's better to admit it."

"You'll regret it. My father's not an easy man," he warned.

"At least I should get back and help with the dishes, or your family will think I'm lazy as well as ignorant."

She retraced her steps. The tears felt warm against her cold face, and she sopped them up with her knit gloves. She felt terribly alone. She should have told Alfred why she was so upset—he was not a mind reader, after all—but he was too irritable to approach. He was not himself around his father.

The cold air put color back into her cheeks. When she returned to the house, she could not find a mirror to check the state of her eyes, but they must have been red, for when she entered the kitchen, Alfred's mother said, "I hope you and Alfred didn't have cross words."

"I'm afraid I embarrassed him with my ignorance." Virginia grabbed a towel. "I didn't realize it was impolite to ask the size of someone's herd."

"Don't you worry two bits about that," his mother said and handed Sue Williams a plate to dry. "When I first came to live here, I didn't know a thing about ranching. I was a city girl. Grew up in Denver, and the closest I had been to a horse was the old nag that pulled the yellow trolley. The first week I was here, I found the prettiest purple wildflowers in the field. I picked a bouquet and put them in the center of the table to brighten the place up. When Samuel saw them, he couldn't stop laughing. I had no idea what was so funny; then he told me that those flowers were larkspur—a cattleman's worst enemy. It poisons the cows."

"You never told me that story," Sue said, laughing.

"Yes, silly old me. But Samuel stood by me while I was learning. He remembers what it's like," she said and patted Virginia's arm. "Would you mind taking him his coffee?"

In the living room, a fire crackled in the stone fireplace, and the children played by the hearth. Photos of prize bulls hung on the wall. Mr. Bowen sat by the window, looking through the black pages of a photo album. Triangular corner pieces held the photographs in place. One yellowed photo of a little boy with a lariat had slipped loose and was hanging at an odd angle. He straightened it.

Virginia handed the coffee to him and sat on the ottoman at his feet. "Is that Alfred?" she asked, peering over the top of the album.

"No, that's my other boy, Shrine," he said and turned the album toward her.

"Alfred's told me all about him. I guess he'd be helping you run the ranch if he were here."

"Shrine wasn't cut out to be a rancher," he said and turned the page.

"Really?" Alfred had spoken of his brother in almost mythic terms.

"He was a cowboy. Alfred never was much of a cowboy, but he's one heck of a cattleman."

"I'm not sure I understand the difference," she said.

"Shrine was a skilled horseman and loved to cut and rope cattle. But he was a terrible manager and didn't have much judgment to speak of. I doubt he could have run a ranch on his own."

She blurted out, "Mr. Bowen, I'm sorry if I said anything to offend you. You know, when I asked you the size of your herd. Alfred told me that I was rude, but I didn't mean to be. I'm learning as fast as I can."

"Alfred would think that." He closed the album and put it on the floor by his side. "Are you strong?"

The question caught her off guard. *Not today* would have been the most honest answer. Instead she said, "I—I don't know."

He looked at her hard. Long hours in the sun had wrinkled his eyes into a permanent squint. "I think you are. And Alfred needs a strong woman. He'll make it. It'll be a surprise to him, but he'll pull through, if he has a strong woman at his side."

Alfred greeted each snow-free day after Christmas with a guilty pleasure, as if he had stolen another day from winter. Snow would force him to dip into his precious supply of hay. Cattle did not have the pawing instinct that horses did, and could not get to the grass under the snow. Once he started feeding the herd, he would have to continue through the winter, and he was not sure his supply would last. A hard winter on top of the drought could easily ruin him. His prospects improved with each snowless day.

But his luck did not last. The first snow fell at the beginning of January. He loaded up the hay rack on the sled and hitched up the two drays. As the team made its way along icy ruts, a sea of brown cows flowed toward him, parted, and went on either side of the sled. Before he could toss the hay to the ground, the cows swiped at the fragrant strands that poked out through the slats.

Feeding would have been easier with a hired hand, but he could not afford help. So he had to stop the horses, climb onto the rack, scatter the hay over the side, climb back behind the horses, and move farther on, advancing across the fields in stops and starts. With two people, one could drive while the other flaked hay onto the snow evenly so that each cow had its own pile, and less hay got trampled or fouled.

Sometimes Alfred wondered if he was trying to take on too much, running the ranch by himself. If Shrine were alive, he could do it through brute courage or energy, if not necessarily smarts. Alfred was smart, but that only went so far.

He was not the only one struggling. Ranchers across the county were in the same dire straits. Cattle were starving. The government was buying cattle for a few dollars a head and distributing the usable meat to people on relief. Just the other day, the *Post* had run a story about a trainload of bony animals that were so hungry that they had eaten each other's ears and tails off by the time the train arrived at the stockyards. Some cattle were too weak to be shipped and had to be killed on the spot.

At least Alfred had hay. More and more, he heard about ranchers who let their cattle starve because they lacked money for feed. What humiliation, Alfred thought. His livestock were his dependents. He could no more imagine cutting them loose than he could imagine starving his family. But he had no room to be judgmental. He might be next.

It was alarming, the amount of land that was passing into the ownership of banks, assurance societies, mortgage companies, and investment partnerships. Last week alone, the county paper carried five legal notices for foreclosures and eight announcements of sheriff's sales. Whenever Alfred started to feel sorry for himself, he thought of the poor man in the adjacent county who had not been able to pay for his false teeth, and had had them confiscated by the sheriff along with other personal property to be sold to satisfy judgments previously rendered.

All around Alfred, families were leaving the land. If his ranch failed, he and Virginia would join the ranks of the dispossessed, people who piled their belongings in trucks and moved about as freely as the dust.

Ever since Virginia moved to Colorado, the precarious state of the ranch was a constant worry to him, grinding down his good humor. He had never admitted this to her, partially out of shame, partially out of guilt for having brought her into such a marginal situation. But he had to think positively. Why should he, like his father, assume he would fail?

Lately Virginia seemed subdued, less spontaneous, and he wondered if she was having second thoughts. He had not been an ideal husband. He felt badly that he could not pay more attention to her when he came home at night, bone tired, fingers numb from cold, always with some new problem to preoccupy him.

He tried so hard to protect her from his financial woes, but they kept growing and threatened to engulf them both. What else was there to do but keep working and try to keep his spirits up, even though there was only the slimmest chance of a positive return on his labor. As his father was fond of saying, "You've got the bear by the tail, and it looks like a very poor time to let go."

Alfred flaked the last of the hay onto the snow, then set the pitchfork against the slats and paused as an odious idea came to him: Had he dragged Virginia into his private need to prove himself to his father? The thought nagged at him. She was an unwitting accomplice. He should have waited for the ranch to become a viable operation before proposing marriage. But he was afraid she would return to her urban life and decide she wasn't cut out for ranch life after all. So he acted impetuously—not his normal habit—and married her as soon as she could arrange to leave Mexico.

He swept out the rack, uneasy with his new insight. The smart cows swarmed around the back to catch the rich dessert of hayseed and chaff that scattered on the snow. Then Alfred returned to the stack yard for another load.

SEVEN

Snow covered the pastures for all of January. As soon as the tips of the yucca and brush showed through, more snow fell to cover them up again. The snow blurred any distinction between foreground and background and obliterated what few contours existed in the land. When Virginia looked out the window, nothing was different from anything else, and it made her feel slightly crazy.

One day she forgot to wind the clock. She did not find out what time it was until she went to town. Not that the exact time mattered. But not knowing added to her disorientation. Time, like the land, became a mass without demarcation.

Chores got her out of the house twice a day, once in the evening and once in the morning, when she pulled on her galoshes and chore clothes in the dark and trudged along the shoveled path toward the shed, her boots breaking through the crusts of ice. Otherwise she was confined inside. Slowly, imperceptibly, the joy had leaked out of her life. During the day, she found herself staring out the window at the snow and thinking about the babies she would never have. She did not tell Alfred. He had enough to worry about without being burdened by her private obsession over a thing that could not be changed. Still, she could not keep her dark thoughts in check: that she would never be as important to anyone as her mother was to her; that Alfred would never have a son to help him on the ranch; that they would never be a family.

In trying to avoid thinking of birth, she found herself thinking of death. What would happen if Alfred died unexpectedly? She would be stuck in this dreary place alone. Her morose mood isolated her, pushed her away from her husband. Many evenings, she wanted to tell him that the woman he was getting to know was not the woman she was. Somewhere along the way, she had turned into a gloomy presence—someone she didn't recognize and didn't like. Life continued around her, but she observed it from a remove. She felt like someone in a darkened theater hall, watching her life on a motion-picture screen, involved in the story from a distance but not actually participating, nor able to change it.

When she first met Alfred at the train station on her way to graduate school, she had been posing as a pregnant woman. She was twenty-five at the time, still able to have babies. Why hadn't they gotten together then? She again remembered removing the pillow from her middle and stuffing it through the window and watching it tumble down the embankment as the train sped away from Alfred. She now thought of her pretend child suspended in a cloud of down, lying among the thistles by the train track.

Virginia sat at the piano bench and watched the steady drip-drip-drip of snowmelt as it fell from the eaves and made perforations in the snow like the holes of the spiral-bound book of Schumann that sat unopened on the piano. She blew the dust off the cover, then opened the book and looked at the strange musical notations: black flags and tic-tac-toe boards, little hats, winged birds, and arcing lines. Some markings looked happy, like dancing feet. Others reminded her of falling water. She wondered if the visual representation corresponded to the sound of the music.

She depressed several keys at random, using one finger, the way she typed. She was not talented in music, painting, or poetry. Her creativity was expressed in her spiritual life.

Alfred had told her that he didn't believe in religion, but she wondered if all art didn't involve a communion with a higher power. He had described to her the stage that he hated in learning to play music, when the harder he tried, the worse the results. It wasn't until he knew the music so well that it became as natural to him as breathing that any real music was possible. It sounded a lot like religion to her.

Her inner life mattered to her passionately. She missed going to Quaker meeting where, surrounded by other people, she could achieve the deep calm she needed in order to think clearly and open herself to surprise.

As soon as the snow melted and the roads cleared, Virginia renewed her efforts to arrange a Quaker meeting. She pinned up a flyer in Dave's General Store, between posters advertising a farm liquidation sale and a Cattleman's Association meeting. She also drafted a letter to her neighbors, with a brief explanation of Quaker silent worship. After introducing herself and giving a little of her background, she wrote:

Traditional unprogrammed meetings occur in silence, with no minister, in keeping with the Quaker belief that the inner light, or "that of God in every man," reveals itself directly to the individual who is still and listens.

During meeting, a person may feel moved to share an insight with the group. The emphasis is on genuineness, not eloquence. When that person stands and speaks, the others need not open their eyes. Given in the spirit of spontaneity, vocal expression is not a breaking of silence so much as it is an articulation of the silence. Each person is encouraged to incorporate the spoken message into their private contemplation, which may lead to an extension of the insight. In many unprogrammed meetings, the spoken messages are thematically linked. In others, there is no connection, and in still others, no one speaks at all. There is no right or wrong way for a meeting to unfold. The emphasis remains on each individual's personal connection to the divine light within.

The silence of Quaker meeting allows us to connect with our deepest core. Many Quaker leaders have been mystics. The power of those gathered together, worshipping individually but supported by the group spirit, can create moments of truth not possible when praying alone.

She reread what she had written and crossed out the part about Quaker leaders being mystics. That would seem too odd to her neighbors. But Virginia personally believed there was a mystic quality to worship. For her, it involved a kind of relaxing, a letting go that allowed her to ease down through layers of consciousness until she reached the core, where she achieved the mystical state of tranquil concentration and everything fell into proportion and clear focus. At its most potent, worship allowed her to connect with her intuitive nature, which was so much smarter than she was but was blocked in daily life by interference from her racing thoughts, which darted forth into the future, and back to the past, preventing her from inhabiting the present. Trying to explain this, however, would scare off her neighbors, and she was already worried, as it was, that no one would respond.

She made copies of the letter by hand and sent them off. Over the next two weeks, a few replies trickled in.

The Saturday before the meeting, Virginia spent the day

cooking. "How many people are coming?" Alfred asked after supper, as he worked at his desk. She opened the oven door and put her hand in to judge the temperature. She still had another pie to bake.

"Six. Let's see. There's you . . ." She added a few more pieces of wood to the stove.

"Me? You said—you assured me . . ."

She watched him squirm for a minute, then said, "Relax, Alfred. I was kidding. You're not the only one who has teasing rights in this house," she said. He laughed at himself, and she continued. "The Ingrams are coming. Do you know them?"

"I heard that Roy is scheduled for a gallbladder operation," Alfred said.

"He's not coming, but his wife, Gertrude, is bringing Roy's mother," Virginia said.

"She must be eighty. I think she's a little senile."

"All are welcome," Virginia said. "Naturally, Eugenia's coming. Never one to miss a social occasion."

"Did you explain to her what meeting is about?"

"Yes, I sent a letter to everyone, though I bet she skipped the explanation. I just hope she doesn't stand up and give us her recipe for Brown Betty, just to fill the silence. Then there's bachelor Jorgensen."

"He needs a bath more than he needs the Lord," Alfred said. He told her about the time he took some medication to the old man in his tarpaper shack several miles from the county line. The room was shin-deep in empty bean cans. "The only thing he ever threw out were coffee grounds. He'd walk out to the front step and empty them right there, in the same spot, day after day. Not a stick of greenery grew anywhere around, but by golly, by that front door were the most beautiful vines you could imagine."

"Well, he may be the only soul I can impress with my cooking," she said.

"That's five. Who's the sixth?" Alfred said.

She stopped to think. "Oh yes, I remember now. A Mr. Edmund. Or maybe Edmund's his first name."

"Never heard of him. What do you know about him?"

"He didn't give any background in the letter. It was post-marked from town, so I assume that's where he lives."

"That's about as queer a group of individuals as I could imagine," he said.

On Sunday morning, Alfred took his horse and left early. "Now I know how to get rid of you if need be," Virginia called out to him as he rode off.

The bachelor Jorgensen was the first to arrive. For the occasion, he had shaved, but had not taken a bath, and he carried with him the smoky odor of unwashed bodies mixed with stale alcohol. Next, Mrs. Ingram ushered in her mother, a beatific woman with gray hair and a sweet vacant expression. The elderly woman didn't appear to know where she was, nor did she seem to care.

Eugenia brought an apple pie with her. Virginia was grateful, since she had burned a pie the day before. She was still not adept at manipulating the drafts to control the oven temperature.

Edmund was the last to arrive. Mr. Edmund, as it turned out—Robert Edmund. He wore a suit of threadbare fabric that was shiny at the elbows. A gaunt man with deep-set eyes and high cheekbones, he had the dignified bearing of a professor or a minister.

People took their places in the chairs, arranged in a kidney shape that followed the curve of the piano. They settled into silence. Virginia could feel Eugenia shifting in her seat. The air was pungent with the bachelor Jorgensen's smell. He had a rattle in his breath and a phlegmy cough. As the silence progressed, he began to snore, and Virginia gently shook his knee. He came awake with a snort and mumbled to himself.

Mr. Edmund bowed his head in dignity. With both feet

planted firmly on the ground, he put one hand over each kneecap and sat with his back ramrod straight. Virginia closed her eyes and tried to ignore the bachelor's snuffling and belching. When she looked up, she noticed that the elderly Mrs. Ingram had her hand raised above her head, as if seeking permission to ask a question. She wore a goofy smile.

Virginia closed her eyes, and when she opened them a few minutes later, the old lady still had her arm up. Virginia leaned over and whispered, "Why do you have your hand raised?"

"I don't know," she said in a loud voice. "What do you think?"

There was muffled laughter, then the meeting continued in silence. Wind circled the house with a steady whoosh. Outside, the windmill clanked, and a large object knocked against the shed. Soon she forgot about the surrounding sounds and settled into herself.

Toward the end of the hour, Mr. Edmund stood up. His jacket hung loosely from his shoulders, like a scarecrow. After waiting a bit to collect himself, he spoke in a quavering voice. "I hesitated to come here." He cleared his throat and waited. When he was able to speak again, he continued. "I was not sure it was the right thing. I came with a heavy heart. I have done something very bad that has caused others great suffering, and I have to live with that." His voice had a two-pitched crackle, like someone who has sung too long without water. "I didn't know how I could possibly continue. And then today, this morning, in this room, I looked inside myself and realized that I could not do it alone. Suffer alone. And I realized there is help, both inside and outside myself. I'm not even sure I believe in God, but today, I felt something I haven't felt in a very long time: hope. And I wanted to say—" He choked up and could not continue. He sat down and tried to collect himself. Virginia kept her eyes closed but could hear bachelor Jorgensen blubbering beside her. She slipped him a handkerchief, and he blew his nose loudly. She was not the only one who was moved.

After the noon meal, Eugenia stayed behind to help clean up, though Virginia would have preferred to be alone. She felt renewed, and she wanted to savor the feeling. But Eugenia wanted to gossip. "What do you think that Edmund fellow did? Kill someone? He doesn't look like a murderer."

Something extraordinary had happened and Eugenia had missed it. Virginia felt sorry for her.

"Maybe he robbed a bank," Eugenia said.

Virginia clanked the hand pump with extra vigor. The water came up from the cistern in a gush. "It doesn't matter what he did," she said. The tent of Quakerism was large enough to accommodate the flawed as well as the unflawed. Eugenia, no doubt, would include herself among the latter.

"But aren't you curious? The way he was talking, I think it must have been something real bad."

Virginia had felt as if Mr. Edmund had been speaking directly to her. That often happened in meeting. What she got out of it was what she was ready for. Not necessarily what she wanted, but what she was ready for. Like Mr. Edmund, she had done something to harm someone back in Kentucky, and it shamed her so much she couldn't admit it to herself, let alone her new husband. Mr. Edmund made her realize that what she sought but could not bring herself to ask for was forgiveness.

"I bet he embezzled money from a church," Eugenia prattled on. "After all, he said he didn't believe in God. I've never known one of those *etherists.*"

Her newly coined word made Virginia picture a hospital room full of anesthetized infidels.

"Whatever it is, he's going to cook like a pot roast in hell for his sins," she continued.

"Please, Eugenia. I don't want to talk about it." Virginia did not believe in divine retribution. Her God was not the punitive authority figure of some religions. Hers was more luminous and personal, intricately complex, but unique.

After that day, Gertrude Ingram's mother went into further decline and was too agitated to sit still for long periods. The bachelor seemed embarrassed by his emotional outburst and did not want to come back. Mr. Edmund, the mysterious stranger, moved and left no forwarding address. Only Eugenia was willing to participate in another Quaker meeting, and this dampened Virginia's enthusiasm considerably. She was disappointed that she was unable to organize regular worship, but the aftermath of her one attempt gave her a boost of hope that lingered into the following weeks.

Monday was mail day. It lifted Virginia's spirits to have something to look forward to. In the mailbox that afternoon, along with the newspapers and catalogs, was a letter from her mother. She hurried back to the house, fixed a cup of tea, then settled in her reading chair and opened her letter. After a cheerful recounting of family news her mother wrote:

> My poor old joints are acting up like crabby old ladies, and I don't know what to do to quiet them. My vinegar tonic has ceased working, and I'm afraid I'll wake up one day and find my joints locked into place, and I'll be unable to clean and cook for your father and brother. Your father is perfectly able to take care of himself, but I stay up nights fretting about Jonathan. I'm afraid I've been guilty of spoiling him, and I know he could do more for himself if he weren't so dependent on me, but what in the world will become of him when I'm in too much pain to do for him?

Virginia had never known her mother to complain. She was of the grin-and-bear-it school and always took things graciously in stride. So Virginia knew as soon as she read the letter that her mother's arthritis must be unbearable, and this saddened her.

For the past seventeen years, Virginia's mother had devoted her life to caring for Jonathan. He had returned from the war with a serious head injury. During the defense of the Champagne front on the Marne River, the blast from an explosion had whipped him backward against a tree. His helmet flew off, and his head took the full brunt of the impact. He was in a coma for three weeks. When he regained consciousness, the doctors kept him in the hospital for a month for observation and then sent him home with an honorable discharge.

Virginia was living at home at the time and attending State Normal College. She looked at her brother and saw the same face, the same body, but he was utterly changed. Even people who did not know Jonathan could sense instantly upon meeting him that something was not right. He did not respond to gestures, nods, or smiles. His wooden voice and blank face made people uncomfortable. The same oblivion that caused the reaction in the first place protected him from its fallout. He simply had no idea how others felt—about him or anything else.

Jonathan was easily confused and could not follow directions. Routine substituted for memory. He knew the way to their father's grocery store and the Quaker meetinghouse by heart, but if he took a different route, he got lost. Once the iceman found him wandering by the neighbor Atkinson's pond looking confused, and gave him a ride home in the wagon.

As a result of Jonathan's accident, a hodgepodge of practical skills that had been so obvious and second-nature to Virginia, such as putting on socks before your shoes, was forever denied him.

When he was tired, he slurred his words and spoke haltingly. Sometimes he forgot words altogether—simple things like *table* or *water*. He needed constant supervision. He was different from a small child, whose lack of knowledge about the world created a predictable set of dangers. A child learns, after putting his hand on a hot burner, not to touch it again. Not so Jonathan. Or not so all of the time. The inconsistency was troubling. You never knew what he was going to do or why.

Virginia poorly understood intelligence. She knew it came in all forms, from the visual intelligence of the artist to the auditory sophistication of the musician, to the free-flowing, associative gift of the poet, and the more precise, inductive talent of the scientist. The doctors said that Jonathan's intelligence was intact, but that provided cold comfort when his memory was gone, and with it his identity.

The accident also affected Jonathan's temper, and he would erupt at unpredictable moments. When their father put him to work at the grocery store, the other employees felt threatened by him. One time when he got upset, he knifed open a burlap sack and hurled handfuls of rice all over the store, like a wedding guest gone amok.

For a short while, Jonathan had a construction job, but he picked too many fights with the crew. Miss Kitty, the librarian and one of Jonathan's biggest supporters, had the altruistic impulse to take him under her wing. She remembered the old Jonathan who made weekly trips to the library and left with a tall stack of books. But Jonathan was no longer able to follow simple instructions. Too often his verbal outbursts disturbed the quiet of the library.

Virginia found herself weighing all the horrible consequences of war and contrasting them to what had happened to her brother. A missing limb, a disfiguring burn, the loss of sight—there were any number of body parts or senses that one could do without and still carry on with spirit and integrity, even gaining admiration from others. Take Jimmy Straits, a neighbor who lost a leg in the war. He now ran a thriving watch-repair business from his house. But Jimmy had only lost a piece of himself. Jonathan had lost himself.

The accident had left Jonathan with one new talent, the way blind people develop superior powers of hearing. Jonathan had an incredible rapport with animals. The most skittish horse calmed down in his presence. Wild cats rolled over his feet when he sat on the front steps. Even birds were not afraid of him. Virginia had watched him cup an injured robin in his palm and feed it with a medicine dropper. These moments confirmed what Virginia knew but so frequently forgot—that gentleness lived beneath his chaos, sullenness, and rage.

The family was hopeful when Jonathan got a job breaking quarter horses for Abner Harkness, who had a farm on the edge of town. His first day on the job, Jonathan returned home much too early, pungent with the smell of sweat and hay. Without washing up, he strode to the rocking chair on the porch and sat beside Virginia, who was studying for a history exam. Staring straight ahead, he rocked with concentrated fury. Pumping with his feet, he moved back and forth, faster and faster, until he was short of breath.

Since the injury, he rocked to comfort himself. Perhaps he found some echo of his childhood in the movement. When he was a little boy, he would wake up in the middle of the night, go to the nursery, and mount his rocking horse. One night when Virginia awoke and heard the nursery floor creak, she tiptoed down the hall and peeked through the door. The room was dove-colored in the moonlight and the ruffled edges of shadows grazed on the floor. The scent of honeysuckle wafted in from outside. She watched him rock with such single-mindedness. This was one of her earliest memories, but it was so vivid that she could feel the room, even now.

"You're back early," Virginia said to Jonathan. The wooden porch let off an angry two-toned pitch under his rocking, like a donkey braying.

"Mr. Harkness is a bad man," he said. He propelled himself back and forth with such force that the chair inched across the floor and came perilously close to the porch's edge.

"Did he insult you?" she said, turning her book over in her lap. Sometimes people treated Jonathan as if he were retarded or hard of hearing. Virginia was alert to any slight. She was not bold enough to march over and have words with Mr. Harkness, but she would send her mother, who was purposeful and firm, a force to contend with when she felt right was on her side.

Jonathan shook his head.

Virginia waited patiently at his side until he wore himself out with his maniacal rocking. Then she was able to find out what had upset him. Mr. Harkness used a method of breaking horses called sacking out. He bound the horses to evenly spaced posts in the corral. To keep the horse from bucking, he tied one of its hind legs to a neck collar. Then he threw a weighted tarpaulin on the horse's haunches. Jonathan had watched as the pathetic animals, wild with fear, heaved and thrashed about on three legs. The more they resisted, the more they injured themselves. Afterward, the animals had swollen necks, bloody pasterns, and raw spots on their coats where the rope's friction had burned off the hair.

"I refuse to work for that man," he said, like the old Jonathan, who reacted indignantly to injustice and cruelty. Every time she saw glimpses of the person he used to be, she allowed herself to hope. Maybe this was it—the turning point—and from here on out, he would slowly regain his old self. But hope, she learned, can be a cruel thing.

One weekend when Virginia was twenty, her parents took the train to Richmond for an uncle's funeral and left her alone to care for Jonathan. At the train station, she met one of her classmates, Jennifer Marsh. Jennifer's blond hair curled out from under her cloche hat, and she wore a dress made out of the thin, shimmering fabric that was all the rage. She invited Virginia to her birthday party that Saturday at the old gold mine.

"I'd love to, but I don't think I can," Virginia said. She desperately wanted to go, but she could not leave her brother unattended.

"That's too bad," Jennifer said, as saucy and energetic as ever. "Jack brought some of his fraternity brothers down from State." She slipped her arm through Virginia's and whispered, "Aren't they cute?" Virginia turned and saw Jennifer's brother Jack joking with several handsome college-aged men. Mr. Marsh pulled up in the car, and the boys piled in and put the suitcases on their laps.

"Gotta go. Come if you can." Jennifer jumped in the front seat. Virginia could hear the laughter as they drove off.

She trudged home. All she had to look forward to was another dreary weekend with Jonathan. He was waiting for her on the front porch, rocking slowly. On a whim, she said, "I saw Jennifer Marsh and her brother at the train station. She invited me to her birthday party. Would you like to go with me?" She would stay by his side all evening and see that he didn't get in trouble.

"Really? You would take me?" Jonathan said, full of excitement. Virginia cursed herself for all the times she had condescended to him, never sure how much he understood.

"Sure. It's at the old gold refinery." She and Jonathan had spent many happy hours there among the ruins, prowling among the piles of dark granite for treasures. "You remember when we used to play there?"

"Don't you?" Jonathan snapped. When he was embarrassed by his memory lapses, he turned hostile.

"Of course," she said, sorry she had brought it up.

Late Saturday afternoon, Virginia and Jonathan took the path that went behind the houses on Ridge Road, skirted the Hedgecock farm, followed the creek, then cut through the Marsh property, and ended up at the gold refinery.

Vines covered the crumbling stone walls and the arched doorway. The roof was missing, but a huge stone chimney rose into the canopy of trees, like a mysterious obelisk. A large circular millstone remained from the days when the refinery was converted to a grist mill, after the War between the States. The early spring leaves had not yet reached their full growth, so the glimmering green canopy allowed a generous amount of sunlight to pass through, illuminating the lichen and moss on the forest floor. As the leaves fluttered overhead, the late-afternoon light played across the walls of the refinery, making them shimmer like water. The place still retained its mysterious hold over her, though it was much smaller than she remembered.

People arrived by the rutted, overgrown road, carrying blankets and baskets of food. Young people milled about the ruins and climbed on the piles of rocks. A couple of boys had crawled up an old pine tree that had toppled onto one of the standing walls.

Jennifer approached Virginia. She was holding a squirming beagle puppy in her arms.

"You remember Jonathan?" Virginia said.

Jennifer smiled at him and turned away as the puppy licked her ears.

"This is Rascals," Jennifer said, pulling the puppy away from her face. "I got her for my birthday. Isn't she adorable?" She ruffled the fur on the dog's stomach.

"Can I hold her?" Jonathan said. Jennifer nodded, and he lifted the puppy toward his chest. Rascals started chewing on the side of his hand.

"Bad girl," Jennifer scolded.

"She's just a puppy. She doesn't know any better," Jonathan said and scratched behind the dog's ears.

Virginia left the two of them playing with Rascals and went to help with the food. Jennifer's mother was uncovering big bowls of potato salad, cole slaw, and bean salad. Stacks of pies remained in the baskets covered with tea towels. Virginia patted out hamburgers, keeping an eye out for Jack and his fraternity brothers.

"Who's the cute guy with you?" It was Amelia, from Virginia's home economics class. She had bangs that covered her eyebrows, and her straight black hair curved into a perfect hook on each cheek. Lipstick outlined a heart-shaped pout.

"With me?"

"Sure—you walked up with him. He's talking to Jennifer now."

"Oh, Jonathan. He's my brother."

"Will you introduce us?"

Virginia had forgotten how handsome Jonathan was. That day, the vacant look was gone from his eyes, but the wildness remained.

"I thought you had a crush on Jennifer's brother," she said, looking warily at Amelia, who had a reputation as being fast.

"Jack's a flat tire," Amelia said, rolling her eyes.

Virginia took Amelia over to Jonathan and introduced her. Jennifer glared at them, unhappy at the interruption.

"Nice to meet you," Jonathan said. It surprised Virginia that, of all the characteristics of the old Jonathan that had disappeared after the accident, his good manners should remain.

She left him in the company of the two women and went to the woods to find a stick for toasting marshmallows. It was still light, and she made her way to the creek, breathing in the pine-scented air and enjoying the slight breeze. She snapped off a slender branch of a young sycamore but could not separate it from the tree.

"Need some help?"

She looked up and saw a young man in knickers, argyle socks, and saddle shoes. He was about her height and had broad, handsome cheeks and kind brown eyes. She recognized him from the train station. "Oh, hi—hi," she said.

"I've got a knife." He cut through the green wood. "Want me to peel the bark for you?"

He put his foot up on a stump and ran the knife along the bark. Blond shavings curled away from the blade.

"I noticed you when you first walked up," he said and handed her the peeled stick. "I thought you might have come with that handsome dark-haired fellow."

"He's my brother."

"Yes, I know. I asked around."

She glowed in the warmth of the unspoken compliment. Why in the world had he noticed her, out of all the other women who wore rouge, stylish bob cuts, and short skirts? Virginia reached up and smoothed back her hair, conscious of how old-fashioned she must look. Her mother wouldn't let her cut her hair.

He introduced himself. His name was Joe, and he was studying engineering at State. They talked a while by the creek, then returned to the party. Joe roasted a hot dog for her and they sat together on a blanket. As darkness fell, the silhouettes of the trees slowly blended with the night into one seamless expanse of black. The reflection of the fire on the walls of the refinery made her wonder if perhaps some of the gold had leached into the stones, so golden did they glow.

After dinner, Joe brought out his ukulele, and people gathered around him to sing. Everyone but Virginia seemed to know the words to "Carolina in the Morning," "Baby Face," and "I'm Just Wild about Harry."

Virginia stood by the fire and roasted a marshmallow. Jennifer came up to her. "Have you seen Jonathan?"

Virginia had completely forgotten about her brother for the past few hours. Her marshmallow caught flame, and she pulled the stick out and waved it around, then offered the marshmallow to Jennifer.

"He must have taken the puppy with him," Jennifer said, licking her sticky fingers. "I can't find Rascals anywhere."

"He's probably out giving her some exercise," Virginia said. She speared another marshmallow and put it in the fire.

"Who? The puppy or Amelia?" It was Jennifer's brother, Jack, who had walked up.

"Very funny," Jennifer said crossly.

"You think I'm kidding? I've been looking for Amelia for the past hour. I can't find her anywhere."

The soft marshmallow drooped off Virginia's stick and plopped into the fire, sizzling.

"That's just like Amelia," Jennifer said, stamping her feet. "Trying to steal my friends."

"Don't tell me you've got your eye on Jonathan?" Jack said. "The guy's a nut case. Everybody knows it."

"Go cook a radish," Jennifer said. "He's more normal than you. At least he's not a flirt like Amelia. I don't blame her for ditching you for him."

Virginia loved her for defending Jonathan.

Mr. Marsh walked up. "What's the problem?"

"Jonathan Mendenhall and Amelia Roberts disappeared together," Jack said. "No one's seen them for an hour. I'm worried about Amelia. If Jonathan tries to take advantage of her, she won't be able to defend herself." Jack had an unerring instinct for what would rile his father.

Mr. Marsh turned pale. "Gather your fraternity brothers, son," he said.

Joe came up, holding his ukulele by the neck. "What's wrong?" he asked, but before Virginia could answer, Jack had recruited him to help.

The search party spread out in the woods, each man carrying a gas lantern. In the dark, the staggered flecks of light looked like star formations. As the men went through the hollow and up over the hill, the lights blinked out of view, but the night air still carried back the plaintive cries of "Amelia."

Virginia waited on a rock, not knowing what to do. What if Jonathan did something wrong and didn't know it was wrong? Amelia was such a tease. She might trigger a stronger reaction from Jonathan than she counted on, not knowing that he no longer knew how to control himself. And then . . . and then . . . Virginia blushed inwardly. What she now had to consider was what she had been forbidden by her upbringing to even think of—the power of unrestrained instincts. Though she could not put it into words, she felt that on some elemental level, she, too, had been drawn to Joe by that power. How else could she explain totally reneging her responsibility to look after Jonathan. She had allowed her attraction to Joe to overcome her good judgment. And look at the fine mess she had made of things.

The singing had stopped, and people now spoke in hushed

tones around the fire. Virginia spotted Jennifer by the millstone and went up to her.

"How could he prefer Amelia over me," Jennifer sniffled. "And it's my birthday."

"You're worth a dozen Amelias," Virginia said and squeezed her arm.

Half an hour later, the search party returned empty-handed.

"We'll have to call in the police," Mr. Marsh said.

"Don't do that," Virginia said. "Please."

"I don't have any choice."

At that moment, they heard a thrashing through the woods. Someone shouted out, "It's Jonathan!"

He approached the fire, holding Jennifer's puppy in his arms. His shirt was ripped and covered with blood. He had torn off a piece of his shirttail and wrapped it around the beagle's paw.

Everyone gathered around him, talking at the same time.

"Where the heck have you been, son?" said Mr. Marsh.

"Where is she? Didn't you hear us call out? We looked everywhere," said one of the fraternity brothers.

"You should know better."

Jonathan looked right and left, his eyes confused and wild.

"Tell us where Amelia is," Jack said and grabbed his arm roughly. "Now."

"What are you talking about?" Jonathan asked.

"It's okay, Jonathan. Just tell them," Virginia said.

Jennifer ran up and saw the puppy limp in Jonathan's arms. "Oh, my poor darling. What happened to you?"

Jonathan handed the dog to her. "She ran off into the woods. It took me a while to find her. She got tangled up in a trap, but I think she'll be okay."

"You mean you weren't with Amelia?" Virginia said.

"Who's Amelia?" he said.

"I'm sorry. We were sure—we thought—"

The overlapping voices and accusations spooked Jonathan.

He backed up, panicked like a trapped animal. Then he broke out of the crowd and crashed down the hill. Soon they heard the sounds of water splashing, and then nothing.

They stared into the darkness. Virginia couldn't move.

Just then, Amelia walked up.

"What's all the fuss?" she said.

"What are you—where've you been?" said Jennifer.

"I left my purse in the car and went back to the main road to get it."

"You've been gone almost an hour."

"What are you, my mother or something?" She looked around to check for adults, then took a silver flask from her purse. "Who's coming with me?"

The fraternity brothers trooped after her. "You coming?" Joe asked Virginia.

She shook her head. He was just like all the others. He didn't care that they had upset Jonathan. All he cared about was hooch.

Virginia took the long way back along a main road. The moon went in and out of the clouds, but it provided enough light for her to see her way home.

When she reached the house, Jonathan was on the porch in the dark, rocking furiously, staring straight ahead.

"I owe you an apology," she said. She felt ashamed of herself for so many reasons.

He didn't reply but continued rocking. His broad hands gripped the rocker's arms as if trying to crush it with brute force. The puppy's blood still marked his face like war paint.

She went inside to the living room. Without turning on the lights, she sat in her great-grandmother's teal rocker that had lulled three generations of Mendenhall babies to sleep. The paint had worn off the arms, and the wood was smooth, burnished by the natural oils released by bare skin against wood.

A stillness fell over the house. She could hear the clock in the hall, the rocking outside, and sounds from the depths of the house that those less familiar might attribute to ghosts—a shifting in the attic, a groan by the back door, a mysterious tap from the kitchen. Warm shadows made patterns at her feet. She sat in the dark for a while and listened to the house's internal sounds, heard only in its silence, the way gentle stomach rumblings become an accepted part of Quaker meeting. After collecting her thoughts, she carried the rocking chair to the porch and set it down beside Jonathan.

Jonathan did not acknowledge her presence but continued rocking fiercely, as if the chair could spirit him away from that spot.

Virginia pushed off with her toes and moved back and forth, faster and faster. She could feel the spindles against her back and wondered if the antique rocker could withstand her roughness.

When her speed matched Jonathan's, she reached over and lay her hand gently on his arm. He did not look her way, nor did he speak, but he slowed down ever so slightly. Gradually they both slowed down, and before long they rocked languidly, side by side.

The moon couched the porch in a soft gray light. Virginia looked over at her brother and realized how much they shared—their mother's strong nose, their father's lanky figure, a childhood in this house. He was her brother and always would be. That night, for the first time in a long time, she was glad of that.

EIGHT

With no clouds, no dust, and no wind, the day seemed as shiny as a brand new penny. The sun warmed Alfred's skin. He took off his jacket but kept it nearby. It was March, and the weather could change in an instant.

Now that calving season had started, he spent most of his time on horseback. That day, he rode the black gelding with white legs. The horse's previous owner had named it Boots. What kind of person would give a horse a cat's name? Alfred wondered. The white leggings resembled socks more than boots—but to call the horse Socks would be an even greater indignity.

He rode over the ground, which was dotted with calves and nursing mothers. He stopped every so often to dab iodine on wet, pink navels, massage the teats of a tight-bagged cow with lanolin, or doctor a calf for scours. As he patrolled the herd, he kept an eye out for cows having trouble giving birth.

At the top of the rise, he paused to look over the cow-calf

pairs that bunched together against the fence. At the beginning, there were only a few scattered births. As the days wore on, the pace would pick up, like popping corn, building to a level of furious activity before it stopped. Now he could still catch four or five hours sleep. That would be cut in half when calving was in full swing. As he looked over the knock-kneed calves attached to the underside of their mothers, he was filled with a sense of well-being.

This was his first calving season. The future of his business was being born under his watchful eye. He and Virginia could not have children, and that suited him just as well. If he did not have a child, then he could not lose a child, and he knew that he could never endure that terrible pain. He remembered his father's grief after Shrine died.

At the border of the cow-calf pairs, he saw one little calf hover apart from the others, gazing forlornly into the group. This pinch-faced orphan—bummers, his father called them, though most ranchers referred to them as dogies—had swollen eyes and a nose cracked from lack of milk. His ribs showed through his dull coat like a Japanese lantern.

The bummer waited for an opening. When a calf wandered away from its mother, the scruffy orphan snuck up from behind and tried to cop a drink of warm milk. He only got a few mouthfuls before the cow noticed the impostor and kicked him away.

Nearby, Alfred spotted a speckle-nosed cow on her side straining her head forward, pushing. He dismounted and went to check her. She was worn out and needed help. By the time he got out the Vaseline and rolled up his sleeve, the calf had slipped out. The birth sac remained intact, clear and bluish like a jellyfish. The calf inside showed no signs of breathing. Alfred punctured the sac with a knife. The calf was dead.

Now was his chance to pair the bummer with a new mother. He snatched the afterbirth and rubbed it all over the nearly starved dogie, scuffing up behind the ears and buffing the rump to allow the smell to penetrate so the mother would accept the substitute calf as her own. He placed the bummer in a heap by the speckle-faced cow, which was now standing upright. The little thing struggled up on wobbly legs, dipped his head under the surrogate mother, and butted the udder to make her let down her milk. The cow did not protest but continued grazing as if nothing had happened. The dogie smacked and sucked, no longer a dogie but an adopted calf.

Alfred was a man who kept no secrets. Virginia had sensed that about him the first time they met. She had wanted, and gotten, a man who would never shock her. He lived his life in complete honesty, while she, who strived for this as a goal, came up so very far short. She had something to hide, and it formed a rift between them.

Lately she found herself going back to what the stranger in Quaker meeting had said. He had made her see that there was nothing to be gained by suffering alone. She wanted to tell her husband what had happened when she was working on the Quaker feeding project in Kentucky.

It had started innocently enough. She was driving her Quaker coworker Alice to the nearby mountain town to pick up supplies. On a hairpin curve, she lost control of the car, ricocheted against a rock wall, then skidded across the slick clay and down the bank. The only thing that prevented the car's headlong descent into a ravine was a slender ridgepole pine. She and Alice were shaken but not hurt. They both crawled out the driver's side and grabbed onto shrubs and saplings to pull themselves up to the road.

Just as they were wondering what in the world they were going to do, a strapping young man appeared through the gray mist. He wore a pair of overalls with no shirt and no shoes. He had the taut, honey-brown skin of a young brave, and his muscles glistened in the rain. "Need a hand?" He looked down the bank at the car and let out a long, low whistle.

"Yep, we got a problem here, sure enough. When the rain stops, I'll come back with the mules and see if we can get her out."

He invited them to come home with him. "My Serina will fix you up in no time flat. We ain't got much to offer, but at least it's dry."

His name was Lemmie Johnson, and he lived up the hollow. They followed the road to the next switchback, then turned onto a path that hugged the side of the mountain.

Lemmie whistled as he moved in long, sure-footed strides. Virginia walked behind him, looking at his broad shoulders and sharply defined arms. His overalls hung loosely on him, and the rain slithered down his bare skin underneath the overalls, below to . . . Good gracious! Maybe he wasn't wearing any underwear. Thinking of this, Virginia forgot to look where she was going and tripped. She lurched forward. Lemmie turned just in time to catch her. His wet skin slid against hers, and she felt a current shoot through her.

"Sorry, I'm so clumsy," she said and thought: *What's gotten into me? Maybe it's a delayed reaction to the accident that's made me quivery all over.*

"Not to worry, ma'am. You're not used to these hills like me." He grinned broadly, exposing perfect white teeth. Most of the miners had brownish, cavity-infested teeth.

Before they reached the house, the rain let up, and the sun, with its odd light, made the leaves shine as if dipped in mercury. The moisture released the scent of pine, which mixed with the earthy smell of the rich forest duff.

They arrived at a small, well-kept house perched above the path. The rain had darkened the unpainted boards. Wildflowers bloomed up next to the porch, and smoke swirled from the chimney. A split-rail fence zigzagged by the path, surrounding the house and a shed that had animal skins stretched across its side.

Lemmie's wife, Serina, came out onto the porch in a plain patched dress. Two small girls—twins—peeked from behind their mother's skirt.

"Go on and get some towels—scoot," she told the twins. They returned with towels, and Serina made everyone wipe the mud from their feet before she'd allow them through the door.

Inside, the cabin was bright with patchwork quilts. Hams and sacks of corn hung on the wall, and rings of pumpkin dried on rods by the stone hearth, filling the room with a spicy scent. Lemmie took several chairs from their hooks on the wall and set them down near the fire.

"These chairs are wonderful," Virginia said, examining the ladder-back hickory chairs with woven seats.

"Lemmie made them," Serina said proudly.

"Just something I do in my spare time," he shrugged.

Their fourteen-year-old son, Jimmy, came in and set his rifle against the door. He was an awkward, gangling youth who didn't seem to know what to do with his oversized arms and legs. His mother introduced them.

"Okay, out with the lot of you. These ladies need to hang their clothes by the fire." She playfully shooed Lemmie and Jimmy out the door. "The young'uns can stay," she said.

"Too bad. I was hoping to find someone to play hidey-go-seek with," Lemmie said.

The twins squealed and ran out the door with him.

Alice and Virginia stripped down to their slips and wrapped themselves in quilts while their clothes dried by the fire.

While Serina warmed up some leftover hominy, Virginia looked out the window. Lemmie had one of the twins on his shoulders. He turned right and left, and said, "I haven't seen hide nor hair of Rosy May. Where in the world could she be?"

The little girl on his shoulders giggled.

A tapping sound came from an overturned wheelbarrow. "Bean, help me out here," Lemmie said.

Inside, Virginia turned to Serina and said, "Bean?"

"He's got his own special names for the twins."

Virginia turned her attention back outside.

Rosy May sprang from beneath the wheelbarrow. Lemmie swung the other twin off his shoulder and chased after both of them, growling like a bear. Soon he was on his back on the leaves. One of the girls draped herself over his chest while he lifted the other, on her stomach, balanced on the soles of his bare feet.

"Me next, Daddy. Me next," the other twin cried.

"He's a good father," Alice observed, caught up in the scene as well.

Serina looked out the window. "Lord have mercy, it's soaking wet out there. I'm going to have a heap of laundry on my hands."

Later in the afternoon, after Virginia and Alice's clothes had dried, Lemmie and his son returned with the mules and pulled the car onto the road. Miraculously, it started up right away. The headlights were smashed, so they could not travel at night, but otherwise the car was still serviceable.

That evening in Swan Hill, as Virginia fixed supper, she noticed how sterile and cold their kitchen seemed compared to the mountain house they had just left. She felt drawn to Lemmie and his family. Their fierce poverty had not daunted their spirits the way life had beaten down the miners.

"I'd give anything for some chairs like the ones Lemmie made," Virginia said. "Do you think he'd be willing to take orders?"

"If he did, I know a lot of people back east who would snap them up," Alice said.

"That's it." Virginia jumped up, possessed by a new idea. "I bet there are all kinds of people here in Swan Hill who could make things like Lemmie. Most of them are only one generation away from the hills."

"I'm sure there are."

"Don't you see? All people do here is wait for the impossible to happen. The mines aren't going to start producing again any time soon. The men have time on their hands. The talent's there. I know it. The only thing that's missing is a place to sell, and we can provide that."

Alice put away the dish towel and grabbed a piece of paper. By the time the chicken was cooked, they had sketched out the beginnings of a plan. They would find out who could make what in town. The following summer, Alice would take a selection of crafts to resorts along the East Coast and take orders. During the winter, the men would have something to occupy their days, and make a little extra money at the same time.

That night, Virginia was too excited to sleep. The car accident, meeting Lemmie—there seemed to be a purpose in it. If she could start a project that would help the people in town regain their dignity, what a wonderful gift that would be. She spent the night scheming and planning and did not fall asleep until the first light crept over the mountains.

In the middle of the week, Virginia drove to Lemmie's house. She found Serina outside hanging clothes on the line. Virginia told her about the plan to sell crafts on the East Coast, and asked if she could talk to Lemmie.

Serina pointed out the path around the mountain, which Virginia followed until she came to a field too steep for animals or machinery. The plowed rows were graduated, one above the other, like theater seats. At the top, Lemmie crouched before a clod of worked-over earth, digging up potatoes. He was barefoot and wore no shirt. The sun slid out from behind some feathery clouds and cast a satiny light over the contours of his muscles. Watching him, Virginia felt her pulse quicken. How much of her plan, she wondered, had been concocted with the thought of seeing Lemmie again?

He saw her and waved for her to come up. She was grateful, this far away, that he could not see her flushed face. He put his hands over the top of the pitchfork and rested his cheek on it, watching her pick her way over the steep rows. She was out of breath when she reached him.

"I was waiting for you to come back," he said, looking directly at her. His gaze made her feel exposed. She shivered and looked across to the distant mountains. Veins of dark evergreens ran along the ridges, with the reds, yellows, and oranges in the hollows.

"What are you thinking?" he said.

"You live in a beautiful place."

"I was hoping you were thinking about me." No one had ever spoken to her so directly.

"Well, I did come to see you with a proposition—a plan," she said.

"I haven't had much schooling, but I reckon I can figure out what a proposition is." She turned red, regretting her patronizing attitude. She told him about her idea for selling his chairs. He stared at her and said, "So you want me to be quaint for the benefit of strangers? No thank you."

She had not meant to insult him. "No, no—please. I was thinking about your workmanship. You're good."

"Good, but not good enough for you."

"That's not what I meant."

He pulled her toward him and kissed her. She was startled, but before she knew it, she was responding in kind.

They kissed for a long time, until she thought better of herself and pulled back. "No, I—it's not right."

"What does your heart say?" he said, looking straight at her with brilliant eyes made bluer by the reflection of the sky.

"It doesn't matter."

"It's the only thing that matters."

At that moment, Lemmie's son, Jimmy, came running up the hill.

"Pa, Mama wants to know if you want lemonade."

She caught her breath. If he had come a few moments earlier, he would have seen them kissing. This, surely, was a sign. As if she needed one. What she needed was a cold shower. It was shameful how she felt, but all she could think about was falling into his arms again.

"We'll be there in a minute, son."

When they got back to the cabin, Serina was waiting for them with two tall glasses of lemonade.

"I'm sorry, I've got to get back," Virginia said.

"Better stay for a drink. You're looking a little peaked," Serina said.

Was it that obvious? She glanced at Lemmie. He gave her a look of longing that made her shudder—Serina was only a few feet away. How could he be so bold? Or perhaps she was imagining all of this. But the kiss. No, that was real. She could still taste it.

Lemmie told her to come back on Wednesday and he would have an answer for her on the chairs.

For the next few days, she had wild swings of emotion. One moment, she felt giddy and girlish. The next moment, she was sick with guilt. She wanted to do the right thing but longed to do the wrong thing, and the longing was much more powerful.

She needed guidance. She spent time with her *Faith and Practice*. The trouble with Quakerism was that it didn't tell you what to do, other than to follow your conscience. But conscience was a weaselly thing, particularly when it intertwined with the heart.

Looking back on the incident, Virginia had deep feelings of remorse. She had craved Lemmie's lips, his touch. But the shame had proven more durable than the longing. It was not right to let Alfred go on thinking she was one kind of person when, in fact, she was another. The duplicity weighed heavily on her, and she resolved that very day to tell him about Lemmie.

Full of fitful energy, she busied herself until he returned. Her nervousness perfectly fit the fussy motion of dusting. March was the worst month for dust. Each time the wind blew, the dirt broke down into smaller and smaller particles so that less wind was needed to move it the next time. Now the dirt had been pulverized into such a fine powder that the slightest breeze created a haze on the plains, and it seeped through the smallest crevices into the house. The day before, the sky had been perfectly clear and blue—a trend, she had thought, but today the air was once again laden with particulates. She dabbed Vaseline in her nostrils to keep the dust from her lungs.

She had barely begun to clean when Alfred surprised her by returning in the middle of the afternoon. He stood outside the door and beat his hands against his coat and pant legs. Dust flew out, as if from an old rug. His face was the color of cinnamon. "You're back early," she said when he came into the kitchen.

"Need to make a run to town." He moved purposefully to the counter.

"I'm going tomorrow," she said.

"Can't wait. Blasted mineral salts ran out on me. The deer must be into them." He reached for the coffee can that held loose coins.

"Let's have tea. We never have tea together."

"I never have tea, period." He reached for the keys to the truck. "Now, where did I put that list? I might as well drop off the laundry." He seemed to be talking to himself.

"I just thought we could talk," she said.

"About what?" The pump made a rapping sound as he drew up water from the cistern and filled his glass.

"Never mind. If you don't have time."

"I have time if it's important."

She sighed. "Go on, we can talk later."

"Do you need anything in town?"

"I could use some cotton stockings," she said.

"Can't you mend the ones you have?" he said.

"They've been mended so many times a new set of holes has appeared above the darning. They might as well be made of net." She raised her hem and held out a leg for him to see.

"We can't afford extras right now," he said and took a big gulp of water.

"Extras? How expensive could stockings be?" she said. She wasn't asking for the silk stockings she had seen in those daring magazine advertisements that featured lusciously-colored drawings of shapely women in diaphanous slips, high heels, and silk-clad legs. She only wanted common cotton hose.

"Anything is too much right now," he said evenly. He poured a little water on his bandanna and wiped his face.

Virginia thought of a little girl she had come across near the school in Swan Hill—what was her name? The girl stood barefoot with her back against an empty railroad car and watched the other children playing in the schoolyard. It was raining, and Virginia was on her way to the school, so she offered the girl room under the umbrella. A big tear ran down the girl's cheek. "I can't go to school."

"Why not?" Virginia asked. The girl so clearly wanted to be with the other children.

"I just can't," she said and ran off through the rain.

Later Virginia found out the reason the child was not in school: she did not have any shoes to wear. The family had only one pair for all their children, and that pair had gone to her brother. As soon as Virginia discovered this, she arranged for the girl—Lizzie was her name; it came back to her now—to do housework in exchange for a pair of shoes.

Virginia had never thought she would be in a similar situation. Yet here she was, unable to afford a new pair of stockings, much less shoes. The humiliation made her cheeks tingle, the way wind seared off the nerve endings and turned the face red. She looked at her husband and said, "Alfred, are you telling me we can't afford stockings?"

"Everything's riding on this calving season. If I lose too many calves—"

The tautness in his voice made her skin stiffen. "What's normal? What can you expect?" she asked.

"In this situation, we can't go by what's normal," he said. It was normal to lose stock from birth, disease, toxic plants, rustling, lightning, or falling trees. Even normal could spell ruin for him. "I'm not even sure we'll have enough money for taxes," he said in a measured voice.

He had not meant to tell her about his financial worries. Certainly not in this way. She had no idea how much strain he had been under.

"You could ask your father for a loan," she said.

"I'll die before I do that." He set the glass down so hard that water sloshed over the edge.

"You'll pay him back. You just need help to get on your feet."

He didn't like Virginia meddling in his business. Borrow money? Never! The old man would probably give it to him. A small price to pay for being right that his son could never make it on his own. But Alfred would not give him that satisfaction.

He set his jaw and said, "Either I make a go of this on my own, or—" The alternative was too painful to consider.

"I don't understand this thing you have with your father. He's on your side. He respects you."

"How do you know?"

"I talked to him at Christmas."

"And how much is he going to respect me if I go borrowing money?"

"It's not your fault. Everybody's having hard times. The weather, the drought—you can't control those things."

"That's a given in ranching. You're always at the mercy of weather. That's the gamble you take. I just happened to start out in one of the driest years on record."

"Exactly. That's why you need help. You don't have to grovel. Just ask him."

"You don't understand my father. As long as you're doing fine, he's fine. You're in trouble, tough luck."

"What are families for, if not to help out in hard times?"

"I'm not going to ask him. Period. Is that clear?"

He took the keys and left.

She sat down, shaken. She wanted to help Alfred, but her help was not welcome. He treated her like an intrusive meddler, as if she had no stake in their problems.

She picked up the dust rag and went to the piano. Like cell mates, she and the piano were trapped in this tiny house together. The ebony surface was a showcase for dust, which was not really dust but some insidious hybrid, too heavy to form dust kittens but too silky to be called dirt. It did, however, settle over everything—the bookshelves, the windowsills, and the piano, always that damn piano. She knew it represented Alfred's history, but everything she did, everywhere she turned, it was him, him, him. She dearly loved Alfred. But somehow she had expected her love for him, her joy of living with him, to fill her up, leaving no room for other problems. But he left early and came back late. The rest of the time, she was trapped in this tiny dust box, sharing the space with this monstrous dust-collecting piano. She ran the rag over the keys. The piano bared its ivory teeth at her.

She had wanted to tell Alfred about Kentucky, but he didn't give her the chance. He was preoccupied. Well, so was she. But he never stopped to notice. He was too engulfed in his own troubles. Both their lives were plagued by absences—a connection to his father, water, and a child, always the child.

Alfred surveyed the sky as he rode over the calving grounds. Old habits. The fluffy, silver-edged clouds to the north were useless beauties. There would be no rain today. For once, he was glad. Damp ground bred bacteria and made the vulnerable calves more susceptible to disease.

In a far corner of the field, he spotted a cow with her tail cocked at an angle. She raised her rubbery muzzle to the sky and lowed plaintively. He got off his horse and checked the cow's rump. He made a mental note to swing back in an hour; by then, the cow would need help.

Working this closely with the livestock, he had developed a sixth sense about animals. It was part of what made him good at what he did. He knew when the cattle needed water or extra feed, which cow was going to calf when, and which cows needed help giving birth. Animals were easy.

He and Virginia had not spoken again about the stockings since their words the week before. His deep shame prevented him from apologizing. What would he apologize for? Being a lousy husband, a bad provider? Financial worries had kicked the manhood right out of him.

Since their argument, they had treated each other with an excruciating politeness. Gone was the warmth, the teasing, the laughter. He wanted to make some offering or gesture that would allow them both to forgive. But what? The only thing he could think of was music. He had never played the piano for her. In music, he could express things that he didn't dare say aloud.

As a musician, his mind worked more like a mathematician than a poet. He was interested in the way everything related to everything else—in precise, predictable patterns, not wild flights of fancy like a poet. It comforted him to know that the A-minor and C-major scales shared the exact same notes. It was the context that made them different. Because the two scales started on different notes and had different related chords, they didn't sound anything alike—one was sad and forlorn, the other happy and bright. The same, but different. A poet could draw a lesson therein, but he could not. He only knew that he wanted to play for Virginia, to express to her intuitively what he saw in the music, and hope that she drew from it what was in his heart.

As he rode across the plains, he thought of what piano piece he could play. Anything technically challenging was out of the question. His hands were out of practice and roughened by ranch work, and did not have the dexterity for rapid arpeggios or trills. He would choose a slower, simpler piece. He could render, from the few notes, heart-aching beauty. So much of music was shaping the silence.

He considered Chopin's nocturnes, or Schumann's "Träumerei," from *Scenes from Childhood.* Finally he settled on Bach's Fifth French Suite—minus the last dance, the jig. No way could he do that with his hands in their current shape.

After supper, Alfred asked Virginia to come sit in the living room. "I want to play for you," he said.

He set a candle on the piano lid. The light reflected against the piano's black finish like a midnight lake, and the oxen-hoof marks made ripples on its smooth surface. Virginia leaned back in her reading chair.

He began to play. At first he was aware of the ivories beneath his fingers, so unfamiliar did they feel, but before long he forgot about the mechanics. Something long dead stirred within him. He felt his mind become alert, his body charged. How could he have stayed away from the piano so long? He closed his eyes— he did not need to look at the keyboard or the music, for his fingers knew their way by heart. Alone with the music, he felt totally, completely himself. Only by pulling inward and letting the music take over could he communicate to Virginia in a deeply felt way what the piece meant to him. The third dance, the sarabande, was a slow lyrical piece, heartbreaking in its simplicity. When he got to the end, he looked up at Virginia and saw that her face was wet with tears. He went to her.

"It's beautiful. A lullaby," she said quietly and wiped the corners of her eyes.

"I guess it does sound a little like a lullaby."

"A song to a precious child."

He embraced her and felt her chest convulse against his. "What's wrong?"

She tried to form the words, but a sob came out instead. He held her, alarmed. This was not the reaction he had anticipated. He meant the music as an offering and had succeeded only in making her sad.

"I'll never be able to—" She was trembling.

"To what?" He couldn't stand to see her so upset. Was she mad at him?

"Sing it," he made out through the blubbering. She was not making sense.

"Why do you say that?"

"You should have . . . have married someone else," she said.

He felt a prickly sensation radiate up his spine. He had been right. She was having second thoughts about him.

"You're not happy?" Her heaving shoulders gave the answer.

"I can't—I can't—" She went no further.

What? Stand to be around him? Take the uncertainty? Face failure? He couldn't bear to hear it. Not now. Not tonight. The music had made him drop his guard. Perhaps that's why he had avoided playing, all these months. It made him too vulnerable.

She was a limp weight against him.

"I can't have a baby," she blurted out.

Suddenly everything came into clear focus. "That's what's been bothering you all this time?" He felt deeply ashamed. He had known she was unhappy these past months but, on purpose, had avoided asking her what was troubling her, because he was afraid he knew the answer: she was disappointed in the ranch and, by extension, him. Rather than risk confirming his fears, he isolated himself and, in doing so, very nearly destroyed what he was trying so hard to protect. "I knew that when I married you."

"Thee does not want a family?" She surprised him by using plain language.

"You're my family." He raised her wet, shining face toward him. He was not good at expressing how he felt. It seemed unnecessary. How could Virginia not know? But now it came to him naturally. The thing he had been trying to say through music, he now gave voice to, and it was the thing that calmed her: "I love you."

✿   ✿   ✿

161

Ever since his talk with Virginia, Alfred had watched her more closely. He worried when the dark spells came over her. Sometimes she would stop washing the dishes and stare across the plains, lost in thought, and he knew that she was thinking about the babies she could not have.

He understood obsession. If she thought about babies half as much as he thought about rain—both things they had no control over—then she must have a very crowded head indeed. He was gone during the day so he didn't know how she spent her time. Living the way they did, surrounded by too much space and time, the possibility of madness was always with them.

That afternoon as he rode the fence line, he looked to the east and saw a dark cloud that started at the horizon and rose into the sky, turning yellowish-brown at the top where the sun permeated it. Above, the sky was a flawless blue.

A forest fire, he thought. The drought had turned the plains into a tinderbox. But as he stared at the roiling mass filled with brown and green spots, he saw that it was not smoke but a wall of dust moving toward him.

The hairs on his arm tingled with the kind of static electricity that preceded a tornado. A coyote streaked along the edge of the pasture, and the field was alive with rabbits escaping the oncoming duster.

The grasses stood strangely still. The cloud moved forward, a creeping, fearful thing. Everything seemed off-kilter—the absence of wind, the electrically charged air, the disturbing quality of the light that fell over the prairie, the feeling that the elements were in suspension, waiting.

Alfred's only thought was to get home to Virginia. She would be terrified. He urged his horse into a gallop. At home, he found Virginia lowering the plywood storm windows.

Before long, the cloud was on top of them. The air became so dark they had to light a lamp in the middle of the afternoon. The wind did not pick up until they sat down to dinner. Then it came with a terrible force, flinging grit and tiny pebbles against the house. In the drafty room, the lantern flame sloshed against the curved sides of the glass chimney, blackening it. Virginia could feel cool currents move about the room and, though she could not see the dust, she could feel it in her throat when she breathed through her nose.

They put napkins over the food and ate hurriedly from under the cloth, heads bent to the table. Afterward she set the dishes on the counter. There was no reason to wash them now.

"I'm so glad you came home," Virginia said. She was grateful she didn't have to go through the storm alone.

"I've got to go back now. I just wanted to make sure you were all right."

"Alfred, you can't go out in this thing," she said, horrified.

"I have to."

"You can't wait 'til tomorrow?" She checked the clock. It had stopped. The dust had seeped into its mechanisms.

"Cows aren't going to stop having calves just because the dust is up. I'm already shorthanded." He was not going to risk losing the ranch by being absent on the most important night of the year.

"Are you absolutely sure?" She tried to keep her voice even. The light of the lantern lurched this way and that, buffeted by the wind. He nodded.

"Then I'll go with you," she said quietly.

"I can't ask you to do that."

"You didn't. I'm offering."

They drove the truck to the pasture. Alfred hunched forward, his chest almost touching the steering wheel, and inched ahead.

She had no idea how he managed to follow the road or find the spot he was looking for, but after a tense ride, he left the truck idling, opened the gate, and drove farther into the pasture.

"Stay close to the truck. I know my way around. I'll cover the far end of the pasture."

"What if I lose you?" she said.

He pressed something cold and metallic in her hand. She felt its sharp edges. It was a whistle. "Use this if you need me."

She watched him walk away. The dust-softened outline of his flashlight drew in on itself until it disappeared completely. She listened to the wind for a few moments and, working up her courage, got her knapsack of supplies and went outside.

A whirlwind broke across her back, enveloping her in a confetti of loose straw and grasses. The sheepskin flaps of her plaid cap warmed her ears, but the cold clung to the bottom half of her face, where she had tied a damp bandanna to keep out the dust.

She flashed the beam of light around her and advanced slowly, feeling the tufts of grass beneath her feet. As she made a wide swath around the truck, she came across several cows that were either not close to calving, or having no trouble.

On the other side of the hill, she heard an animal bellow. She found a cow on its side, its breath coming in labored heaves. It was clearly in trouble. She flashed the light at the cow's tail. One leg of the calf appeared through the orifice, along with a pink nose still shrouded in the birth sac. Panic collected at the base of Virginia's spine. One of the calf's legs was stuck. The mother needed help to reposition the calf.

She felt the sharp contours of the whistle in her pocket. She brought it toward her lips until she felt it hit cloth—she had forgotten that her mouth was covered with the bandanna, like a bandit. She paused. Alfred was somewhere nearby. In the past two weeks, she had watched Alfred pull calves. If she got into trouble, he would come to her aid. Knowing that calmed her. She would handle this on her own.

The wind enveloped her in gauzy whorls. She covered the mother's nose with a gunnysack to filter the dust, and set the flashlight on the ground so that its beam pointed to the cow's hind legs. She pushed her sleeve above her elbow and slathered Vaseline over her arm. It gleamed in the pale beam of light.

With all her strength, she pushed the calf's head back into the birth channel, as she had seen Alfred do. The mother's muscles clamped down on her arm with surprising power. Virginia persisted, and pushed her arm further in, but the pressure was too much for her. She withdrew her aching arm and lubricated the other one.

The flashlight rolled away, its light looping down the incline. Virginia was working by feel now. She reached into the moist warmth of the cow and felt the hollow of the calf's nostrils. To the side, she felt the sharpness of a cloven hoof. The mother bellowed with each contraction.

"Come on, Mama, you're doing fine. You're going to make it," she said.

With the wind pushing against her back, Virginia felt for the calf's other leg. The cow bore down on her arm. Finally Virginia got hold of both legs together and repositioned the calf's head so the mother could do the rest.

Virginia dropped to the ground, exhausted. While she rested, the mother strained then relaxed, strained then relaxed. Soon the calf's two front legs cleared the opening, followed by its head and rib cage. The calf showed no signs of breathing. For the next few minutes, nothing happened. The mother had stopped pushing.

When Virginia regained her strength, she took the calf's front legs, one in each hand, planted her feet, and pulled with all her strength. The calf slipped loose so quickly it sent Virginia reeling backward. She landed on her seat, legs spread out. The calf lay in a steaming puddle of blood and afterbirth.

With the liquid still in its lungs, the calf gurgled. Virginia cleared its nose of phlegm and rubbed it hard with a gunnysack. The calf sneezed and sent snot flying all over her.

The mother struggled to her feet and butted Virginia aside. With her tongue, she stroked her newborn in long, rhythmic motions, tenderly stiffening the hair and drying it off. She licked against the grain so the hair stood up in ridges. She nudged the calf up, but the newborn was stretched out inert. The dust that had collected on its wet hair looked like hoarfrost. If the newborn did not get to its feet and start moving, it would have little chance of surviving the cold.

Virginia half carried, half dragged the calf back to the truck and deposited it on the passenger's seat. She climbed into the driver's seat and turned on the heat. The vent brought with it dirt from the outside. Virginia rubbed the sticky red mucous from her arms as best she could. The idling truck's headlights cut two fuzzy channels through the darkness.

As the cabin warmed up, the calf perked up and started bawling. Before long, it burrowed its nose under Virginia's arm and nudged it upward. Then it knocked softly at Virginia's elbow and began sucking on it.

"You're hungry, aren't you, sweetie?" she said. "I'm sorry, I can't help you." Virginia's chapped lips hurt when she laughed, and she tried to keep her mouth from widening out, but the rambunctious calf made her smile. It butted its head against the dashboard; it sucked at the gearshift; it placed its mouth around the door handle. Suddenly the cabin was too small to contain the vibrant, pulsing life.

She got the calf out of the truck and set it in the path of the headlights. It got up on wobbly legs, then collapsed, then tried again. Finally, after a few tentative steps, it was on its feet. By this time, its mother had found them. Instinctively, the calf sought its mother's udder, but the cow pushed it away, almost toppling it. Then she licked the calf and, after several tastes, was satisfied that it belonged to her, and let it nurse.

Virginia felt exhilarated as she watched the newborn and its mother. Covered with dried blood, mucous, phlegm, manure, and dust, Virginia thought: *There's nothing in the world I'd rather be doing than this.*

NINE

The next morning, Virginia awoke to a world transformed. Dunes sprawled over the yard, their ridges knobbed like dinosaur spines. Bushes had disappeared beneath drifts. The wagon by the shed held a cargo of dust. Its wheels were buried halfway up the spokes.

Virginia walked to the shed, leaving a trail of hollows where her feet had been. Inside, mounds of dirt had collected where the gaps between boards admitted light. The animals seemed undisturbed, though the irregular white patterns on the milk cow's dark hide had turned brown, like a map of dirty lakes.

After only two hours of sleep, she felt exhausted but totally alive. She hung the lantern on a nail, got out her stool, and set to work. The milk hit the empty pail with a metallic whoosh. As the pail filled, dust floated to the top like undissolved cocoa.

She leaned her forehead against the cow's warm side and cat-aloged the enormous cleanup tasks that awaited her after the storm. Only a few days earlier, she would have felt overwhelmed by the sheer volume of labor. But last night something had changed, and she felt like her old self, recharged and ready to take on any challenge. She could take apart the separator and wash the pieces individually. She could take the dishes out of the cupboard, rub it down, and wash each dish. No problem. She could remove the dust from the floor—not enough for a shovel, too much for a broom—and remove all the sheets she had placed over the furniture and piano and take them to town to be laundered. She could do it all.

No longer did every movement seem like an effort, every idea a fluid that resisted flow. Now her thoughts ran clean and effortlessly, soaring like the nighthawks that inhabited the evening skies—sometimes planing, sometimes diving, always graceful. In her exuberance, she hit upon an idea that made her sit up and catch her breath. Her idea was this: she should invite her brother to come help them on the ranch. Alfred desperately needed an extra hand; her mother needed a break; Jonathan needed more independence. Everyone would be well served. In her excitement, Virginia pulled the cow's teats faster and faster until the animal lowed in protest.

Over breakfast, she told Alfred about her idea.

"Does Jonathan know anything about ranching?" he said, helping himself to more bacon.

"Not ranching, exactly, but he's always had a knack with horses."

"I can't afford to pay him." He sopped up the runny yolk with his toast.

"I'm sure he'd be willing to work for room and board."

She could see he was intrigued by the idea.

"But could he do the work? I mean, I thought he had—problems."

"Oh, he'd need supervision. A lot of times he can't remember things, so you might have to tell him more than once. But he's a good strong worker."

"I'm willing to take him on. But what about you?" He set

down his fork and looked at her hard. "It will be a big responsibility for you."

"Let's face it. You can't keep up this pace. It's too much work for one person."

"I have two people. Last night—you were a big help. I couldn't have done it without you."

"It was nothing."

"It took guts to go out in that storm and help me."

"Only if you're a beginner like me."

"For goodness sakes, woman. Can't you let a fellow give you a compliment? A well-deserved one at that."

She laughed at herself. "Thank you," she said simply.

"That wasn't so hard, was it?" he said.

"Actually, I surprised myself last night," she said. "You know, I'm not bad at this ranching business."

After spending the morning cleaning, she gathered the laundry and drove to town. The air was muffled and quiet, the way it is just after a snowstorm. Last night's wind had ground the silt to a fine whitish powder, then sculpted the drifts into unexpected contours that created a strange, lunar beauty against the cloudless blue sky. In one place, a drift reached the highest strand of the fence so the barbs stuck out like sand spurs at regular intervals along the ridge. The roads had vanished completely under the dust. Virginia drove on the high ground between the bar ditches. The dust fluffed up around the truck and sifted down again, blurring the fresh tracks she had made.

In town, the talk at Dave's General Store was all about the storm. A holiday atmosphere prevailed as men gathered around the stove to trade hard-luck tales. Edgar Ingram had been forced to postpone his gallbladder operation because the doctors couldn't sterilize the instruments. Harley Feathergill's ceiling had collapsed under the weight of the dirt that had blown into his attic.

"No trick a' t'all to tell where these things came from," said

Harley, who seemed enlivened by the misfortune. "The red ones are from Oklahoma, the dirty-yellow ones from the Texas–New Mexico plains. This one here's brown. I got it sittin' in my living room, a present from Kansas."

Virginia found Dave on a ladder, his head hidden by the over-alls and hats that were hanging from the rafters. "We're clean out of brooms and wash pails, Mrs. Bowen," he said. He took a cowboy boot from the ceiling and turned it upside down. Dirt dribbled out. He dusted the boot off and hung it back up.

"At least the storm's good for somebody's business," she said, looking up. "What about coffee?"

"I personally ain't going to dust off every individual bean in that bag, but if you'll take it as it is, we got it."

She paid for the coffee, then drove to Ida Pinska's house to drop off the laundry. No one had entered or left Ida's since the storm—she could tell by the unmarred drifts around the house. She waded through dust to the back stoop. There she dipped her toe into the dust, as if testing cold water, in an effort to find the flat platform of the steps. From inside came a low keening sound. She opened the door a crack.

"Ida, Ida, are you here?" she called out. She pushed the door harder. It made a wedge in the dust, like a windshield wiper.

Ida sat with the heels of her hands against the edge of the kitchen table. Her mouth hung slack, and her face was smeared, as if with camouflage paint, where tears had turned the dirt to mud, streaked, and then dried again.

"What's wrong?" Virginia said, setting her dirty laundry on the table. As long as Ida followed her daily routine, she was fine, but anything out of the ordinary befuddled her.

"My beauties. They're gone."

"What are you talking about?"

"My cats are buried alive."

"They'll find their way home. Don't you worry," Virginia said, though she noted she had seen no animal tracks near the house.

"Where did they go?"

"I don't know, but cats have good survival instincts."

Ida looked as if she wanted to believe Virginia.

"Why did all this dirt come visit me?" she said, looking around the room as if noticing it for the first time. The dust was so thick on the floor that the chairs and tables seemed to be floating.

"We had a huge dust storm," Virginia said. "Alfred and I were out all night with the calves, and when we came back we had to shovel the porch before we could get the door open to go inside."

"You mean the dust came to your house, too?" She paused and considered this fact. "I thought I was being punished for being bad."

"The storm was a natural act. It was created by God, but he didn't do it to punish anyone. Especially not you," Virginia said.

"Even if I've been bad," she said and turned her head downward in shame.

"You haven't been bad, dear," she reassured Ida.

"I lost my beauties."

"They'll come back. You did not cause the dust storm, honey. Trust me."

A look of relief passed over her face. Then confusion. "Then why? Why did we have a storm?"

"I don't think anyone can answer that," Virginia said, smoothing Ida's hair, trying to calm her. "Were you scared last night?"

Ida's eyes got wide. "Yeah."

"You poor dear. Here all alone." Virginia wiped the dirt from Ida's face. Even with Alfred at her side, the storm had been terrifying. But to face it alone, the wind howling, dust filling the air and making night out of the afternoon. Virginia couldn't imagine anything worse.

"Come on. I'll help you get started. You haven't had anything to eat today, have you?"

"What about my beauties?" Ida's tapping foot stirred up the dust.

"I'll find them. Now let's get to work."

Outside, Virginia took the broom handle and poked up under the house where the dust had built up in drifts. The handle slid easily through the loosely-packed dust. She prayed she would not hit a solid mass. Surely the dozen cats Ida kept had found a way to safety, as Virginia had so confidently predicted on the basis of no knowledge whatsoever.

She dug under the front porch where the cats lived. She felt something heavy on her shovel, and her stomach clenched. What would she tell Ida? She brought out the shovel and emptied the contents on the ground. When the dirt fell away, she saw that it was a feeding bowl. Only a bowl. In the course of the afternoon, she uncovered a number of bowls, several wood scraps, and a rake head. But nothing else.

After several hours of digging, she went back to the kitchen. She had already stayed longer than she intended, and she needed to get back before dark, since the dirt-covered roads were not navigable at night. She found Ida on the floor with several cats in her lap. The gray one's head moved back and forth as its salmon colored tongue flicked across the padded part of its paw. A darker-gray cat preened itself in her lap. The white cat's fur remained pristine, not a speck of dust visible.

"Why didn't you tell me the cats were back?" Virginia said, thinking she could have saved herself an hour's digging.

"I didn't think about it," she said innocently. She looked so happy that Virginia could not stay mad at her.

"Well, I'm glad they found their way home," she said. "Now I need to get on the road."

"Wait a minute." Ida stood up, and the cats scattered on the floor, creating clouds of dust. Ida went to the next room and returned with the laundry Virginia had left the week before, clean and tied in a neat bundle.

"How did you keep them clean? Virginia asked.

Ida motioned for her to follow her to the bedroom. She nodded to the other bundles in the unmade double bed. "I slept with them," she said.

"That was clever."

Ida looked pleased. Virginia paid her. Ida pulled the chamber pot from beneath the bed, opened the lid and blew into it. Dust puffed out like smoke from a pot.

"Ida, remember what I told you about hiding the money?"

"I did hide it. Under the bed." She dropped the coins into the pot.

"But if you show people where it is, it's not hidden."

"But you wouldn't take my money, Mrs. Bowen. I know that."

"But someone else might. You need to get in the habit."

"Okay, Mrs. Bowen. I'll do as you say."

Virginia wasted no time in writing her mother a letter proposing that Jonathan come work on the ranch. A positive response came back immediately. "Jonathan is not one to show emotion," her mother wrote, "but when I read him your letter, he was animated with joy. You know how he loves horses and animals. And though I hate to admit it, I think he will be happy, though a bit nervous, to get away from his mother." It would take several weeks for Jonathan to get ready, but he had already purchased his train ticket and was scheduled to arrive on the second of May.

That April, it did not rain. Occasionally the sky clouded over and rumbled and the wind picked up, but the rain never came. Day after day, the sun shone hot and hard on the parched earth. Virginia took advantage of the summerlike weather to stake out a garden. With the temperature in the mid-eighties, she could not imagine that the danger of frost existed until the second week of May.

The first day she worked under the hot sun, her pale skin burned. She asked Alfred if she could use the stained Stetson that hung in the storage room that had served as a post office in the days the bachelors owned the ranch. He said, "I have an extra bandanna you can put around your head."

"I need a brim to keep the sun off."

"Don't you have a hat?"

"Well, I've got that gray Quaker bonnet that belonged to my grandmother, but I'd feel ridiculous wearing it."

"That's perfect. It's got a wide brim."

"What about the neck? My neck will burn. If you don't want me to use your hat, just say so."

He shifted on his feet. "It's too big for you."

"Why are you being so touchy about a silly old hat?" she said.

"It's not a silly hat. It'll still turn water and hold its shape in a rainstorm," he said.

He offered her a billed cap with GOMER'S SEED stitched across the front. She decided instead to wear her grandmother's bonnet.

She started digging that same day. The sun-baked earth was difficult to turn over—not at all like the airy dust she had shoveled from under Ida's house—but she found the physical labor exhilarating. She went to bed exhausted, woke up aching. After she had prepared the site—much smaller than she had originally envisioned—she planted the seed. Each evening after supper, when the sun had lost its potency, she hauled water from the windmill by the house and poured it on the rows that would soon be potatoes, squash, beans, tomatoes, and sweet corn. Each morning, she awoke with excitement and went to the garden to see what changes had occurred overnight. She marveled at the way the tender shoots split the earth and displaced crumbs of dirt. She waited for the seedlings to put out two leaves, then four.

She was happiest when she was in the garden. All thoughts and worries left her as she crouched down and worked among the clicking and buzzing of insects. She felt she was contributing something tangible to their lives. The dirt that daily defeated her in the house was the source of her greatest pleasure in the garden.

The morning of Jonathan's arrival, the chores took longer than expected, and she and Alfred arrived at the train station twenty minutes late. She checked the main board for the schedule, then hurried to the quay. The train was gone, the platform deserted. A porter wheeled an empty baggage cart past them.

"Excuse me, but have you seen a tall man with black hair, about thirty-five?" Virginia asked him.

"Does he have a beard?"

"I—I don't know," she said. It bothered her that she could not answer such a basic question.

At the far end of the platform, she spotted a box tied with raffia string. Beside it was a battered cardboard suitcase. She ran to check the tags. It was Jonathan's luggage.

"What are we going to do? Where could he be?" Virginia said.

"He can't be too far off," Alfred said.

She nodded, in a daze. What was she thinking? She knew Jonathan was not reliable. She knew about his condition. The trip from the East Coast was difficult, even for an experienced traveler. He had to go halfway across the country and change trains twice. Each time, there was a possibility that he would get lost, lose track of time, miss the connection, or get on the wrong train. But no, his bags were here. So he had to be here somewhere. But where? He may have wandered off or forgotten about his luggage. Images raced through her head—an ambulance with lights flashing, cars stopped by the road, rubberneckers craning to see. The doctors would ask Jonathan whom to contact, and he would not know. He was no longer a child with his address pinned to the pocket of his shorts. But his memory was no more reliable than a child's.

Alfred carried Jonathan's luggage back to the truck. Frantic, she went to the main terminal. If they were lucky, he would still

be in the station. No trains were scheduled to arrive or depart for another hour. The cavernous space was filled with rows of high-backed wooden benches. She moved quickly. Her breaths came in short pants. She had to find him. Boldly she walked up to every man between the age of twenty-five and fifty. She waited outside the men's rest room. Those leaving gave her funny looks. She was not deterred. She had to find Jonathan. Otherwise something terrible would happen, if it hadn't already. And it would be her fault. All her fault. What would her mother say? She had entrusted Jonathan to her, and already things had gone awry. Now he could be wandering around Lower Downtown, with no sense of where he was or how to get in touch with her. Maybe he had fallen in with hobos and taken off riding the rails. Or had he been shaken down by street toughs, or wandered off with a stranger? He was an easy target. He had no sense of direction.

She had not taken into account the perils of having Jonathan live with them. Bringing him out to Colorado was a half-baked idea. If Jonathan could not keep track of his luggage, how was he going to keep track of the cattle?

Alfred returned. Still no Jonathan. They checked Lower Downtown. Outside a flophouse, men with grainy unshaven faces milled about. A few sat cross-legged on the cement and played cards or craps. One man slept on the sidewalk, his back against the brick wall, his head slumped between his knees. The creases in his neck were black. There was no shortage of derelicts and hard-luck cases. Rather than pity them, she felt threatened by them. Jonathan did not belong among these men with no money, no jobs, and no families.

She had lost him. It was her fault. She was supposed to be the responsible one, yet she had lost Jonathan. Growing up, he had been the responsible sibling. She had been the prankster—carefree, mischievous, always getting into scrapes. One quick accident of war was all it took to reverse their positions.

Virginia was in college when Jonathan returned from Europe. After she graduated, she stayed home to help. She cooked and cleaned house, washed and ironed. The bad associations she had of those hard years of domestic labor had colored her enthusiasm for doing housecleaning chores on the ranch. She watched as her sweet father grew more and more sullen and disappeared daily into the darkness of the motion-picture theater—a habit he kept from her mother. But Virginia knew. She timed supper to come out when the afternoon matinee let out of the Rialto. She felt more secure knowing where to find him if things got bad, and they needed a male presence in the house, someone of heft and bulk who could take Jonathan down if his temper got out of control.

An emptiness hovered at the heart of the house now that all of her mother's attention was focused on Jonathan. He sucked the joy out of the air. He was morose, volatile, and unpredictable. Virginia vividly remembered what it was like in those years, coming home from college classes—the hard knot in her stomach as she put her hand on the doorknob, having no idea what to expect. Everyone had their way of coping. Her father had the movies, she had her books. Before, she had taken her faith for granted, but now she found solace in it. That was when she began to study Quakerism in earnest. And her mother— who knew what kept her going? If she resented making sacrifices, she never let on.

The Mendenhall house looked like a school, with slates, chalk, and erasers in all the downstairs rooms for lists, words, messages, and reminders for Jonathan. Each item in the house was labeled in large letters: STOVE. WINDOW. BUREAU. Jonathan had to relearn his vocabulary. Cue cards with sequential steps helped him dress by himself. Everything was designed to help Jonathan lead a normal life. In the process, Virginia's life was destroyed. She felt trapped. She rarely went out, and was embarrassed to have friends over to the house. Yes, now she could finally admit it. She was embarrassed by Jonathan. She did not want to answer questions about him or have her friends witness the tension in the house.

These feelings made her feel ashamed. Jonathan had been her role model, her best friend, and her protector. Why could she not rise to the occasion, like her mother? She felt that somewhere, deep inside her, there was a richer, truer, more generous self, if only she could gain access to it.

Virginia would never have left home had her much wiser mother not nudged her out—pushed her, really—realizing that Virginia needed to get on with her life. Her mother encouraged her to go to graduate school. She did not, however, encourage her to stay away. Virginia did that on her own. In the nine years since she had left home, she had only returned to visit twice. That was all. She had abandoned her brother. Perhaps that's why she had invited Jonathan to come live with her—to make amends for being such a coward. During those nine years, she couldn't bear to see him. Twice she had been swayed by her mother's cheerful letters. Jonathan had made great strides, she said. But when Virginia saw him after long absences, she could barely tell a difference, and she realized that she and her mother had different standards. Virginia was comparing him to the old Jonathan. Her mother was comparing him to the damaged son she lived with every day, for whom each minor improvement was a triumph. That must have been where her mother got her strength—in the minor improvements that looked like triumphs.

Because her brother was not dead, Virginia had not been able to grieve for the loss of him. But the old Jonathan was dead. Now she would have to come to terms with a new Jonathan who was a combination of the old brother she had revered and the one whose personality had been rearranged by an accident of war. He was now thirty-five. He had been the altered Jonathan almost as long as he had been the original.

Virginia and Alfred reached a street in Lower Downtown that

was crowded with saloons. Noise spilled out the doors and onto the sidewalk. It was midafternoon, and the drinking had already begun. A year and a half after Prohibition was repealed, and saloons had sprung up like wildflowers after a rain. They paused in front of Pike's Peak Saloon. As Virginia headed for the door, Alfred held her back and insisted he go in while she waited in the hotel across the street.

"You don't know what Jonathan looks like," she reminded him. She straightened her shoulders like a temperance soldier and marched in. The room was blue with smoke. Wild game heads mounted on the walls peered at her from the shadows. Someone had spilled a beer. A river of foam ran along the lip of the bar. She checked the face of each man at the bar.

They combed the other bars. No Jonathan.

"We need to contact the police," Alfred said.

Her panic returned. Police. Something had happened to him. Alfred thought so, too. The police would need help identifying Jonathan, and she couldn't help them. She didn't even know if he had a beard or a mustache. She had been given the chance to make up for her reprehensible behavior in deserting Jonathan, and already she had failed him.

It was starting to get dark, and the sidewalks were in shadows. As they returned to the truck, she saw a lanky figure approaching. She would recognize that loose-limbed walk anywhere, even in outline form in dim light.

"Jonathan!" she cried. She broke away from Alfred and ran toward her brother. "We've been looking all over for you," she said when she reached him. He had a full black beard that showed threads of gray. His hair stood out at funny angles. His pant leg was caught in the back of his boot, and part of his shirt-tail was untucked. But he was in one piece.

"Aren't you going to say hello, Sis?"

"Look at you. Where were you? Have you been drinking?" she said.

"No, why?"

She hugged him for several seconds. "I was worried sick. I thought I had lost you."

"You're just like Mama," he said.

She kept a grip on his arms but leaned back in order to get a better look at him. "It's so good to see you." She hugged him again before introducing him to Alfred.

"You've got your hands full, dealing with Sis here," Jonathan said, shaking Alfred's hand.

"I hope you're not as ornery as she is, or I'm in big trouble," Alfred said, grinning.

"Where in the world have you been all afternoon?" Virginia said.

"Looking for these." He pulled up his pant leg to show off a pair of new cowboy boots with intricate stitching in the black leather.

"You spent all the money Mama gave you? That was supposed to last six months," Virginia chided.

His smile was unrepentant. "Can't work on a ranch without cowboy boots."

"Those are too nice for ranch work," Alfred said. "Better save those for town."

Back at the ranch, she and Alfred showed Jonathan to the room in the shed beside the saddle room. The former post office had wooden cubbyholes along one wall. The other walls were made of unpainted plywood and exposed wood framing. The room smelled of horses and leather. A squat, claw-footed stove sat in a box of sand. The iron bed was made up with an olive-green wool blanket and a pillowcase with a flowered motif that their mother had embroidered—the only extra pillowcase Virginia had.

Jonathan dropped his suitcase on the floor and tried out the bed. The coils of the springs groaned under his weight. He noticed a cowboy hat hanging from a hook—Alfred's old Stetson.

"Is this for me?" he said, his eyes wide. Virginia looked at Alfred. She knew he was funny about his hat.

"See if it fits," Alfred said.

Jonathan put it on and turned to them for approval.

"How do I look?" he said.

"Like my brother, Shrine," Alfred said. "It was his hat, and I'm sure he'd be glad for you to wear it."

Fourth Month, Thirtieth Day, 1934

My Dearest Virginia:

Ever since your father sold the grocery store, he mopes around the house. The only thing he can think to do with himself is go to the movies. But I can't complain about someone whose temperament has made our married life nearly half a century of unbroken happiness. After Jonathan leaves, I intend to go to see a motion picture myself. That's one of the many new things I want to try out, now that I have some free time. The new house will keep me busy enough. Did Jonathan tell you? Since he decided to go out west, we bought a smaller house. It's more manageable with my creaky old joints. We're not moving until Jonathan leaves—he's so opposed to change of any kind that it would upset him. But I have no sentimental attachment to the house. The truth is, I'm always reaching out toward things that are in front and forgetting things that are behind. I find the new things so much better than old that it seems a pure waste of time to mourn over the old.

I'm confident that Jonathan will be happy living with you. I'm afraid I smothered him in an attempt to help him, but I know you will give him the independence he needs. He should not require great effort on your part. Just an understanding of his special condition so that you can create the kind of home where he can thrive.

Being the old worrywart I am, I must give you a few words of advice. You may take them or leave them—one thing I've learned over the years is to be perfectly indifferent to whether or not my advice is taken.

Don't be fooled by Jonathan. He can seem so healthy that you might forget he is not like the rest of us, which can lead to surprises. Keep instructions simple. Complicated things confuse him. Any task needs to be broken down into parts. His temper can flare up at the oddest times. Don't take it personally if he lashes out at you. Just try to change the subject. Most times, he won't even remember that he erupted. He's an excellent worker, but he doesn't have one whit of common sense. That's why I was always afraid to leave him alone. If the house were to burn down, I'm not sure he would do the right thing. He tends to fall apart when things go wrong.

The hardest thing to accept is the inconsistency. Sometimes he's perfectly normal, and you'd affirm that nothing is wrong with him, and then he'll do something so inconceivable it's frightening. Just be prepared for anything.

He still has trouble reading. He can't keep his mind on the words long enough to let them sink in. But he loves to be read to. I am sending along several books he likes—Rudyard Kipling, Daniel Defoe, and, of course, my favorite, John Greenleaf Whittier.

One thing I despair of. Writing is difficult for him. Could you possibly get him to dictate the letters to you? Otherwise I'm afraid I'll never hear from him, and I couldn't bear that.

So, it is with sadness, but also great joy, that I entrust my beloved son—your dear brother—to your care. In the meantime, I shall bask in the first free day I've had in thirty-six years without children or responsibility.

Love,
Mama

Virginia folded the letter Jonathan had brought with him and walked out on the porch. The leggy outline of the windmill stood against the sky, and pale moon-shadows draped softly across the ground. The sky was shot through with stars, incandescent in a way that only the prairie sky can be. Despite the great nightly beauty, Virginia felt the weight of the responsibility that she had taken on, and she felt all alone. Looking up at the unimaginably large sky, she thought: *This is a place where things can go wrong.*

The next morning at breakfast, Jonathan sat at the table, ready for his first day of work. He wore the Stetson.

"The hat rack's behind you," Virginia said.

"Yep, I see it," he said and made no effort to use it. There was something about a man and his hat that Virginia didn't begin to understand.

"How do you like your eggs?" she asked.

"Fine."

"No, I mean how do you like them cooked?"

"I like them better that way."

Exasperated, she said, "Sunny-side up or over easy?"

"Over easy."

She cracked two eggs into the popping oil and watched the clear part turn white and fill with bubbles.

Alfred came in. "You ready for work?"

"Sure thing," Jonathan said.

Virginia caught Alfred's eye and touched the top of her head while glancing over at Jonathan's hat. He looked at her blankly. Jonathan wasn't the only one who had trouble with inferences. Men! She decided to forget about the hat.

They sat down to eat. Virginia picked up her fork and pierced the yolk of her egg. The yellow oozed onto the plate. Before she took a bite, she looked up and noticed that Jonathan was holding out his hands, palms up, to both her and Alfred.

Virginia cleared her throat and put down her fork. She had

forgotten that Jonathan was used to having a Quaker blessing before meals. Since Alfred was not a Quaker, they had not gotten into the habit of giving silent thanks before meals. She took her brother's hand and offered her other hand to Alfred. Eyes closed, hands linked, they gave a silent blessing.

Afterward, Jonathan eagerly took a mouthful of egg. Then he spit it out.

"Ugh. What did you do to those eggs?"

"I thought that's how you like them."

"They don't taste like Mama's."

Virginia was quiet during the meal, not willing to admit her feelings had been hurt. She was aware that she was not a good cook, but Alfred never complained.

After breakfast, Virginia went with the men to the horse pasture. Jonathan surveyed the grazing horses. "What about that one?" he said, pointing to a chestnut stallion.

"He's a balky thing. Hasn't been legged up," Alfred said.

"I can handle him," Jonathan said.

"If you get him on strange ground and he doesn't know where he is, then he'll start paying attention to you."

Jonathan started across the pasture with a bridle.

Alfred watched him. "Let's see what he's got."

The horses were not hobbled, and when the stallion saw Jonathan, he tossed his head and took off running in the opposite direction. Then, much to Alfred's surprise, the horse stopped, turned around, and let Jonathan approach him. Without protesting, he let Jonathan slip the bridle over his head.

"Well, I'll be darned," Alfred said.

Jonathan led the stallion to the fence and saddled him up.

When Jonathan mounted, the horse sidestepped. Soon Jonathan got the animal calmed down and rode over the hill. Alfred watched him go. Jonathan handled the horse with such confidence, just like Shrine. Alfred almost expected to see an empty sleeve flapping in the wind.

While Virginia watched her brother disappear from view, it occurred to her how easily one could get lost out on that endless expanse, where everything looked the same. If Jonathan started back and veered off a little to the east, he might miss the house completely, as she did once when she was ten. She had followed an orange-and-black-striped butterfly into the woods behind her Uncle Jake's house in North Carolina. When she lost track of the butterfly and turned back, the house was gone. She had gotten turned around. She walked and walked, but nothing looked familiar. One stand of trees looked just like the next. She knew she needed something to ground her—a stream, a field, a farmhouse. But all she encountered were trees and more trees, terrifying in their similarity. The best course, she decided, was to stay in one place and let someone find her. She sat on a springy cushion of chartreuse moss and leaned against a tree. She wrapped her arms around her bent legs and rested her cheek against her knees. Her brother would find her. She knew he would not let her stay lost. Yet as the afternoon wore on and the angle of the sun diminished, she saw no signs of him. Doubt set in. It was almost dark when she heard her name. It was Jonathan's voice. The trampling in the distance got closer, and soon he appeared.

"You gave us all a scare," he said.

Now, looking back, she felt saddened to realize that Jonathan probably didn't remember the incident. He had lost so many memories, and with them his history and his coherence. So much of what we are is fused with memory, she mused. Looking over the scrubby rolling hills, she saw no sign of her brother.

"What if he can't find his way back?" she said to Alfred.

"The man knows his way around a horse. That much is clear."

"Do you think it was the right thing, bringing him out here?"

"Now I have to deal with two Mendenhalls instead of one."

"No seriously."

"Seriously?" He squinted against the sun. "Either it will work or it won't, but worrying about it isn't going to change it."

"Like the rain you never worry about?" she teased.

He laughed. "I'm better at giving advice than taking my own. Never claimed otherwise."

"I'll remember that," she said and slipped her arm around his waist. "Look, there he is," she said. They both turned toward the crest of the hill. Jonathan galloped into view, through a cloud of dust, and headed down the slope toward home.

TEN

In May, the land still wore the shabby leftover clothing of winter. The curled tawny mats at the base of the grasses looked like shaggy buffalo pelts. The creek beds were as dry and cracked as chapped lips. A few brown twisted leaves clung stubbornly to the shrubs. Others had been pushed off by the growing buds and made a scratchy sound as they circled the powdery ground, then swirled upward to form the innards of dust devils.

All Alfred's spare moments were spent worrying about food. In a normal year, he would not have to feed the cattle this late into the spring. But this was not a normal year. He let the bulls and heifers forage on their own. Hunger made them less finicky. But he had to feed the nursing mothers, and his haystacks were alarmingly low. At most, he had a two-week supply left. If rain had not fallen by then, he would have to think of other solutions. In town, he had talked to a rancher who burned the thorns off the prickly pear and fed his herd a diet of the chopped-up cactus. "Is that good for the cattle?" Alfred asked.

"A little better than a fence post," the man replied.

Tumbleweed was not much better than a fence post either. If the tumbleweed was young enough and the cattle desperate enough, they might eat it, the way starving people might eat cardboard: it provided no nutritional value, but it exercised the jaws and filled the stomach.

In this country, grass determined everything. Sometimes it seemed as though he raised grass, not cattle. He no longer talked about rain, as if talk would keep the rain away. But he frequently scanned the sky, kept an eye on the changing configurations of clouds, and listened for the telltale rumble that promised relief.

Having Jonathan with him made his life both easier and harder. Easier because he had an extra hand; harder because he had to train Jonathan, and that was no easy task. It required patience, and patience was not in Alfred's nature. He tended to speed through life, always anxious to get one more thing done, and done quickly. With Jonathan, Alfred had to slow down. When he explained how to do something, Jonathan would stare at him with an impenetrable expression. The seconds would tick by—probably no more than five or six, but the pause unnerved him. When Jonathan finally answered, he let the words out a few at a time, then paused and let a few more out, like someone feeding a lure onto a trout stream.

Jonathan was incapable of interpreting facial expression, whether a subtle flinch in the cheek or the more blatant dropped mouth or rolled eyes. Though Alfred was direct and plainspoken, he had been brought up to be polite, and he favored subtle. But subtle did not work with Jonathan. Any face was a poker face to him.

Jonathan responded in a visceral way to tone of voice rather than actual words spoken. He was quick to pick up anger or danger. He grasped them with his body, not his mind, the way animals pick up things people cannot.

He pondered questions that had never occurred to Alfred:

"Does the dust on birds' wings make it harder for them to fly? When a cow eats dirt, does mud build up in its stomach and cause pain? Why don't birds fall off their perches when they sleep? Why don't flies fall off the ceiling?"

One day when they were moving the heifers from one pasture to another, Alfred paused at an unusually narrow gate. "I don't know if we can get them through here," he said.

"No problem," said Jonathan. "Cattle like to move in single file."

"Why do you say that?" Alfred asked.

"Look at the cow paths. They're only a foot wide."

"Well, I'll be darned," Alfred said and looked at the beaten-down paths through the pasture.

This was not a man lacking in intelligence or observation, Alfred noted.

Jonathan had a soothing way with horses and seemed to know intuitively what they thought and how they would react. Alfred called him the Quaker trainer. Jonathan didn't use a halter or a heavy lead rope, only a thin piece of twine. "A horse can feel a fly on its back. Why not twine?" Jonathan told him. He looked at things through the horse's eyes, as if he were inside its skin.

Alfred scoffed at Jonathan's theories until he watched him at work with a blaze-faced brown mare named Sassy. He had bought her cheap from a trader who specialized in Indian ponies crossed with government remount studs, which were used for breeding for the cavalry. The result was a horse that was tough but not too big. Alfred could tell by the spark in Sassy's eyes that she was difficult but razor sharp, and he was not disappointed.

Alfred watched as Sassy, attached by a thin lead rope, trotted around Jonathan counterclockwise. Every time the horse tried to turn her haunches to him, he waved at her and forced her back into motion. Soon the horse learned to turn toward him rather than try to escape him. A tender exchange developed between Jonathan and the animal. Later, when the horse had learned to trust Jonathan, he put a saddle on her. No test of wills, no bucking or twisting or death-defying antics. Sassy stood there and let Jonathan mount her as if she had been saddled all her life.

Jonathan loved physical activity but avoided anything that required planning or thinking. In this way, he reminded Alfred of Shrine. Both were quick to take the brazen course of action, never the wise, well-thought-out plan. In all other ways, the two were different: Shrine had a short, compact build, whereas Jonathan was long-limbed. Shrine was independent and didn't like to be told what to do; Jonathan preferred things spelled out. Shrine liked to show an animal who was boss; Jonathan was gentle and patient. But the differences didn't matter. There was something about the daily rhythms of working the range with Virginia's brother that stirred up Alfred's memories of his brother, both good and bad. He carried with him a low-grade feeling of remorse that hovered just beneath the surface, like a shadow in the still edges of a backwater.

It was Shrine who had taught Alfred to rope calves. Alfred had had no desire to be better with a lasso than his brother. That would only have spawned a brutal rivalry. Alfred only wanted to be proficient enough to avoid embarrassment. But he had a secret weapon: he loved to learn. He knew that one day he would surpass Shrine, for he had curiosity and determination, and his brother did not. Shrine shied away from the things he was not good at, while Alfred would tackle anything. Looking back, Alfred saw that in his own quiet way, he was just as competitive as Shrine. The difference was that Alfred had competed with himself, whereas Shrine competed with Alfred.

Still, Alfred vividly remembered Shrine's humiliating criticisms and belittling comments as Alfred was learning to rope. Now that he found himself in the role of teacher, Alfred made an effort not to be too hard on Jonathan. This required discipline, for Jonathan was anything but a quick study.

Roping required agility, speed, and superior horsemanship—

all of which Jonathan had. But it also required depth perception, which he lacked. No matter how much he practiced, he could not judge the correct distance when throwing the lariat. He would fail to take into account the horse's speed and the quickness of the calf, and he would throw the lariat too far or come up short. But he kept practicing. He'd spur his horse into the herd. Pandemonium reigned as he lurched among the cow-calf pairs, sending them thundering in all directions. Alfred began to suspect that rope practice was just an excuse for Jonathan to show off his horsemanship. He might not be able to rope, but nobody was better at handling a horse and executing quick turns at breathtaking speeds as the horse galloped after a bolting calf, dodging boulders, thorny undergrowth, gullies, and rocky ledges.

Alfred's father had taught him one important thing about ranching—more than one, but the one that stuck was to disturb the cattle as little as possible so they would gain the maximum amount of weight. Contented animals were better producers.

"Maybe you should practice roping on something stationary, like yucca or a bale of hay," Alfred told Jonathan. He tried to keep his advice plain and direct. If he put more than three or four sentences together, Jonathan would lose track.

Jonathan shifted in his saddle and stared down at him. Jonathan had shaved off his beard the first week on the ranch, and now his square jaw jutted forward. "That's no fun," Jonathan said, and again Alfred was reminded of Shrine.

"Ranchers aren't rodeo cowboys," Alfred explained. "We're on horseback for a living. I can't have you getting the calves and mothers all riled up."

Alfred waited silently for Jonathan's answer. The seconds ticked by.

"Why not?" Jonathan said, as if there had been no time lag. His mind was like a rusty machine, capable of working, but in its own sweet time.

"Every pound of weight they gain is money in the bank. If

they lose weight escaping you, that's like throwing money away."
He paused, then assured Jonathan, "You're a gifted rider. You'll
get the hang of roping. It takes practice, like anything else."

He watched to see if Jonathan was taking it in. Jonathan usually understood about half of what Alfred told him. The problem
was, Alfred never knew which half.

Over the winter, brush, tumbleweed, and debris collected in the
dry ditch that ran through the ranch. One day, Alfred asked
Jonathan to help him clear the channel. On the way there, they
rode past the area where Alfred kept the bulls. They were powerful animals with thick necks, massive shoulders and chests,
and long curving horns. Alfred called them the Old Boys Club.
The bulls had gathered at the fence and gazed with longing at
the cows in the next pasture.

"These boys make me nervous. We better move 'em out,"
Alfred said. He did not trust the few strands of barbed wire to
hold back all that virility.

"Now? You said we were going to clear the ditches," Jonathan
said.

"I need to move the bulls now."

Jonathan jiggled his foot in the stirrup. "Why didn't you tell
me before?"

"Didn't think of it." Alfred had noticed how Jonathan needed
to know beforehand what they were going to do. He locked into
plans, turned them over and over in his mind until they were no
longer strange.

"I don't understand," Jonathan said petulantly.

"I don't care if you understand. You'll do as I say." Alfred recognized that tone—authoritative and bullying. It was Shrine
speaking through him. He vowed to be more vigilant.

They rounded up the bulls and herded them through the gate
at the far end of the pasture. When they had moved the last one
onto the range, Alfred counted heads. As a rancher, he was

always counting. He came up one short and scanned the land-scape. On the plains, you couldn't tell how near or far a thing was. By contrast, the clouds lent a great sense of depth to the sky. Purple smokelike wisps hung in front of more distant clouds, separated by bands of blue. In the middle distance, the edges of plump, silver-lined clouds bled into the matted white of the flatter clouds behind them.

Alfred spotted the missing bull in the distance. Jonathan was circling the animal on horseback, twirling a lasso above his head.

What the hell's he doing? Alfred thought. *Surely he wouldn't—no, no one would be that foolish.* Virginia had warned Alfred that her brother had no common sense, but until now he had not understood what that meant. Trying to rope an animal that out-weighed his horse by two to one, on rough open terrain where you could go for miles without an obstruction—that, for sure, quali-fied as lack of judgment.

He watched as Jonathan tossed the lasso. By some miracle—call it beginner's luck, only this time it was bad luck—Jonathan landed the rope around the Hereford's downward-curving horns and dallied the rope around the saddle horn, in a textbook example of technique.

The angry bull charged across the range, dragging Jonathan and the horse behind him.

Jonathan cried out for help.

Alfred spurred his horse into a full gallop and followed the moving plume of dust.

He could not get ahead of the bull, and even if he could, he would not be able to turn it. When a bull charged, it did not look right or left, but simply ran—something Mexican bullfighters were familiar with.

"Cut the rope." Alfred yelled to be heard over the thundering hooves. The thorny greasewood whipped against his legs, exud-ing a faint odor of creosote.

"No knife," came the reply.

The bull had too much of a head start for Alfred to get a rope around his hind legs and trip him. But he couldn't let the animals run themselves out and die of exhaustion.

Instead, Alfred overtook Jonathan and, as the two horses and the bull ran at full speed, he gripped tight with his knees, reached over, and made several passes with the knife. Finally the rope snapped. The bull continued down the range. Jonathan brought his horse to a stop and got off. The horse was panting and lathered up underneath the saddle.

"What do you think you were doing?" Alfred said, dismounting.

Jonathan was pale with fear. It took him a while to answer. Alfred saw that he was shaking.

"We could have been killed," Jonathan said.

"We?" Alfred said, still out of breath.

Jonathan looked down.

Alfred stepped forward and touched Jonathan's shoulder to reassure him. "After lunch, I've got a gathering job for us to do. Are you up to it?"

"You bet," Jonathan said eagerly.

The man had no common sense. But anyone who would go through what he had just been through and get up immediately, ready to start again, was someone worth working with.

Alfred mounted his horse and went in search of the bull. The last thing he needed was for the high-dollar animal to wrap the dragging rope around a bush and choke to death.

When he returned, Jonathan had built a fire and was warming the stew Virginia packed for lunch.

"Did you put the bull back with the cows?" Jonathan said.

"Of course not." Alfred filled his plate.

"Why not?"

"We're trying to prevent premature pregnancies."

Jonathan looked at him, obviously not comprehending.

Good God, Alfred thought. *Does he not know the facts of life?* It occurred to him that it was entirely possible that Jonathan did not. He had left for the war when he was in high school, and even if he knew anything then, the accident may have erased that knowledge, along with other memories and facts. Living with his Quaker mother for so many years afterward, Jonathan was not likely to relearn whatever had been lost.

Someone should tell him. But who? Alfred felt an itch around the collar. He did not want to be the one. But if not him, then who? Certainly not Virginia.

Man to man, he would tell him straight out. He poked at the fire with a stick. Suddenly all the bravado went out of him.

"Have you ever known a, um, woman?" Alfred said and cleared his throat. He took a mouthful of stew.

"Of course. My sister, my mother." Jonathan's fork clicked against the speckled blue enamel plate.

This was not a productive course. Perhaps nature would provide him with a better example.

"Do you know why we keep the bulls separate from the cows?"

"Of course."

Alfred sighed with relief.

"To keep them from chasing the cows," Jonathan said and poured Alfred a cup of coffee. "It's bad to chase cows."

Grain floated to the top of the tin mug. Alfred took a gulp. A few rudimentary facts would be necessary, after all. He'd give anything to get out of an explanation, but the man needed to know. He cleared his throat and straightened his back.

"You know, a man is different from a woman," Alfred observed. He took his bandanna from his pocket and wiped his forehead.

Jonathan tilted his head and stared at him, his lips parting. Alfred could tell by Jonathan's baffled look that he was not following.

"A bull is different from a cow, you will admit," Alfred forged bravely on. He drew some crude hieroglyphics in the dirt with the stick.

"Yes, more ornery," Jonathan said knowingly.

This line of reasoning was going nowhere. Alfred changed tacks.

He finished his stew and poured a tiny bit of water from the canteen to clean off the plate as best he could.

"Nature has provided men and women with certain urges that help continue the race," he said.

Jonathan looked down at the dirt scribbles, as if this would give him a clue.

Alfred backed up and tried again. "Do you know what a husband and wife do together at night in bed?"

"They sleep?" Jonathan had the perplexed, tentative tone of a child who wants to please and knows the adult knows the answer.

Alfred sighed. "No, they—" He brought his hands together and made an explosion of sound.

"They clap?" Jonathan was trying to follow his thinking.

"No, no, no. They"—Alfred interlaced his fingers—"come together in love."

It was clear Jonathan was confused by the ineffectual pantomime.

"Jonathan, I'm talking about the birds and the bees," he said in total exasperation.

"I'm allergic to bees," Jonathan said.

The man was infuriatingly literal-minded. Language had to be concrete for him to understand, and Alfred's natural modesty was forcing him to resort to euphemism.

He turned to a less oblique example. "Have you seen a horse mount another horse from behind?"

"Of course."

"Do you know what they are doing?"

"Copulating," Jonathan said.

"Exactly!"

"That's what you've been talking about all this time?" he said. "Why didn't you say it?"

❀ ❀ ❀

"When are we going to eat?" Jonathan asked one day at noon. He stood behind Virginia as she prepared the meal, so close she bumped into him when she moved from the sink to the stove in the main room.

"The cornbread's taking longer than I thought," she said. Jonathan and Alfred were home for a rare midday meal. That afternoon, she was going to take Jonathan into town to show him where to find the general store, Ida's house, and the filling station. Virginia did the errands every couple of weeks. But since the drive was an hour each way, it would be a big load off of her to have Jonathan take over.

"It doesn't matter if it's underdone," Jonathan said, tapping his toe against the linoleum. He was nervous about going into town. Anything new made him apprehensive. She was not completely calm herself. Since his arrival, Jonathan had proved himself to be more reliable than she thought, but she was still not entirely sure he could handle the town errands on his own.

"You don't want to eat this cornbread with a spoon, do you?"

"I don't care."

"Well, I do. Now shoo. I can't think with you breathing down my neck." She playfully swatted him away.

He sat down. His fingers drilled against the table, like a radio sound-effects man simulating Tom Mix's faithful steed, Tony the Wonder Horse. She had listened to that radio show in Philadelphia, when she had electricity and a radio, and when the life of the cowboy was an imaginary world of lawbreakers and straight shooters, totally foreign to anything she had experienced.

"Don't you have something better to do? You've heard of the watched pot?"

He leaped up and paced around the room. "Now how much longer?"

"If you're hungry, take a piece of bread." He could be maddening.

"No, I'm not hungry. Can I do something to make it go faster?"

What she really wanted was for him to leave the room so she could cook in peace. But she gave him the job of setting the table.

"Put the plates and glasses face-down on the table," she said.

"Why?"

"So the dust won't get in them."

"How long before we eat?"

"I don't know," she said. "Soon. Fifteen minutes, half hour. Now stop pestering me. If you keep asking me, it's going to be longer."

He set the table, then said, "Now what can I do?"

She sent him out for more firewood, just to get him off her back.

She checked the table after he set it. As she suspected, it was a mess. He had placed the knives and forks parallel to the edge of the table, the spoons at odd angles. There was no order. No matter how many times he set the table, he could not remember what went where, or even grasp the concept that the silverware should be perpendicular to the table's edge. The simple task was actually complex to him, or rather, it required the very thing that Jonathan lacked: an ability to put together several sequential steps. Knife to the right of the plate, spoon beside it, fork to the left. Three separate steps. Jonathan's mind did not work like that—at least not anymore. But he wanted to be helpful. That was just like him.

As soon as the cornbread came out of the oven, they ate. Afterward she took Jonathan to town for a dry run. Dust coated the leaves of the elms along Main Street, giving them the fuzzy look of items forgotten in attics. The lettering on signboards had disintegrated under the blasts of flying grit. In the middle of the road, a sleeping dog begrudgingly got to its feet and ambled off when they parked in front of Dave's General Store.

Inside, the men had pulled their chairs around an enormous

galvanized washtub under the ceiling fan. A large block of ice sat in it.

"I want you fellows to meet my brother, Jonathan," Virginia said. "He's helping us out on the ranch."

"Is it dusty enough for you around here?" a rancher said.

"Yep," Jonathan said. He was a man of few words, which was a good thing, since each of the words betrayed him. She took his arm and tried to hurry him along before the men noticed there was something queer about him.

"Did you hear the one about the gopher?" Harry Thurston said.

Jonathan's face pinched inward, and his eyes worked over-time.

"Dug his hole three feet in the air," Thurston said.

The men guffawed. Jonathan's muscles tensed, the way a horse does before it bucks. His injury had robbed him of a core part of his personality—his sense of humor. Jokes were too abstract for him.

When the laughter died down, Jonathan was still standing there, slack-jawed, staring. The men fell silent.

"It's a joke," Virginia said gently.

"Three feet in the air. That's a good one." Jonathan laughed in a wild, uncontrolled way and the ranchers looked down, uncomfortable.

"Dave around?" Virginia said through a false smile. She was mortified.

They pointed to the back of the store.

Virginia showed Jonathan around the store and introduced him to Dave. They picked up a few items and drove to the edge of town to drop off the laundry. Ida sat on the front step, sur-rounded by cats. One cat was stretched out in her lap. Two curled around her feet, like plush slippers. Others sat on the bottom step. When the truck pulled to a stop, Ida stood up and the cats scattered under the house.

When Virginia introduced Jonathan, Ida said, "Oh, you're

Mrs. Bowen's brother. I know I'm going to like you." Wisps of brown hair escaped from under a kerchief that was tied around her head. The frizz framed her forehead like a mist.

Ida and Jonathan began talking about cats. Jonathan crouched under the house. Several cats approached him, circumspect. He remained still and let them sniff him. When they were used to him, he picked up a calico kitten and rubbed her head. The kitten closed her eyes in pure bliss.

"They usually won't let a stranger touch them," Ida said, observing him from beside the lilac bush.

Virginia remembered how, in North Carolina, the wild cats would come to Jonathan, but would not let Virginia near them.

"You got a rotten step here," Jonathan observed from beneath the porch. He set the kitten down.

"I know," Ida sighed.

He backed out on all fours, stood up, and brushed the dust from his jacket. "I'll fix it for you if you want."

Virginia smiled. Ida had a gift for getting other people to do things for her. Whenever Alfred brought the laundry by, he would always reattach a picket, tack a new screen on the door, hang a clothesline, or replace a lock. Virginia was so self-sufficient, she marveled at the way Ida attracted help. When people offered to help Virginia, she would rush in with protests, not wanting to inconvenience them; Ida, on the other hand, accepted with such heartfelt gratitude that people felt good about themselves. Virginia thought of herself shoveling dirt from under the steps and cleaning the house after the dust storm. Now she waited while Jonathan replaced the step.

The following week, Jonathan went into town by himself with a written list of instructions. Virginia was in the kitchen when he returned. She felt relieved when she heard the truck drive up. She never worried about him when he was on the plains with Alfred, but in town anything could happen. "Put the change in the can on the top shelf," she said when he came in the kitchen.

"There's no change," Jonathan said and set bags of oatmeal and flour on the table.

"What about the money from the cream?" She had come to depend on those few extra coins.

"Here—for you." Jonathan handed her a brown bag with half a dozen sticks of red licorice inside.

"Oh, Jonathan, you shouldn't have." Had he remembered it was her favorite candy? Or perhaps Dave had told him. She reached eagerly into the bag, then thought better of it and said sternly, "We have to watch every penny."

"Go on, try one," he said.

She put an end in her mouth and let the sweetness seep in. "What am I going to do with you?" Virginia said and tousled his hair.

Eleven

The next week, Jonathan went to town with the laundry but was not back by suppertime.

"Should we go ahead and eat without him?" Virginia said to Alfred. She fiddled with the rickrack on her apron.

"Save a plate for him," Alfred said.

"Did the truck have plenty of gas?" She always worried about that. If he ran out on the desolate dirt road, it would be hours before someone passed by. And Jonathan always crumbled in an emergency. Alfred assured her the tank was full.

After supper, she busied herself with a crossword puzzle. She hated crosswords. But that night, she could not concentrate on her book, and she hoped that the effort to find obscure or arcane words for meaningless objects would keep her mind occupied. Every noise distracted her, and she got up several times to look out in the dark for the truck's headlights.

"What in the world do you think's happened to him?" she said, giving up on finding a nine-letter bird that started with "gy."

"I could ride into town, but it would take a while on horse-back."

"How long?"

"I don't know—four, five hours, depending. I've never tried it."

"Let's wait a little longer." She went out to the porch and looked across the prairie. A coyote's lonesome call traveled through the night, and she felt in a more immediate way the true nature of their isolation. With no truck, they were stranded. The nearest phone was half an hour on horseback, and that was going at pony-express speeds. There was nothing to do but wait.

At quarter to ten there was a knock on the door. It was the sheriff's deputy, a young man with a sparse mustache who looked barely old enough to shave. "Do you know a Jonathan Mendenhall?" he said.

"What happened to him? Is he all right?" Virginia opened the door wider.

"He's in jail, ma'am," he said.

"Oh, dear. Alfred. Alfred, come here. Jonathan's in trouble."

The three sat at the kitchen table.

"What happened?" Virginia asked. Under the oilcloth, she laced her hands and pressed her fingers into the space between the tendons, the way she did at the dentist.

"Best I could make out, he'd been drinking in the bar," the young man said.

"Jonathan doesn't drink," Virginia said. She felt Alfred's hand on her knee.

The deputy continued his story. A Mexican sheepherder from Dalton's operation ordered a beer at the bar. A ranch hand who worked for Knudsen, north of town, started making fun of him. Jonathan got involved. A fight broke out. They kicked over tables, broke glasses. The cowhand lost some teeth. The bartender pressed charges and demanded that Jonathan pay for the damage.

"Was he hurt?" she asked.

"Nothing serious. He'll probably have a hell—I mean, heck—of a shiner on him tomorrow. Pardon, ma'am." The deputy nodded to Virginia.

"What about the other man—the one who made the original remarks?" Alfred said.

"Oh, you mean the sheriff's brother-in-law?" the deputy said, without irony.

Alfred straightened his spine against the back of the chair. "I see."

The deputy looked nervously to the side.

"Well, did anyone ask the Mexican for his side of the story?" Alfred said.

"Ain't nobody speaks Spanish."

"I do," Alfred said. "I'll interpret."

"I don't rightly know how the sheriff would feel about that."

Alfred stood up. "Well, Jonathan's been in jail long enough. Let's get him out."

Alfred drove into town with the deputy and posted bail. Virginia stayed up and fretted, refusing to look at the clock in the belief that she would be less tired in the morning if she didn't know how late she had stayed up. Finally the truck pulled up. Jonathan came in, shoulders stooped, face turned down. The cuts on his forehead had crusted over.

"You're a sight to behold," she said and sat him down at the table.

He rocked maniacally in his chair.

She poured a bowl of water. "Hold still," she said and put a hand on his shoulder to make him stop rocking. "Look up at me. This way." He turned his face to her. "No, a little to the right." She dabbed water on his wounds. "Some vinegar will fix those cuts right up. You know, Mama and her vinegar cure," she said, supplying the details to prod Jonathan's memory, but he did not react.

"You're mad, aren't you, Sis?" He winced and looked down.

She wrung out the cloth, then pressed it to his forehead. "You had the best of intentions, I have no doubt. But surely there was a way to resolve the problem without fighting."

Light from the lantern reflected off the glossy oilcloth. The water in the bowl took on a rosy tint.

"He was minding his own business, not hurting anyone," he said. "And he was this much shorter than that cowpoke." He held his hands a shoulder width apart.

She sighed. His instincts were Quaker to the core, but his inability to control his temper made him settle his disputes in a most un-Quaker way.

"So you're not mad? I don't want you mad at me." He gave her a plaintive look. He needed to be loved like a small child—forthright and unrestrained.

"You've got to learn to tame your temper."

"Mama taught me a way."

"What is it?"

"She told me to sit down, breathe deeply, and recite the Quaker queries."

Virginia turned away as she rinsed out the cloth so he could not see her smile. The thought of Jonathan in a rowdy bar silently reciting the Quaker queries was ludicrous. Even she could see that.

Several days later, Jonathan and Alfred went to town to meet the Mexican sheepherder, who had agreed to come with them even though Dalton was docking him a day's wages. Alfred served as interpreter while the Mexican told the sheriff his side of the story.

Jonathan and Alfred did not return until late that night, after Virginia had gone to sleep. She woke up when Alfred got into bed beside her. The lantern cast an oval of light on the side table.

"Did you get it straightened out?" she said, sitting up and rubbing her eyes.

"They're not going to press charges, as long as he doesn't get in trouble again," Alfred said. He had talked with the sheep-herder, the bar owner, and a few witnesses. From what he could piece together, the Mexican had come to the bar and ordered a *"cerveza."* The ranch hand next to him said, "We speak English here, Pancho." The sheepherder turned to him and said, "My name Jorge, not Pancho." The ranch hand yelled the Spanish pronunciation of the name—"WHORE-hay!"—around the room and made crude jokes about the Mexican's sexual habits.

The Mexican did not need to understand English to understand the laughter. "Go back to your own country and stop taking jobs from the citizens of Trinity County," the ranch hand snarled in his face. The Mexican punched him. The ranch hand came after him swinging. Jonathan stepped in between them. Mayhem broke out. Others jumped in. Soon the room was filled with flying glasses, spilled beer, overturned chairs.

"Way I figure it, you got a roomful of men who were unem-ployed, financially strapped, barely holding on, and drinking. It didn't take much to start an old-fashioned brawl," Alfred said.

"What about damages?" Virginia asked anxiously.

"We got lucky. The bartender dropped the damages, too."

One worry down, many to go. Jonathan was a wild card. Some day, when he did the wrong thing at the wrong time, the conse-quences might not be so easy to smooth over.

"I hadn't spoken Spanish in a long time," Alfred said. "I wasn't even sure I could remember, but it came back quickly. I spent a lot of time in Jalisco. That's where Jorge's from. He's not taking jobs from anyone. You think Dalton would fork over the money to hire an American? If the sheriff's brother-in-law has a problem with Mexicans taking jobs, he should talk to the people who hire them, not the ones who take the jobs."

"Maybe I should take over the errands," she said. They had made bail once but could not afford to do it again. Jonathan was supposed to help them save money, and all he had done since his arrival was cost money.

"He had a piece of bad luck. To tell you the truth, if I were in that situation, I'd do the same thing."

She, too, secretly admired her brother, but that did not prevent her from worrying. Trouble followed him around.

"He'll make mistakes," Alfred continued, "but let him make them on his own and learn from them." He blew out the lantern. "Now you can stay up all night fretting if you want, but I'm going to sleep." He kissed her, pulled the sheet to his chin, and shut his eyes. Soon he was breathing evenly.

The moon softened the darkness and filled the room with a soft gray light. She looked tenderly at Alfred's face in the pale moonlight. He had stood up for Jonathan. She loved him for that. What a kind, generous man he was. Part of the reason she wanted a child was to see how Alfred's face would look reproduced on the face of a son or a daughter. Their child would have the best of each of them—her imagination and adventurous spirit; his height, his hands, his heart. But it was all a dream. They would never have a child.

When she was small, she used to pick out the silhouettes of elephants, unicorns, and dragons among the leaf shadows that floated across the ceiling in her room at night. On the ranch, there were no trees to cast patterns. The ceiling hovered above her, a muted gray plane, a blank canvas for her heartache.

Not long after that night, Alfred stomped into the kitchen after work and demanded to know where Jonathan was.

"In his room, I suppose," she said and held up a coral-red flower with a spicy scent. "Look what I found on my walk. The first sign of spring."

"Can the cows eat it?" he said bitterly. He had been working on the windmill all day, and his hands were hatched with tiny cuts.

"Oooh, cranky, cranky," she said, trying to humor him. "What's gotten into you?"

"That brother of yours," he said, pulling off his boots. "The windmill in the east pasture was making some clanging noises. I asked him to check the water, and he told me he already had. Today I rode by, and doggone if the thing wasn't clogged up and the water tanks empty."

"I'm sure he just forgot." She poured Alfred a glass of buttermilk.

"There are some things he can't forget. Do you think he'd ever forget to give his beloved Sassy water?"

"Jonathan's going to make a few mistakes in the beginning. That's what you said."

"A mistake is one thing. Lying is another," Alfred said gravely.

"My brother does not lie." Of that, she was certain. He had not mastered the complex emotional reactions necessary in deception.

"He tells me he did something and I find out he didn't. That's lying, in my book."

It wasn't like Alfred to be so unforgiving.

"We knew he had a faulty memory when we asked him to come live with us. Maybe you should be more careful about the things you ask him to do."

"All I need is straight answers. That's all I ask. But I can't run this operation if I can't depend on him to tell the truth."

"Did you tell him that?" she said.

"I tried, but he acted insulted."

She sighed. "Let me see what I can do."

After dinner, she looked out the window and saw Jonathan on the porch in a rocking chair. Light had almost faded from the sky, leaving a few wisps of color. The nighthawks looped in the sky. Jonathan watched intently as they beat their wings rapidly, then sailed through the pink light.

She pulled a rocking chair beside him and watched the birds, enjoying the few moments of silent companionship. Maybe she would put off talking to him. Why ruin a nice moment?

After they sat there quietly for a while, she said, "Jonathan, I need to talk to you."

He did not give any signs of hearing her and continued to focus on the birds. His ability to concentrate on one object and block out the rest of the world always amazed her.

"Jonathan, look at me."

He turned to her, irritated, as if he had been interrupted while watching a movie. She chose her words carefully. "You know, every day I make a list of things I need to do. Otherwise I have so much on my mind I can't keep track. It helps me remember."

He stared at her for several seconds, his mouth parted. She waited uncomfortably.

"So?" he said finally.

"It might be a good idea for you."

"Why?"

"So you don't forget things." She tried hard not to patronize him, but she didn't want to talk over his head either. "Alfred told me he asked you to check the windmill, and you said you had, but when he rode by, the cattle didn't have any water." She spoke without judgment, simply stating the facts.

He leaned forward in his chair and began to rock. The wide planks of the porch creaked under his weight. She remembered the closeness they had felt on the porch in North Carolina, after the birthday party at the gold mine. This moment had none of that loveliness.

"I know you didn't mean to—you just forgot. It's nothing to be ashamed of. Since the accident, your memory—"

"Nothing is wrong with my memory." He gave equal emphasis to the words, with space between them.

She looked at him with surprise. Could he possibly believe that?

"You treat me like a freak." His white-knuckled hands curved over the edge of the armrest as he moved forward and back with intense concentration.

"I make lists, too. You know me. I can't keep track of all I have to do."

He locked his knees, and the chair abruptly stopped. "You were always p—p—" With his finger, he traced the word on his palm. "Perfect." When he was upset, he sometimes forgot words. Writing them out helped retrieve them.

"I forget things, too. That's why I write them down."

He started rocking again. She put her hand on his arm, applying pressure to slow him down.

"Jonathan, I didn't mean to upset you. All we're asking is for you to be straight with us. If you forget, that's nothing to be ashamed of. I do it; Alfred does, too. We just need to know. Alfred can't run the ranch if the cattle don't get water."

He looked confused, as if listening to a foreign language in which he could pick out a word here and there, but the meaning eluded him.

Darkness had fallen over the plains, obscuring the nighthawks. "You want me to—go."

"Oh, no, Jonathan. That's the last thing on my mind."

"You tell me not to lie, but you're lying now." He jumped off the porch and disappeared into the dark yard. She heard the door to the bunk room clap against the frame.

What had gone wrong? It was such a small matter, and suddenly it had flared into childhood resentments, jealousy, and inadequacies. They had never argued like this when he was . . . when he was . . . she whispered the word to herself: *normal.* She hadn't counted on how hard it would be to live with Jonathan, to never know how much he understood, what was getting through to him. She was also peeved at Alfred. He had forced her into this confrontation with her brother, and now everyone was agitated.

The following evening after supper, Jonathan went to work with the horses and she followed him. She rested her forearms over the top of the wooden fence and watched. Jonathan and Sassy appeared to be engaged in a game of tag. The young horse playfully kicked out her back legs. The wind lifted her mane. With her nose, she butted Jonathan's stomach. He laughed, circled around, and touched the horse on the hindquarters.

They frolicked about until they stood head to head. Jonathan held both arms out, then tagged her on one side of her head. The blaze-faced mare nipped at Jonathan's hand, then dodged him when he tried to tap her other cheek. The frisky horse nickered in delight. With animals, Jonathan was so natural and uninhibited that it made Virginia's heart ache. It also confirmed her suspicion that somewhere behind Jonathan's wooden exterior flourished the playful spirit of the old Jonathan.

When Jonathan finally noticed Virginia at the fence, he came over. Sassy followed.

"Alfred says you're a genius with horses," she said.

"Really. He said that?" He seemed pleased.

"Yes, like how some people can play the piano by ear. They just have a knack. It's something they're born with."

He opened his hand, and the horse nuzzled his palm. Virginia had suspected him of taking sugar for the horses—an expensive treat—but now was not the time to bring that up.

Sassy neighed and put her head over the rail. Virginia jerked to the side so the horse wouldn't touch her.

Jonathan looked at her in revelation. "You're afraid of horses," he said.

"You were right about Tommy Turnbull in high school. You said he was mean as a snake," she said.

Since his arrival, she had been careful never to say: "Do you remember?" For invariably he did not, and reacted hostilely. Instead, she tried to re-create a memory, like a storyteller, providing details that might spark a sense of familiarity. She told him about how he had helped her sneak out to meet the doctor's son, then added details he could not have known: how their wild horse ride had ended at the Hedgecock farm when the horse stopped at the fence but she did not. One important thing she left out: the horse's death. For that would be the one detail that Jonathan retained out of the whole story. She described his fight with Tommy, and the shock he created at the table that night when he announced his decision to go to war.

During the recounting, she watched him closely, hoping to catch a glint of recognition, but she could have been talking about anyone. His memory was gone, and with it his past, the gradual accumulation of experiences that created the history that bound them together.

The horse blew air out through her lips, and Virginia flinched.

"This girl's not going to hurt you," Jonathan said, rubbing Sassy's neck. "Here, you try." He took Virginia's hand and put it on the horse's neck. Virginia tentatively stroked.

"See? Not so bad."

"Will you teach me to ride?" she said.

He smiled. "Really? You want me to?"

The sky was the lovely transitional blue that follows sunset and precedes dark. From a nearby field came the sound of neighing; from the other direction, a bird's song.

"Do you really write things down?" Jonathan said.

"I do. Just a word or two to jog my memory."

"I think I'll try it."

At the end of May, neighbors came from the surrounding ranches to help Virginia and Alfred brand their calves. Branding was a community tradition. In the coming weeks, they would return the favor to their neighbors. Young women came to watch the single men, the children came to get out of school, the wives to feed their husbands, the old folks to relive old memories. Everyone came to have a good time. It was one of the few days in the year that people socialized. After the work was done, the host family fed the crew.

Virginia was determined to put on a good spread. Being a newcomer, she wanted to make an impression, and she certainly wasn't going to do it with her horsemanship.

The morning of the branding, she got up at three to start the cooking. Her stomach was feeling upset, and she thought back to what she might have eaten the night before. Suddenly, a horrible thought occurred to her: it was her own cooking that made her sick. What if someone at the branding were to get sick because of her food? Well, she couldn't think about that now. There was too much work to do, though being around food in her condition was not pleasant.

The men arrived a couple of hours later on horseback and scattered over the ranch, rounding up the cow-calf pairs and herding them back to the corrals near the house. There, the calves were cut out from the mothers.

Jonathan dug a fire pit at one end of the corral. Men stacked firewood nearby and hauled buckets of water, in case the fire got out of control.

Virginia was making pies in the kitchen when Eugenia Dalton arrived. Her husband was a sheep man and had not come, but Eugenia was not one to miss a social occasion. Or the chance to dispense advice. When Eugenia looked over the spread Virginia had prepared, she said, "Oh dear, you've only fixed one kind of potato?"

"That's not enough?" Virginia said, alarmed. She had never prepared food for so many people, and had made things simple on purpose.

"It's just that men usually like a choice," she said.

"Alfred's never said anything," Virginia said. It distressed her, the thought of Alfred wanting different kinds of potatoes and being too nice to ask.

"I always fix mashed potatoes, baked potatoes, and scalloped potatoes."

Virginia had developed a visceral reaction to any sentence that started out "I always." About pies, Eugenia said: "I always like to put more cornstarch in. Otherwise it's too juicy and the crust gets soggy." Or: "I always use vegetable shortening—it makes a flakier crust." Every sentence that contained "I always" contained an implied criticism.

A knock came at the door. It was Chance Greene, a brash young man in his thirties who lived with his mother several ranches over. He held his hat in front of him. "Excuse me, ma'am. Your husband sent me for the ear hole punchers. He said he left them on the desk."

"Sure, come on in," Virginia said, and led him to the living room. While she looked for the punchers, he stared at the piano with curiosity. He ran his callused fingers across the ivories, then tried a few notes.

"That's a fine piece of machinery you've got there, ma'am," he said.

"Thank you, Chance," she said, smiling. She handed him the punchers, and he left.

"He's a nice young man," Virginia said.

"Handsome, too," said Eugenia. "He's sweet on Lucy, one of the Swenson girls." Eugenia's mind was filled with the details of other people's lives. "She's the one in the red shirt talking to—wait a minute." She leaned closer to the window. Her enormous bosoms dipped into the sink. "Is that your brother?"

Virginia looked out the window. Women and children had gathered around the main corral, waiting for the action to begin. Some sat on the top rails, as if at a rodeo. Jonathan leaned his forearm across the wooden slat, cocked his head forward, and listened intently to a woman in a red shirt with curly blond hair—a real beauty. The woman was holding Jonathan's coffee cup for him and feeding him doughnuts.

Virginia had noticed that Jonathan had a powerful effect on women. He was silent and handsome, a combination many found to their liking.

Eugenia went back to rolling the crust. "I wonder what she's doing."

"Eugenia, I think Lucy can get along nicely without your supervision." She slid the pie into the oven, snapped the door shut, and left to watch the branding.

The air was filled with the uproarious racket of bawling calves who were separated from their mothers for the first time. The fence creaked under the weight of the spectators. Dust swirled everywhere.

In the main corral, Alfred organized the men. Competition existed for who would rope the calves. The single men wanted to show off their skill in front of the ladies.

"Greene, you start off," Alfred said, addressing Chance.

"You told me I could go first," Jonathan said to Alfred. His sheer size made him threatening.

"I changed my mind," Alfred said. Jonathan had not yet mastered roping, and Alfred didn't want him to embarrass himself in front of the neighbors.

"Yeah, this ain't no job for greenhorns," Chance said, adjusting his chaps. He looked Lucy's way to make sure she was watching.

"You can pitch in toward the end," Alfred told Jonathan.

"You gave me your word." Jonathan grabbed the rope from Alfred and mounted his horse, ready to rope the first calf out of the chute. Rather than cause a scene, Alfred shouted to the men in the adjacent corral to run the first one through.

A male calf trotted into the dirt ring and looked around nervously, startled to find himself surrounded by spectators. Once the calf sensed danger, he bolted in the opposite direction. Jonathan followed, twirling the rope above his head. When he sent it sailing, the loop landed behind the calf's ears, then trailed along its back. The calf trotted along the side of the railing. Women and children perched on the fence yelled and waved their hats to force the calf back to the middle.

"Give her another try." Alfred shouted to be heard above the livestock.

Jonathan urged his horse after the calf. Amazingly lithe, the calf ran the length of the corral. Jonathan galloped at full speed toward the fence. People jumped off and scattered. His hat flew off and rolled in the dust. The lasso fell short of the calf, but he stopped the horse before crashing into the fence. One of the children scrambled under the bottom rung and retrieved the hat.

From the sidelines, Virginia looked Lucy's way. She had lost interest and climbed off the fence. No man worth his chaps lost his hat. That was as humiliating as botching the roping.

"Why don't you work the ground?" Alfred shouted to Jonathan.

"Once more," he said and looked toward the empty spot on the fence where Lucy had been. His horse faced the panting calf, whose tongue lolled outside its mouth. Bareheaded, Jonathan tossed the rope at the stationary calf. Again he missed.

"Hey, Three-loop, time to give someone else a shot," Chance shouted.

The nickname stuck. One of the kids from the side said, "Yeah, Three-loop. Give it up."

Jonathan's face turned red. Chance was at the far end of the corral, near the fire. Jonathan glared at his rival, then reluctantly moved to the side.

Chance mounted his horse. He clasped the loop in his armpit as if it were a hen and pursued the calf. A couple of cranks and both arm and loop vaulted forward in one fluid motion, as if the rope were an extension of his arm, and landed on its target. He dragged the bawling calf toward the fire. There, rasslers threw it to the ground and pinned it by the neck and rear legs.

A team of workers surrounded the calf, like doctors around an operating table, each performing a different function. Chance castrated the calf, then cut a V-shaped notch out of the bottom edge of his left ear. Another neighbor used dehorners to scoop out the tiny horn buttons, and a third person vaccinated the calf. Alfred wore one heavy leather glove and held the other like a potholder as he took the gray-hot brand out of the fire. As the brand sizzled on the calf's heaving side, Jonathan covered his ears with both hands, his elbows angled out like chicken wings. Thick yellow smoke rose as the brand made its way through the hair and to the skin. The calf cried out in pain. Alfred withdrew the brand and scuffed the spot with his gloved hand.

Without warning, Jonathan lunged at Chance and pulled him away from the calf by the scruff of the neck. The ring of bobbing hats parted. Chance backed up and kept Jonathan at bay with the castrating instrument held in front of him like a weapon. Jonathan wheeled around and knocked the syringe from the man charged with vaccination. The neighbor with the dehorner jumped out of Jonathan's way. When Jonathan reached Alfred, he made an upward chop and knocked the branding iron from his hand. It flew toward a knot of neighbors by the fire. They scattered, and the hot iron fell in the dust. The smell of burned hair mingled with the sweetish odor of heated, close-packed cattle.

The calf struggled to its feet, bucking and lowing for its mother.

"What do you think you're doing?" said a stunned Alfred.

"You're hurting the calf," Jonathan said.

"Goddamn it. It's only for a second."

"I don't care. You're hurting it!"

Virginia climbed over the fence and ran toward her brother. Neighbors turned away, embarrassed by the spectacle. The disoriented calf trotted along the outside fence, but no one paid it any attention.

Jonathan's breathing was uneven, his eyes erratic. When she reached him, she put her arm around him. "Come with me" was all she said. Words were of no use now.

She firmly guided Jonathan to the gate. He lowered his head, as if he knew he had caused shame, but he followed her without resistance.

Neighbors had congregated in small groups and were talking in hushed tones. Virginia walked Jonathan through the crowd, looking neither right nor left. A young boy cried out, "Three-loop," but his mother quickly shushed him. When they passed

Chance, he put his body between Lucy and Jonathan, as if to protect her.

When the dust settled, the corral was a mess—firewood scattered about, hats blown off, metal instruments flung here and there. The calves in the next pen bellowed. The men retrieved their instruments.

"All right, bring on the next one," Alfred said, as if nothing had happened.

Virginia took Jonathan directly to the bunk room. She felt a surge of loyalty for her brother. When she had invited him to come live with them, she had bound herself to his fortunes, his progress, and his happiness. What she had not counted on was that his pain would become hers. She felt it as a physical thing that had weight and girth. Yet she was powerless to protect him, or even comfort him. She left him in his room, then went to serve the meal.

TWELVE

June came, but the rain didn't. The land was like a great parched desert, congenial only to grasshoppers. Weeds and thistle competed with the grasses for what little groundwater was left. Farmers watched their crops shrivel up under the searing heat. The grasshoppers finished off what was left. The hungry grasshoppers would eat anything, including paint off the houses and wood from hoe and rake handles. National Guardsmen trucked sawdust from mountain sawmills to the plains, where it was mixed with bran, molasses, sodium arsenite, and banana oil to make a death brew for the hoppers. But farmers, already forced to borrow money for seed, had none left over for poison.

Ranchers were no better off. Some sold off their herds rather than watch them starve. The market was glutted, and prices plummeted. If Alfred sold his calves in the fall for dirt-cheap prices, he would not have enough money to make ends meet. His only hope was to fatten the calves over the winter and sell them as yearlings in the spring, on the bet that prices would improve by then. To do that, he needed money for hay to hold the calves through the winter.

He had put off asking for a loan, knowing he was unlikely to get one. But no matter how he worked the figures, he could not come up with a way to get by without borrowed money. So he had made an appointment with the banker Roy Gilman. Now he was on his way to town, dressed in newly polished boots, a dress shirt, and string tie. His hat sat on the seat beside him. He was too tall to wear a hat in the truck. He also wore his good luck charm: a fancy belt buckle he won at the county rodeo when he was seventeen.

In the truck, he rehearsed what he was going to say to the banker. He needed to appear confident, competent, upstanding. And there was a time when he had been all of those things. But desperation sucked the essence out of a man.

Through the truck window he heard a strange whirring, like a downed power line. Before he knew what was happening, he drove into a swarm of grasshoppers. Their hard bodies cracked against the windshield in tobacco-colored splatters. A few slipped in through the cracked window, whirled about the cabin, and ricocheted off the glass. He stopped the truck and swatted a newspaper at the whirling invaders. When the swarm had passed, he drove on.

First drought, then pestilence. The whole thing had a Biblical ring. Alfred liked to work with a certain number of limitations—it forced him to be creative. But there was such a thing as too many limitations, and he had passed that point long ago. All his background, personality, and training had taught him to do things in the best way possible, not to hold back. Now cutting corners had become second nature. Getting by was what counted. Not doing well, just getting by. What was the least amount of water the cattle could survive on, the least amount of feed? Could the cows go without vaccine? Was salt absolutely necessary? Everything was a game. Shave here, economize there, cut out completely. It was degrading. It went against the grain. But this was his life. It was everyone's life, here on the plains.

Outside of town, he passed an open-bed truck headed to the rendering factory. The truck was filled with emaciated cows that had died from heat exhaustion or been slaughtered by ranchers who could no longer support them. The carcasses had been tossed into the truck, their legs hacked off at the joint to make them fit. Oozing, bloody limbs poked through the slatted sides or stuck out on top at odd angles. The sight sickened him.

He arrived early for his appointment and went to Dave's General Store to kill time. Tacked to the wall by the door was an announcement of a liquidation sale at the Burton ranch the next week. Alfred refused to go to the sale, even though he might pick up equipment at rock-bottom prices. It was too heartbreaking to see the family's possessions tagged and set out on the dusty ground for people to paw through.

What would a sale look like at his place? he wondered. The things he cherished most would bring the least: the piano, his Spanish dictionary, a few Mexican novels, some old sheet music. The piano had come cross-country in a covered wagon and survived a stampede of oxen, but with its shaggy bark legs and tinny tone, it was worth nothing to anyone else. He imagined piling his unsold belongings into the truck after the sale and heading west. The legs of the chairs and tables would stick out above the truck, like those of the cattle carcasses he had passed on the way to town. Both told a similar tale of failure.

At two-thirty, he went across the street to meet Roy Gilman. Rumor had it that he was one of the biggest landowners in the county. He privately contacted the struggling ranchers and farmers—he had inside information on who they were—and bought them out for a ticket and a token: a ticket to California and a token payment for their land. Anxious to avoid the humiliation of a public sale, many took his offer—how many was anyone's guess.

Alfred waited outside Gilman's office. The transom above the door was tilted open, allowing fragments of conversation to drift out: another poor wretch groveling to borrow money. Alfred didn't want to see who it was, and didn't want the other fellow to see him, so he ducked around the corner and waited until the door opened and the rapid click of boots faded down the hall.

When the coast was clear, Alfred knocked on the door. A pudgy man in his fifties opened it. He wore a short-sleeve shirt and a tie. Alfred shook Gilman's hand, which was as smooth as his bald head. Never trust a man who doesn't have calluses, his father always said.

"If you don't mind sitting here for a minute, I'll be right back with you," Gilman said, patting him on the shoulder in an overly familiar way.

Alfred waited. On the wall, a calendar from Gates Rubber in Denver showed men at work in the factory. *Poor fellows,* Alfred thought. *Doing the same thing, day in and day out.* Of course, those men had regular paychecks. There was something to be said for that. He tried to imagine what it would be like to work on an assembly line. He would wither and die, he was sure of it.

Every day on the ranch was different. That's what he loved about it. To be a good rancher, he had to master so many things. He thought of his father. His father broke and trained horses, understood breeding stock, studied breeding lines, and over the years had built up his herd of cattle. He could tell by looking at the cows which ones were going to calf and when, which ones were barren, and which had lost calves. He knew which cows were sick and which were just thin. When an animal got sick, he was the veterinarian. He was also a tracker and could distinguish a coyote track from a dog track, an antelope from a sheep, though they looked remarkably similar.

Alfred's father was an expert in land management. He knew every square foot of his ranch and how to use it to the best advantage. He knew how much grass was required for each head, and how the pastures varied from wet years to dry years.

He knew the locations of patches of weeds that could be dangerous to the herd. He knew how long to keep the animals in one place to get maximum use of the grass without destroying the root systems that would regenerate the grass for future use.

His father had to be a businessman, too. He kept the books, bargained with dealers for feed, figured out the best time to sell to get the highest profit. He also had to be a diplomat and get along with his neighbors, because he depended on them at branding time and other times of the year. His father was a builder and a carpenter who kept up miles and miles of fences. He built toolsheds, barns, and additions to the house. He was a mechanic and a handyman. When something went wrong with a truck or tractor, he had to fix it himself. Alfred had seen his father cannibalize old machinery to weld together a makeshift part that kept a truck running for months.

His father had developed all these skills over a lifetime, and it would take Alfred just as long. But now time was running out. He would not be able to face his father if he failed. He dreaded his father's reaction more than Virginia's. His father would never understand.

Mr. Gilman returned and took a seat at his desk.

"What can I help you with, Mister—" He glanced down at a piece of paper. "Mister Bowen," he said.

"I came to see about a loan," Alfred said.

"You bank with us?" he said.

"Yessir, I do."

"And how long have you been with us?"

"About a year." He had forgotten that he was a relative newcomer. No one at the bank knew him; no one could vouch for his honesty, even though he felt more a part of the community than this lily-palmed bureaucrat.

"So you're just starting out."

"Yessir, but I grew up on a ranch." Alfred cleared his throat. He might as well be an itinerant worker. *I wouldn't lend myself money,* Alfred thought. *Why should he?*

"Why'd you decide to start out at a time like this?" He laced his fingers and placed his two index fingers together.

"It just worked out that way. I was living in Mexico—"

Mr. Gilman raised his eyebrows, which seemed to lift up his entire face. A mustache of sweat had appeared above his upper lip, and his moist, jiggling arms seemed devoid of bones, like a slug. "Mexico, you say?"

Every question turned up some deficiency. "Yes, I was working for the YMCA," Alfred said, hoping that the organization, at least, would be familiar to Gilman. "I have a family here now," he continued, in an attempt to cast himself as a stable character—a citizen with ties to the community who would not pull up stakes and take off. Alfred could just as easily have been trying to convince Gilman to post bond.

The ceiling fan was making a funny click. It would not run for much longer. Alfred thought: *I can fix that, and I bet this man can't.* But the idea gave him no satisfaction.

"Any children?" Gilman asked, tapping his middle finger on the desk.

"No, not yet. I've been married less than a year." He felt disloyal to Virginia, hinting that children might be in the future, all in a flailing attempt to present himself as a family man. Instead, he had only succeeded in raising further questions in the banker's mind. "I normally wouldn't be in here, but the drought—"

Gilman sighed. He wore a large class ring. The gold had worn away, so the name of the university was no longer legible. Gilman rapped the ring against a metal file drawer. "See this here? These folks all want the same thing you want. I can tell you right now that a good many of them won't be in this county a year from now. The weather is a cruel thing, Mr. Bowen."

Gilman asked him some questions about the business and his loan obligations. He made some notations on a form.

Alfred waited for what seemed an interminable time as

Gilman scratched some figures in his folder. The only other sound was the ticking of the clock and the click of the fan, whose pitiful efforts to keep running Alfred now saw as a metaphor for his life. He took a deep breath and wondered if Gilman could hear his heartbeat from across the desk.

Gilman stood up.

"Mr. Bowen."

Alfred knew the answer from the tone of Gilman's voice.

"I know I can make this work," Alfred said. He was begging. He hated himself.

"I'm glad you believe in yourself. But it's not my fault that the price of grain's going up and the price of cattle's going down. You know the math as well as I do."

Alfred would grovel no more. He got up and started for the door.

"Mr. Bowen."

Alfred turned around. He knew what was coming: a ticket and a token. Would Virginia forgive him if he decked the unctuous bastard?

"Yes?" Alfred said and pressed his lips together.

"Don't forget your hat."

On his way back, the fields were running. Tongues of dirt had migrated onto the road in places, and the wheels of the truck thunked as they passed over them. Alfred's mind was a muddle. How could it be otherwise, in a world where you couldn't even count on the earth to stay in place?

He wanted to blame Gilman, but the fact was, Alfred was a bad risk, just starting out—a greenhorn. Was it arrogance or blind stupidity that made him think he could do this? Perhaps the trait he thought of as perseverance was nothing more than folly.

When he reached the turnoff to the ranch, he had the sudden urge to keep going straight and leave all his responsibilities behind. An empty truck and an open road—he would drive until the ocean wouldn't let him drive any farther. But the truck turned in, as if on its own, like a horse to the barn.

At the house, he paused outside the kitchen door. It was closed to keep out the dust, but through the crack he could hear Virginia singing. He wanted to sit on the steps and listen, let her happiness fill him. Or perhaps, like birdsong, happiness had nothing to do with it.

He walked into the kitchen and she stopped singing.

"I've never heard you sing before," he said.

She seemed suddenly shy. "I didn't know you were there, but I couldn't help myself—I felt like singing." Then her face filled with radiance. "Alfred, we're going to have a baby."

He stared at her, unsure he had heard correctly. "What?"

"A baby. We're going to be parents."

He felt so many things at once, and so quickly, that he didn't know what he was feeling.

"I suspected last month, but I didn't dare dream. I mean, it wasn't supposed to be possible. But it's true."

"That's, that's—wonderful," he said weakly, knowing his response was inadequate. A baby made his failure to provide more complete.

"It's more than wonderful. It's a miracle. What did I do to deserve this?"

"And you're absolutely sure?"

"Alfred what's wrong with you? You're not happy?"

"It's—I never—I just don't want you to be disappointed." He had never found a use for pretending, but that was what was called for now. And he could not do it.

Her face started to puff up the way it did before she cried.

"I'm happy for you. Really, I am," he said, without realizing what he had said.

She backed away from him as if he had struck her.

They stared at each other.

"This is not my baby, Alfred. This is *our* baby."

And then she cried. Big heaving sobs. He put his arms around her. "Of course it's our baby, Shoo-fly." He pulled her toward him and smoothed away her tears with his thumb. "I just got so used to thinking one way. I'm no good at surprises."

She smiled. He smiled, too, and allowed his heart to admit a spark of joy.

"It *is* amazing, isn't it?" he said.

"Yes, truly."

Sixth Month, Eighth Day, 1934

My Dearest Mama,

Oh, joy of all joys, what I have wished for and waited for for so long has happened. I am overcome with a happiness that I never thought possible. I am going to have a baby. This is something I never thought could happen to me. Oh, I do think God is watching over me. And I thought he had forgotten me. Oh, mother, I am so full of love and happiness. I wish you were here to share it with me. Is every mother so possessed? This is the most perfect moment of my life—until, that is, the child is born.

Virginia sealed the letter and walked to the mailbox. Her mother would not receive the news for days, but at that very moment she felt close to her.

She had still not told Jonathan about the baby, afraid he might be jealous or fearful. He had not noticed the change in her. Men were so dense sometimes. For days, she carried herself like a priceless vessel. Suddenly her life seemed almost intolerable in its richness. The smell of bread baking and the flames in the stove filled the house with a warm domestic glow. She even had the urge to knit, newly enchanted by the idea of tiny sweaters, miniature caps, and wee booties.

For the first time, she understood the transcendent rapture the early Quakers must have felt at the discovery of a profound unity with something too small to see and too big to imagine.

They described it as the light within—a spirit that was universal yet made everyone unique, a spirit that made all things new, gave all of creation another smell.

As she walked back from the mailbox, it began to hail. A torrent of white chunks fell from the sky, like a meteor shower. She ran into the house, grabbed all the galvanized tin buckets she could find, and sprinted to the garden, where she covered as many tomato plants as she could. The ice had formed high above the clouds, encapsulating the dust particles to form marble-size pellets with swirling brown eyes. The cold hailstones stung, then melted on her warm skin, leaving little deposits of mud. She looked as if she were covered with moles.

The hailstorm lasted only a few minutes but left a wreckage of denuded stalks and shredded leaves. She thought of the hard clay soil she had dug, how she had softened it with manure in order to give breathing room to the roots, and how she had hand-carried the water to the fledgling plants. After all her loving attention, the garden had been reduced to sauerkraut in under three minutes.

She looked over the beaded, glistening earth, surreal in its beauty, heartbreaking in its destruction. She had come to accept the harsh land, with its unpredictability and brutal indifference. But how would she feel bringing up a child on these wild plains?

Several evenings later, Virginia was reading aloud to Jonathan on the porch. He sat with his long legs stretched out in front of him, his head against the back of the rocking chair. She was reading from George Eliot's *Middlemarch,* and it looked as if the good-hearted Dorothea was going to fall for the pretentious and gloomy Mr. Casaubon. Virginia wanted to shake Dorothea and say, "No! You're making a terrible mistake." Dorothea was the kind of cheerful do-gooder Virginia had met so often in Quaker circles.

To hold Jonathan's interest, she tried to make the reading as dramatic as possible. For Mr. Casaubon, she adopted a low, lugubrious voice, then changed to a sunny, lilting voice when she read Dorothea's dialogue.

In the middle of the chapter, Jonathan walked off into the yard without a word. He did that sometimes—just wandered off. He simply lost track of what he was doing.

"Jonathan!" she called after him, but he did not answer. So much for her dramatic talents.

She turned ahead a few pages to see what happened. Perhaps she should pick a book he was more interested in, and save *Middlemarch* to read on her own. The story was complicated, with many characters. Jonathan preferred the strong rhythm and short verses of poetry. Virginia didn't like to read poetry to him, particularly his favorite, Edgar Allan Poe. Last time she read Poe aloud, she couldn't purge her mind of the rhythm, and for days afterward she went around the house pulling the broom and passing the dust cloth to the interior drumbeat of "Annabel, Annabel, Annabel Lee."

She closed the novel and went inside. Alfred was at the desk, surrounded by piles of bank statements and an open ledger. For the past several weeks, he had seemed distant. He had told her about being turned down at the bank. She sympathized with the weight on his shoulders, yet she resented that he was not happier about the baby. Everything was money, money, money. Couldn't he forget about these dreary financial worries, for a short time at least, and celebrate with her? She understood that he wasn't connected to the child in the same way she was—he did not carry it inside him, entwined with his body, his dreams, and his imagination, and for this she felt sorry for him—but he had shown so little joy of late that it hurt her feelings.

"Do you realize how much it cost to get the truck fixed last time?" he said. "And look at this." He showed her a list of prices realized from the cattle auction. "If prices don't improve by fall, there's no way we'll come out," he said with a ragged edge in his voice.

She didn't want to talk about markets or money. She had other things on her mind. For example, where would they put the baby? The double bed took up most of one room, and the piano filled the other. There wasn't space for a crib.

"Do you think we could finish the basement?" she said. It was not an ideal space, but it was all they had.

"We can't afford it now," he said without looking up.

She frowned, angry at being so easily dismissed. She had spent a lot of time thinking about remodeling. That's how her mind worked these days—racing from one plan to another. One moment, house improvements, the next, schools.

"Just listen to my idea," she said.

"I don't have to. I know we can't afford it."

"Then maybe we should sell the piano," she said.

He looked at her in disbelief. How could she be so insensitive? He returned his attention to the ledger.

"Did you hear what I said?" she said.

Exasperated, he said, "Virginia, I'm trying to figure this thing out now."

"Aren't you glad we're going to have a baby?" she said plaintively.

"Don't you see? With a baby on the way, the pressure is worse," he said. Did they have to stand on a soup line for her to notice the depth of their troubles? "I can't fail."

"You won't. I have complete confidence in you," she said.

"You're not seeing what I'm seeing here." He threw the pencil on the ledger.

Jonathan came into the room. "Are we going to finish the chapter, Sis?"

"I thought you'd lost interest," she said.

"I don't like Mr. Casaubon. He's not a man of character. I hope Dorothea doesn't marry him."

She sighed and picked up the lantern and the novel. "Let's find out what happens," she said.

✽   ✽   ✽

Despite their financial troubles, Virginia passed the days in airy euphoria. The tiny life inside her made her examine her own life. She felt a deeper connection to Alfred. Embarking together on this shared responsibility strengthened her sense of purpose and commitment. She felt closer to her mother and father in North Carolina. Continuing the family line made her reach back, as well as forward, tapping into familial bonds that, like a lasso, encircled them and, when pulled, bound them together.

When she daydreamed, she did not conjure up pictures of a cooing infant swaddled in blankets, but of an older child of indeterminate sex. The facial features were ill-defined, like the image of someone she knew so well that details no longer mattered, or like God, who had for her a luminous presence without a specific form. Her imaginings were more like mood moments, tableaux of happiness that always contained, at their center, the sunny, open face of her child.

She wanted her child to have a spacious mind, a generous heart, and a sense of humor, to carry life's burdens lightly. He would be surrounded by good books, music, and progressive ideas. He would learn the value of hard work, which would make him confident in his own strengths and able to overcome his weaknesses. He would learn Quaker values of tolerance, inner peace, fairness, and community service.

Virginia's mother had a simple standard: let your life speak. By that she meant that there should be no split between the inward and the outward life. Virginia wished the same for her child.

Despite her buoyant moods, Virginia could slip, quicksilver, into obsessive worry. In her darkest moments, she imagined the dust penetrating her womb.

The life growing within her had made her see dangers where before she had seen none. No amount of vigilance could protect her child completely. Look at Jonathan. His accident made her realize how life, in a split second, could change irrevocably.

One day Virginia found Jonathan in the kitchen sifting through the drawers.

"What are you looking for?" she asked.

"The keys to the truck." His movements were fidgety, his eyes feral.

"We don't have any errands to do," she said and laid a hand lightly on his arm to calm him.

"I need to get to town," he said.

"Why?" Every time he went into town alone, he got in trouble.

"You need the laundry dropped off, don't you?" he said with such an urgency that for a moment she almost gave in.

"It can wait another week. We can't waste gas," Virginia said, knowing full well that reason meant little to Jonathan when he was like this. Once he got in a rut, he became panicky if he didn't get his way.

"I've got to get to town," he repeated. "Hand over the keys."

She was frightened by his single-mindedness. She did not want this to break down into a contest of wills.

He opened another drawer and tossed the contents onto the floor.

She stood between him and the drawer and closed it with her hip. "Jonathan, enough," she said firmly.

"Where are the keys?" He was shouting now. Straightened to his full height, he stood a full head above her.

"You know me well enough to know I'm not going to give them to you," she said. The wild look in his eyes frightened her.

"You-you-you," he repeated in staccato rage. His face was red.

He pulled his fist back, ready to strike. She grabbed a chair and put it in front of her like a lion tamer. He came toward her. She stumbled backward, then tossed the chair down, slipped into the other room, and closed the door. She pulled the upholstered chair up against the door and collapsed into the seat, trembling.

She spread her fingers over her belly and sat there, unable to move. Through the window, she saw her brother heading to the horse pasture. The sky was filled with dark clouds. She wished he would go away and never come back. Her life would be so much easier. She could not—would not—have violence at the core of her home. Not with a baby on the way. That changed everything.

If she asked him to leave, where would he go? Her mother had moved to a smaller house and no longer had room for him. Maybe he could find work as a hired hand. But jobs were scarce, and even if he found one, he would not last. It took someone with patience to understand how to get good work out of him.

She had never been afraid of her brother before. Worried, yes, but never afraid. But that afternoon he had tried to hit her. And he might try again. He was too volatile. She couldn't handle him. What if he did something to the baby? That clinched her decision. She would ask him to move out.

She felt the door jostle against her back, and the fear returned. Then she heard Alfred's voice. She slid the chair back to its place to open the door. Alfred was picking up the overturned kitchen chair. He looked at her.

"Jonathan tried to hit me."

"He what?" Alfred set the chair down hard.

"To be fair, he doesn't know about the baby," she said. She still felt quivery.

"It doesn't matter. To hit a woman—to hit anyone. I will not have anyone raise a hand in this household."

She smiled. He was starting to sound like a Quaker.

That night at supper, she set a place for Jonathan but he did not come.

"He left on horseback. I don't know where he went," Virginia said.

She hoped he was miserable and wracked with remorse. More likely he wouldn't even remember. It was not fair to blame him for his condition, any more than she could blame a blind

233

person for being blind. But it was no longer a question of blame but of safety.

Outside, the sky darkened and the wind picked up. The bushes and the brush gave off a dry rattle as the brittle leaves scraped against each other. A prolonged crack issued from above, like a tree split down the middle. Out the window, she saw an arrow of light pierce the plains. She glanced at Alfred but did not say a word, as if she had heard nothing, seen nothing. They had gotten their hopes up too many times before.

"Do you think we did the right thing? Asking Jonathan to come live with us?"

Alfred set down his fork and looked out the window, waiting. "He's your family," he said.

His tone was flat, and she could not tell if he meant *He's your family, so we had no other choice but to take him in,* or *He's your family—you decide.*

"With the baby coming—his volatility worries me." Thunder rolled. She closed her eyes for a moment. "The truth is, I'm worn out. I don't really want him here."

She looked over at Alfred for an indication of what he thought. He was a man of strong opinions, but that evening he kept his own counsel. He only asked that she be absolutely sure, in her mind, of what she wanted before she talked to him.

Another protracted crack sounded above them, as if the heavens had finally given way under an unbearable weight. Then sharp and discrete pings hit the tin roof, like bullets.

"My garden!" she cried. She left her unfinished meal on the table and ran to the back of the house, where she kept the buckets.

If it was hail, she only had a few minutes to protect the tomato plants. She stacked the buckets and hugged the tower of tin to her chest. It was the late side of evening but not yet totally dark. The pearly gray of one side of the sky blended into the duller, darker gray of the other. As she hurried to the garden, she slipped but caught herself before she fell. She steadied her unwieldy load and noticed a strange sensation: her arms were wet. Could it be rain and not hail? She beat back hope and pressed on. The fat rain drops hit her with such force that they felt like lead pellets. By the time she reached the garden, her dress was soaked through. Only then did she give in to the fact that it was not hail but rain, blessed rain, that was slicing through the semidarkness and turning the dust to mud.

Lightning shot up from the ground in a single thread, then forked into tributaries of light. Next a horizontal skein zipped across the flat gray sky. Then she was treated to a circular display of light chasing its tail. The charged sky was as unpredictable as it was thrilling. Involuntarily, she emitted oohs and aahs, as if watching Fourth of July fireworks.

The thunder came fast now, one roll still unfinished when the next began, leaving Virginia no time to count, as she had done as a child, parsing the distance of the lightning at one mile per second: thousand-one, thousand-two, thousand-three . . .

How quickly things can change. One day she thought she would never have a child, the next day she was pregnant. One day she thought the drought would ruin them, then the heavens opened up. Only a short while ago, she was convinced that change could only be for the worse. But here she was, under the glorious sky, soaking wet and filled with hope.

She held out her arms palms-up and looked up at the sky. The rain fell sharp and hard against her face. She opened her mouth and let the clean, pure drops fall against her tongue.

Alfred arrived with more buckets. "Can you believe it?" she said.

He had lost count of the times he had imagined, dreamed, willed the rain to fall, and then been disappointed.

Lightning flashed, and for a split second the garden disappeared into whiteness. A crack of thunder sounded, followed by lightning, and the sky seemed to split momentarily along a thin, jagged fault line. Rain came down furiously. On the plains, nothing happened in moderation.

Rain dripped from his thick eyebrows. He wanted to join her in celebration, but he knew what she did not: one rainfall would not be enough. Certainly not this gulley-washer. It was coming down so fast that the ground, which had become hardened like a stomach expecting a blow, repelled the water rather than absorbed it. Might as well serve a starving man a dozen apple pies—his shrunken stomach will only allow him to eat a few bites before he gets sick. The rest of the pies are wasted.

Alfred watched water sheathe over the ground. It sought out the slopes and poured down in gullies over the garden without soaking in. Alfred said nothing, because he needed her hope, false though it was. Hope made life tolerable.

So he rejoiced with her, dancing in the mud, holding her slippery hand and making a damn fool of himself under the gushing heavens.

The next morning, when Virginia went to do her chores, she saw Jonathan rubbing down his horse. He had been out all night. He came whistling to breakfast and sat down, full of spirit and good humor. He didn't apologize. He had forgotten the incident altogether.

But Virginia had not forgotten. She waited until evening, after the dishes were done, and told him that she needed to talk with him. She suggested they go for a walk.

The sun was low in the sky when they started off across the plains. The air was fragrant with resin, humus, and other smells released by the dampness. One good rain was enough to turn the fields green. Clusters of blue flax sparkled among the grasses, their delicate flowers like teardrops from the sky. Other wildflowers had bloomed overnight. Only yesterday, the grass was brown and lifeless, and crackled under their feet. All along, it had been lying dormant under the earth's surface, waiting for renewal.

Neither she nor Jonathan spoke. Virginia looked downward as she walked, careful to avoid the scattered clumps of grizzly gray cactus hidden beneath the grasses.

Suddenly a meadowlark fluttered from beneath her feet and gave out a distressed cry. The bird bobbed through the air on broken wing and landed off to the side.

"Oh, the poor bird. I wonder if we can help it," Virginia said.

Jonathan squatted. "Look," he said. With a stick, he held the grasses back like a curtain to reveal a nest in a thatch of grass. It was filled with white eggs speckled with purplish brown.

She reached out to feel the eggs, but Jonathan stopped her. "Don't touch," he whispered, almost reverently, mindful of the need not to taint the nest with human scent.

He backed away, pulling Virginia gently by the arm, and the bird flew back on two perfectly good wings. Her crippled flight had been a mother's ruse to divert their attention from the nest.

They walked over the next ridge. The house was now hidden from view. Virginia stopped by an outcropping of rock. They sat in silence and listened. The *coo-coo-ee* of the turtledoves competed with the meadowlark's evening song.

When she looked out over the plains, she saw too much sky, too little land, too few trees. Her idea of beauty was still steeped in the rain-drenched lushness of the East. Jonathan, however, seemed so at home here, as undomesticated and turbulent as the land. He understood the language of the plains, while she was still unversed in its rudimentary grammar.

"Isn't this beautiful?" Jonathan said with a look of complete contentment. He threw a pebble sideways, as if skimming a stone on water. "Someday I want to get my own spread," he said, watching the stone skim across the tips of the grasses. "Something I can pass on. Not as big as this. Just a few acres, so I can breed horses."

It broke her heart to hear him. She was not even sure that Alfred, with all his talent, intelligence, and drive, was going to make it. That's what the land did. It encouraged dreams, then dashed them.

Jonathan sifted through the gravel for more stones. He picked one up and examined it closely.

"There used to be an ocean here," he said.

"I don't think so," she said patiently.

"Then what's this?" He handed her a fossilized clam the size of a silver dollar. Bits of sand clung to its fluted edges. She held it between her fingers and stared. Here they were, in the middle of a drought, a thousand miles from the nearest coast, but what she held in her hand was unmistakably a clam fossil. Millions of years ago, this expanse had been an ocean floor. Jonathan did not have any trouble accepting that.

He looked over the sea of grass. "I wonder how the pioneers did it—kept from getting lost when everything looks the same."

She had often wondered the same thing.

"Remember that time you got lost at Uncle Jake's?" he said.

Her mouth dropped.

"You don't remember?" Jonathan said.

"Of course. How could I forget?"

"For about an hour, I was sure you were gone forever."

She felt tears come to her eyes.

"You said you wanted to talk to me about something, Sis," he said.

"Nothing important," she said and dropped the fossil in her pocket.

THIRTEEN

The dry creek that cut through the hay meadows ran only in times of heavy rain. Alfred depended on the ditch for irrigation. After the downpour the night before, the flow in the ditch would be strong enough for him to take out his allotment and get water to his hay fields in time to sprout the seeds. With a little luck, he'd have an abundant crop with enough hay to feed the cattle the following winter.

The morning after the rain, he was animated with excitement as he rode to check out the ditch. When he got there, he stopped his horse and looked down in disbelief. The creek was bone dry.

How could this be? Agitated, he rode north to the property line he shared with Dalton. When the water was running, it flowed from Dalton's ranch to his. Perhaps it had gotten clogged on his neighbor's property. Tumbleweed and old sticks had to be cleared out every spring, otherwise the debris trapped dirt and created a natural dam. Most ranchers conscientiously kept the pathways clean. But if Dalton maintained his ditches like he maintained his fences, Alfred knew that it was entirely possible the blockage was on Dalton's property.

He stopped at the fence separating Dalton's property from his. He looked up the length of the creek bed, which ran straight north and then veered off to the right out of view. He could see no obstruction, but he was still suspicious.

"I wonder if Dalton's tampering with the ditch," Alfred said at supper that night. "I wouldn't put it past him."

"That's a serious charge," Virginia said, "and you do no one any favors by speculating." In the West, where water was precious, he might as well have accused the man of cattle rustling.

"He's diverting water, you can bet on it," Alfred said.

"How can you be sure?"

"He's capable of it." Alfred couldn't say that of anyone else in Trinity County. All a man had was his reputation, and when that was sullied, he opened himself up to all kinds of speculation.

"We're all capable of anything, under the right circumstances," she reminded him. Virginia had never met Mr. Dalton, and his wife Eugenia was no favorite of hers, but accusing them of stealing was another thing entirely.

"I'll ask the Mexican who works for him—what's his name?" Jonathan turned to Alfred.

"Jorge."

"Yes, I'll ask Jorge."

"You'll do nothing of the kind," Virginia said, reminded of Jonathan's barroom brawl. As Quakers, both she and Jonathan had been raised to bear witness against injustice. But Jonathan's inability to control his temper made him an unreliable advocate for quiet resolution.

"Look at you. Both of you. We can't go accusing people of serious things without proof," Virginia said.

"If you wake up in the morning and the ground's wet, do you have to see the drops falling to know it's rained?" Alfred said.

"If you accuse him and he's innocent, we've still got to live together as neighbors."

"Some neighbor. He doesn't keep up his fences, he doesn't help at branding."

"Well, I don't expect we'll catch him over here tuning the piano or changing the tire on the truck, but let's give the man the benefit of the doubt," she said.

"I guess I could start with the water commissioner."

The next morning, on the way to the county seat, Alfred passed fields that had been abandoned, others that had been furrowed. If more land had been left in native grasses instead of plowed up, he thought, the dust wouldn't be such a problem.

With the weather and the hoppers, everyone was looking for a place to lay blame. The ranchers blamed the farmers for plowing up the land. The farmers blamed the ranchers for overgrazing. The cattle ranchers fingered the sheep men. Sheep chomped off the grass close to the roots so it was harder to regenerate. Truth was, no stockman worth his salt would allow overgrazing, which jeopardized the grass that was his lifeblood.

In town, Alfred went to see the water commissioner. He was a tiny man who wore elevated boots and an extra-tall hat that would have fallen into his eyes, had it not been for his oversized ears.

Alfred told him about his neighbor.

"Do you have proof?" the commissioner said.

The real proof was Dalton himself. The man was no-count. Anyone who met him would tell you that. But Alfred explained to the commissioner that he had not gotten a trickle of water from the ditch after the downpour.

"No water ain't proof. It's just more of the same, like everybody's experiencing." The commissioner had a barking way of speaking, like a contentious lapdog.

"Do you think he's going to come knocking at my door and volunteering the information?" Alfred said.

"If I had a gallon of water for every suspicion a person had, we'd have enough acre-feet to pull this county out of the drought."

Several days later Alfred saddled up his horse and rode to Dalton's ranch. Most neighbors would allow him to cut across their property. Not Dalton. Alfred had to travel miles by road to get to the house, which was only half a mile as the crow flies. From there he followed the rutted track that went past the lambing sheds in the flats. Farther on, he crossed the dry creek that ran onto his property. Pebbles and dirt dribbled toward the dry gully as his horse jig-trotted down the embankment.

Once he got beyond the crook in the creek bed and looked over the rise, he saw fields of deep green that made a swath beneath the horizon. He squinted and looked again. That saturated shade of green was not native to this part of the world. It was a color produced only with water, and plenty of it. The other grasses had received their fair share of rain, and those fields had not turned that color. There was no question in his mind: those pastures were getting irrigated. So what had happened to the water before it got to him?

He picked up the trail on the other side of the creek and followed it until he came to an old sod house hunkered down under a rise. There, he turned toward the sound of bleating sheep.

At the corral, Alfred found Dalton working with two Mexicans. A sheep lay on its side between the rancher's legs. With his knee, Dalton pinned its folded front leg to the ground to keep it from moving. Clippers in hand, he shaved around the sheep's rump with a quick, efficient motion. The ground was littered with commas of wool.

Nearby, a Mexican flipped a sheep on its side, then set to work. In the corner, sheep huddled together, waiting to be clipped. Red numbers were painted on their backs. The sheep hooked their necks over the backs of other sheep so the group formed one interlocking mass.

The clipping reduced the maggots and kept the scat from matting the wool. It was a chore the sheep rancher could have avoided doing. Alfred had pegged Dalton as lazy, but now he realized that he had it wrong: Dalton would do anything that benefited himself. Taking the extra time to shear the sheeps' rumps made the wool more valuable and increased his profits. But he could not be bothered to fix a fence to prevent his stock from eating the neighbor's grass. Why should he care, as long as the sheep were getting fat?

Dalton stood up and the black-faced sheep struggled to its feet and scurried to join the others in the corner of the corral. When Dalton saw Alfred, he climbed over the railing.

"You got fence problems?" he said. He was a heavyset man with a great stump of neck that fell straight from his ears to his collarbone. His chin was indented like a cloven hoof. An early bout with acne or chicken pox had left his face scarred.

"Nope," Alfred said and offered no further explanation. His hands rested loosely on the saddle horn.

Dalton looked up at him from beneath the brim of his hat, then patted his chest pocket for tobacco. He rolled a cigarette. His hands were glossy with lanolin and left greasy fingerprints on the paper.

"Nice rain we had a couple nights back," Alfred said.

Dalton put the cigarette in the center of his chapped lips, lit it, then, moving his mouth, rolled it over to the side. "Could always use more."

In the corral, Jorge painted tar on the sheep's bag where he had nicked it with the clippers.

"The ditch down our way is dry as a bone," Alfred said, looking directly at him. Sheep bleated in the background.

Dalton scowled. "You don't say." He had a thick mustache the color and texture of tobacco.

"Yeah, I was surprised." Alfred kept his voice steady. He didn't want this man to sense any weakness.

"Up our way, it was more commotion than rain. Lot of thunder and carrying on." Dalton put his boot on the bottom rung of the fence.

Alfred had to be careful about making accusations, particularly with no proof. "I figured something on your property might be clogging up the ditch," he said, as if the blockage had occurred without Dalton's knowledge or intervention.

"Not that I know of." He flicked the cigarette off into the distance. Alfred watched the tip glow, then wink out. Fire was a real danger, with the drought. A cigarette could turn a grass field into a wall of running flames in an instant. One brief rain had not altered that.

"It's hard times," Alfred offered.

Dalton had a steady, pitiless gaze, but Alfred did not back off. "Your fields look nice and green," he observed.

"Now do they?" Dalton's voice was low and rasping. He walked to his horse. A rifle was tied behind the cantle of the saddle. He adjusted the strap.

The hair on the back of Alfred's neck stood up. He was not armed. Guns so upset Virginia that he no longer carried one with him unless necessary.

"Well, I best be heading back," Alfred said.

Dalton nodded but didn't offer anything else.

Alfred rode the long way home. He had arranged to meet Jonathan at the windmill at noon. The rain had washed the grasses clean, and new shoots were everywhere. He looked with satisfaction as the cows wrapped their rough tongues around the tender stems and snapped them off. Their eyes rolled contentedly as they worked the grass to the back of their mouths.

Water had overflowed the tank next to the windmill and the cows trod in mud that covered their white socks. Such a waste of water, Alfred lamented. He looked up at the narrowing wooden skeleton with a ladder up the side. He had never thought of turning the windmill off. Then again, he had never thought there might be an end to the water. But once it was gone, it was gone for good.

Alfred pulled the wire that connected the windmill. The blades folded up and the rudder drifted in the wind. The creak-ing sound drew to a stop, and a strange silence fell over the land. From a distant field came the bellowing of bulls.

Jonathan rode up. "Talk to Dalton?" He let the reins drop so the horse could drink.

"He's not owning up, but I'm more convinced than ever that he did it. I just can't prove it."

"Why not follow the creek and see?"

"It's not right to go on his property without his permission."

"What he's doing's not right either."

"*If* he's doing it. Right now, all I've got is a hunch—and some emerald-green fields he had trouble explaining away."

They went back to work and didn't speak about Dalton again.

The next morning, without telling Alfred, Jonathan rode north alongside the dry gulch. In some places, it was a natural coulee with steep vertical sides, in others, a man-made ditch. Sometimes the sides sloped so gently it resembled a slough. At Dalton's property line, a barbed-wire fence stretched across the cut in the earth. The ground had slid out from beneath one of the posts, leaving it dangling in midair, held aloft by the tension in the wire. A funnel of shale and gravel angled beneath the post. Jonathan backtracked to where the sides were less steep and guided Sassy into the dry creek. When he reached the fence, he dismounted, climbed the bank, and, digging his heels into the crumbling earth, held the dangling post over his head, leaving just enough room for his horse to pass under it.

As he continued on Dalton's property, the gulch was deep enough to hide most of the horse, but not her head and shoulders, which glided above ground level like a target at the county-fair shooting booth. The wind had quieted down, and the only sounds were the creak of leather and the horse's crunching steps.

Jonathan rode for a long time under the blistering sun before coming to a man-made dam. It was built up with packed mud, rocks, old fence posts, tumbleweed—even an old cookie sheet.

Fragments of debris jutted out from the dirt like ancient treasures at an archaeological site. He got off the horse and took the pickax from the back of the saddle.

He drove it into the sloping dirt wall and pulled himself up so he could look on the other side of the dam. What water had not seeped into the ground had been lost to evaporation, and now all that was left was a muddy soup. In his haste, he slipped and tumbled down the other side, breaking his fall with the heels of his hands. The ax landed with a splash. He fished it out of the muck and started to work. He wrestled some dead branches and an old board from the packed dirt and pitched them up on the bank. With the pickax, he opened a hole at about chest level.

Suddenly a shot rang out, and a muddy jet of water spouted at his feet. He jumped back, the mud sucking at his boots.

"Hey, you!" came a voice from above.

Jonathan held the ax under its head and looked up. Dalton stood on the bank. Jorge stood beside him but gave no sign that he recognized Jonathan.

"You're trespassing," Dalton said. He held his rifle at his side.

Sassy was on the other side of the dam. Jonathan was trapped.

"Get out of there," Dalton said.

Jonathan scrambled up the bank, leaving deep skid marks in the dirt. Disoriented, he left the pickax behind.

Now he stood on the bank facing Dalton. The sun was in his eyes.

"Who are you, anyway? What are you doing on my land?" Dalton said.

"Looking for water," Jonathan said.

"This is my spread," he hissed, like air being released from a tire.

Dalton bunched up Jonathan's shirt at his chest and brought his face close.

Jonathan kicked away the rifle. Dalton took him down with his body weight. They rolled down the bank, feet tangled together, and landed with a splash. They thrashed about. The slimy mud made it hard to get a purchase. Dalton spotted the pickax Jonathan had left and dove toward it, freeing Jonathan to climb up the side.

Dalton came after him. When he reached the top of the bank, the Mexican offered him his hand, but as he pulled Dalton up, his grip slipped, and Dalton slid back into the creek. This gave Jonathan time to vault onto his horse from the bank.

Sounds of slurping, splashing, and cursing came from the other side of the dam. Jonathan galloped down the ditch for a ways. He heard a shot above his head. He leaned down with his chest against Sassy's mane and galloped until the creek veered to the right and he was out of danger.

At home, he rubbed down the horse, then let her loose in the pasture.

Virginia was headed for the shed when she met Jonathan carrying his saddle. She looked at her brother. His skin was caked with dried mud. "Where in the world have you been?" she asked. In a drought, mud was a rare sight.

"I went to Dalton's," he said proudly and set the saddle on the ground. "You want proof he's damming up our water, here's proof." He flaked some mud off his chin.

He looked at her expectantly, like a puppy waiting to be rewarded with a biscuit.

"Jonathan, you didn't get in a fight, did you?"

"I didn't start it."

Jonathan was so anxious to help, so hungry for praise, but Virginia could sense the situation slipping out of control. She lowered her head and thought a minute. There was still time for her to ride to the Daltons' place and get back before dark. If she waited, Alfred would return and discourage her from going—forbid her, even.

"Sis, are you mad?"

She sighed and looked up. "No, but I'm going to talk to Mr. Dalton."

"Ginny, no!"

He rocked forward and back on his heels and moved his fingertips rapidly against his thumbs. She could feel the incipient panic in him, and she tried to defuse it.

"I'm going to reason with him," she said calmly. She lay a hand on the dried mud on Jonathan's arm. It felt like a pastry shell beneath her fingers.

"I don't—I can't—please say it again."

When he was excited, he had trouble patching together the meaning of even simple sentences. She repeated her intention to go visit Dalton.

"No, you can't. I won't. He's no good." He looked right and left. He stuttered and repeated himself.

For reasons she did not understand, he had not expected this reaction from her. Caught unprepared, he did not have the suppleness of mind to adjust his thoughts. He depended on predictability; he needed time to dull the edges of strangeness.

With alarm, she watched his deterioration, unable to stave it off. His lip twitched, his eyes winked, his pupils darted about. When he thought, he could not feel. When he felt, he could not think. He was awash in emotion.

"You can't. If that man—you'll never—it's not my fault—"

His mind was like a flood that dislodged things from their place until they bobbed and floated and bumped into each other, out of control in the rising water.

"Jonathan. Slow down. One thing at a time. Nothing's going to happen to me. Is that what you're worried about?"

Verbal fragments spewed from his mouth like shattered glass. He grabbed her arm and squeezed hard. He was too agitated to concentrate on anything, even his own unraveling.

"Jonathan, you're hurting me."

He loosened his grip.

"My fault. My fault. Alfred will hate me."

Suddenly he bolted. She watched him scramble over the gate to the horse pasture and run up the hill. The grazing horses scattered.

Virginia caught the Sorrel and saddled her. After nightly lessons from Jonathan, she was still not entirely comfortable with horses, but she could manage on her own. Jonathan had taught her to ride without a bridle. She learned to use her weight and her legs to guide and stop the horse.

Virginia backtracked to the dirt road and headed for Dalton's ranch. She was unsure what she would say to Mr. Dalton, but she felt charged with purpose. She wanted to smooth over any damage her brother had caused, and clear up the misunderstanding about the water. She knew Alfred would not be happy with her for interfering, but she felt led. When she acted, she listened to her conscience, not to codes of ethics or authority figures, even those close to home. Something about the growing life inside her multiplied who she was and what she could do. She had to set an example for her unborn child. It mattered. Now everything mattered.

The Daltons' house was not visible from the county road, but their mailbox rose above the rolling waves of grass like a buoy. She picked up the mail before turning into their ranch.

She found Eugenia sterilizing Mason jars in a large speckled blue vat on the stove. Squash was piled on old newspapers on the table.

"I was admiring your garden as I rode by," Virginia said and set the mail down on the counter. She felt a twinge of envy when she compared Eugenia's verdant plot to the shredded remnants of her garden. Like a tornado, hail felt so personal, devastating some areas and leaving others nearby untouched.

"I always save the bathwater for the plants," Eugenia said, and Virginia cringed at that dreaded opening, "I always." But Virginia, too, hauled bathwater to her garden.

"I could use some help chopping," Eugenia said, transferring a colander of squash to the sink.

"Actually, I came to see your husband."

"Why do you need to see him?" Eugenia eyed her with suspicion.

Virginia felt the urge to say, "I *always* come to see my neighbors' husbands," but reproached herself for being petty. It was not Eugenia she disliked, but herself when she was around Eugenia. "It's a private matter," she said.

"Okay, but at least come into the living room and see my salt and pepper shaker collection."

She led Virginia to a bookcase crammed with miniature ceramic replicas of chickens and dogs and rabbits and teapots and German half-timbered cottages—four shelves of colorful figurines with holes at the top for the salt and pepper to come out. Virginia tried not to show her impatience as Eugenia recounted the stories behind her prized shakers—their provenance, who gave her which sets, how she had outwitted a hapless salesperson and gotten the rarest, most collectible pair for a song. As she prattled on, Virginia thought: *Who would want to dust these tacky little knickknacks?* After going through the collection in exhaustive detail, Eugenia finally gave Virginia directions on how to reach her husband. Virginia slipped out quickly, before she received a pop quiz on the collection.

Outside, Virginia put her foot in the stirrup and raised herself onto the Sorrel, aware that Eugenia was watching her through the window. Virginia made a mental note to thank Jonathan. It was because of his riding lessons that she could pass muster under Eugenia's critical eye.

Virginia continued along the overgrown path. The righteous wave of purpose that had possessed her earlier was gone, and as she moved farther and farther from the house, she realized she was a solitary woman on a deserted road and felt very small and afraid.

Soon she came upon a herd of sheep grazing contentedly on the new grass. Before long, she saw three horses coming toward her. She pulled to the side and waited.

One of the riders was a young Mexican. His slight size and smooth skin made him look young—maybe fourteen or fifteen—though the lines around his sunbaked eyes made her think he might be in his twenties. The other Mexican looked slightly older. The man on the bay horse had pitted cheeks. His clothes were crusty with dried mud.

They stopped.

"Mr. Dalton, I'm Virginia Bowen, Alfred's wife." Her horse sidestepped, skittish.

He squinted at her from beneath the brim of his hat. The scars on his cheeks had the mottled look of sponge painting. "Eugenia's back at the house," he said. The two Mexicans sat rigidly on their horses, without expression.

"I came to see you."

He raised his eyebrows and tipped his hat back.

He signaled for the Mexicans to continue on. He rested a loose fist on his saddle horn and looked at her long and hard, like a man at a poker table trying to gauge the others' moods without giving any clues to his own. "Nobody told me you was pretty."

Self-conscious, she hooked a stray strand of hair behind her ear. "I've come to apologize," she said. "My brother, Jonathan, came onto your property earlier today without your permission."

He wiped his mouth with the back of his hand and looked at her. "That was your brother," he said. A statement rather than a question. He got off his horse and she followed his lead. He sat on a rock, picked up a piece of grass, and started chewing on it. He said nothing but continued looking at her. His stare unsettled her.

She was used to silence as a positive, healing force, but this was something else entirely. She felt the courage seep out of her, and knew she had to act quickly before she lost her nerve.

"Friend, I'm here to see if we can come to some agreement about the water." It did not come out as neutral as she had intended. She realized, to her dismay, that her legs were quivering.

He spit out the grass. "Bowen sends a woman to do his dirty work." This seemed to justify him in some way.

He got out a cigarette paper and sprinkled tobacco in a line. He had thick, stubby fingers and dirty fingernails.

"Alfred doesn't know I'm here, and I'm sure he wouldn't be happy if he did." The sky was huge and made her feel naked and unprotected.

"Then why'd you come?" He frowned, and the notch in his chin deepened.

"I'm asking you to reconsider your position." She looked straight at him and soon became aware that she was holding her breath. She let air out in a measured way so it would not come out as a sigh. "We have senior water rights."

For a moment, he looked chastised, like the class bully who takes on a kid younger than himself and is surprised by the kid's spunk and gumption. But he quickly recovered and said, "Ain't nobody owns water from the sky." He took a deep draw on the cigarette and glared at her. Smoke dribbled out of his nose.

Virginia did not want to get into an argument about water rights, which she poorly understood. "You did wrong by taking the water."

The tendons in his neck stood out, and he got up abruptly. "Don't go meddling where you got no business."

He hitched up his pants.

The discussion had taken an ugly turn, and she needed to get it back on neutral ground.

"All we're asking is our fair share of the water." She glanced down the road, hoping the Mexicans would return. She felt threatened.

He ran his tongue across his chapped lips. His boot crunched against the ground as he moved toward her.

"We can discuss this reasonably and come to some agreement," she said, backing up. "We do not want to deny you water. We just want what's rightfully ours."

He continued toward her in slow sinister steps. The upper part of his lip curled up and disappeared beneath his mustache.

She stumbled over a loose stone and lost her footing. She

scrambled up from the ground. Sheep stuttered in the nearby field.

He pinned her against the fence, and she felt a sharp prick in her back. "Mr. Dalton, we've all been under a great strain. Please. I want you to think about what you're doing," she said.

She pushed him away, but he pressed his thick body on hers. Mud flaked off his shirt.

She arched her back to avoid the barbs. This close, she could smell his sour breath. His teeth were full of brown holes, as if riddled by buckshot.

"These are hard times, Mr. Dalton," Virginia said and turned her face away to avoid his kiss. She felt his lips scratch like dried snakeskin against her neck. "We're all trying to hold things together, and you've got two children to think about."

He gave a little convulsion, like a sneeze. She closed her eyes as the spittle sprayed across her face. When she felt his weight withdraw, she opened her eyes. To her utter shock, she saw that he was crying.

He sat down on the edge of the bank and pressed the heels of his hands into his eyes. "I can't feed my family. What kind of man am I if I can't feed my family?"

She glanced at the butte across the way. Erosion had eaten into the side, which was concave and ragged brown at the edges, like a sampled but discarded apple.

She wanted to reach out and comfort him, as she might a small child, but given the circumstances, she did not want any physical contact. So she sat beside him and spoke to him quietly until the moment had passed. Ashamed, he got on his horse and rode off.

Virginia remained in place, too shaken to get up immediately. After regaining her strength, she mounted the Sorrel and headed home.

She filled her tin tub with water and scrubbed herself vigorously, as if memory itself were a new layer of contaminated skin and if she rubbed long enough and hard enough she could wipe out that rancid breath, those rotting teeth, that pocked skin. But no matter how many times she lathered the washcloth or scrubbed her skin, she still felt dirty.

Perhaps he had sensed some ugliness in her. Was it possible that what she had done with Lemmie in Kentucky had tarnished the light within, so that it no longer functioned as a healing force, but only as a beacon attracting unwanted attentions? She shuddered. Her skin bled in places.

When Alfred returned from work, he heard her splashing behind the rigged-up curtain in the kitchen.

"Virginia, what's gotten into you? You just had a bath a few days ago." As he lectured her about the need to conserve water, she pressed her cheek against her knee.

She didn't want to tell him about Dalton. Perhaps she had imagined the threat of violence—she had been so overwrought that she didn't trust her instincts.

When she did not respond to Alfred's reprimand, he looked behind the curtain. "What are these scratches on your back?" he said.

"I backed into a fence," she said, trying to keep her voice strong.

"I don't understand how you could have done that."

"No, you do not," Virginia said evenly.

It wasn't until she heard Alfred draw the curtain shut that she felt tears on her face—the only water that was free and readily available.

Fourteen

In July the temperature rose into the high nineties for days on end and did not fall off much at night. The hot winds sucked the moisture out of the soil and offered no relief from the heat. Under the brassy sun, the prairie looked brittle. The sweet memory of rain was only that—a memory.

The drought was back, as if it had never been interrupted. The established grasses with deep roots could withstand the heat, but the newly sprouted seedlings shriveled up and died. The Russian thistle, propelled by the wind, spread its opportunistic seeds across the prairie.

One day, a Mexican arrived on the Bowen's porch. He was dressed in a fancy shirt and string tie. Virginia recognized the sheepherder from Dalton's ranch.

"*¿Está Señor Juan?*" he said, his eyes fixed on his newly polished boots.

She struggled to remember the Spanish she had learned in

Mexico, but the only words that came to mind were from high-school French.

"*Entrez,*" she said and opened the screen door. He looked around nervously.

"Please. *Por favor,*" she said and opened the door wider. She pulled out a kitchen chair. "I'll go get Jonathan."

She went to the bunk room and returned with her brother. He smiled when he saw the sheepherder.

The Mexican stood up and pumped his hand. "The water, she now comes to you," he said with a mischievous smile.

"What about the dam?" Jonathan said and drew a picture with his hands.

Jorge made an exploding sound with his mouth and opened out his fingers in a star burst. "Dam is bye-bye," he said.

Jonathan pointed to Jorge. "You?"

The Mexican shrugged and smiled sheepishly.

Jonathan clapped him on the shoulder. "You're a true friend."

The drought continued through the summer. There were a couple of showers, but never enough water to fill the creek bed. One day in August, Virginia was at the woodpile filling the canvas carrier with kindling. The sky was the color of vegetable stock, and the air was so dry that the smell had gone out of the sagebrush. Suddenly the sound of a bell carried across the prairie. She looked to the north and saw a rolling black cloud that started at the horizon and churned upward. Its bilious brown edges bled into the sky and created a strange bronze light.

Another dust storm, she thought wearily, though storms were rare from that direction. She despaired of going through the drill yet again. Back at the house, she collected rags to stuff under the doors. Before she had gotten far in her preparation, Alfred galloped up on horseback and yelled "Fire! At the Daltons' place."

Jonathan took care of the horses. Virginia collected shovels, pails, and gunnysacks. Alfred put the large tin bathtub in the back of the truck and filled it with water from the windmill.

They arrived at the Daltons' at the same time as Chance Greene and his mother. A neighboring rancher stood in the front yard and gave directions to the arriving neighbors.

"Where's Eugenia?" Virginia asked.

"Inside. My wife's with her. She's got a bad case of the nerves," the rancher said.

Virginia was relieved to learn that the Dalton children were in school. The one-room schoolhouse was in the opposite direction from the fire.

Chance's mother offered to drive to the nearest phone, ten miles away, to call the fire department. Chance hoisted his shovel and gunnysacks into the back of the Bowens' truck and jumped in with Jonathan. Virginia rode beside Alfred as he drove toward the smoke on a far hill.

At the outer edge of the fire, trucks were parked at odd angles along the road. Men unloaded shovels and buckets and hurried toward the flames. Virginia had not seen this many people together since branding.

The wind blew from the east, pushing a low wall of fire across the dry grass. It advanced with a terrible flapping sound, with no creeks or rivers to stop it.

Alfred and Jonathan unloaded the large galvanized-tin basin. Most of the water had sloshed out on the trip over. Virginia had no idea how they were going to fight a fire of this size with so little water.

"You go over and help the women," Alfred told Virginia and looked toward a group of wives who had set up a first-aid station on the tailgate of a truck. Virginia nodded, but she had no intention of staying back. She wanted to fight the fire with the men. Every hand would be needed.

Dalton arrived in his pickup. Half a dozen men gathered around him. Some leaned on the handles of their shovels, others held buckets. Virginia shrank back, afraid Dalton would give some sign of recognition. She felt sick to her stomach, seeing him again.

Alfred looked back at the house in the distance, barely visible over a low rise. "I'm heading back to the house, to dig a trench around it."

Dalton eyed him suspiciously. "Fire ain't headed that way," he said.

"One shift of the wind and it will be. Fire's mercurial," Alfred said.

"You can throw around all the high-dollar words you want. Fact is, the sheep's over there." He pointed to the west, toward the path of the fire. "Besides, the road will stop the fire."

"Could be, but I'm not taking a chance."

Fury colored Dalton's face.

Alfred ignored him. "Who's going to give me a hand?"

He scanned the faces of the men around him. Chance looked nervously from Alfred to Dalton.

Jonathan stepped over the imaginary line and stood by Alfred.

After a few tense moments, Alfred said, "Oh, hell. It's his spread." He walked toward the blue Ford truck.

After Alfred left, Virginia followed a group of men headed in the opposite direction of Dalton. She was afraid of Dalton, even around this many people. Her worries were groundless. With all the commotion and activity, Dalton never looked her way. He worked in one part of the field and she worked in another.

Closer to the fire, she watched to see what the men around her were doing, and followed their lead. She dipped the gunny-sack in the water and worked on a small area. It took several passes to put out the knee-high flames. She could feel the heat through the thick soles of her oxfords. Aware that she had to pace herself, she tried to slow down. Each time she ran back and wet the sack in the sooty water, it felt heavier and heavier.

Sparks flew over her shoulder like lightning bugs and alighted on neighboring grasses, moving the fire forward.

Behind the fire, the prairie was naked and black, as if lava had crept over it.

As the fire grew, so did the number of people fighting it. In one part of the field, men dug trenches. In places where the dust had collected in drifts, firefighters shoveled the loose dirt onto the flames.

Several dozen sheep had clumped together in a corner of the field. On one side, the flames had closed off their escape. On the other, the fence posts had caught fire. Some sheep had backed into the sizzling-hot barbed wire, and the acrid smell of burnt wool permeated the air. A group of men wetted down a pathway to the trapped sheep. They yelled, shooed, and swatted, but the sheep, moving as one mass, refused to be funneled through the fire.

Finally, Jorge arrived on horseback with two border collies. The horse would not get close to the fire, but the dogs streaked across the field, following Jorge's whistle. Fearless of the fire, they nipped at the heels of the sheep and herded them along the narrow path between walls of fire.

Concentrating only on the small area around her, Virginia lost track of time. In her haste to get to the fire, she had forgotten the most important thing of all—drinking water. Her tongue felt dried and cracked like an old shoe. Her eyes watered from the smoke. Her sooty face was streaked with sweat. Caught up in the communal vitality, she worked far past her endurance.

Suddenly the wind shifted and the fire veered south, toward the road. Now the fire was headed directly toward Dalton's house a quarter mile away, a distance the hungry fire could lap up in no time. Dalton had counted on the road to stop the fire, but the road was no match for the wind, which sent ribbons of flame over the barrier and ignited the grasses on the other side. Once the fiery mass got a toehold, it was off and running toward the house.

It happened so quickly. No one was prepared for it. Men abandoned shovels and buckets in the field and ran for the trucks. A rancher gave Virginia a hand and pulled her into the back of the truck as it was leaving. The scene had an aura of war—a rapid retreat, soldiers running for cover, faces blackened with camouflage.

From the truck bed, Virginia watched as the fire moved down the rise. She understood why the Indians called wildfires the red buffalo. Moving forward, it was a glowing, frightening thing, with a personality and form all its own.

Back at the house, Alfred had hitched up the team and was plowing a furrow around the house, the shed, and the hay that was piled loosely next to the shed. The hay was the real danger. A single spark would transform it into a tower of flame. The fiery twists that broke off and traveled on the wind would endanger the house and shed.

Knowing how poorly Jonathan reacted to crises, Virginia looked around for him. When she found him working next to Alfred, digging a trench by the house, she felt a gush of love for Alfred. He always looked after Jonathan.

The firefighters regrouped in the front of the house to decide how to proceed. So much equipment had been lost in their hasty retreat.

Virginia felt woozy. She stumbled backward and put the heel of her hand behind her to support herself against a truck. One of the wives brought her a glass of water.

"Are you all right? Maybe you better stop," she said.

"No, I'm fine. This is just what I need." She drank the water and poured the last drop on a handkerchief to wipe her face. Refreshed, she picked up a wet burlap sack and went looking for Alfred. He was now by the shed with a torch, setting fire to the grasses. Why in the world would he be doing such a thing? She looked again. Sure enough, Alfred waved the torch over the tips of the grasses, which crackled up in tongues of red, yellow, and orange.

When Dalton saw him, he turned to the men gathered in the yard and yelled, "Stop him!" Dalton ran toward him, waving a shovel over his head. The men followed. Virginia watched in horror as an angry crowd surrounded Alfred.

"What are you doing?" shouted one man. He snatched the torch from Alfred and threw it into an area that was already burning.

Dalton poked a finger in Alfred's chest. "You've had it in for me ever since you moved here, haven't you, Bowen?"

Alfred swatted Dalton's hand away. "You're wasting time," Alfred said. "This is going to save your house. Now get on the other side of the trench and put out the sparks that jump over."

Now Virginia understood. The fire Alfred had set on the other side of the trench was burning away from the house and toward the larger fire, eating up the grass so when the two met, there would be no fuel left to carry the larger fire to the house.

A woman came out of the house in distress and found Virginia. "I can't get Eugenia to leave. She's not even giving advice, so you know she's not herself. Maybe you could talk some sense into her? She won't listen to me."

Virginia went inside, where the shouts of firefighters were muffled and the air was milky with dust and smoke.

"Eugenia," Virginia called out cautiously. "Eugenia, are you in here?"

A thin voice came from the back bedroom. She found her in a rocking chair facing the iron bed, with her back to the window.

Eugenia looked at Virginia without a sign of recognition.

"Eugenia, it's me. Virginia," she said, realizing that in her tattered clothes and black face, her neighbor might not recognize her. "You've got to leave now."

Eugenia looked at Virginia in confusion. Her knuckles were shiny from gripping so hard.

"We can't wait any longer," Virginia said urgently. "The fire could cross the trenches at any moment." Virginia tried to pull her stout friend up from the chair, but Eugenia gripped the chair with such force that her tendons popped up in relief.

"Everything I have is in this house," she said, her jaw set.

"I'll help you gather your things. Just tell me what you want."

"My salt-shaker collection."

"Okay, you go on out, and I'll get them and bring them with me."

"I'm not moving 'til I have them in my hands. That collection is the only nice thing I've ever owned."

Virginia moved quickly. She could not find a box, so she stripped the bed and took the linens to the bookcase in the living room. She quickly wrapped the ceramic salt shakers in the sheet and stuffed them in the pillowcase. A black pepper shaker in the shape of a cat slipped out of her hand, cracked on the floor, and lost an ear. She picked up the pieces, wrapped the ear with the other shakers, and brought the bundle back to Eugenia.

"Okay, I got it. Let's go."

Eugenia crossed her arms in front of her, securing the lumpy pillowcase to her chest and clamping onto the arms of the chair. "I'm not going anywhere."

Virginia could see it would do no good to argue. She ran outside and found Alfred. Her eyes stung, and she was out of breath. "Eugenia's gone off. She's not in her right mind. Someone's going to have to take her out by force."

Alfred and Jonathan rushed inside the house. Several minutes later, they reappeared carrying Eugenia. She was still in the rocker, holding tight to her salt and pepper shakers. They set Eugenia and the rocker in the back of a truck.

The fire moved toward the house like a wave. But when it arrived at the swath that Alfred had already burned, it had no more grass to feed its hungry appetite. The flames lapped at the charred earth, then died, just as Alfred had foreseen.

By the time the pump truck arrived with more community volunteers and a tank of precious water, the danger was over.

The exhausted men gathered around Alfred and clapped him on the back. "Glad you were on board, partner," one said. "Good work," said another.

Dalton busied himself gathering equipment. He skirted the knot of men around Alfred.

"Dalton, you're one lucky son of a gun," said one of the fire-fighters.

Dalton approached the group reluctantly. "I appreciate all you folks have done."

"Alfred's the one you should thank," another rancher said.

Dalton rubbed the toe of his boot in the dirt, as if putting out a cigarette. He shifted a stack of gunnysacks from one arm to the other.

"Come on, man. It ain't going to kill you to acknowledge his part."

The men looked at Dalton expectantly.

Dalton could not look Alfred in the eye. He turned his head toward the scorched fields and muttered, "I owe you one, Bowen."

"No problem," Alfred said and left to get Virginia. He found her leaning against the side of the house. Her blouse was torn beneath the arm. Her eyebrows were singed, and her stick-straight hair had frizzled around the temples where it burned to the edge of her scarf. He gently smoothed away a black smudge below her eye. "You're a sight to behold. I'm going to have to trade you in for a new model," he said.

"I don't know how much longer I can last," she said. Then her feet buckled, and she slumped down.

Alfred caught her as she fell. "Let me get you some water," he said with dismay.

"I'm fine," she said weakly. "I just need to go."

On the way home, ashes floated down on the windshield like dark snowflakes. The fence posts were still smoldering, and threads of smoke rose from the blackened fields. But the Daltons had lost no livestock and no buildings. The fire would actually do the fields good—clean out the dead stalks and allow light and air to reach ground level. The following year, Dalton's fields would be verdant and rich. If it ever rained.

＊　＊　＊

Several days after the fire, Virginia awoke to sharp pains below her waist. With intensifying alarm, she stayed in bed while Alfred fixed himself breakfast and did the chores. After he left, she felt another wrenching spasm and tried to tell herself: *That's not so bad. A simple upset stomach. I must have eaten something that didn't agree with me.* She didn't want to overreact. Throughout her pregnancy, she had been acutely sensitive to every twinge in her body. But she knew that the excruciating pains were not normal. Something had gone badly wrong.

Alone in the dark, she placed her hands over her belly and lay perfectly still, convinced that if she did not move, she could preserve the life inside her. Her pulse throbbed in her palms and transferred through the thin fabric of her nightgown to her belly. She imagined the light surrounding the seed inside her, protecting it. She would will herself to keep this baby. If humans were capable of extraordinary feats in times of crisis, like lifting a car off a child, then she should be able to do this very simple thing. Everything depended on her remaining calm. But how could she, when her own body was doing violence to the growing life inside? *Please, God. Please,* she beseeched. *The pain is fine. Just don't let me harm the child.*

When morning light came into the room and lay warmly over the bed, a pain pierced her lower parts and shot up her spine. She felt her insides harden and contract. Then a warm liquid slipped from her, and the place below her heart emptied.

She rose, stripped the bed, and soaked the sheets in precious cistern water. She rubbed the white cotton until she had worn the skin away from her knuckles. As she emptied the water beside the steps, she watched the ground darken and soak up the blood. With fresh water, she worked on the sheets some more, but no matter how hard she scrubbed, a vestigial stain remained, in pale pink, darker at the verges, the phantom image of her child.

She was too embarrassed to let Jonathan take her soiled

sheets to Ida, so she bundled them up and drove to town herself. She acted quickly, while she was too numb to feel.

She found Ida in the backyard taking laundry off the line. Ida folded a sheet in half and smoothed out the wrinkles with a flip of her wrists. The sun-starched sheet gave a crisp *crack*. She folded it over several more times and put it in the basket. With her luxurious plumpness and flushed cheeks, Ida gave off a glow of good health.

Virginia closed her eyes and held the damp bundle close to her chest. The laundry, flapping in wind, sounded exactly like flames. When she opened her eyes, she stared at the pristine sheets on the line, pinned corner-to-corner, so perfectly white, no secret to hide, no grief to disclose. She had bundled up her sheets in a tight knot so the blood would be in the interior. She handed the bundle to Ida.

Virginia wanted to leave quickly, but Ida insisted that she look at her most recent sewing project.

In the kitchen, a dozen cat-food bowls lined the baseboard. A tabby cat shot out from under the table and disappeared into the bedroom. When Ida leaned over to set the laundry down, a black cat sprang from a crouched position onto her shoulders and wrapped itself around her neck like a vibrating stole.

Ida went into the other room and returned with the cat still draped around her neck. She set the cat on the floor, then showed Virginia her treasure. It was a baby's quilt.

"That's very nice," Virginia said without really looking at it.

"You don't like it?" Ida said, hurt.

"Of course I do, dear. It's lovely," she said flatly. "Who are you going to give it to?"

"It's for me," she said proudly.

Stunned, Virginia looked at Ida's loose fitting dress and understood her radiance. "Oh," was all she could say.

Ida ran her hand lovingly over the quilt's puckered surface. "It's beautiful, isn't it?" she said with unabashed euphoria.

"You're very lucky," Virginia said.

Suddenly the room seemed to tremble. The cat smell over-powered her, and she had trouble breathing. "I have to go," she said urgently.

"You look pale. You can lay down in my room."

But Virginia was already out the door.

By the time Alfred returned from work, Virginia was back in bed. She dreaded telling him. He had never seemed that excited about the baby, and if he reacted the wrong way now, she knew she would never forgive him.

She lay flat on her back, arms at her side, and stared at the ceiling. At the moment, she could feel nothing. In her acute numbness, she chastised herself for not grieving profoundly enough.

When she heard Alfred in the kitchen, she closed her eyes and pretended to be asleep. She heard him clump loudly into the room, stop at the door, and continue on his tiptoes. In hushed quiet, he changed his clothes.

When she opened her eyes, he was staring at her.

"Alfred, we lost the baby," she said, her senses blunted.

He sat on the bed beside her. "I'm sure you're imagining things. Everything will be fine."

"No, Alfred. It won't."

His eyebrows drew together and he searched her blank face. "So it's certain?"

She nodded.

He absorbed the news for a moment, then said, "How are you feeling?"

"Not very good."

"Oh, heart of my heart." He pulled her to him and held her tight. Then his body went limp, and he was a dead weight against her. She felt anesthetized, unable to respond to his grief.

After a long time, Alfred pulled back and leaned against the headboard. "I knew I shouldn't have picked out names," he said.

"You didn't tell me," she said, surprised that he had given it any thought.

"I was going to consult you. It just seemed a little premature."

"Faith if it was a girl, right?" she said in a monotone.

"I thought of that, but I figured you might want to name her after your mother."

"And if it was a boy?" she said.

"Samuel."

"After your father?"

"Samuel was my brother's name, too. His nickname was Shrine."

For the first time, she felt the full force of her sadness. "Oh, Alfred," she said, clutching him. The tears came freely now. "What is to become of us?"

Over the next few weeks, the loss settled in. The absence felt as real as if a limb had been torn from her body. But she did not stop working. The cow had to be milked, the chickens fed, meals cooked, rooms cleaned. It was the routine that carried her through.

She expected the sadness to diminish gradually, imperceptibly, until one day it would cease to exist. But morning after morning, she could see no change. She learned to live with the grief, which hovered around her like a noxious gas—formless, odorless, but strong enough to kill.

She would never know if her loss was due to the fire, the smoke, the dust, or the exhaustion. Or maybe darker forces were at work. As her mind roamed over the possibilities, the what-ifs and if-onlys, she was drawn back, not to the fire, but to the thing that had happened almost two years before. A terrible thought began to form. Her efforts to ignore it only gave it greater credence. The thought was this: she was now suffering the consequences for what she had done in Kentucky, the thing she had never told Alfred about—or anyone, for that matter, because she was so deeply ashamed.

The day Lemmie kissed her on the mountainside was not the last time she had seen him. She had promised to return the following Wednesday to find out if he would be willing to make ladder-back chairs to sell at Eastern resorts. She had mixed feelings about seeing him again. True, she had given him her word. But she was also titillated by the danger of it. If only Alice could go with her, but Alice was in Bluefield, West Virginia, at a meeting of Quakers organizing feeding projects in various hollows in Appalachia.

She decided to go, but she put on her ugliest dress and vowed not to be alone with Lemmie. Technically speaking, she had not done anything irreparably wrong. But the Quaker sense of right and wrong was not based on technicalities.

She found Serina in the front yard stirring clothes in an iron kettle over an open fire. Her sacklike dress hung loosely around her.

"Lemmie's in the orchard," she said.

"I'll wait here until he comes back," Virginia said and sat on the steps.

"He's not coming back afore nightfall, or thereabouts. He told me to send you along. The same path you took before, 'ceptin' when you get to the second fork, take a left."

She followed the path along the side of the mountain until she came to a small apple orchard. A ladder leaned up against a tree. She looked up into the branches for Lemmie and did not see him approach her from behind. He lifted her up and twirled her around. She felt his strong arms and heard his deep laughter, but all she could see was a kaleidoscope of red, orange, and yellow leaves—luminescent chips of color reorganizing themselves into different patterns. When he set her down, the world continued to spin. She saw his face weaving toward hers and then felt his soft lips on hers. She kissed him, wishing she didn't enjoy it so much.

Afterward, she put her hand to her head. "I must look a

fright," she said. She was in her plainest dress, and her hair had come loose from its bun.

"You look real pretty." He kissed her again, but this time she resisted.

"No, Lemmie. This has got to stop."

"What in the tarnation's the matter? You come back, didn't you?"

"I came back for your answer on the chairs," she said, knowing her response was disingenuous. There were so many things between her and honest expression: breeding, religion, education, everything that constricted her true feelings. He spoke with the directness of a child.

"What do you want?" he said.

"It's—it's not right. Serina."

"No need for Serina to know." His eyes were lighter than the sky.

"Please, I've come to talk business. Let's go back to the house." If they were around Serina, Virginia would be safe.

"Come this-a-way. I'll show you my favorite spot."

He started off into the woods and then turned back. "Coming?"

She stood in place.

"Don't worry. I ain't going to make you do anything you don't want to do, rest assured. That's not how my mama raised me up."

What scared her was what she wanted to do.

She followed him through the woods. He held out his hand and helped her over a fallen pine tree that formed a bridge across the stream. "This is where I get the hickory for the chairs," he said and ran his strong hands along the bark. The simple motion seemed so sensual to her. "Now's the best time to gather up the timber, when the sap's down. Keeps down the warping."

He stretched out on his back on a tuft of ground softened by the leaves. He held his arms behind his head and chewed on a grass stem. She sat beside him. The sun funneled between the trees. Overhead, a hawk circled in the sky. "If this isn't near about the prettiest spot in the world, then I don't know what is," he said.

Unfortunately, her ugliest dress was also the easiest to get off. In her adult life, she had never been naked in front of another person—much less a man. But it somehow seemed the most natural thing in the world. His kisses were tinged with the sweet smell of grass. As he ran the tips of his fingers over her skin, she shivered and felt like a snake that had shed its hardened skin, exposing the long-dormant layer underneath.

She did not know what to expect, but she certainly did not expect this: his tongue on her skin, darting its way down across the highly charged surface until it was almost more than she could bear. She tossed her head back and forth, trying to suppress her cries but unable to stop the sounds completely. Then he moved down, past her belly button, to the soft swollen cleft that she had given so little consideration to in her life. She arched her back and moved toward him, forgetting about him as the sensation converged in pure hot surges. And that was only the beginning. He moved on top of her and was inside her and their bodies moved rhythmically then rearranged themselves like a puzzle with many different ways to be fit together, until much, much later—an eternity later—when he, less inhibited than she, let out a cry that was swallowed by the sky.

Afterward, they lay in each other's arms, his sunbaked skin dark against her pale complexion—different colors, different backgrounds, but for one brief moment, none of that mattered.

By the time they got back to the house, the sky was awash in color. Serina stood at the stove, wiping her face with the back of her hand. Her face was drawn and wan.

"Hard day?" Lemmie said, placing his hand on the small of her back.

"I'm plumb wore out. You go on and take the young'uns to

the revival," she said, holding her hands over her stomach. "This one here isn't going to let me get through these last months without a fuss."

Virginia looked closer at Serina's sack dress and noticed for the first time that she was pregnant. Euphoria gave way to remorse as Virginia realized what she had done. "I need to hurry back," she said.

"Lemmie, why don't you walk with her. It'll be pitch black before she gets to the road," Serina said.

Then Virginia remembered: her headlights. They had not been repaired since the accident. How could she have been so careless? She explained the problem to Lemmie and Serina.

"You can stay here. Won't be no problem a'-tall," Serina said. Did Serina have to be so kind? The house was tiny. There was no room for guests. She dreaded being trapped with Lemmie's family. But she had no choice.

"You want to stretch out before supper?" Serina asked. "You can use Jimmy's bed."

"I don't mind if I do," Virginia said, desperate to get away.

Darkness had settled in the corners of the room. Outside, the trees and the barn formed a flat silhouette against the bruise-colored sky. As Virginia was lying down on the bed she found a leaf attached to the back of her dress. Why hadn't Lemmie told her? As she brushed it off, Jimmy came in the room with a lantern, back from the day's work.

Virginia leaned back against the iron headboard. "I don't know if your mother told you. I'm staying for the night."

He said nothing. His face was beyond the lamp's reach, but she could feel his scalding glare.

"You been messing with my pa?"

"Pardon?" She felt the contours of the corn husks beneath the mattress ticking.

"You heared me right." He was only fourteen, but he had Lemmie's directness.

"Didn't your father tell you? He's going to make chairs for

me," she said, her voice quivering. She put her hand to her chin. It was chafed from all the kissing.

Jimmy held the lantern up so the light flooded his face. He looked exactly like Lemmie—dark skin, light eyes, dark hair. But his face was so raw; all the hurt was in its lineaments.

"I ain't staying in the same house with the likes of you," he said and left.

Virginia stared into the dark. She could hear laughter from the kitchen, and the sounds of clanging pots. The smell of fatback hung thickly in the air. She had never been so miserable.

At supper, Serina was tired, Jimmy sullen, and Lemmie quiet. The meal was mercifully quick. After clearing the table, they set out for the revival. Serina begged off, and Jimmy refused to go. The others walked along the narrow mountain path.

Virginia felt a growing sense of doom. She could not undo what was already done. She would have to live with the consequences. Damnation was not a part of the Quaker religion, nor was guilt, but conscience was, and that was even more insidious.

When they reached the cabin, she could see bobbing lantern lights as people approached from all directions. Men were passing planks through a window and setting them on overturned pails for benches. Inside, the twins scampered to the back of the room to join the other children.

"He knows. Jimmy knows," Virginia whispered to Lemmie as they took a seat several rows back.

"That boy's got more yearnings than he knows what to do with, and it's got him all wrought up. Don't pay him no never mind," Lemmie said.

"Don't you remember? That first day in the field. He was there."

The congregation hushed, and a man with an unkempt beard and bad teeth got up and placed his Bible on the table beside a lantern. Shadows filled the sockets of the preacher's eyes. His face was pale and skeletal. He talked about Doubting Thomas, then led the followers in a chant.

I am the man, Thomas, I am the man.
I am the man, Thomas, I am the man.
Look at the nail prints in my hand.
I am the man.

When he got to the words "nail prints," the preacher wiggled his fingers above his head, palms outward. Soon the room was swaying. Shadows throbbed on the wall. Someone in the back row banged on a pan. From the other side of the room came the shout, "Lord have mercy."

To Virginia, who had known the quiet of meeting as the only form of worship, the commotion was alarming. She needed silence to collect her thoughts. Amidst the delirium, the heat, and the smoky smell of bodies, she couldn't pray, she couldn't think, she couldn't probe her shame.

The noise did not bother the twins. They curled up on the table in back, head to foot like puppies, and slept soundly.

A man dropped to his knees and raised his arms toward the ceiling. A few others followed suit. The shadows rippled on the wall like tendrils.

The chant picked up. People clapped and shouted. Soon the whole room was swaying with the voodoolike chant, and all the words started blending together: *Siam the mayan Thomas, siam the mayan.*

The mass wail rose to a crescendo, then waned to a murmur as a man with a bandage on his nose came to the front with the preacher. "I've been cleansed by the Lord. The sin's gone out of me," he cried and ripped off his bandage. The ooze from the open sore glowed in the lantern light.

The preacher picked up the bandage, held it over his head, and cried out, "Nothing but the blood of Jesus." When the chanting straggled to a halt, he continued his sermon. Spittle spewed from his mouth and landed in his beard, glistening like dew. He spoke of concepts foreign to the Quaker religion— God's army, sinners, eternal damnation, and hell, where people burned like a roast in an oven for all eternity. He described a fearful and vengeful God, a character no more familiar to Virginia than a fairy-tale monster. The preacher punctuated his words with sharp cries of "Ha!" followed by wild laughter. His hoarse voice rose to new heights, cracked, then descended.

From beside Virginia came a bloodcurdling screech. Without warning, Lemmie flung himself to the floor on his stomach and began kicking his feet and moving his arms like someone trying to swim out of water. Virginia panicked. Was he having an epileptic fit? She looked around the pulsing room. No one paid attention to his writhing. Then she realized he was speaking in tongues. He sputtered words that she could make no sense of, though she recognized a few. The patter from his lips was rhythmic, repetitive, punctuated by grunts and growls. The preacher helped him to his feet and tried to calm him, but the force would not let loose. It hit him in gusts of vibrations that wrenched his body, made his shoulders jerk back and his arms fly up in uncontrollable spasms. As the congregation chanted, the preacher walked Lemmie around, as if cooling off a horse.

The packed room, the flickering lights, the smell of unwashed bodies, and Lemmie's yelping eruptions made Virginia's heart pound with strange terror. Much as she tried, she could not banish the harsh realization that she, Virginia Mendenhall, had had relations with a pregnant woman's husband.

On their way home, she and Lemmie walked single file over the path, each carrying one of the sleeping twins. Lemmie did not speak, as if all his words had been expelled in the fit of religious ecstasy.

Back at the house, Virginia could not sleep. *Siam the mayan Thomas, siam the mayan* echoed in her mind like a primitive drumbeat. When the first signs of day lightened the sky, she slipped out the door without saying good-bye. She turned back for one final look and she saw Jimmy leaning against the barn, as if he had been waiting for her all night. That image of him would haunt her for years to come.

For the next week, she could not get out of bed. Alice brought her tea and soup. The thought of telling Alice what had happened added to Virginia's turmoil. She could not bear to lose Alice's respect. But she finally confessed, and instead of being judgmental, Alice took charge of the situation. She contacted her aunt, an English nurse who had married a Mexican anthropologist. The aunt agreed to let Virginia stay in their house in Mexico City until Virginia got her strength back.

How strange, Virginia reflected, that if she had not gone to Mexico, she never would have seen Alfred again. From the moment she agreed to married him, she felt obliged to tell him about Lemmie, but each time she tried, something intervened. The longer she waited, the less inclined she was to tell him. Recently she had given up telling him altogether. But after she lost the baby, the weight of the secret had become almost unbearable, linked as it was, in her mind, to a much deeper loss. That she had defied the doctor's predictions once was a miracle, and miracles don't happen twice. Everything came with a price. The price she paid was this: that something precious would remain forever beyond her reach.

FIFTEEN

"Does thee know what day this is?" Virginia asked Alfred one morning at breakfast after Jonathan had left to saddle the horses.

"It's Thursday," Alfred said, as she knew he would.

"Yes, it is Thursday, but it's another day as well," she said and thought: *It is only women who note milestones, memories, the passing of time.*

He reflected a moment but could come up with nothing.

"It's the anniversary of the day we were married," she said.

His face brightened. "So it is. And what a beautiful day it was. I remember that park we went to after the ceremony. What was the name of it?"

"City Park."

"Oh yes, the swans on the lake, the pavilion with the mountains in the background, and you wore that purple dress that makes your eyes look purple."

"Why, Alfred Bowen. I've never known you to wax sentimental," she said, warm in the glow of the shared memory.

He looked sheepish. "There's still a thing or two you don't know about me."

"There are a few things you don't know about me, too." She offered this in playful riposte but realized, as soon as she had said it, that she had presented herself the perfect opening to tell him about Lemmie.

"What's wrong? You look like you swallowed a bug," he said.

"I never told you why I went to Mexico."

He had asked once, long ago, but had not insisted on an answer, and never mentioned it again.

Now she told him about Lemmie. Not in great detail—there were only a few details that mattered, but those were the ones that reflected on her character. She talked fast, her eyes fixed on the table, knowing that if she stopped, she would never get it out. When she finished, she looked up at Alfred. His breathing was erratic, and his face was inflamed. The white of his scar bulged out in relief, as if the pressure coursing through him were trying to escape through his forehead.

"You're upset," she said, alarmed.

"How did you expect me to react?"

She hadn't given it much thought. She had pondered, in considerable depth, her own shame and discomfort, without ever trying to imagine how he might respond, though her resistance to telling him meant that she knew, on some level, what his reaction might be.

"I never saw him again. I didn't write," she said, then added, almost as an afterthought: "He couldn't read, anyway."

"But you would have written? If he weren't illiterate?" he said.

"No. I mean, I don't know. I never thought about it." Perhaps she expected too much, that he could forgive her. "It was an impulsive moment. I can't explain it, and I'm not going to defend it. But I felt dishonest not letting you know."

"Well, I wish you hadn't told me," he said. He held his chin rigid in a way that caused prickles to fan out from her spine.

277

"Then I'm sorry I did," she said.

They both fell silent.

"Alfred, say something. Don't scare me like this. What are you thinking?"

"I'm thinking I better leave before I do something I regret." And he was out the door.

He spurred the Sorrel into a gallop. If he slowed down, he might start thinking, and he didn't want to think. He was not used to being so stirred up, and didn't like it. He had been caught off guard. Her revelation cast doubt on all kinds of things and shook him to the core.

He felt rage in his throat, wind against his face. *Virginia, how could you?* he thought. *What got into you?* It didn't fit his view of her. If she could do this, what else might she do? It was the unpredictability, the opening up of possibilities, that disturbed him so. The grit in the air scoured his cheeks. His bandanna scratched his neck as if it were sandpaper. But Alfred kept galloping until finally, mercifully, he stopped to give the horse a rest.

The Sorrel stood, sides heaving. A white lather foamed beneath the saddle. Alfred had violated his cardinal rule. He had used the horse for his own purpose, to work off steam, without consideration for the animal.

He sat on the ridge and looked out over the hay fields. In a good year, he should get two cuttings. That year, he had only gotten one cutting, and a sorry one at that. There was not enough hay to hold the calves over the winter. He knew what that meant, but he couldn't bear to face it now. Life was hard. He had been brought up to accept that and not complain. What he was not prepared for was the way hardships clustered together. Virginia. The baby. The ranch. He knew one loss had no connection to the other, and yet . . .

He looked out over the unforgiving land. Everything he

could see was his. But for how much longer? Maybe the Indians were right: no one owned the land. Not even the dead.

Virginia stared at the table of dirty dishes, unable to get up. Was this it, the crack that would shatter the crystal? Those euphoric days of the past autumn were nothing but a memory. She felt numb, unable to think, her mind thick with grief and confusion.

Jonathan came in and filled his canteen from the pump. "Where did Alfred go in such a hurry?"

"I don't know," Virginia said. She felt, in a real way, the thing she had been trying to deny: fear.

Jonathan sat at the table and pushed aside a dirty dish. The fuzzy dust that had collected on the hardened egg yolk looked like mold.

"He didn't tell me the plan for today. He always tells me the plan." Jonathan tapped his foot rapidly against the floor.

"He'll be back. Can't you find something to keep yourself busy until he does?"

His fingers drilled relentlessly against the table.

"Jonathan, please! That's getting on my nerves." He looked hurt. "I'm sorry. I didn't mean to raise my voice. I just need quiet now."

"I want to talk to him, Sis. To both of you." He scratched his back with a fork. "It's important."

"It'll have to wait. He went off somewhere to be by himself. Something's troubling him."

"What?"

"It's a private matter."

"I'll go find him."

"Jonathan, let him go. He needs to be by himself. He's upset with me."

"I can understand why," he said.

"Jonathan!"

"You're perfect," he said earnestly.

She laughed ironically. "Right. I'm perfect. That's my problem."

"It is," he said.

"What news did you have to tell us?" she said with a weary sigh.

His face brightened and he stopped fidgeting. "I'm getting married," he said proudly.

Somehow this possibility had never crossed her mind. She wasn't even aware that he knew any women. Dazed, she scraped her chair back. She felt it again: the fear.

"Who are you marrying?" she asked.

"Ida Pinska."

In an instant, she put everything together and the realization came crashing down on her. "Oh," was all she could manage to get out, as the cauldron of her undigested emotions came dangerously close to spilling over.

Virginia slapped the paintbrush against the wall, up and down, working off her fury without regard for the splatters that covered her arms like albino freckles. She was fixing up the bunk room in the shed, in preparation for Ida's arrival.

She was furious at her situation and furious at Jonathan. By one action that took no thought, no planning, no consideration, he had thrown everyone's life into disarray. What an idiot she had been to give him the chore of dropping off the laundry. A baby! And Jonathan was without a thought in the world as to how to provide for it.

Why was it fair that Ida could have a baby and she could not? Why? It would be one thing if Ida could care for the child. But the dear sweet-tempered girl was not the brightest light. In town she managed to take care of her wild cats, but they were savages, survivors—not a helpless infant. By default, the responsibility for the baby would fall to Virginia, and that was the last thing she wanted. Not after all she had been through. She tried to think of ways to diffuse her resentment. It was not Ida's fault.

It was no one's fault. But instead of acceptance, she felt only rage, silent rage, tearing her insides out.

She didn't want Ida in the house, didn't want to be reminded of what she could not have. She tried to come upon some way she could live with this, but she only felt more distressed. Alfred's estrangement, their lost child, Ida's fertility, all became wrapped up in the drought. She was surrounded by dust, dryness, dearth, and death.

She had no one to blame but herself. It had been her inspired idea to bring Jonathan out to live with them. Poor Alfred. Suddenly he was put in the position of having to support not two people, but five. Oh, it wasn't fair. It was not right. She smacked the brush against the rough boards, which soaked up the watery paint and took on a sickly pallor.

As upset as she felt, this much she knew: no bride deserved a room like this. The ends of nails stuck through the unpainted walls, a square of cardboard replaced a missing window pane, and tattered tar paper curled from the ceiling. Jonathan didn't care about his surroundings, but Virginia knew from the spotless way Ida kept her house in town that she would not be comfortable living in this room.

She had found a partially filled can of white paint in the shed. When she added paint thinner to stretch it out, the paint turned a bluish white, like milk freed from its butterfat. By the time she reached the fourth wall, the paint ran out.

After supper, she approached Alfred and asked him if she could buy more paint. He was at his desk, hunched over the ledger. Ever since she had revealed her secret, the frosty chill between them had not thawed, but they could still discuss business. It was the only thing that was safe to talk about.

"A quart's all I need to finish the room off," she said.

"Don't waste your time," he said. "We won't be here much longer."

She recognized the color of his face: the same color as the raw wood that had soaked up the diluted white paint.

"You've decided to sell the calves?" she said quietly.

"I have to." The words hung in the air like a death sentence.

His face was filled with defeat. "We can't hold them over 'til spring?" she said, almost at a whisper.

"I've thought of every avenue and option, but I can't put it off any longer. We simply can't afford the feed."

"So what happens next?" she said, numb with fear.

When he finally spoke, his voice was controlled but brittle. "We can stay here and wait to be run off, or we can sell out and move west."

She thought of how difficult the move would be for Jonathan and Ida, but she was sure he had considered this, too, and she didn't want to make him feel any worse.

"What about all of our things? The piano?" she said.

"It made it halfway across the country. That'll have to do," he said without remorse.

She knew it had to be an indication of how dire the situation was that selling the piano no longer seemed like a bad thing to him. This brought it home to her: they were going to lose the ranch. Time was, when she would not have minded leaving. She had felt ambivalent about the featureless land, the suffocating dust, the parsimony of nature. The land demanded so much— more than she had to give—and yet somehow, somewhere in the struggle, the land had reached up and included her in it.

"What about talking to your father?" she said.

"You know the answer to that," he said with finality.

True, they had been over that ground before, but she could conceive of no pride so strong that he would not ask his own father for help.

"We could go back East," Virginia suggested. "I could see if they'd take me back at the American Friends Service Committee."

He winced, and she saw that her offer only served to humiliate him. Everything she did these days seemed to hurt him.

"You'll need to stay home and take care of Ida and the baby," he said.

"She lived alone for years. She can take care of herself."

"But is she responsible enough to—" He paused.

"I know what you're saying, but"—she shook her head furiously—"I don't want to take care of a baby. Not someone else's baby."

Alfred looked at her as if, for the first time, he understood.

"I'm sorry," he said with sympathy, but made no move to touch her.

"Having a baby is the easiest thing in the world. But I can't do it."

She wanted desperately for him to hold her and make the pain go away. But their estrangement was too great. The tension in the room was more than she could bear, so she went outside.

The moon was not out, but she could see well enough to follow the road. The stars showed through the perforated sky like braille. If only she could touch them, she might understand their meaning. Somewhere among the glittering patterns of light danced the soul of her unborn child. She felt a cold, hollow space beneath her heart where, once, her own child had slept. It was empty, and always would be.

Virginia put off writing to her mother about Jonathan's situation, hoping each day that something would change. Her good Quaker mother would be heartbroken. A child out of wedlock. A shotgun wedding. It would be an affront to her values. Her mother led a sheltered, pious life and would not be able to make sense of this. Virginia dreaded putting her through the pain. But she felt obligated to tell her. With the wedding date approaching, Virginia could delay no longer, and sent off a letter.

The following week, she got a response. "My dearest Virginia," the letter began: "I read thy news with great joy."

Her mother must not have received her most recent letter,

Virginia thought with dismay. She checked the date in the corner and continued reading:

This is so much better than I could have dreamed for Jonathan. He now has someone to care for him and love him, and likewise he has someone to love. No one should go through life without that. People belong in families. It is one of life's great blessings. I don't know what I would do without thy dear father. For so long I was afraid that Jonathan would have to spend his life alone. I'm delighted to find out that now he, too, can know the warm closeness of marriage. Jonathan is not a person who fits in our world, and if he has to do things a little differently, so be it.

As for what others say—why does thee care? Truth is not governed by outward laws and moral codes, but by the inward leading of the light. Tolerance and respect are after the manner of Friends, not small-minded judgments.

I hope thee won't take their situation on thy shoulders. People must make their own way. Experience has taught me that one cannot play Providence successfully, even in one's own family.

I believe that God presents us with obstacles and unforeseen events for a reason. Hard times are the training ground of the spirit, where we learn how much, through our own pain, we have to offer others. But this takes time. And in time, darkness will give way to light, and thee will have empathy with a world of suffering thee previously didn't know existed.

Virginia finished the letter, but instead of feeling better, she felt chastened. How could her mother advise Virginia to keep out of their lives? Perhaps she had not made clear the limits of Ida's capabilities, but her mother certainly knew how irresponsible Jonathan was. *People must make their own way.* This, from a woman who refused to leave Jonathan alone during the fifteen long years she cared for him? And now she was proposing to let him make his own mistakes with a baby?

Ida and Jonathan were married by the justice of the peace. The Lutherans, who had provided Ida with charity baskets at Thanksgiving and Christmas and had helped set her up in the laundry business when she first came to town, would not allow her to marry in the church.

The day after the wedding, Alfred had to go to the bank but needed Jonathan on site to repair the windmill, so he offered to help Ida move. In town, she waited for him on the bench across the street from the bank. She sat on the edge of the bench and leaned back, her stomach protruding, her knees apart so that her skirt formed a hammock between her legs.

Alfred made his withdrawal at the teller's window, then exited the bank. Across the street, a little girl cried out, "There's the Cat Lady." She broke away from her mother and ran up to Ida, her blond pigtails bouncing. The mother caught up to the little girl, grabbed her arm, and pulled her away from Ida.

Alfred felt anger building as he waited for a car to pass. As he crossed the street, he heard the little girl say, "But Mama, she saves the kitties."

When he reached the bench, Ida jumped up and grabbed his arm, her face puddled in sadness.

"Today's a good day for candy," Alfred said. "What do you say we go to Dave's and pick us out some?"

Ida did not smile. "That woman hates me, doesn't she, Mr. Bowen?"

"What she thinks has nothing to do with you," he said evenly.

Her lower lip quivered. "I don't like it. Why does she hate me?"

"Some folks have got a very narrow view of what's proper. But that's her problem, not ours. Now, what's your favorite kind of candy? I favor butterscotch myself."

As they walked up the steps to the general store, the men on the porch abruptly stopped talking.

"What's the matter, fellows? Cat got your tongue?" Alfred said.

There were a few embarrassed laughs. One man spat into the old paint can they used as a spittoon.

"Well, I hear you got a new member of the family," Harley Feathergill said.

"Right. Soon to have two," Alfred said, speaking of what was on everyone's mind. "You fellows know Ida Pinska Mendenhall, I trust."

One man coughed. The others avoided Alfred's gaze. None looked Ida's way.

"Well, congratulations, I guess," Harley said.

"You guess right, Harley," Alfred said and took Ida's arm. They went inside to pick out some candy.

At Ida's house, Alfred made her rest on the front porch with her bag of penny candy while he filled the back of the truck with her belongings. Stripped of the curtains and clotheslines, the ramshackle place looked like one of the deserted houses of farmers who had given up and headed west for jobs. Alfred felt such sadness when he passed those houses. One in particular got to him. The owner had meticulously enclosed the orchard and garden with a fence of closely-placed boards that served as a windbreak. Abandoned, the enclosure had collected so much dirt it resembled a sandbox. The twiggy tips of the plum trees stuck out above the dust, and nothing was alive in the garden except for the blue-flowering bull nettles, which no amount of wind, dust, or sand could hinder.

Alfred loaded the truck with Ida's washtubs, scrub boards, wooden paddles, and baskets. Since she would not be able to continue her laundry business on the ranch due to the quality of the water, Ida had wanted to sell her laundry equipment, but Alfred insisted that she keep everything, just in case. The case, which he did not mention for fear of worrying her, involved starting up again in a new location.

As he loaded the boxes onto the truck, Alfred found himself pondering the future. He was a planner, a dreamer. The future felt as real and concrete as the present. That was because the future was always rich with possibilities. No more. He had not planned exactly how they were going to move, or where. He knew that eventually they would have to move, but for the moment, he just tried to get through one day, then the next.

By the end of the afternoon, Alfred had cleared out the house. The only job that remained was gathering the cats. He had never kept pets on the ranch, because of the coyotes. But when he had suggested to Ida several weeks before that she find homes for her cats in town, her eyes had filled with tears and she said, "People brought the cats to me because nobody else wanted them. They have nowhere to go." His resolve melted.

When all the cats had been gathered into two burlap bags, Alfred set the bags on the floor of the truck, by the gearshift, and they drove home.

The bags percolated with activity. The cries and moans from inside had a strangely human sound. When Alfred made a sharp turn onto the county road, the bags shifted against his leg, and he let out a cry as claws pierced through the burlap and the denim of his pant leg. It was like rubbing up against a cactus.

"My poor beauties," Ida said. "If I sing, it calms them. Do you mind?"

"Not at all."

Her voice was sweet and wild, like a bird's song. The music had a soporific effect on the cats. They stopped squirming, as if drugged.

"You have a lovely voice, Ida."

"Thank you, Mr. Bowen," she said, looking pleased. "I could never learn the words, so I just sing any old thing, but the cats don't mind."

She sang tunes his father used to sing around the campfire at Bear Park. The crotchety old man turned sentimental over the tale of the cowboy from Laredo, or the trail rider with his two-dollar horse and forty-dollar saddle. "Bury Me Not on the Lone Prairie" made him teary-eyed. Alfred could never understand how his father, who had such a hostile attitude toward the piano, could have such a deep love of song. He taught Alfred all five verses of "Home on the Range," including one that Alfred suspected his father had made up, since the mountain references didn't fit with the rest of the song:

> Oh, I love those wildflowers on this mountain of ours,
> The Steller's jays who love to scream,
> And I love the white rocks and the antelope flocks
> That graze on the mountaintops green.

As Ida sang, Alfred joined in.

He realized how much he missed music. Time was when he hummed wherever he went—in the truck, on the range, around the house. He hummed folk tunes, sonatas, popular songs. Music was such a part of his life. Recently the music had gone out of him.

They continued singing—sometimes alone, sometimes together—and for an hour, Alfred forgot about his troubles. When he reached their mailbox, he wanted to continue down the road so they could sing some more. He didn't want the feeling to stop. But when he pulled into the ranch, the urge to sing drained out of him.

Jonathan went about the ranch whistling and walking with a lighter step than before. Even his normally stone-faced demeanor could not conceal his happiness. He glowed in Ida's presence and seemed to delight in her every move.

In many ways, theirs was a good match: Jonathan's wooden face showed no emotion, and Ida's malleable features were totally transparent; Jonathan needed affection but didn't know how to ask; Ida gave it without hesitation. Despite her considerable bulk, she moved with the exuberance of a puppy. When he returned from the range, she romped toward him and covered him with kisses.

If someone had asked Virginia earlier whether these two people belonged together, she would have said no unequivocally. Her once-brilliant brother with this childlike woman? Out of the question. But in the brash ways of the heart, the match worked. In Ida, Jonathan had found someone who would never judge him, never criticize, never demand—she would only love him, and under her effusive attentions, he blossomed.

Ever since Virginia had lost her baby, the physical affection between her and Alfred had waned. There was no more silliness, no more hugs, no more teasing. He no longer picked her up from behind. She was no longer his Shoo-fly or his *bonita Cuaquerita*. The crack in their marriage had turned into a chasm, and she did not know how to bridge it. A secret, once told, could not be withdrawn, unlike love.

Being around the giddy newlyweds reminded Virginia of what she and Alfred had lost. One night, she lay on the bed beside Alfred, not touching. It had been weeks since they had made love. Apparently he had deemed her too tainted, and that's how she felt. Sounds of laughter drifted through the darkness from the bunk room. After a stretch of silence, Virginia heard a yip, like a coyote's call. Were they—could they be— She tried to stop her imagination. How did that work, with Ida's swollen belly? The fact was, two people, each with their own limitations, could still enjoy the pleasures of love. Did they have their own secret language, gestures, movements? She shuddered at her indecent curiosity and covered her head with a pillow.

During the day, Virginia longed to be alone, but there was always Ida to take care of—sweet, trusting Ida, who had no clue she was a burden. Ida was eager to please, and copied Virginia's every move. If Virginia held the broom handle with her left hand above her right, then Ida would hold the broom the same way. If Virginia cut up carrots in slices instead of sticks, Ida would cut the carrots in the same way. Virginia felt tempted to flap her arms, stick out her tongue, and walk with her hands above her head just to see if Ida would follow suit.

Ida followed her around in the two tiny rooms, like an imprinting gosling.

"Ida, honey, you don't have to stay so close. I need a little breathing room."

"Yes, Mrs. Bowen," she said and dutifully put some space between them. But it wasn't long before she forgot and moved in behind her again.

Everything about Ida irritated her: the way she chewed her food with her mouth open, the way she cleaned her ears with the end of a wooden match, the way she snorted when she laughed, the way she sat on the edge of the chair and arched her back as if trying to balance her rounded belly on the ball of her spine. Virginia tried to improve her attitude, but jealousy ate at her. Ida was having the baby she could not have. And with Ida underfoot, she was reminded of that fact every blessed moment.

Meanwhile, grief hung in the air, as thick and sticky as pollen. Some nights Virginia was startled awake by the smell of smoke. After checking the house, she returned to bed. It was at these times, after Alfred had fallen asleep, that he would appear—her fleeting child, imploring for her help to be born. Then, just as quickly, he would be gone, as insubstantial as the dust.

SIXTEEN

One autumn day after the chores were done and Alfred and Jonathan had left for work, Virginia said, "Ida, I'm going to be gone all day today."

Ida clutched the broom to her chest like a dancing partner. "Where are you going, Mrs. Bowen?"

"Please call me Virginia," she said, as she had many times before. It took many repetitions for Ida to learn. "I'm going on some private business."

"I want to go with you."

"This is not something you can do."

"But what will I do alone?" Ida said with a startled look in her eyes.

"You were alone when you lived in town."

"But I was lonely."

Virginia remembered the time before her marriage. The loneliness she felt then was preferable to what she felt now with Alfred, for her current loneliness was shaped by the memory of happiness and the knowledge that it was missing.

Virginia had decided to ask Alfred's father for a loan of hay so they could keep the calves over the winter. She needed to act before Alfred sold the calves at fall auction. She had not asked Alfred's permission, knowing he would not approve.

She toyed with the idea of asking Ida not to mention the trip, but Ida had trouble keeping instructions straight, so Virginia decided to say nothing and hope that Ida would not say anything about her absence. She would be back before supper.

As she drove west, the jagged mountains appeared at the horizon, so faint they could almost be mistaken for sky. Feathery clouds blended with the white of the snowcaps. Unlike the plains, the mountains provided a focal point—a place for the eyes to stop. She was nervous about approaching Mr. Bowen, but a loan was the only chance they had to save the ranch.

After driving for most of the morning, she reached the foothills and felt lightheaded. By the time she arrived at the ranch, she had developed a throbbing headache. Alfred's mother greeted her warmly. "We didn't know what time you'd arrive, so we went ahead and ate lunch. Can I fix you a plate?" she said.

"No thanks, but what I'd really like is an aspirin. I have a terrible headache."

"You poor dear. It's altitude sickness. It hits you if you aren't used to it. Water's the best thing."

"Thanks. That should fix me up," Virginia said. "Is Mr. Bowen here?"

"He's expecting you. You remember where the office is, don't you?"

Mr. Bowen was at the desk, going through a stack of bills. He stood up and shook her hand. "Pull up a chair," he commanded. She moved a straight-backed chair in front of the desk and felt as if she were back in school again, visiting the principal's office for some transgression.

She started off by telling him about the status of their herd and the improvements they had made to the property. A year earlier, she hadn't known the difference between a heifer and a steer, yet here she was, talking knowledgeably about their operation with a real master. He appeared to listen with interest.

After they had talked a while, he said, "So why are you telling me this? Your letter was not clear."

"I didn't mean to obscure my purpose," she said. "I just wanted to give you the background in person. The reason I'm here is to ask for a shipment of hay on loan. We will pay you back in the spring when we take the yearlings to the sale barn."

"And where is Alfred?"

"He doesn't know I'm here. He never would have asked you."

"Why not? Because he thinks too highly of himself, or too little of me?"

"He has a chip on his shoulder. Actually, I think it's more like a Rocky Mountain–sized boulder," she said with the hint of a smile.

"And you feel good coming here, behind his back?"

Her smile disappeared. He had zeroed in on her weakest point. She was being sneaky.

She drew a deep breath. "No, I don't. But this time—" She paused. Alfred would be mortified if his father had even a hint that they were on the verge of losing the ranch, so she did not tell him, though this would have strengthened her appeal. "This time I felt it was the best course of action," she said.

"You've got gumption, I'll give you that. But let me tell you something. I don't approve. A husband and wife need to be of the same mind on all the big decisions."

Her headache was back. She had brought on his condemnation. At Christmastime, she had felt some kind of connection with him, but now she saw that she was sorely mistaken.

"I agree with you generally, but—" She wanted to ask him: *What do you do when you and your spouse differ, and survival is at stake? When you see a way out and the other person— blinded by pride, hubris, or plain old stubbornness—does not?*

"But what?" Mr. Bowen said.

She felt herself starting to unravel. Gone was the confidence she had felt earlier when she discussed their ranch work. Now her request seemed like abject groveling. She needed to leave before she broke down and disgraced herself further.

"I'm sorry I bothered you with our request."

Perhaps he had never been near failure, or didn't remember what it was like. To preserve Alfred's pride, she could not tell him how close to the edge they were. It was not a fair exchange. Begging rarely was.

She got up to leave.

"Hold your horses," he said and she froze. "You make a request and you don't wait for the answer?"

"I was under the impression that you had already given it." The thought occurred to her that he was going to draw this thing out, to torture her further and teach her a lesson. She sat down, chastened.

"What do you think Alfred's going to say when a truckload of hay arrives at his doorstep and he doesn't know anything about it? Will he be angry?"

"I suspect he will be."

"But you still want the delivery?"

"Yes, sir."

"Don't 'sir' me."

"Yes, sir—I mean, Mr. Bowen." She could not so easily slip out of formality.

"And if the loan came from another source—other than me—would he still be angry?"

She thought a minute, wondering if this was a trick question.

"Don't suppose that I don't know my son," he said.

"Then you know the answer," she said, looking him level in the eye.

He began to talk of other things, and she had trouble concentrating. She had no idea if he planned to come through with the loan or not. She was also aware that it was getting late. After a while, she said, "I need to get on the road if I'm going to be back before dark."

"Well, thanks for stopping by," he said, as if she had made the three-hour drive for a friendly chat.

"And what have you decided about my request?" she said, cringing inside. It felt more uncomfortable to ask this time than the first.

"Oh, for chrissake, of course I'll do it," he said and waved his hand as if swatting at a fly. "You're kin."

"Oh, thank you so much, Mr. Bowen. We're so grateful. Thank you."

"Enough," he said impatiently. He stood up and gave out a slight groan.

"Are you okay, Mr. Bowen?" she said, getting out of her chair.

"Doggone bum leg." He hobbled toward her. "I'll arrange delivery from this end. Just keep in mind—You're the one who's going to have to bear the brunt of his anger."

"I know," she said gravely. "Your son can be very hard on people, and when they disappoint him—" A little sob escaped her lips. It caught her totally unaware. Alfred's disappointment in her had taken a terrible toll, more than she realized. Horrified, she covered her mouth with her palms and flicked away the tears with her fingers. "Pardon me, Mr. Bowen," she said and struggled to regain her composure. She had immense respect for him, and it pained her that she had displayed such untoward emotion in his presence.

"Yes, he can be. But keep in mind—he's hardest on himself." He offered her his elbow. "Now, if you wouldn't mind giving an injured old codger your arm, I'd be honored to escort you to the truck."

The following week, Alfred stopped to check the mail on his way back from the county dump. He always looked forward to mail days, when the *Denver Post* arrived. He closely tracked the national news, with President Roosevelt proposing one federal relief program after another. Italy and Germany dominated the international news. There was rarely any information about Mexico, which interested him most. The week before, he had read a front-page article that calculated 850 million tons of topsoil had been swept off the Southern Plains in the preceding twelve months. He puzzled over the statistic. Who arrived at such a figure? How had they taken measurements? And what did a ton of dust look like? He had shoveled enough of it to know that dirt was heavy. A ton wasn't as much dirt as it sounded. So maybe the estimate was not out of line.

The barren clouds hung in the sky, as useless as they were beautiful. That day, the wind moved the topsoil around. On blustery days like this, a lot of real estate changed hands. He opened the mailbox and removed the newspapers and letters. Dirt had gathered in the grooves of the corrugated-metal bottom. *Add another pound to that 850 million tons,* he thought. He looked through the mail and recognized his mother's spidery handwriting. He opened the envelope and read her letter:

Dear Son,

I hope Virginia is feeling better by now. I'm afraid she had a touch of altitude sickness. The drought has not affected us as much in the mountains. We've been blessed with a good hay crop this year, and we're happy to share it with you. We hope the delivery will tide you over until spring.

The corners of his eyes quivered, and he bit his lower lip. Had Virginia gone behind his back? That didn't sound like her. But there was no other explanation. She had gone begging to his own parents without his knowledge or permission. Anger rose in his throat like acid. Gunning the motor, he headed home, the rear tires spitting pebbles.

When he was younger, he used to cringe when he heard his

father say about a neighboring rancher, "He's no stockman." He could not bear to think of his father saying that about him. But what else could his father think, with Virginia shamelessly importuning him to bail them out. *You're no stockman.*

Virginia was in the kitchen canning tomatoes when Alfred came in with the mail. The table was covered with tomatoes of all different sizes, some misshapen, others colored with translucent yellow and green patches. The canning lids, like so many gold wafers, were boiling on the stove in a small pan beside the large blue-speckled canner.

These were the tomatoes she had saved from the hail, then babied through the season, spading around the base of each plant to allow the roots to breathe, and trudging back and forth from the windmill with buckets of water. The labor-intensive tomatoes were a luxury. Canning them was, for her, a pleasure.

Alfred threw his mother's letter on the table by the tomatoes. "What do you have to say about this?"

She wiped her hands on her apron and picked up the letter.

"Yes," she said when she finished. "I went to visit them last week." She had been waiting for a chance to broach the subject, but she had waited too long.

He took one of the hollow canning rims and squeezed. It crumpled in his hands. "How could you do this without my permission?" he said in a tone that reminded her of his father.

"I knew you'd never do it. That's why I went." She pulled an empty Mason jar out of the boiling water with tongs and began to spoon in the blanched tomatoes.

"Did it ever occur to you there's a reason I didn't ask my father for hay?"

It had, in fact, occurred to her, but she couldn't for the life of her figure out what the reason might be. He was too proud to ask his own father for help, but he was not too proud to go to the county, for that's what they would be forced to do. She couldn't imagine herself lining up in front of the post office on Tuesdays for the rice, beans, flour, and peanut butter that were distributed by the county government. Maybe he had not looked into the faces of the relief recipients, but she had—the averted eyes, the slumped posture of dismay, resignation, and shame.

"If you had a son, wouldn't you help him out?" she said.

"Of course."

"Then why won't you let your father help you?"

"I would never treat a son the way my father treats me."

She fell silent. She realized she could not talk about a hypothetical son without feeling a deep ache. He did not notice her pain, and for this she resented him.

"Your father's a rancher. He understands the pressure you're under. Besides, he's not giving us the hay. It's a loan. He knows you better than you think," she said.

"Then why didn't he offer in the first place?"

"He didn't know we needed it. In case you've forgotten, you haven't spoken to him since Christmas."

"Well, he could have guessed."

"So now he's supposed to be a mind reader?" Virginia said.

"You don't know what you're doing." His breath came hard. Maybe she had made the wrong choice in asking for help.

"I know how proud he is of you. You should have heard him bragging at Christmas. When I went to him this time, he was happy to lend us the hay," she said. Her hand trembled so much she could not get the tomatoes into the mouth of the jar.

"I don't doubt that," Alfred said bitterly. "A small price to pay for being right."

"About what?"

"That I can't make it on my own," he said.

"You've got too much pride for your own good," Virginia said.

He glared at her. "You don't understand me."

"And you don't understand him."

"I'll thank you not to meddle in my affairs," he said and left.

The following week, Alfred drove to the mountains. He hated Virginia for interfering. As if it weren't enough to be on the brink of failure. Now he had to humiliate himself further with his father. *You're no stockman.*

Alfred had been silly to think that he could make the ranch work. It had been a pipe dream. Nothing more. He had proved himself a failure, as his father would have predicted. But beaten down as he was, he still had his dignity. No one could take that away from him.

His father had an expression: "Man up to it." This involved making the tough choices, doing the right thing, taking it like a man. When Alfred was growing up, his father had used this expression for things both small and large. When Alfred whined about going outside in the subzero weather before school to break up the ice in the water tank, his father would say, "Man up to it." When he lied to his teacher about losing his homework, his father insisted that he go to her and "man up to it." And then there was the time his beloved Streaker had to be shot, when it hurt most to hear those words.

Now he was traveling to his father to man up to it. He refused to let his father think that he was the kind of man who would send his wife in his place to beg for help. He wound his way along the serpentine road as it snaked down to the valley and looped around back to the house. The aspens had turned early, their golden spangles bright against the dark evergreens. Red and gold vines twisted through the trees in the woods. Alfred could see the slashes where deer had rubbed off the bark with their antlers. A shot sounded in the woods. Already the hunters were out.

The hayfields in the valley had been mowed and stacks of loose hay, high as a house, were piled at the edges. In the mountains, hay was more important for winter feeding because snow stayed on the ground for longer stretches. His father always put off feeding hay for as long as he could. "It's just like relief," he was fond of saying. "Once you start giving it to them, you'll never get 'em off it." Now it was not the cattle but his son who would have to go on relief.

He passed a pasture of replacement calves that had been held back from market to improve the quality of the herd. Each year, his father culled out the mothers that did not bear calves or produce milk. He had a gift for breeding, and his herd was famous throughout the valley. He bred for size, ease of calving, milk production, general conformation, straightness of back, and meat production.

He drove by the outbuildings and parked in front of the house. The original log cabin, which was now the kitchen, had been purchased by his grandfather, who added a main room and a bedroom built of logs he had hewn by hand. The dark adze marks were still on the logs. When Alfred's father brought back a wife from Denver, a second story was built, and another bedroom was added when Shrine was born. Each addition had a different ceiling height and roofline. From the time Alfred was a junior in high school, he had had to duck his head to go up the stairs. When he returned from Mexico, he had forgotten how to accommodate his size to the quirks of the house, and he banged his head on the door frame. A bruise swelled above the scar Shrine had left when he hit him with a rock.

Now as Alfred stood by the front door, he did not know whether to knock or simply walk in, which rattled him more than he would have liked to admit. The door was unlocked. He pushed it open and called out. There was no answer.

In the dark hall, he looked around and waited for familiarity to wash over him, some sense of belonging, some childhood memories to make him feel at home. But everything looked alien, even the sixteen-point elk antlers that had held hats since Shrine's sixteenth birthday, when his brother had bagged the bull—one point for each of his years. Boots and galoshes were in a heap on the floor beneath the antlers. His mother had long ago given up the battle of getting the men to leave their shoes by the back door.

Alfred pulled a boot free from the bottom of the pile, upsetting the equilibrium. Several boots and galoshes tumbled down the steep sides. He held a dress boot of fine stamped leather, polished for town, though traces of mud remained on the soles.

The heel was run over. It had belonged to Shrine. That boot had been there for—how long now?—more than twenty-five years, by Alfred's calculation. That's how long Shrine had been gone. Yet everywhere he looked, there was evidence of Shrine's presence: his boots, the hat he wore to square dances, the photograph of him holding a ribbon by a prize Hereford—as if his parents had nicknamed him Shrine in preparation for what the house would become to him.

Alfred heard voices from the kitchen. *Of course,* Alfred thought. His mother was preparing a special meal in honor of his visit. He could count on her. Suddenly he felt incredibly hungry. He dropped the boot on the top of the pile—it would take another twenty-five years to make its way to the bottom—and wended his way to the kitchen. There he found his father at the table, braiding rawhide strands to make a riding whip called a quirt. A large pot was heating on the stove. Alfred watched the old man's crusty fingers agilely plait together the carefully scored strands of rawhide around the tine of a pitchfork, used as filler for the riding crop. His father did not look up from his work, and Alfred wondered if perhaps he was hard of hearing.

"I didn't expect to find you in here," Alfred said.

His father grunted by way of acknowledgment. There was no greeting, no small talk, no "How are you, how's the ranch, how's Virginia?" His father's attention was focused on a complicated twelve-strand pattern of plaiting. "You can still do that," Alfred said with admiration.

"These old fingers still have a little quick in them," his father said without looking up. Alfred watched him for a moment, unclear where to go from there. He was amazed by the old man's dexterity. Even if Alfred still used quirts—which he hadn't since Jonathan arrived at the ranch—he did not have the patience or skill to make one himself.

Alfred sat at the table in the silence, the only sound the switching of the leather strands and an occasional "Damn" from his father.

Bent over the rawhide, his father showed his balding head. He usually wore a hat, and Alfred was surprised to see how thin his hair had become. His father was not a vain man, but he had always been proud of his thick mane.

His father seemed to forget Alfred was there, and soon he began mumbling.

"Talking to yourself?" Alfred teased.

"At least I'm assured of an intelligent answer," he said.

Full of nervous energy, Alfred got up and looked in the cupboard.

"If you hold off a minute, I'll fix us something." His father had reached the delicate stage where he had to turn the rawhide strands back on one another and fold them into the end that formed the tail of the whip.

Alfred got up and paced around. "Where's Mama?"

"In town," he said and did not elaborate.

Alfred felt hurt. "When's she coming back?"

"I don't know. You should have told us you were coming." He pressed his finger to keep the plait in place while he pulled another strand around.

"You didn't get my letter?"

He shook his head.

This presented problems. In the letter, Alfred had laid the groundwork for what he was going to say. Now he would have to start from scratch.

They fell into silence again. The water boiled, and steam rose from the pot.

"I wanted to talk to you about—"

His father cut him off. "Wait. I'm almost finished here." Alfred's father had never been much of a talker, nor had he ever been able to do two things at once.

"There." His father held the riding whip up for Alfred's inspection, then got up and took several stiff steps toward the stove. "Now let's see where your mother keeps things." He dipped down on one leg, then pulled the other behind him.

"Something wrong with your leg?" Alfred said, alarmed to see him move like an old man.

"Horse threw me. Lucky it didn't require serious plaster." He dropped the quirt into the boiling water, then opened the cupboard.

He clattered around helplessly among the shelves until he found a pair of tongs. Alfred couldn't tell if the old man was addled by age or simply baffled by women's work.

"I'm sure your mother will be sorry she missed you," his father said and fished the quirt out of the water with the tongs. He tied a rock onto the end of the quirt and hung it on a hook to stretch it out. Then he took down a tin of rice.

"Now, I'm not sure what she does with this—"

"I'm not hungry. Let's go to your office," Alfred said.

The window faced south and looked out over the horse meadow. The curtains had faded under many years of exposure to the sun, which was more potent at this altitude. Bits of barks adhered to the log walls. Alfred was surprised by how much emotion the room brought back. No matter how old he grew, whenever he came back to this room he would always be nineteen and announcing to his father that he was going to college. The walls themselves had retained the memory of his father's disapproval.

On the desk was a framed photo taken on Alfred's twelfth birthday, with him and Shrine both astride Streaker.

"Do you still think about Shrine?" Alfred asked his father.

"Every day."

"Every day?" This surprised Alfred.

"Son, you wouldn't understand unless you've lost a child of your own," he said.

"I do understand." He paused and felt a stitch in his chest. "I'm just surprised it's every day."

"I remember him in my prayers."

Alfred gave a start. His father had never gone to church. Alfred didn't even know he prayed.

His father lowered himself into the desk chair and seemed unaware that he had let out a faint groan. He got out his calendar. "I believe we need to schedule a delivery."

"I didn't know Virginia came to you. It was her idea," Alfred said. "I'm sorry."

"Why be sorry?"

"She doesn't know how things are."

His father swiveled his chair around. "And how are they?"

"Each month I barely eke by, putting off the inevitable, hoping that the next month will be the month I turn the corner. Now I can't do it any more."

"So you're just going to call it quits? Is that the responsible thing to do?"

Alfred felt a convulsion of anger. He had always been the responsible brother. If his father credited him with nothing else, he would have to give him that. Shrine was the cutup, the daredevil, the irresponsible one, and his father had loved Shrine the most.

"You've always had the same damn problem," his father said, shaking his head.

When Alfred was nineteen, he would have let a remark like that pass. But not now. "I may not have succeeded, but I made a damn good run of it, starting out during the worst drought on record."

His father shook his head sadly. "You don't understand. You never have."

This riled Alfred further. He started to leave. He would not stand for this treatment.

"Sit down," his father said in the authoritarian way he had that made everyone obey. Alfred obeyed.

"What I meant was that you never believed in yourself. *That's* your problem."

"But I—I—"

"Son, why not take help where you can get it?"

"Why do you want to help me?"

"Is there anything unusual about that?"

"Then why did you throw me out?" Alfred said.

"What are you talking about?"

"When I was getting ready to leave for college, after Shrine—after he, you know—" Alfred went hoarse, then regained his voice. "You said if I walked out, it was the last time—not to bother coming back."

"Perhaps it was a moment of anger."

He was rewriting history, and Alfred would not let him get away with it.

"When I came back from Mexico and wanted to go into ranching, you didn't offer to cut me in or help me out in any way." How vividly Alfred remembered that dinner. It still stung.

"I wanted you to make it on your own. I knew you would. Then you wouldn't spend the rest of your life wondering, like I have."

Alfred searched his father's face and saw no sarcasm, no subterfuge, no stonewalling. He was speaking the truth as he saw it.

Alfred was taken aback. His father had never expressed any doubts about his own abilities. But he hadn't started the ranch on his own; he had inherited it from Alfred's grandfather.

Alfred looked across the meadow. The willows had not yet turned color. He thought of all the years he had believed his father to be too arrogant, too proud, or too self-absorbed to forgive his son, while all the time, at the root of his father's actions, there had been a deep self-doubt. This realization shook Alfred to the core. If he had so badly misunderstood his father, how well could he know himself?

"So will you accept delivery?" his father said. He reached over to shake Alfred's hand and seal the deal.

"We're both too old for that," Alfred said and clasped him to his chest.

SEVENTEEN

Alfred rode his horse along the ridge with the wind at his back. His mind churned. The hubris had been knocked out of him. By carrying a grudge, he had lost valuable years with his father. Who knew what might otherwise have developed between them? It was not too late, but past years could not be replaced. He had thought he knew his father better than he did. He had thought he knew Virginia better than he did. He would not repeat the same mistake with her.

His pride and jealousy had separated him from his wife at a time when they most needed each other. He couldn't save the ranch without her. Or rather, he could but didn't want to. Their lives were like two separate strands woven together to make a rope that was stronger for being entwined.

A little farther along the ridge, he came upon a mound of stones he had never noticed before. At first he thought it was a campfire that someone had carefully covered to prevent from spreading. But when he got off his horse and took a closer look, he realized that this was no haphazard pile of stones. Each one had been thoughtfully placed to create a sturdy structure that would withstand years of wind, snow, and—in the good years— rain. This was not a land that gave up stones easily. Several generations ago, someone had searched far and wide for enough rocks to make a gravestone.

A wavering wedge of geese honked overhead, draping their purple shadows across the plains. Sprays of silver-green graced the coulees where the Russian olives grew. The morning light raced along the backs of the grass, which bent over and caught the sun in different ways, creating shimmering variations. The prairie was always in motion. Beautiful and innocent under the golden sun, it could turn cruel in an instant. Brave pioneers had passed over these lands in wagon trains, the promise of a new world glimmering before them. They had endured hardships more grueling than anything he had encountered, and their perseverance had made things easier for those that came after them. Alfred's life was built on their backs. The pyramid of progress: his mother and father, his four grandparents, eight great-grandparents, and on and on, backward in time, each generation benefiting from the labors of the last. Along the way, there were deaths, and this humble pile of stones honored one of those deaths: a father or a mother, a husband or a wife. Or perhaps—and it was this thought that made Alfred's heart clutch—a child.

Suddenly he felt a strong urge to be with Virginia. Not at lunch, not after work, but right then. He jumped on his horse and sped home. He found Virginia in her chair, staring blankly into the room. She looked up.

"What is thee doing home at this odd hour?" she said.

"I want to be with you."

And then he did something he had never done before. He put his head in her lap and cried.

* * *

She had gotten her husband back. He had forgiven her. While this unmerited gift did not cure their problems, it made them feel so much more manageable. The arithmetic of love defied intuition: only when given away did it multiply. Their reconciliation confirmed something that had been building inside, deep and indestructible, that bound them together.

As the months passed, Ida's belly continued to grow. Her ankles swelled up so much that she had to wear her oxfords without shoelaces and walked without lifting her feet from the floor. Her face was puffy, and her wrists were cinched in like the joints of balloon animals. The swelling worried Virginia, but otherwise Ida was in fine health.

They spent Christmas together at the house, which they decorated with a one-sided scrub cedar cut from a nearby bluff. Ida surprised Virginia and Alfred with knitted scarves. Virginia had no idea when Ida could have stolen the time to knit them. But she was touched by the gift.

It was a bitter cold winter. For a month after Christmas, the temperature did not rise above freezing, even during the day. One morning in late January, Virginia came up from the root cellar with a pail of potatoes. "I feel moisture in the air," she told Ida. "I think we're in for some snow."

After Virginia peeled the potatoes, Ida offered to help cut them. Virginia gave her the cutting board and showed her how to do it. Ida eyed the potato, then carefully positioned the blade above it. After a nod of approval from Virginia, Ida drew a deep breath and brought the knife down, creating a perfect slice.

Ida was concentrating so hard on the next slice that she did not look up when Jonathan came into the kitchen. "I'm headed to town, Sis. Have you got the errand list ready?" He slipped a slice of raw potato into his mouth and crunched down.

"Don't," Ida said crossly and pouted. "That was my sample."

"Here, I'll make you another," Virginia said and quickly cut another slice. She jotted down a list of the errands for Jonathan. Alfred needed vaccine for the cattle. The truck needed gas. "Ida, do you have any dirty clothes to add to the laundry?" she said. Ida shrugged. Now that Ida was out of the laundry business, she didn't show enough interest in it even to gather her dirty clothes together for Jonathan to take to town. Virginia handed Jonathan the list and got the laundry for him. As he headed out the door, she said, "Oh, I forgot about stamps. You know how mother worries if she doesn't hear from us every week." He returned with the list and she made the addition.

After he left, Ida showed Virginia the potato slices she had cut. "How am I doing?" she asked.

"You're doing fine," said Virginia.

Ida cocked her head and scrutinized the slices. She wore her skirt unhooked and rolled at the waistband. The apron that was tied under her breasts barely covered her belly. "Are you sure?" Ida said.

"Of course. They don't have to be perfect," Virginia said.

"But if it's not good enough, you'll tell me, won't you?" Ida said.

"You're not going to find anyone in this crew who'll refuse to eat a potato just because it's misshapen. It'll taste just as good."

Ida pondered this for a moment but was still not satisfied.

"But if I don't do it right, will you make me leave?"

"Leave where?"

"Home."

"Good heavens, no. What ever gave you that idea?"

"My stepmother. I wasn't clever enough for her."

Virginia looked at Ida, her shoulders sloped down, her eyes fixed on the potato in front of her, and tried to imagine how hard it must have been for her when she was forced to fend for herself in town. For the first time, she admired Ida's strength.

She pulled up a chair beside Ida. "You know your cats. Would you ever turn one out?"

"Oh, no. Never."

"Well, you're part of the family now, and nobody's going to turn you out."

"Really?" A bright smile came over Ida's face. She put her arms around Virginia and gave her a warm hug.

"My baby is a grasshopper," Ida said. "Feel." She arched her back and pushed her stomach forward.

Virginia placed her hands lightly over Ida's belly. Through the apron, she could feel little jumps against her palm.

"I do believe your baby has the hiccups."

"Really?"

"That's what it feels like to me."

Ida placed her hands next to Virginia's and waited. "It tickles," she said and started giggling. Virginia joined her.

Some time shortly before dawn the next morning, snow began to fall. When Virginia went to the outhouse to empty the chamber pot, her footfalls indented the fuzzy snow cover. She loved the clean look of fresh snow and the tickle of the flakes against her cheeks. She paused a moment to listen to the lovely sound of snowfall—which was no sound at all, really, but neither was it silence. It was too cold to tarry long.

She did the chores and fixed breakfast. Midmorning, as Ida swept the kitchen, a low moan escaped her lips, and her hand slipped along the shaft of the broom.

"Are you feeling poorly?" Virginia asked.

Ida started sweeping again. "I feel all right, I guess."

"Is it the baby?"

"He's been acting up of late."

"Here, let me fix you a cup of tea. That will fortify you," Virginia said. She cleared off the papers from her reading chair so Ida could sit down.

"No, I'll just keep working. It helps keep my mind—" She stopped as another wave of pain tightened her features.

"This is one time you can allow yourself to be pampered," Virginia said and led her to the chair.

It was early, awfully early, for Ida to be having labor pains. The midwife had predicted the end of February, beginning of March. Of course, a due date was not an exact science. Still, this was not a good sign. Perhaps it was a false alarm.

To be safe, Virginia took Ida to see the midwife, who lived a fifteen-minute drive over dirt roads and then ten more over blacktop. The midwife was a short plug of a woman with tight coils of gray hair like a pot scrubber and crooked fingers that were still agile enough to allow her to deliver most of the babies in Trinity County. She examined Ida and predicted that she would give birth in a week.

Virginia was not reassured. When they returned home, she made Ida sit in the chair with her feet up. "Now when you feel a change, you let me know," she said.

The snow continued falling all morning. It was hard to believe anything that light could fall so fast. Already the tracks Virginia and Ida had left in the snow upon returning from the midwife had filled in.

Virginia decided to pass the time by reading to Ida from *Bleak House*—a luxury usually reserved for the evening. Dickens was the only author the entire family could agree on, and they had filled many evenings listening to the story. Ida was illiterate, and Jonathan read so haltingly that even Ida became impatient when it was his turn to read aloud, so by general agreement the task of reading fell to Alfred and Virginia. Alfred's reading voice was flat as the prairie, yet Virginia loved to listen to him. Some neighbors in the county had radios, and at Dave's General Store they would gather to discuss recent episodes of *Amos 'n' Andy*. But Virginia had no desire for a radio. She much preferred the human voice to a disembodied actor's voice coming from a box.

While Ida knitted, Virginia picked up the story where they had left off the night before. She would fill in Alfred and

Jonathan later. She read with great liveliness, making a special effort to dramatize the story. She adopted a low bass voice for Jarndyce, the owner of Bleak House, and a girlish, vulnerable voice for Esther, his ward. Now that only Ida was present, she even tried out an English accent. Every so often, Ida's knitting needles stopped clicking and she tucked her hands under her and squeezed the bottom of her thighs. Virginia would put her finger in the book and wait for Ida to pick up her needles after the pain had passed, before beginning to read again.

After one pain, Ida said, "Am I doing okay? I want this to be just right. I don't want to mess this up."

"You're doing just fine," Virginia said and patted her on the arm.

By late afternoon, Ida's pains started getting sharper and closer together. Virginia helped Ida across the snow-covered yard to her bed. Before long, Jonathan and Alfred would return from work—not a moment too soon—and could go fetch the midwife, who had clearly miscalculated: there was no way this baby would wait for a week, though whether it would come in thirty minutes or thirty hours, Virginia had no idea.

The room was overheated. Virginia cracked a window, but snow blew in and she quickly shut it. At least the snow kept down the dust. She had been worrying for weeks about the sanitary conditions for the baby's birth.

Virginia was afraid Ida would protest when she shooed several cats out the door, but Ida was tossing and turning on the bed and didn't notice. When the pain got to be too much, she let out a cry and put a pillow over her face to muffle it.

Virginia pulled the pillow gently away. "Don't do that, honey. You're going to smother yourself and the baby. It's okay to cry out. If it helps you, take this." She gave her a clean pillowcase and showed her how to put it between her teeth.

As Virginia set a kettle of water to boil on the woodstove, Ida's water broke. Virginia remade the bed and bundled the sheets in the corner.

Ida's face was sweating, red from exertion. Virginia felt Ida's forehead. It was burning hot. She pulled a chair up to Ida's bedside and sponged cool water on her face to make her more comfortable.

Before long, Ida bit into the pillowcase, grunted, and thrashed her head about.

"Make it stop," she said, panting.

"Honey, I would if I could. But it'll be over before you know it, and a beautiful baby will make you forget the pain."

"I don't want a baby anymore."

"Come on, we'll get through this."

Before Ida could respond, a heart-wrenching cry escaped her lips.

At that moment, Jonathan came through the door. When he saw his wife writhing in pain, he dropped the bridles he was carrying and jerked Virginia from the bedside. "You're hurting her. Stop hurting her," he said.

"She's okay. This is perfectly normal." Virginia tried to sound as if she had everything under control, but her voice was shaky.

"No she's not, and you know it."

Ida arched her back and let out another terrifying sound.

Jonathan moved toward Virginia, his body coiled and ready to strike. His face conveyed rank panic, and she knew that he had slipped into one of his states when his mind came unhinged and he could not focus or think; all he could do was feel. She had seen him like that once or twice, but she did not know how far he would go. She felt a deep sense of foreboding.

"Listen carefully, Jonathan," she said as she inched toward the door. She spoke in calm tones, as she would to a snarling dog. "I need you to go get the midwife. Do you understand?" She spoke very slowly.

"You're trying to get rid of me."

Ida let out a long grunt, and blood dribbled from between her legs. When Jonathan saw the dark wet spot on the sheets, he bolted for the door, leaned out, and vomited into the snow beside the steps. Virginia gave him a shove from behind, but he wedged his boot in the crack and came back in before she could close the door.

Now she was afraid she had really upset him. Matted strands of hair lay damp on his forehead, and his toe tapped the floor in intense agitation. His reddened eyelids twitched, and his eyes conveyed a feral alarm. He brought his face close to hers and spoke in barking phrases she could not make out.

He pushed her so hard she fell to the floor, which was muddy from the tracked-in snow. The kettle started to whistle, adding to the chaos. *Please come, Alfred, please come,* Virginia repeated to herself. Unwilling to take her eyes off Jonathan, she moved along the floor on her bottom, crablike, with her arms behind her, feeling for the iron leg of the bed.

Jonathan overturned a row of cat bowls as he moved the rocker to the door, blocking Virginia's exit.

Crouched against the wall at the foot of the bed, Virginia kept her body perfectly still. She did not want to call attention to herself or catch his eye. A black cat that had escaped her eviction rubbed against her. The kettle screeched on the stove. Ida twisted on the bed, caught in her own world of pain. Virginia held onto Ida's foot so as to offer the comfort of human touch.

Jonathan was now rocking maniacally in front of the door. He stared straight ahead as the rocker plunged forward, then swung back at unnatural speeds.

The overheated room smelled of blood, cats, and sweat. The shrieking kettle did not drown out Ida's cries, each higher pitched than the last, urgently climbing the scale. Jonathan covered his ears and held his elbows outward like wings as he rocked and rocked, letting out a low steady noise from his throat to block out Ida's pain.

He was not himself. He had entered a state of pure fear. Somehow the idea that Virginia was hurting Ida had set off a flood of primitive feelings. He would rock himself out of this state, if only Ida could wait. But the baby was waiting for no one.

The sheets were bunched up at Ida's feet. As Ida lifted her bottom off the bed, Virginia looked up through the iron railings and saw, between Ida's legs, the crown of the baby's wet head. She would have to act now. It would not do to be in a state of excitability. Jonathan was feeding off her mood. If she composed herself, he might calm down.

From her crouched position, Virginia looked over at her brother, who was rocking furiously. In an instant, a picture came back to Virginia, and she was back in the dark hall of their house in North Carolina where, unnoticed, she had peered into a shadowy room and watched her brother on his hobby horse.

And it came back to her that here, about to be born, was a Mendenhall child, a link from the past to the future, not her genes, but her blood, her family. And Jonathan didn't seem as threatening anymore.

Ida let out a long grunt, and the top of the baby's head pushed out a bit farther. Now Virginia had the courage to get up from the floor.

"That's it. Attagirl. You're doing it," Virginia said to Ida, the fear gone, replaced with certainty and wonder. She could do this. She would do this. They would all get through it.

Possessed of calm, Virginia approached her brother and put her hand on his forearm. "Jonathan, your baby is about to be born, but I can't do it without your help."

The rocking slowed, and his body relaxed. "You mean you need me?" he said.

"Yes. I need you to saddle up Sassy and go find Alfred."

"What about the midwife?"

"There's no time. This baby has a mind of its own."

After Jonathan left, she washed up, elevated Ida's bottom with a pillow, and positioned herself at the foot of the bed. Ida's face turned a purplish red as she grunted and bore down. With each push, the baby's head emerged, inch by agonizing inch.

"You've got it, now come on," Virginia said, but Ida seemed worn down. Her cries were weaker now, and a fever set in. Just when Virginia was worried that Ida would exhaust herself before the baby was out, Ida gave one final, determined push. All at once the baby emerged, gray and unimaginably, impossibly small. It was a girl. She did not make a sound, did not move. Virginia held her breath. Then came a sharp hack, followed by a cry, surprisingly loud for such a tiny creature, and Virginia let out a joyful sigh. "Ida, you have a daughter. A perfect baby daughter," she said.

Birth was not a miracle. Life itself was the miracle—that people carried on, against all odds, in the face of hardship, sadness, death and the rare moments of elation that made it all worthwhile. In that moment, religion seemed very simple to her: the Lord gives; we thank.

Virginia did the best job she could with the umbilical cord. Then she washed the baby and laid her on Ida's chest. Ida stared at the mewling infant and whispered weakly, "She's mine?"

Virginia lifted Ida's hand and put it around the newborn, but Ida's hand flopped to the side.

Virginia was alarmed. All the color had drained from Ida's face, and she was listless, barely aware of what was going on around her. Virginia patted her cheeks softly. "Ida, look at me. How are you feeling?" Ida closed her eyes, and her head rolled to the left. "Don't go to sleep now. Just stay with me."

Virginia propped Ida up on her hip, then laid the infant on the bed next to Ida's breast. The child nosed her mother's nipple, not seeming to know what to do, then latched on and started sucking. Ida looked at the child through half-closed eyes but was too weak to respond.

Virginia felt a glimmer of terror. She didn't know what to do and in what order. Her concern for the child was now replaced with concern for the mother.

Where were Alfred and Jonathan? If only they would come. Ida was barely conscious and breathing shallowly. Virginia had to get her to the doctor, but that was an hour's drive away. The midwife was only thirty minutes away, if she could just get that far.

Virginia moved quickly, knowing that every moment counted.

Outside, it was bitter cold and the snow came down furiously. Smoke from the chimney fused with the blurry white of the falling flakes. Already the bunk-room stairs were hidden under the drifts. It was a blizzard, for sure.

Virginia cleaned off the truck windshield and started the motor to let the cabin warm up. There was still a little daylight left. If they set out now, they could make it to the midwife's by dark.

She rushed around the house gathering the things she needed. She brought a Mason jar of milk and bread for Ida, who would be hungry if she roused. She brought quilts and diapers for the baby. She checked the back of the truck to make sure the chains were there if she needed them. She prayed that in her haste, she would not forget anything essential. She left Alfred a note saying that she planned to spend the night in town or at the midwife's. They would not be able to drive back in this storm.

Virginia wasn't strong enough to carry Ida to the car, so she wrapped her in quilts and dragged her, leaving a trail in the snow. She managed to get Ida into the passenger seat and propped her upright. Virginia stuffed a wooden crate full of blankets and nestled the newborn there, on the seat between them.

They set out. Virginia had to slide the crate closer to her in order to shift into fourth gear. The road was hidden beneath the snow, but she had gotten good at following the contours of the land, driving on the high ground between the bar ditches. It was a skill she had picked up when dust, instead of snow, covered the road. Now, however, with no sun and no shadows, it was harder to read the land, and as the sun fell farther, it would be harder still.

The wheels slipped a bit, but she wasn't worried about running into another car. No one used this road except the mailman, and he wasn't due for another day.

Outside, the fields were downy, the air pristine. Inside, the truck cabin was warm and cozy.

The infant slept quietly in the crate beside her. She was not born with a squashed face like most newborns. The baby's face was delicate and serene, as if, by necessity, she had emerged from the womb a little further along than most.

Virginia glanced over at Ida and felt relieved when she saw the blankets gently lift up and recede. The sleeping mother and child seemed so peaceful that Virginia almost forgot her sense of emergency.

"We're going to be all right, girls," Virginia said to her sleeping passengers. She felt flush with optimism and still elated from the birth.

When they got to the blacktop, Virginia had to make a decision: right, to the midwife, or left, to the doctor? The midwife was closer, but Virginia was unsure of her since the mistaken prediction of birth. And she was certain Ida needed serious medical attention. So she turned left, toward town.

About ten minutes further on, the road got slicker and several times the truck fishtailed. The small of Virginia's back tensed up and her shoulders tightened. The driving was more difficult now. Had she chosen the midwife, they would be there by now.

She didn't want anything to interrupt their forward progress, but when she veered off the road and almost lost control of the truck, she realized she could not make it without chains on the tires.

She stopped the truck and got out. The frigid air made the hairs in her nose stiffen up. She was wearing Alfred's boots and an old sheepskin coat that had hardened and cracked at the elbows. She covered her mouth with the scarf Ida knitted, and got out the chains. The cold of the metal pierced through her cloth gloves. The chains went on easily, and she felt a slight moment of pride. A year earlier, she would not have thought herself capable of putting on chains.

Now the wheels held more securely to the road. After she had been traveling for another five minutes, she felt the truck surge forward, then coast along, then catch and glide forward again. Finally, it rolled to a stop. The headlights made weak tunnels into the falling snow. What could possibly be wrong? She turned the key. The engine turned over but did not catch. The heater kept blowing, but now cold air came from the vents. She let the truck rest for a minute and tried again. Then she caught a glimpse of the dashboard.

"Jonathan!" she cried aloud as the terrible realization sank in: they had run out of gas.

She laid her forehead on the steering wheel. Then she sat up and took a deep breath. "Stay calm," she told herself. "You'll think of something." It was too dangerous to let emotions over-take her now.

She watched the flakes alight on the windshield and disap-pear in streaks down the still-warm glass. Why hadn't she checked the gas? She knew how unreliable Jonathan was. From this one innocent mistake, the consequences were—they were—she couldn't think about it now.

From beside her on the seat came a tiny squeak, muffled by the blanket.

"Ssshh. It's going to be all right," Virginia said. With her thumb she rubbed the soft part of the newborn's head, where her skull had not yet come together. The pale fuzz was so sparse she couldn't even tell what color it was—blond like Ida's or dark like Jonathan's.

She wanted to get everyone fed and strong while there was still heat in the cabin. She leaned over the crate and shook Ida gently. Ida stirred and let out a low moan but did not open her eyes. "Here, Ida. I want you to take this. It'll give you strength." She put the jar of milk to Ida's lips and poured. It dribbled down her chin. Virginia wiped Ida's mouth.

"Okay, Ida. I'm going to give you the baby. I'll hold her."

She loosened Ida's clothing and put the baby to Ida's breast, but this seemed to agitate Ida and she twisted and groaned, almost knocking the child.

The baby started to cry. Virginia lifted the child to her own chest. "Come on, sweetheart, bless your little heart. You're mommy's sick and you're hungry and I don't have any milk to give you." She was unsure how much nutrition the infant had gotten from Ida immediately after birth, or how much she needed. Virginia unscrewed the jar of milk, dipped her finger in, then put it in the baby's mouth. The newborn wouldn't get much milk, but maybe this would keep her from getting dehydrated.

Snug in the crook of Virginia's arm, the infant slurped and sucked on Virginia's wet finger. After a while, Virginia placed the baby on her shoulder and patted her back. The joyous belch of life.

The truck cabin lost temperature rapidly. Jonathan had forgotten to deliver the laundry while he was in town, and the bundle was stuffed on the floor of the passenger side. Virginia untied it and separated out the dirtiest clothes. One thing about ranching—the dirty clothes were exceptionally filthy. She used the jackets and jeans that were stiff with manure and blood to line the well of the driver's side. This stopped the cold air from blowing up through the ring of space around the clutch and the brake. She wadded up clothes and placed them along the back window for insulation. Shirts she stuffed in the crack of the window, the way she did at home on bad dust days. She put a pair of crusty jeans on under her skirt. Alfred's boots were loose enough to fit several pairs of extra socks. She stuffed laundry between Ida and the door, then piled extra clothes on top of Ida's inert form. The cleanest clothes she stuffed around the baby.

Time passed, and the infant was mercifully quiet. Ida's silence made Virginia nervous. Virginia frequently beamed the flashlight on Ida to check her breathing. At least she was not getting worse.

Later in the night, the child woke up wailing. Virginia took off her glove and stuck a finger down the child's backside. Sure enough, her tiny diaper was wet. Virginia didn't dare put on another one—her cold hands were too clumsy for the fine work of safety pins. She took off the wet diaper and put it on the dashboard.

The windshield was now completely white, and snow climbed up the side windows. They were encapsulated in snow. Virginia thought of the tombs of the ancient Egyptian pharaohs who were buried with all the belongings they would need in the afterlife. What would an archaeologist make of this rag-stuffed capsule?

She dared not go to sleep—she had to be vigilant and watch over the baby and Ida. To keep herself awake, she kept up a constant patter. When she wasn't talking, she sang songs her mother had sung to her—"Itsy Bitsy Spider," "Old MacDonald," "Farmer in the Dell"—or was it vale? Her voice was small and cold. The notes came out on a pillow of fog. Some songs, she could remember the rhythm but not the words, so she made up nonsense syllables.

The temperature kept dropping. Ice formed on the inside of the window. Her ears hurt. She used a tea towel to tie down the sheepskin flaps of Alfred's cap.

While the mother and child slept, an eerie quiet filled the cab. The light was strange—darker than day but lighter than night. She could not move her toes, but she could still move her legs, so she stomped down on the clutch and the brake, alternating rapidly, trying to get some feeling back in her feet.

She must have drifted off to sleep, because she awoke with a start and for a moment didn't know where she was. She looked through the opaque windshield and made out two blurry plates of light. She rolled down the window. Snow fell into the truck cabin. Summoning her strength, she yelled into the darkness. She was met by silence. And darkness. There was no light. There was no car. There was no one coming to rescue them. She had imagined the whole thing.

The commotion brought Ida out of her stupor. She opened her eyes a crack, moved her head from side to side, and mumbled nonsense phrases. The baby started to howl.

"You're hungry. Poor thing. You've been good for so long. Virginia reached for the flashlight and heard something clack against the windshield. It was the diaper, frozen solid.

She got her fingers around the flashlight, but knew only by looking that she held something in her hand. She had become disconnected from her body.

Virginia pointed the beam of light around the truck's cabin. She located the jar of milk by the gearshift, but it had frozen. She put the jar between her thighs to thaw it.

"Don't cry, sweetheart," she said. "I'm doing the best I can." A few tears turned Virginia's eyelashes brittle, and she realized how dangerous crying was. She checked the baby's eyes. They were dry. The infant had not yet started to produce real tears.

The milk was not melting. To speed the process, she held the jar against the side of her neck. Chill darts spiked down her back. Virginia gritted her teeth and held the cold glass there a little longer. She could only stand it for a short stretch at a time. In between, she put her naked palm against her neck to transfer some warmth.

Virginia felt chilled to the core. Even her internal organs ached. If she felt that way, what must the cold be doing to a newborn, with lungs the size of robin's eggs? Ida's extra weight would protect her from the cold, but the loose skin of the tiny newborn provided no insulation whatsoever. Now Virginia's worry shifted from mother to child.

The milk remained a solid mass, but enough liquid thawed along the edges of the jar so Virginia could wet her finger. The baby showed no interest in sucking. When Virginia put her finger to the baby's mouth, she tossed her tiny head and bawled, inconsolable.

"You're cold, aren't you? It's no fun being out here, is it?"

She took off her other glove, cupped both hands over her nose and mouth, and breathed into the enclosed space. When her hands were warm, she placed the concave pockets of her palms against the baby's soft cheeks and curled her fingers over the top of her head. Soon the baby stopped crying.

Virginia remembered how, on the coldest nights, she snuggled up to Alfred, skin to skin; how his body glowed like a warm coal and protected her from the cold more than any number of layers could. Virginia realized that the warmth of the human skin might keep them alive.

She fumbled with her own clothing to loosen it, then placed the infant against her bare skin. The child's downy head fit under her chin. Against her skin, she could feel the rise and fall of the infant's chest.

Virginia felt a warm liquid sliding down her stomach, and she started laughing. It was a sign of life. Even in these difficult hours, the baby did what babies do.

"You're going to be just fine," she said. The vibration of her voice seemed to soothe the infant, who drifted peacefully off to sleep. It was hard to believe the tiny weight against her chest could evoke such emotion—love so strong it felt like heartburn.

It must have been toward morning when the child woke up and started coughing. "I can't do anything for you, sweetheart. We've just got to make it through 'til someone finds us."

Virginia felt the infant's tiny chest hardened, then her rib cage pushed off from Virginia's chest as she emptied herself of air in fierce eruptions. A string of coughs left the baby exhausted and gasping for air. With each tightening of the muscles came a violent expelling of breath. Against her bare skin, Virginia felt each explosion as if were part of her own body.

Ida was still in a stupor. Stretches of snoring were interspersed with low moans. It was a blessing that Ida didn't know what was going on.

Virginia tried everything she could think of to soothe the child. She bounced her, rocked her, patted her back, sang to her. Nothing worked. Virginia felt completely undone.

"You're a real little trouper. You can do it," she said, but she found it harder and harder to keep up the comforting patter.

She had never thought of coughing as a violent act, but now she had no doubt that it was. She felt the infant's stomach harden as she expelled air with a ferocious thrust. Her unformed muscles clenched in an act of unimaginable intensity.

The child was coughing so hard she could barely breathe. Then the coughs began to weaken, like a windup toy running down.

Virginia prayed. She decided to ask for something small and specific—that the coughing stop—instead of something large, a trick she had learned at Christmas as a child, when she noticed that if she asked for something large, like skates, she would not get it, but if she asked for something small, like socks, she was never disappointed.

The coughing stopped, and they both slept. Toward morning, Virginia awoke and saw a bobbing light. Convinced she was hallucinating again, she tried to lean forward but felt a lump at her chest, as if she had grown a new heart overnight. Confusion overtook her. She closed her eyes. Soon there was a knock at the window, and a gloved hand cleared a circle on the glass. A face appeared.

It was Alfred. He had hitched up the team to the sled and had come to get her. He opened the door. Jonathan was standing behind him, out of Virginia's sight.

"It is thee," was all Virginia could say.

"Jonathan told me about the gas. He didn't remember until this morning."

Jonathan pushed Alfred aside and blubbered. "How's Ida? How's my daughter?"

Virginia clutched the baby to her. "Don't touch her," she snapped. Weakness had eroded her diplomacy. He recoiled as if electrocuted. One look at Jonathan's face, and she realized the hurt she had caused.

Alfred made his way to the passenger side and checked on Ida. "She's weak but still holding on," he said.

Jonathan and Alfred set to work with a broom and a shovel to dig out the truck. They filled the gas tank with a gallon of gas they had brought from home. They cranked the engine.

"Jonathan, you drive them to town and I'll take the team back," Alfred said.

"Please, Alfred. Will you go with us?" Her weak voice was barely audible.

"But Jona—"

"Please," she said.

Jonathan looked at her and then turned away. His bottom lip trembled and his eyes changed shape. His absent expression still conveyed a bone-chilling shame.

Alfred looked at him, uncomfortable. "Does that suit you?"

Jonathan said nothing but leapt up behind the team and steered the horses toward home.

The cabin was getting warm, but Virginia had lost all feeling in her fingers and toes. The heat caused shooting pains to radiate through her limbs. She felt prickly all over, as if her entire body had fallen asleep. The pain increased as she warmed up, and she could not stop shaking. Ida's face was drained of any color, but her fever was gone. The baby cried and coughed a little but seemed unchanged by the harrowing evening.

She knew the child would be all right. Anyone as resilient as this baby would not easily succumb to cold. Throughout the night, the infant had maintained the unflappable surety she was born with. Virginia had once had that kind of faith. Once.

In town, Virginia waited while the doctor attended to Ida and the baby. When he came back to examine Virginia, she was too weak to talk. Alfred asked the doctor about Ida.

"She's one lucky lady," the doctor said. "The cold air may have actually helped keep the fever down."

"And the baby?" Virginia was able to utter with her last strength.

"I wouldn't have guessed the little critter could survive, but she's going to be all right."

Alfred looked proudly at Virginia. "She saved the baby's life."

Virginia did not respond, but she knew the truth: it was the baby that had saved hers.

EIGHTEEN

The doctor put Ida and the baby in the hospital in Fort Morgan for a week for observation. Ida's infection cleared up rapidly with medication and proper care. As she regained her strength, the nurses taught her how to care for her daughter. The doctor predicted that the baby would probably be susceptible to colds all her life, but that otherwise she had suffered no lasting damage. After a week she was growing and thriving.

When Alfred brought them back to the ranch, Jonathan was waiting on horseback at the mailbox. He galloped alongside the truck for the half mile to the house. While Ida took the infant to the house, he hitched Sassy and came inside, taking the three steps of the stoop in a single leap.

"Here, your papa wants to feast his eyes on you," Ida said. She placed the baby on her back, on Virginia and Alfred's bed. The baby's sparse hair stuck to her head in downy swirls.

Jonathan clasped his hands behind him and leaned over to examine the gurgling infant. She folded up her pudgy legs and kicked, active and alert. Her tiny hands curled up the way plants turn in on themselves in a drought to avoid losing moisture to the sun.

"Woo," Jonathan said, rocking on his heels. "Woo woo."

He burrowed a finger into the child's fist and gently unfurled her hand. He counted the fingers. Beaming, he turned to Ida and said, "She's perfect."

"Go on. Pick her up," Virginia said.

He backed up and said, "Oh, no. I couldn't do that. No, no." He looked around the room, as if ready to bolt.

"Sure you can. You're her papa," Virginia said.

"What if I drop her?"

"You're not going to drop her. Just cup your hand under her head. Here, I'll help you," Virginia said. She had not forgiven herself for snapping at Jonathan in the snowstorm. But he did not seem to remember the incident. That was one good thing about his faulty memory: he never carried a grudge.

She wrapped the blanket around the baby and gave her to Jonathan. Then she showed him how to support the baby's head with his hand. He pulled his daughter to his shoulder and crooked his cheek against her tiny head. A look of unadulterated joy crossed his face.

"My, my," he said and laughed. He moved his head back so he could see the child's face. She squinted at him. He laughed again. "Well, I'll be," he said and made a face.

"You know what she really likes to do?" Virginia said, smiling. "It's something you're really good at."

"What could that be?" Jonathan said.

"Rock."

They named the baby Amanda, after Jonathan's mother, but Amanda was too big a name for such a small child, so they called her Mindy. Ida was a doting and attentive mother. Giving love unstintingly was something she knew how to do. When Virginia watched Ida with her daughter, snuffling, kissing, and playing, she understood the purity of a mother's love—a love that existed in some perfect realm where intelligence or responsibility did not matter.

The weeks passed quickly. As Virginia grew more comfortable leaving Mindy alone with Ida, she began to spend part of each day on the range with Alfred and Jonathan, returning each evening in time to fix supper. She loved working outdoors. She now felt a deep kinship with the land and a bond with the livestock—connections born of hard work and long hours. When calving season came around, she was at Alfred's side.

By May, the yearlings had fattened up and were ready to be herded to Brockton. Virginia was pleased that Alfred deemed her competent enough to help him make the two-day cattle drive on horseback over back roads and trails. Jonathan stayed home to look after the rest of the herd. Virginia wouldn't have missed this trip for anything. Their future—whether they could keep the ranch—was riding on the price the yearlings commanded at the sale barn. Alfred's father had carried them through the winter, and now nothing would save them but a solid price for their yearlings. And that price would be determined by factors beyond their control: who came to buy cattle on that particular day, who bid against each other, who was out having coffee when the Bowens' lot went on the block.

If Alfred was nervous, he did not let on. There was too much work to do. They gathered the yearlings from different parts of the ranch and checked the draws and gullies, making sure none was left behind. On the morning of the drive, they eased the yearlings out of the holding pasture and onto the dirt lane. The trick was to keep the cattle moving slowly. Any unnecessary exertion would cause them to lose weight, and now every pound counted.

They rode by fields of sun-fragrant sage, past the Ebberson place, and the Munsen ranch. When they turned onto a trail through the open grasslands, Alfred rode point. She brought up the rear, nudging along the lazy yearlings who stopped to tear at the tender grasses in the swales or lie down in the shade of the junipers. She skirted the rocky stretches of the trail—the sandy soil farther out was kinder on the horse's feet. The animals lumbered along, each one kicking up dust for the next. Straggled out across the plains, the herd looked bigger than it was.

Alfred was so far ahead that she lost sight of him, but this did not make her nervous. She had a new confidence in her abilities. As she rode along, she had ample time for reflection and was lulled into tranquility by the sounds of the wind through the grasses, the bovine grinding of molar on molar, and the guttural belching, punctuated by the occasional reassuring plop of bodily waste.

Two years earlier, she could never have imagined herself herding cattle across the prairie. Quakers had long acknowledged a close relationship between physical effort and spiritual awareness. This idea was at the heart of the Quaker work camps and the Appalachian child-feeding program. But up until now, Virginia had never made the connection with ranch work. Now she realized how putting her heart and soul into hard physical labor had taught her things that no amount of sedentary contemplation would. Generosity, endurance, capacity for cooperation, even passion revealed themselves through hard physical labor. Work made visible the values she cherished: simplicity, genuineness, and living at the core.

She caught up with Alfred at Back Creek. The thirsty cattle crowded around the creek, which the drought had reduced to a trickle. By nightfall, they had reached the Jackson land, where Alfred had permission to keep the herd in a fenced pasture overnight. After cooking over an open fire, Virginia and Alfred unrolled their sleeping bags side by side. Virginia got in hers and looked up at the sky. Cloud cover blocked out all but a sprinkling of the most persistent stars.

"You know, with our luck, it'll start raining tonight," she said. "I didn't even bother to pack any rain gear."

"Would that be good luck or bad luck?" he said, rolling up his shirt to make a pillow. "Think about it."

"I don't know. What is luck, anyway?"

"A darn lie. I don't believe in good luck any more." He slipped into his sleeping bag.

"How could you say that? We're all healthy. That's good luck."

"The country's still in a depression," he said. "That's bad luck."

"We're doing exactly what we want to be doing. That's good luck."

"The drought won't let up. That's bad luck," he countered.

Neither of them spoke what was most on their minds: they might lose the ranch. That was too close, too specific. Better to stick with generalities.

"We're here together," Virginia said.

"That's not good luck," he said.

She felt unexpectedly hurt, though it was only a silly game. Then he quickly added, "That's just plain good."

He rolled over and kissed her. "Is there room in that sleeping bag for me?"

"You dear sweet thing. There's always room for you. Be careful, though. The ground's rocky over here."

He joined her in the sleeping bag and they made love like porcupines—very carefully.

Up and out early the next morning, they reached Brockton by noon. At the sale barn, they picked up their pen assignments. After they got the cattle and horses watered and fed, they walked around and looked at the stock.

The maze of pens held every possible type of cattle. There were Angus and Herefords, longhorns and mixed breeds. There were old bulls for the bologna trade, old butcher cows for hamburger, young calves to be sold as veal, heifers to replenish the herd, prize bulls that would fetch hefty prices. Alfred paused at each pen and sized up the animals that would be run through the auction the following day. Virginia watched him and thought: *He's a stockman through and through.* She felt a clutch at her chest, knowing that their future would be determined by split-second decisions—a wink, a nod of the head, an imperceptible flick of the finger.

When Alfred returned to their pen, he took off his hat, wiped his face with a bandanna, then surveyed his yearlings. "Can't complain about these folks," he said, resting his boot on the bottom rung of the fence. "You won't find a more finely muscled group anywhere."

"No, you won't." She shared in his pride, for she, too, had had a hand in raising them.

Main Street was crowded with stockmen in freshly pressed hats and women in their best outfits. Music spilled through the opened doorways of saloons and hotels. Laughter and shouts could be heard above the music, along with the stomping of boots on the wooden floors. Ranch families were so isolated that any gathering was an excuse for a festive occasion.

Virginia was in no mood to celebrate. She knew what she wanted to do. She had been dreaming about it during the long dusty days of the cattle drive. That night at the hotel, while everyone else was out dancing, she filled the claw-footed tub down the hall, eased herself into the steaming water, and indulged herself in the divine luxury of water on demand. She rested her head against the curved porcelain, closed her eyes, and felt the water lap against her earlobes. She breathed in the steam, letting the moisture penetrate every pore, as if her body could store up the sensation, the memory of wetness. She stayed in the tub until her fingertips puckered and turned pale. When someone knocked on the door, she called out that she would be out in a moment, horrified by her own selfishness. She took another, quicker bath the next morning, before she and Alfred set out for the auction.

At the sale barn, tiers of cement rose around a dirt ring that was enclosed by metal piping. Large doors that slid open sideways were operated by rope and pulley. Outside, men on horse-back moved the cattle through alleys, into holding pens, and finally into the ring. The auctioneer sat on a platform high above the ring. He wore a kerchief over his throat to protect his voice, which was as valuable to him as an opera singer's was to her. The scale master and the clerk sat at the table beside the auctioneer. Pneumatic tubes ran from the platform to the back office, where the cash transactions were settled.

The arena was crowded with ranchers in felt and straw hats, farmers in bill caps, and women in jeans. A few women wore dresses. Some people had come to sell, others to buy. The buyers included a mix of feedlot owners, commissioned buyers, and packers, who bought large lots, as well as farmers who only wanted a couple of calves.

Virginia and Alfred found a place beside a sixteen-year-old boy who had pincers instead of a hand—a reminder of how dangerous ranching could be. The boy had pale skin and black hair, just like Jonathan, and seemed at the same time both innocent and experienced beyond his years. Virginia remembered that same look on Jonathan when he returned from the war, except Jonathan's limbs were intact—it was his spirit that had been amputated. With the baby, he had gotten some of his spirit back.

Odd lots were auctioned off first—old bulls, cows with cancerous eyes or lumpy jaws. By late morning, the auctioneer started selling off large lots of cattle by the hundredweight. Suddenly the door to the ring opened and a sampling of Virginia and Alfred's yearlings flooded into the arena. With a crack of the whip, the ring man sent the animals running along the pipe fencing that separated the ring from the seats. Another firecracker-like crack, and the startled animals changed directions. One spirited yearling charged at the ring man with lowered horns. The ring man jumped behind one of the permanent curved-metal shields until the cow moved past him and rejoined the others.

After a year of caring for the cattle, attending to their every need, Virginia and Alfred were reduced to spectators. She felt the cold iron of the armrests against her skin. The serious bidders had already looked the animals over and knew which lots they would bid on and how much they were willing to pay. Virginia knew that her and Alfred's fate had already been decided, but this did not reduce the drama. Alfred sat stiffly beside her, his mouth closed, his jaw tense.

The auctioneer picked up his megaphone, and the bidding began.

"Tell me, what do you give for them. Whaddaya whaddaya whaddaya give?"

The ring man waved his leather-clad hand over the audience, as if bestowing a blessing. When he identified a bidder, he whipped his hand into a fist, as if catching a fly, and shouted the bid back to the auctioneer. Several of the yearlings crowded him, and he jumped back, snapped his whip, and, in an instant, turned his attention back to the crowd to search for bidders.

"Gimme gimme gimme three on 'em. Give me three." When the auctioneer paused for breath, he rapped the table sharply several times to keep up the rhythm. The man in front of Virginia tweaked his mustache in time to the music of the words.

The auctioneer's job was to sell, and he worked the crowd into a frenzy. He did it with his voice—the speed, the tone, the timbre: fast, then slow; up then down; loud, then soft—all to coax the highest possible price out of the buyers.

"Yes!" shouted the ring man, pointing behind Virginia with the butt end of his whip.

"Let me hear three twenty-five. Three twenty-five."

The ring man let out an Indian-style whoop and looked at the rancher to Virginia's left, who used the toothpick in his mouth as a signaling device.

"Now three fifty. Three fifty. There. Way up high." The auctioneer pointed to a man on the opposite side of the arena. The personalities of the bidders were beginning to emerge.

The man in front of Virginia was in the running. As the bids increased, he kept his head down. Virginia stared at the shiny backs of his ears.

The young man beside her fanned himself with the smeared blue mimeographed program, which was clipped in his pincers. The man on the other side spit into one of the large red coffee cans that were placed at intervals under the seats.

The auctioneer goaded, cajoled, joked, and bullied. All in rhythm. His voice was his instrument, and he played it like a pro, feeding on the excitement, the competition, the surge of emotion. With impeccable phrasing, he varied his rhythm and tone, teasing the audience with his voice, thrilling them with an unexpected twist.

"Three seventy-five. Three seventy-five. Four. What say, Jerry?"

She looked around, careful not to draw attention to herself. In this game of studied indifference and rapt concentration, subtlety reigned. There was a great shrewdness in the cryptic conversation between the ring men and the bidders. She knew she could scratch an ear and not walk away with the top bid. These men knew who was playing and who had an itch.

The ring man was having a conversation in sign language with a man in the front row, who was obviously a regular.

"Four over here. Now four twenty-five! Four twenty-five."

The ring man scanned the crowd. The man with the shiny ears had dropped out. No one else was bidding. Virginia held her breath.

The auctioneer dropped off to a normal voice. "This lot's under the money, folks. Look at 'em. You've got a lot of thickness in these individuals, a lot of weight to sell. Now let's get down to business."

The auctioneer had an interest in getting the highest price, since the barn took a percentage. He picked up the pace again.

"I'm at four fifty bid, at four fifty. Who'll go to four seventy-five? You tell me."

She was caught in a hypnotic trance. Their livelihood depended on this man.

The auctioneer looked at the man with the toothpick and said, "Are you going to be a one-timer? Give me five? What say, five?" He turned to the audience, "That's five cents a pound, folks. Can't do better'n that?"

The voices faded, and her mind drifted. Hard to believe it had all come down to this—this fleeting moment. After all the midnight births, the subzero feedings, the dust-choked days of gathering and herding. After all this—

She was jarred out of her thoughts when the word "Sold!" rang out through the arena. The bidding was over. Their lot was sold and she had no idea how they had come out. This was the moment she had anticipated for weeks, and she felt like the cymbal player who has but one clap of the cymbals to play in the entire symphony—and misses the cue.

She started to whisper something to Alfred, but he shushed her as he leaned forward to hear the name of the man who had bought their yearlings. She realized that she didn't even know the number they needed to reach in order to pay off their debts and taxes. Even if she had heard the final bid, she wouldn't have known what it meant. They waited while several other lots were auctioned. She felt Alfred's presence beside her, but he was not giving off any clues.

Finally he said, "Let's go."

Outside, she said, "How'd we do?"

"Respectably."

She waited. When he didn't say more, she said, "So we made enough to keep going for another year?"

"Almost. But not quite."

She was stung. It seemed that everything they tried to do was almost good enough. And in the end, the only thing that mattered was the "not quite."

It seemed so anticlimactic. That was the end of their ranching career? Just like that? She had believed, had counted on, someone—somehow—seeing them through. It didn't seem possible that this had not happened.

Alfred did not seem upset. She was confused. Perhaps he had a plan, another rabbit to pull out of the hat. "Aren't you going to react?" she said.

"We did the best we could."

They were losing the ranch and that was all he could say?

A serenity surrounded him. She wasn't sure what, exactly, she expected of him. That he would fall on the floor and howl in pain? Obviously not, but something more than his unnerving equanimity. The darker side of being steady was—well, being steady.

Then she asked the question that she had dreaded asking. "If we didn't have the medical bills—"

"That doesn't matter. The only thing that matters is we'll leave with a good name."

Alfred listened to the creak of the saddle as they rode along the dusty roads. Without the yearlings, the trip home was much quicker. He and Virginia didn't speak. There was no need to. He knew that she was disappointed and was, in her own way, making the adjustments she needed to make.

What was a man worth? He was worth the best he was capable of, no more. And that's what Alfred had given. He knew that she knew that, although, in the end his best had not been enough.

For him, the failure had come in increments. That's the only way he could ever bear it. At each stage, he accepted what he thought he could never accept. Now, that it was truly, finally, over and he knew he would lose the ranch, it did not seem so bad. In fact, there was a relief in the finality. You try your best, you do what you can, you toil and sweat and struggle and pray, and somewhere along the way you realize the achievement is not the goal itself—the achievement is the person you've become in trying to reach the goal. Still, there was no way to avoid the disappointment.

What he had expected to get out of ranching was not riches but a good life—the kind of life where he went to bed dead tired, with aching muscles, sunburn, blisters, and bruises, the only reward being a good night's sleep, which was reward enough. And then to awake with gusto, ready for the day, knowing that no matter how small his contribution—a doctored calf, a mended fence—he was adding to the world instead of subtracting from it. And that was what he feared losing. It was the work, not the land, that kept him vibrant. Yet the work was impossible without the land. And the land was impossible to keep without a profit.

But it took more than one failure to make a man. If he followed the failure with success, then the failure would be forgotten. If he stopped now, if he let this defeat define him, then without a doubt he would be a failure. But he was not stopping.

He looked out across the drainage basin and saw a sea of bluestem grass—a valley grass. The cloud's purple shadows lay softly on the grass, like garments held aloft on the stalks. The green made a startling contrast to the subtle gradations of brown and sorrel and tan and rust that painted a magnificent mosaic across the plains. He understood now why brown was the predominate color in this country. The sky was so blue, and there was so much of it, that the ground needed to be earth tones to offset it. Otherwise there would simply be too much color.

Soon he would have to think about packing up the truck as one of banker Gilman's refugees, with a ticket and a token. But that was tomorrow. Today he felt bittersweet. He would not leave empty-handed. The land would forget, but he would never forget. The grass could exist without cattle, but the cattle could not exist without grass. In the end, it was no contest. And maybe that's as it should be.

He glanced over at Virginia, who now looked quite confident

on horseback. She was a good, steady partner. Once she adjusted to losing the ranch, she would be ready to start a new life with him. He had no doubts.

By the time they arrived home, night had fallen. The little house on the hill was dark, as if it had already been abandoned, but light glowed from the bunk-room window.

Virginia and Alfred found Jonathan and Ida rocking by the woodstove. Ida was knitting. The click of the needles sounded strangely similar to the cattle's horns knocking against each other on the long drive. Mindy slept peacefully in the cradle at Ida's feet.

Alfred told them what had happened at the sale barn, speaking quietly so as not to wake the baby. "We came up a little short."

"How short?" Jonathan said.

"Short enough so we'll have to close up shop and move on."

"You mean—leave the ranch?"

"I'm afraid so."

Jonathan stared into space, his eyes vacant. Then he abruptly got up and went outside. Virginia had forgotten how much any change upset him. The move would be harder on him than anyone else.

She returned to the kitchen. Everything was spotless. Ida had been at work. Returning to this dear, sweet house, Virginia felt a rush of warmth. The cupboard was well provisioned, the house clean. But then she remembered the grim future that lay before them.

As she prepared supper, a lead weight attached itself to her mood and pulled her down, down, down. When the stew was ready, she called Ida and Jonathan to the table, then sat beside Alfred, her shoulders slumped. Neither spoke. Before long, Ida arrived with the sleeping infant nestled against her shoulder. Jonathan carried a pillowcase that was bunched up at the end. It was filled with something heavy and lumpy.

"This is for you." He pinched one corner of the pillowcase

and emptied the contents onto the table. Hundreds of coins slid out, as if from a slot machine. The coins clinked against the plates, rolled between the silverware, and formed piles. Some twirled on their edges, tottered, and fell flat on the table. Others rolled off the edge of the table and onto the floor.

"Where did this come from?" Virginia said, slightly alarmed.

"Ida's savings." He smiled proudly at his wife.

"How much is it?"

"I don't know. I never counted it," Ida said.

Virginia and Alfred stared down at the money. There were quarters and nickels and pennies, but also quite a few silver dollars and wadded-up bills. The coins emitted a metallic odor, like blood. No one moved. No one said anything.

"I can't take your money," Alfred said, his voice barely audible.

Virginia looked at Ida, who was aglow with the radiance of young motherhood. Mindy had just stirred awake. She was hungry and started to cry. Ida rearranged the blanket to make Mindy more comfortable. Oblivious to what was going on at the table, Ida nursed the baby.

"Brother, thee is too generous, but we can't accept," Virginia said, touched to the core.

Jonathan's face was strong and determined. "It's not for you. It's for me. Us." He put his hand on Ida's arm. "We want to raise our family here." He spoke with conviction, and Virginia was carried back to the time before Jonathan's head injury, when he was the stronger of the two siblings and always prevailed in any battle of wills.

Virginia let out her breath slowly and waited. She looked over at Alfred. His pride was a mighty and terrible thing.

"Alfred?" she said gently. It was a question.

He held her gaze, then turned to Jonathan and said, "Thank you."

ACKNOWLEDGMENTS

I am greatly indebted to Elizabeth Jensen, Quaker rancher, who shared her life story with me. The events and characters in the novel are fictional, but the spirit and integrity belong to Elizabeth. Born in 1900, she almost made it to a new century. Sadly, we must face it without her. This book is in her memory.

I would also like to extend a warm thanks to ranchers Roberta Z. Crouse and Amy Davis, who read the novel for accuracy; Bill McBean, Andrea Barnet, and Malcolm Gay, who read early drafts and made valuable suggestions; Richard and Marietta Wright, my earliest and most fervent champions; Lydia Chávez and Mary Jane McBean, who kept me going through high moments and low; Amanda Patten, for her shrewd editing; and finally, to Gail Hochman and Joscelyn Gay. I'm especially grateful to Ursula Hegi, for her support and encouragement.

Authors whose books I found helpful in my research include Linda Hasselstrom, Teresa Jordan, Dayton O. Hyde, Jo Jeffers, Lois Phillips Hudson, Gary Penley, Cynthia Vannoy-Rhoades, David Lavender, Caroline A. Henderson, Mary Kidder Rak, Hal Borland, and many others.